The First Death

The demon named Pig reached out with its narrow, taloned fingers and snared the diseased thread of Peter Barry's exhaled breath. It tugged on that invisible thread. Peter's eyes popped open as he fought against the demon's strength to pull air into his lungs. He looked up in terror and finally saw Pig. The breath snapped fully into the demon's hands as he gasped out his last words.

"My God. You are real."

Pig just grinned—and waited.

THE WORLD OF DARKNESS

mage

Such Pain

Based on
THE ASCENSION

Don Bassingthwaite

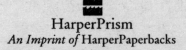

HarperPrism
An Imprint of HarperPaperbacks

This is a work of fiction. The characters, incidents, and
dialogues are products of the author's imagination and are
not to be construed as real. Any resemblance to actual events
or persons, living or dead, is entirely coincidental.

HarperPaperbacks   *A Division of* HarperCollins*Publishers*
                    10 East 53rd Street, New York, N.Y. 10022

Copyright © 1995 by White Wolf Fiction
All rights reserved. No part of this book may be used or
reproduced in any manner whatsoever without written
permission of the publisher, except in the case of brief
quotations embodied in critical articles and reviews. For
information address HarperCollins*Publishers*,
10 East 53rd Street, New York, N.Y. 10022.

Cover illustration by Janet Aulesio Dannheiser

First printing: April 1995

Printed in the United States of America

HarperPrism is an imprint of HarperPaperbacks.
HarperPaperbacks, HarperPrism, and colophon are trademarks of HarperCollins*Publishers*.

❖ 10 9 8 7 6 5 4 3 2 1

For my friends and teachers—
especially Mom and Dad.

Acknowledgments

I'd like to thank the people whose support and inspiration made this novel possible. My appreciation goes out to Stewart Wieck and Phil Brucato of White Wolf Game Studio, and to my friends and critics, Stephen Powell and Lisa McDavid.

PROLOGUE

Mike stood pressed back against the building, his fingers splayed out against the rough stone. The wind tugged at the ends of his hair, occasionally sending strands of it drifting across his face. Sometimes the wind would gust suddenly and tear at his body. Sometimes Mike just wanted to let the wind blow him away.

There was too much noise. Sirens from police cars and ambulances. Shouts from the crowd on the street eighteen floors below. Traffic from other streets and all of the noises of San Francisco. Mostly, though, there were the voices. Whispering to him. Reminding him of the dark things he had done—all of the little things he had forgotten, all of the big things he had tried to forget. Mostly they reminded him of his biggest secret, a betrayal of trust and friendship long ago. He squeezed his eyes shut as if that could somehow keep the voices away.

"Can you hear me?"

For a moment, Mike couldn't distinguish the real voice that he was hearing from the voices that whispered to him. When the words were repeated, though, he heard them and turned to look at their source.

A woman had joined him on the ledge. She wore a harness with a safety line attached to it. Her body language screamed "cop."

"What are you doing?"

He almost laughed. "Just stepped out for some fresh air."

"Planning on staying out here long?"

"I don't know." He leaned his head back against the side of the building. "Maybe a little while longer."

"It's kind of cold."

The sun was going down. This side of the building was already in deep shadow. The street below was a dark chasm. *Cold and dark*, whispered the voices. *Like your heart. You tried to kill someone. How can you live with yourself? Do you deserve to live at all?*

"It's too noisy," Mike blurted.

The cop gestured, smiling. "It's nice and quiet inside."

It's nice and quiet down there in the dark, said the voices. Some of them added, *If you go with her, you'll have to tell them all your secrets. You'll have to tell them about us. They'll think you're crazy.*

"No."

The woman's smile faltered for a moment. "Come on inside. It'll be okay. Trust me."

Can you trust yourself?

Tears flooded Mike's eyes and cascaded down his cheeks. "No." There was no fighting the voices. They were right. Mike clung to the wall for one last moment. Then he hurled himself into the void. Halfway down, he screamed as he realized that the voices were still with him.

On the street below, one man smiled as Mike fell. Saffleur touched the small statuette that nestled in his breast pocket. The talisman had done its work. He didn't have to know what the young man's deep secrets had been. The power of the talisman would have brought them to the surface of the young man's mind, reminding him of them over and over until he would do anything to get away from his own secrets. The talisman was a relic of a time long past, a carving of a woman with the head of a beetle. Ancient texts and even more ancient legends called it the Great Lady. As powerful as his own magick was, Saffleur could not have reproduced the Great Lady's effects.

Sometimes Saffleur longed for the old days of the Mythic Age, before the Technocracy had imposed its scientific vision upon the fabric of reality, locking out the visions of other mages. He had been the same age as the young man when the great Technomancer Copernicus had fixed the nature of the universe in 1543, initiating the decline of the non-Technocracy Traditions of magick. His first teacher had remembered the height of the Mythic Age. The Great Lady predated even the wonders of the Mythic Age.

But magick had no place in the modern world—or so the masses of humanity, the Sleepers who had not yet been Awakened to magick, believed. Magick was all around them, the alteration of reality through willpower. Mages were uncommon, though certainly not rare. Even the Sleepers themselves worked magick in a way, creating the fabric of reality out of their unconscious, consensual beliefs.

Since the end of the Mythic Age and the rise of the Rational Age, however, the consensual beliefs of Sleepers had included consensual disbelief in magick, a disbelief encouraged by the Technocracy. Reality would strike back now against any mage who dared work magick openly in violation of that disbelief. Such open, vulgar magick attracted the dangerous, damaging force that mages called Paradox. There were ways to avoid Paradox, though. A mage could disguise his magick, rendering his workings indistinguishable from coincidence and lucky chance. It didn't necessarily matter what form the magick took as long as the mage's will was done. Just because the evening news and the police reports stated that a young man had committed suicide here tonight, that did not mean that a mage had not wanted him dead and used magick to make it so.

Saffleur nodded in tribute toward the body that lay on the pavement as paramedics stepped forward and placed a white sheet over it. The young man had died the Good Death for a great cause. His death had been as necessary as it was inevitable. Soon this life cycle would be complete and the Angel would pass back and forth across the dark waters on Saffleur's behalf. Again.

Saffleur peered through space, searching for the Angel. He found him drinking coffee in a seedy little restaurant halfway across the city. A television in the restaurant was displaying a news flash of the young man's death; the Angel's face was already pale, and the hand in which he held his coffee was shaking. There was no time to lose in performing coincidental magick now. Saffleur would have to risk offending reality with vulgar magick in order to reach him at the proper time. He stepped briskly through the dispersing crowd and into a nearby alley.

Out of sight of the Sleepers on the street, the mage performed a few steps of a curious dance and vanished. The air rippled slightly with the Paradox created by the impossible event.

"Have you heard from Aaron yet, Bill?"

"No." William Pierce shook his head. "I phoned his hotel in Geneva two hours ago. They said he had picked up his messages."

"Damn him." Peter Barry's body spasmed with a fit of coughing. "Fuck it, Bill, that wasn't funny!"

"What?"

"I heard you snicker!"

"Believe me, I didn't." William stood up and poured his friend a glass of water from the pitcher on the table beside the bed. "The little shit isn't worth it."

Peter accepted the glass and shifted around as best he could to sip at it. The tube that ran down his congested throat and connected him to the oxygen tanks made swallowing awkward, but he managed it. He sat back again with a sigh, as if even the act of drinking was too much of a strain on his deteriorating system. "He wasn't so bad when he was little. Before Barbara died. Lord knows that was hard enough on me."

"Don't think about it, Pete."

"I don't have much else to think about." He drew a ragged breath, then exhaled with a strained wheeze. "I wish I'd never taken up smoking."

"Everybody did it when we were young. You couldn't be a man without smoking. Hell, you couldn't be anybody if you didn't smoke. It was just what we did."

Peter managed a weak chuckle that turned into a hacking cough. "Now you can't even light up in most buildings," he gasped after a moment. "Damn anti-smoking lobby! You know they're increasing taxes on cigarettes?"

"Damn Democrats."

Silence fell in the room, broken only by Peter Barry's labored breathing and the humming of the old electric clock by his bedside. The air in the room was warm and very close, heavy with the smell of disease. Peter refused to allow the window to be opened. William wondered if his friend had finally fallen asleep when Peter spoke suddenly.

"Do you think I did the right thing, William? Was I too hard on him?"

"It was a hard time for you. It wasn't your fault."

Peter waved his hand weakly. "I mean sending him away."

"You had to get Aaron out of the house. He could have broken down any minute. England was a good place for him."

"I know. But I haven't seen him in so long."

"He was on the television again last week. Another paternity suit."

"At least it's women." Peter groped suddenly for the basin that sat beside him on the bed and coughed into it. William glanced away. Peter had been coughing up blood for some time now. "Maybe some good came of all of it." He sighed. "So why do I feel like I've been paying for the most prolonged orgy since Nero?"

"Probably because you have. You should have cut him off after he finished school."

Peter shook his head. "He's still my son. I feel like I owe him something. Poor bastard doesn't have the financial sense of a wet dog." He wheezed again and reached out to seize William's hand. "Bill, do me a favor. Make sure Aaron doesn't spend it all too quickly."

"I will, Pete."

"Thanks. Thanks for everything." He let go. "Now go on and get out of here. Jean must be getting tired of you spending all your time with me."

"I brought some things with me. I thought I'd stay over tonight in one of the guest rooms."

Peter smiled. "Thanks, Bill. Good night."

"Good night, Pete. I'll let you know if Aaron calls."

"Thank you. Leave the lights on."

Peter Barry watched his friend slip out of the room and close the door quietly behind him. He sighed again, looking around his bedroom. At least he had the money to die at home with dignity instead of in some wretched hospital. His gaze settled on a framed photograph—he and Barbara on their honeymoon forty-five years ago. A black-and-white snapshot was tucked into a corner of the frame as well. Barbara holding Aaron at the hospital twenty-nine years ago. Or was it thirty? He had never gotten around to getting a proper frame for the little picture.

There were other photographs of Aaron around somewhere. In a box in a closet someplace. Peter had thrown them all in there after . . . He glanced at his cane, leaning in a corner of the room, and squeezed his eyes shut. He had been so angry, and later so frightened. He rolled over onto his side and tried to go to sleep. He almost hoped Aaron didn't call. Peter wasn't sure he could face talking to him.

He was on the verge of sleep when his eyes popped open again. Peter lifted his head and looked around the room. He could have sworn he had heard someone else in there with him. There was no one. Old, sick man, he told himself. Your imagination is starting to play tricks on you. He closed his eyes again.

The demon crouched precariously on the heavy, dark wood headboard above him smiled and ran a long, pointed tongue around its lipless mouth. It was invisible to mortals when it wanted to be. William Pierce had not registered so much as a glimmer of its presence, but Peter Barry, one foot already in the grave, could sense it vaguely. Earlier, he had heard it snicker as he cursed his son. It leaned down close to Peter's face, relishing the fetid odor of decay on his breath. As it sat up again, eyelids slid slowly down over gleaming yellow eyes in the closest approximation to a human blink the demon was capable of.

The demon's name was Pig, an appealing enough sobriquet that a young Aaron Barry had given to it. Pig sat and watched as Peter Barry's breathing grew regular in sleep. It had been rather annoyed when he had sent Aaron away. Aaron had been its playmate. It was tired of waiting, though. Pig wanted Aaron back again, but he wouldn't come home as long as Peter was alive. It was looking forward to a reunion.

Pig reached out with its narrow, taloned fingers and snared the diseased thread of Peter Barry's exhaled breath. It tugged on that invisible thread. Peter's eyes popped open as he fought against the demon's strength to pull air into his lungs. He looked up in terror and finally saw Pig. The breath snapped fully into Pig's hands as he gasped out his last words.

"My God. You are real."

Pig turned Peter Barry's dying breath into a cat's cradle strung between its claws, grinning and waiting for Aaron.

1

The room beyond the glass was dark. Pitch dark, save for a pool of light that shone down on a Victorian parlor sofa and chair and on a tea table with a silver tea service and on the man and woman who sat taking tea together. The darkness beyond the pool of light might have been described as sinister and threatening. It was intended to be.

Kate Sanders looked down at the array of readouts displayed on the computer monitors before her. The room where she sat was as much in gloom as the other room, deliberately darkened to maximize the effectiveness of the two-way mirror that separated them. The monitors were the only sources of light here. She reached forward and pressed the button that activated a microphone set among the computers. "Optimal stress conditions achieved, Julia." Kate flicked a number of other switches. "Beginning recording of session six, subject: A. Richardson."

In the other room, the woman sitting on the parlor sofa touched her ear and the miniature earphone there to acknowledge that she had received her assistant's message. She picked up the teapot and smiled at the man in the chair. "Another cup, Mr. Richardson?" Julia's words were softened by a quiet, upper-class southern drawl.

Microphones around the room conveyed her words to Kate. Cameras hidden in the darkness transmitted pictures to be displayed on her monitors, covering the scene from every conceivable angle. Other instrumentation recorded more unconventional details. Andrew Richardson's fine china teacup rattled in its saucer as he held it out for Julia to fill. On one of Kate's monitors, the red line indicating his heart rate jumped momentarily.

"I'm terribly sorry, Miss Brennan," he apologized.

"That's quite all right, Mr. Richardson." She smiled at her guest, putting him at ease. Julia was a reasonably pretty woman. An ordinary observer might think she was in her late thirties. Actually, she was almost 150 years old. She wore a very conservative skirt and blouse, and steel-rimmed glasses. That wasn't the way she appeared on one of the larger monitors that Kate watched. On that monitor, she was truly a vision of beauty, wearing the costume of a southern belle and sitting on the veranda of an antebellum plantation mansion. Her face was radiant. Her smile was dazzling. Kate glanced up out of the window and then back down at the monitor again. In this idealized vision, there wasn't even a sign of the ugly scar that cut along Julia's right cheek and into her scalp. Richardson himself appeared in the picture on the monitor, offering Julia a mint julep from a silver tray.

"He's thinking of you," she reported to Julia via the microphone. There was a trace of amusement in her voice.

"Mr. Richardson?" the older woman asked without missing a beat, scowling only slightly in reproof of Kate's levity.

The man shook his head. "I'm sorry. I must have been daydreaming."

"A bad habit, Mr. Richardson." Julia poured a precise drop of milk into her own teacup and stirred it carefully. "I wanted to ask you again about the person who drew up your blueprints." She gestured at a set of plans spread out on the table in front of them. A number of elements on the plans were circled in red ink: support beams that ran in strange directions, odd concavities in the wall, complex webs of wiring that seemed unnecessary, and specifications for colored floor tiles to be arranged in certain intricate patterns.

"Oh, yes." Richardson stared at the blueprints as if in a daze. The image of Julia on Kate's monitor dissolved into an image of the blueprints. Besides the red ink, there were other stains on the paper in this view. Richardson's eyes kept returning to a phantom spray of blood that was spattered across the plans. He looked up at Julia, but the picture of the blueprints remained on the screen. "I wish I could tell you more, but they were simply delivered to me by the consortium that's building the club. I really don't know who designed them. I was hired to make sure they were followed to the letter."

Julia encouraged him with another smile. "Well then, why don't you tell me about the consortium?"

He flushed. "I'm afraid I don't know much about that either."

Ghostly figures of big men with shadowy faces sitting around a wide conference table appeared on Kate's monitor. Punching commands into a computer, Kate focused on one of the faces and tried to enhance it. The shadows remained nothing more than shadows. "False memories identical to those previously observed," she muttered into the microphone.

"Think hard, Mr. Richardson," suggested Julia, frowning. "Is there anything you haven't told me before?"

"I don't believe so." He furrowed his brow, staring

off into the darkness around them. For a moment, Kate felt as though he were looking straight at her, but his gaze moved on. His heart rate began to rise, and the picture on her monitor grew worse the longer he stared. The shadows on the monitor became more frightening and began to reach out for Richardson, now a pale, hapless, doll-like figure at the foot of the table. "I've never met them. I've never even seen one of their names, and I'm the top man on the project. They're very mysterious. Maybe they want to be distanced from the scandal the club is going to cause—you should see some of the advertising the marketing agency we're working with has done for the opening!"

"We're losing him, Julia!"

Julia laughed, a musical, tinkling sound, and laid a hand on Richardson's arm, bringing his attention back to her. The picture on the monitor grew clear again, the threatening businessmen banished by a return to that southern veranda. "Scandal doesn't interest me, Mr. Richardson." She took his teacup from him, though he resisted with numb fingers, and added pleasantly, "But, please, I want you to try and remember absolutely everything."

The teacup was Kate's signal to throw another switch. Richardson screamed and clutched at his head. Julia sipped at her tea as he curled up into a whimpering ball on his chair. The images on the monitor beside Kate began to flicker past with incredible, almost impossible, speed. She kept her eyes on a readout, however, waiting as a computer-generated curve approached its peak. The growth of the curve mirrored the speed of the flickering pictures. The moment the curve peaked, the monitor screen went completely white. "Full recall induction reached," she told Julia. "You have twenty seconds."

"Mr. Richardson," Julia said firmly, "concentrate

and tell me everything you know about the consortium that is building the club called Pan's."

"I don't know anything!"

"How do you communicate with them?"

"They send me letters by courier! My pay is automatically deposited in my bank account!"

"Yes, you've told us that before. Have you ever heard of the *Traditions*, Mr. Richardson? Are you aware of any significance to these elements of the project?" She indicated the circles on the blueprints.

"What? No!"

"Do you remember anything about the letters? Anything special about them?"

"No! No!" He gasped suddenly. "Wait! One of them had a handwritten address when all of the others were typed!"

Julia glanced at Kate. Kate shook her head. "No clear picture." Julia frowned and produced a pencil and paper.

"Can you duplicate that handwriting for me please?"

He looked at the pencil and paper as if they were alien artifacts. "I don't think I can. I don't think I could do that, Miss Brennan."

"Of course, you can." She nodded at Kate, who hit a button on the panel in front of her.

Richardson's hand shot out as if of its own accord and seized the pencil. Richardson himself watched in amazement as it wrote out the address of his architectural firm in a narrow, cramped, almost illegible handwriting that was not at all like his own. Julia picked up the paper when he had finished and nodded in satisfaction. "Thank you, Mr. Richardson."

The man gasped in release as Kate turned off the switch she had turned on a few minutes before. The curve on her readout fell, and a picture slowly reformed on the monitor. Julia again, but this time she sat at the conference table of the mysterious consortium. She still had a beautiful smile, however. "Thank you, Miss Brennan," Richardson mumbled in reply.

Kate pressed another button on her panel. A large man in a black suit stepped out of the darkness and laid a heavy hand on Richardson's shoulder. Richardson started and began to turn in surprise. The man in black merely reached toward a small box that was attached to his belt, and Richardson stopped moving instantly, his face white with fear. He meekly followed the man in black into the shadows.

"Ending recording of session six, subject: A. Richardson," Kate said into the microphone. "File: San Francisco 2556-10. Investigation: Pan's. Recording Supervisor: Kate Sanders, New World Order 3-8003."

She turned on the lights, washing away the darkness in the interrogation area as well as in her own little monitoring room. To some people, the interrogation area was scarcely less intimidating with the lights on than with them off. It was a cold room, the floor and walls starkly white. The parlor sofa and chair were incongruous, but they were only there because Julia found that her subjects were more cooperative when they had been lulled by comfort. Kate supposed that she had grown used to the room.

Complex electronic equipment and computers lined the walls and stood in units on the floor. Suspended over the chair Richardson had been sitting in was an array of spiky, spindly sensors. They fed into the monitor that she had been watching. A Sleeper seeing the array would not have thought it anything other than another piece of equipment. If the Sleeper had been told that it was a mind probe, they might have laughed and said that was ridiculous. Still, they would have looked at the spikes and the spindles and wondered just how long it would be before scientists really did develop mind probes. They wouldn't have suspected that the machine was magickal.

In essence, of course, science was a kind of magick, albeit the safe, predictable magick of the Technocracy itself, using machines, chemicals, and solidly formulated laws to accomplish the desires of the will. After all, what was the functional difference between a mind probe and one of the Traditions' mind readers? None. The only difference was that the Technocracy's magick flowed with reality, while the magick of the Traditions chanced the accumulation of Paradox by working against it. Sleeper society had accepted the magick of science to the exclusion of all other forms of magick. The Technocracy had worked for centuries to make sure that it did.

Julia rose from the couch and walked into the monitoring room. "Well?"

"Nothing," Kate said apologetically. "He really doesn't seem to know anything about the mages behind Pan's."

"You mean the probe picked up nothing that the simpler probes had not already picked up." Julia brushed past her assistant to examine the readout on a computer monitor. She ran her finger along her scar in an unconscious gesture as she read. "He must know more, Kate. There must be a clue in his mind somewhere, and I'll get it if it kills him. Has the Syndicate reported any luck in tracking down the consortium's accounts?"

"No," Kate responded simply. She was always uncomfortable around Julia after an interview. Perhaps it was the contrast between Julia's warmer, more pleasant, interrogation demeanor and her normal personality and hard, cold accent. Long years of working toward the absolute order that the Technocracy sought tended to wear down the unique facets of individual mages' personalities and behaviors,

especially when the mages worked for the New World
Order as she and Julia did. Their Convention was even
more rigid and hierarchical than the other conven-
tions of the Technocracy, like the mechanistic
Iteration X or the corporate Syndicate. The New World
Order gathered information and watched for deviation
from the prescribed, rational uniformity of
Technocratic reality in Sleepers and in each other.
Julia had been working for the New World Order for a
long time indeed. She had been one of those who had
developed the paradigm that made mind probes con-
ceptually possible in scientific theory and thus permissible to Technomancer magick.

Sometimes Kate mourned the eventual loss of her
own light Kentucky accent. Any sacrifice might be
worth it, however, if she could advance as far in the
ranks of the Convention as Julia had. She watched
carefully as Julia skimmed through the data that the
probe had collected—data that she had already ana-
lyzed. Promotion would even make it worth putting up
with Julia's heavy-handed, sometimes demeaning,
supervision. Julia was one of the best mages of the
New World Order in San Francisco. Her previous stu-
dents had risen swiftly, though none had so far
escaped her shadow. Kate intended to be the first to
surpass her instructor.

"Kate?"

"Yes?"

Julia thrust the paper on which Richardson had
written at her. "Run a handwriting comparison on
this." She looked up and added, "Has anything come
in from the cameras you set up around Pan's?"

Kate took the paper and obediently dropped it into
a device that resembled a desktop digital scanner. As
any technician or clerk could have. She shook her
head in answer to Julia's question. "None. But it's
only been a couple of weeks."

"I think we may need a more active, in-depth investigation."

Kate's stomach clenched in frustration. Pan's had first come to the attention of the Technocracy when a Technomancer working in the city planning office had noticed the magickal elements that were being worked into the club's architecture. An agent of Iteration X had figured out that the elements could be employed in a ceremony that might turn Pan's into a node of magickal power. Since no Technomancer would have gone to such trouble in hiding the design, it seemed clear that it was the mages of the Traditions who were behind Pan's. The investigation had been turned over to the New World Order. The first plan of response had been predictably reactionary. Pan's would be destroyed outright before the construction could be finished and the new node activated. Kate had argued for, and won, a more practical approach. She didn't want to see that plan discarded.

"I thought you supported monitoring Pan's as opposed to simply demolishing it. This way, we can apprehend the mages who—"

"Investigation in addition to the cameras," clarified Julia, waving her concerns aside. "I like this idea, Kate, but I think it would be better if we were to broaden our search strategy. No one can hide their trail completely. We need to put somebody in a position to follow up on fragmentary information. I want you to get a job at a television station."

"You want me to work as a reporter chasing rumors?" Kate could hardly believe what she was hearing. She had worked her way up to a position in the New World Order regional headquarters, and Julia was sending her back down. "Aren't there other Technomancers working in the media already that would be better?"

Julia shook her head. "All in mainstream news. Any

rumors that are circulating about Pan's will be in the field of entertainment and society. Our coverage there is very thin. We've ignored it for far too long on the assumption that it was beneath our notice, but some of the most disruptive influences come out of that area." She paused, thinking. "Perhaps it would be even better if you were to work under an experienced reporter, someone used to the rumor mill."

Kate clenched her teeth, then slowly released her breath. It was for the good of the Technocracy, she reminded herself, and the Technocracy worked for the good of humanity, guiding it toward a safe, orderly future of Ascension. The Traditions were squabbling, fragmented groups with no clear paradigm for reality and Ascension, resentful of the Technocracy's hold on the world and claiming that the Technocracy was doing more harm to humanity than good. They couldn't have been more wrong—the Technocracy labored for stability, a bright future in which humanity was safe from the unpredictable influences of unregulated magick upon reality. If the Traditions mages behind Pan's were to succeed in activating the site as a node, they might do untold damage to the reality that the Technocracy had so carefully crafted. Working as a reporter might be a step backward for her personally, but she had joined the New World Order and the Technocracy to work for the advancement of humanity as a whole. She swallowed her pride. "Yes, Julia."

"Excellent."

The computer attached to the scanning device gave a beep, and the results of the handwriting comparison flashed up on the screen. "Whose is it?" demanded Julia as Kate typed in a few commands, bringing up more detailed information from the New World Order's other databases.

"A bicycle courier who delivers to Richardson's office. Probably the one who brought the packages to him."

"Do you have an address for him?"

"Yes."

Julia hit a button on the console. Almost immediately, a man almost identical to the one who had taken Richardson away and likewise dressed in a black suit, entered. Julia ran off a printout of the information on the courier and handed it to him. "Bring him in," she instructed the man in black. "I want to ask him some questions. And arrange for the disposal of Andrew Richardson. I don't think we'll be able to get anything more from him, and he's seen too much here to be permitted to leave."

2

Aaron Barry stepped out of the cool, dim interior of the private plane and into the bright sunshine that beat down on the tarmac of San Francisco International Airport. For a moment, he drank in the sensations of the sunshine on his skin and the cool wind off the Bay in his hair. He closed his eyes, savoring the feelings, ignoring the clamor of the airport. The sunlight felt different in other parts of the world, harsher in Australia, more seductive in France, sharper in Thailand. It had been too long since he had felt the sunlight in San Francisco, though. He tried to describe its qualities to himself: deep but slightly out of focus, sweet, heady. He opened his eyes and inhaled deeply. It was good to be back.

Slipping on a pair of sunglasses, he turned his attention to the small crowd of reporters who stood clustered around the base of the airplane stairs. "Okay," he shouted, "let's get on with this." He plucked at the lapels of his jacket—rich, dark plum in color and tailor-made in Italy—as he walked down the stairs. "As you can see, I'm in mourning."

As if his words had opened a floodgate, questions

rushed in at him from all sides. Cameras whirred, snapping innumerable pictures of his tanned, elegant features and sharp, blue eyes. Microphones and miniature tape recorders were shoved into his face. He waded calmly into the thick of the fray.

"How does it feel to be home after fourteen years?"

"Fantastic. I love this city."

"Any comment on the O'Reilly paternity suit?"

"Never met the woman."

"How about the Neville-Harris suit in England?"

"I was wearing a condom, and I have the pictures to prove it."

That one got a few laughs and broke the ice. The questions became more prying and personal, probing into his famous indiscretions. Torrid, infamously perverse sexual affairs on six continents, both fact and rumor. The suggestive modeling campaign for that French designer. The spectacular car crash on the German autobahn. The controversial rendezvous with the daughter of the Japanese prime minister in a Rio de Janeiro hotel. Mostly old news, but this was the first time that San Francisco reporters had really had the opportunity to interview their hometown, internationally famous "bad boy." San Francisco had its libertines, but none of them had Aaron Barry's flair for scandal.

Or Aaron's flair for dealing with the media. He posed for the cameras, mugging shamelessly while making sure that they also caught him at his absolute best. The most outrageous questions met with the most outrageous answers. Insipid questions met with even more outrageous answers. Nothing was sacred. Things that were left unsaid were usually shrouded in so much innuendo that speculation ran rampant. It drove his lawyers to the brink of madness; several had retired, prematurely bald from the stress (or so that particular rumor went). And every few months, there was some juicy new tidbit that kept his appeal from getting stale. Aaron reveled in the attention that the media lavished on him.

"Aaron, what are your reactions to your father's death?"

The question brought an abrupt hush over the crowd. Aaron's father was a taboo topic. Reporters across the world knew that Aaron and Peter Barry had not gotten along. Peter Barry's presence was what had kept his son away from San Francisco. Aaron had once personally thrown a reporter out of a press conference for daring to ask about his father. The reporters gathered at the airport drew in their breaths collectively. A few with more mercenary tendencies raised their cameras and jockeyed for the best angle from which to capture the incident that must surely follow.

Aaron himself stiffened and turned slowly to face the reporter who had asked the question. The man swallowed hard as he found himself staring up into the blank, dispassionate darkness of Aaron's sunglasses. "Sorry, Aaron. Forget I asked. Really."

"No." Aaron shook his head. There wasn't a trace of levity in his voice, but neither was there anger. "It's a good question, and one I should answer." He raised his voice, speaking to all of the reporters. "Listen up, because this is going to be the one and only time you're going to hear me comment on Peter Barry. My father was a bastard. There was no love lost between us. The period of my mourning is going to be short. Incredibly short."

He bit off his words and looked around. The reporters were silent. He returned his attention to the reporter who had first asked the question. "You seem surprised. Were you maybe expecting some other answer?"

"Ahhh . . ."

"Good. Do you have any other questions?"

"Ummm . . ."

"Then get out of my face." Aaron turned away from him brusquely. Several reporters edged nervously out of his way. "Anybody else got more questions?" The reporters shifted uncomfortably.

"I do." A woman dressed in a fashionable designer outfit stepped forward into the silence, confronting him brazenly. Her cameraman slipped around to focus on the two of them. "Tiffany LaRouche, Aaron. KKBA entertainment news. You were involved for some time with the controversial European rock star Aphrodite?"

"Involved is such a polite term, Tiffany. We had intense, wild, erotic sex." Aaron flashed her a smile. "But we split up on good terms almost a year ago."

"Good terms? Aphrodite was considering entering a convent."

He shrugged as more cameras were trained on the exchange. "Relatively good terms, then. What's your point?"

Tiffany held out her hand. A smartly dressed young woman with blond hair passed her a videotape. Tiffany waved the tape in the air. "This is an advance copy of Aphrodite's new video, due to be released next week. The song is called 'Sour Thrill.' The video uses some of Aphrodite's more explicit home movies. Many cuts feature one particular naked man with his facial features blacked out. Informed sources say that it's you." Tiffany smirked triumphantly. "Would you care to confirm that?"

Aaron slid his sunglasses down on his nose and looked at her over the top. "I don't know, Tiffany. I haven't seen the video. Maybe you or your assistant . . ." He reached out and snagged the blond woman's hand. His eyes flicked across her press identification card. "Kate? Maybe Kate would care to bring it by my place, and we could . . . confirm it together." He kissed the palm of Kate's hand.

Cameras zoomed in on the shot faster than bursting

fireworks. Kate flushed slightly and looked questioningly at Tiffany, seeking guidance. The entertainment reporter frowned and shook her head. This was a great shot. Kate glanced back to her hand and met Aaron's eyes over his sunglasses. He smiled, warmly and lasciviously. His tongue flicked out to lick her palm. Kate snatched her hand back, her flush changing from embarrassment to outrage. For a moment it seemed as if she might slap his handsome, grinning face, but then Aaron stuck out his own hand in a friendly greeting. A joke. Wary of the cameras, she shook his hand coldly. Aaron chuckled and turned his smile back toward Tiffany.

"I guess we'll just have to see what the video looks like when it comes out then, won't we?" He smiled at all of the reporters as he began pushing his way toward a waiting vintage Rolls-Royce. "I have to go now. Papers to sign, fortunes to inherit."

"The video, Aaron!" screamed Tiffany. "What about the video?"

Aaron climbed into the Rolls and rolled down the window. "Maybe. Maybe not. Aphrodite has had other lovers. *Lots* of other lovers, believe me. I can give you references. Ask them. I'll see you around." He caught Kate's eye and blew her a kiss as the Rolls pulled away.

" . . . and sign here, sir. And here. And here. And that's all." The lawyer indicated the final lines in the papers requiring Aaron's signature. Aaron leaned back with a sigh of relief and shook the cramps out of his hand. It seemed as if he had been signing paper after paper for hours. As he looked at the pile that had accumulated in front of him, he realized that he probably had. All necessary for the smooth transition of his father's financial empire into his hands.

He cracked his knuckles. "So what does it all mean, Tom?"

"Sir?"

Aaron indicated the papers on the desktop with a sweep of his hands. "Bonds. Stocks. Futures. Real estate. I didn't even know my father owned a vineyard in Sonoma."

"A small vineyard, sir. Your father believed in diversification."

There was a derisive snort from the corner of the room, where an older man sat on a hard, straight-backed chair. Aaron swung around toward him. "Something funny, William?" he asked caustically.

"Only marginally." William Pierce sat up a little bit straighter and adjusted his tie. "Diversification is a very sound business practice."

"Hmm." Aaron turned back to Tom. "What does it mean if you put it all together, though? What does it make me?"

Tom blinked. "Wealthy."

"I know that! How wealthy? Wealthier than the"— he gestured toward a window—"whoever it is that lives next door?"

"The Changs," William supplied with a slightly sour expression. "They bought the Gorevales' house and moved here from Hong Kong."

Tom smiled. "Oh, yes, sir. Wealthier than the Changs by far." He coughed politely. "You're probably one of the wealthiest people in the neighborhood, which is saying a fair deal for a neighborhood like Nob Hill. I'll be conservative and say that you may well be one of the five hundred wealthiest people in the world. Or close to it."

The sharp lines of Aaron's eyebrows rose in mock surprise. "Really?" He leaned back farther and put his feet up on the desk. It was his father's desk, the immense oak monolith that had so frightened him as a child. His father had been old-fashioned enough to do some of his work out of the family mansion. He fiddled with his father's old fountain pen, then said suddenly, "Clean out your desk, Tom. I won't be needing you anymore."

"S-sir?"

"I don't want conservative estimates. You're fired. And you might as well get started on your desk tonight, since you won't need to come in tomorrow."

"But . . ."

"Good-bye, Tom." He pointed at the door. The lawyer still wore a stunned look on his face as he let himself out. For a second the click of the latch echoed in the silence; then Aaron sat back in his chair and laughed.

"Oh God! I thought he was going to have a heart attack."

"Not that you would have cared if he had, I'm sure." William rose from his chair and stalked around in front of the desk to confront Aaron. His face was pale with rage. He rested his hands on the desk and looked down at the man a spoiled teenager had become. "That was the most stupid thing I have ever seen in all my years as Peter Barry's financial adviser."

"I'll get someone else."

"Who? No one knew all of the legal intricacies of your father's accounts the way he did."

"They'll learn." Aaron shrugged expansively and folded his arms behind his head. "Besides, they're not *my father's* accounts anymore anyway."

"A change in the man does not make a change in the accounts. They'll still run the way they always have."

Aaron chuckled. "Don't count on it, William. My business sense might surprise you yet. And just what was that comment about 'diversification' supposed to mean?"

William's knuckles whitened on the desktop. "You are no different than you were as a child."

"Oh, I wouldn't say that. I've changed. I've grown up." He stood and walked over to the window. Peter Barry had kept heavy curtains drawn over the windows of his study for as long as Aaron could remember. The first thing he did when he had walked into the room earlier that afternoon was to throw the drapes and the windows open. He looked out the window, past the Changs' house and west toward the setting sun. He smiled nastily in the fading light. "By the way, I like the family pictures in the Christmas cards your wife's been sending me. Your daughter Sharon is what? Nineteen now? Probably in college . . ."

"Stay away from her."

"Why? Afraid I'll be a bad influence? Or just afraid of how she'd take to a little 'diversification'?"

"Damn you!" If he had been fifteen years younger, William might have lunged across the room. Instead, all he could manage was a slightly threatening advance. "Stay away from her, you pervert!"

Aaron laughed in his face. "Afraid I'm going to seduce her and lead her into wicked ways, William?" His laughter tapered off to an evil smirk. He studied the look of outrage on William's face. "You are, aren't you?"

"It's a possibility, isn't it?" William struggled to keep a level tone of voice.

"Not really, actually." Aaron returned to the desk. "She has a face like a cow."

He smiled as the study door slammed shut behind William. He pulled a sheet of paper out of one of the desk drawers and crossed off William Pierce's name, along with Tom's. He almost wished that it had been harder to get rid of his father's old friend. He had never gotten along with William, even as a child. He strongly suspected that it had been William who had suggested to Peter Barry the possibility of shipping Peter's "disturbed" son off to a boarding school in

England. Aaron would have enjoyed being in a position of authority over him.

He ran down the rest of the list. Mostly old employees of his father's. Men like William, entrenched in the old ways of doing business and so set in their morality that they regarded Aaron as a source of evil second only to the devil himself. Men he wanted gone. Some of the names on the list were decent, competent people. Like Tom. He briefly considered hiring the lawyer back.

No. He wanted people working for him who were more than competent. He wanted people who were dynamic, innovative, and hungry. He couldn't fire everybody, of course. He needed to keep some people around who knew what they were doing. He could do some heavy pruning, however. He had rather more business sense than his father or William would have given him credit for. He dropped the list into the "out" tray on the desk. His father's old secretary would take care of making up the pink slips on Monday. Her name was on the list as well.

Aaron smiled, warm with a sense of accomplishment. He looked around the study. Once this had been his father's inner sanctum. Aaron had not been allowed inside unless his presence was desired, a demand that had usually left him shaking and nervous. Now it was his. He closed the windows on the gathering night. The study was his, just as the rest of the Barry mansion and his father's financial empire were his, with all of the power that that entailed. He looked around the study a final time, then turned to face the door. But not without a trace of dread in his heart.

The door was big and heavy and intimidating. He hesitated for a moment before reaching for the doorknob. When he walked out of the study, he would be alone. Alone in the Barry mansion for the first time in fourteen years. Alone, in spite of all of his money and power. He didn't want to think about what that might mean. He had waited almost two weeks after his father's death before returning to San Francisco. The media had speculated that he was snubbing his father one last time by avoiding the funeral. In truth, he had been working up the nerve to enter the Barry mansion, delaying his return until the last possible moment. Swallowing, he opened the door and stepped through it.

The hall was silent. Absolutely silent. Somewhere downstairs, the cook would have arrived to prepare his evening meal. He had considered the financial wisdom of retaining a cook who came in to prepare just one meal a day, but in the end had decided to keep her on just to have someone else in the house during the lonely, quiet hours of the late afternoon and early evening after the housekeeper had left. She was probably banging away in the kitchen, but the sound didn't travel up to the second floor. His great-grandfather had constructed the Barry mansion in the late 1800s, with good, thick walls that killed sound in the house. Of course, his great-grandfather had had eight children. The mansion had been built to accommodate them—big and quiet. What had once been a house filled with children and at least minimal noise was now, however, as still and silent as a tomb.

His feet sank into the carpeting without a sound. He passed a grandfather clock, its mechanism long broken. Full night would have fallen outside. He would go out in a few hours, he reminded himself, the thought like a mantra. He would go out to places where there were people, and when he came home, he would not be alone. He would go out to places where the hair on the back of his neck did not stiffen as if someone were walking down the hall behind him. . . .

He spun around, breathing rapidly, hands up

defensively, eyes darting left and right. The hall, with its antique carpets and dark wood trim, was empty. As, he supposed, it should be. He felt childish. He didn't have to worry. He could take care of himself, now. He had spent fourteen years preparing for his return.

So why had he broken out in a cold sweat?

He turned the corner at the end of the hall. To his left were the main stairs running down to the first floor. To his right . . . Aaron looked down a short corridor. At the end of it, he could see the head of the steep, narrow servants' stairs. They would be just as he remembered them from fourteen years ago, dark and treacherous, worn smooth by the feet of servants long past. He stood there for a moment. His heart was pounding. He waited.

And waited.

Time seemed to thicken, dragging past in slow moments. The thing that he had dreaded for so many years was going to happen sooner or later. He was hoping that it would be later, but almost—*almost*—he wished that it would happen sooner and be done with. If it was going to happen sooner, it would happen now, when he was at his most vulnerable. Alone and frightened.

But it didn't happen. The sudden appearance of the dark, inhuman creature that he had learned to dread never came. Aaron would have to wait, just as he always had. The demon would strike when it wanted to, when he least expected it, never when he was prepared. "Damn you, Pig," he snarled at the walls.

The little nightclub he eventually wound up in several hours later was nothing if not trendy. In fact, once the novelty of the place wore off in a few months, Aaron strongly suspected that it would be reduced to nothing. The music was innovative, but it had the kind of faddish edge to it that indicated short-term appeal. It was also simply far too loud. The decor was barely a notch above average. But Aaron wasn't there for the music or the decor. He was there for the people.

The place was packed with the pretty and the trend-conscious, with a large enough smattering of the famous and semifamous to lend it a flashy, out-of-the-ordinary, star-studded atmosphere. The people here lived to be seen. The bouncers at the door kept the mundane out, while making sure that the line in front of the club moved forward at a suitable snail's pace. A longer line enhanced the club's prestige, or at least said something about its attitude.

Aaron had bypassed the line altogether. Fame had its advantages. Once he was inside the club, everyone was too busy affecting pretention to admit that they were at all impressed by the presence of the scandalous Aaron Barry. Oh, but they were impressed all right. He could recognize it in the way people glanced at him just a little more frequently than normal, in the way they moved out of his path, giving him that extra bit of room accorded to celebrities. They just refused to show their fascination openly for fear of appearing less than sophisticated. He made eye contact with one staring woman. She blushed and looked away.

Someone spoke rather timidly at his side, barely loud enough to be heard over the music. "Excuse me?" Aaron glanced down to find two young women and a young man standing there, looking at him sheepishly. One of the women smiled. "You're Aaron Barry, aren't you?"

Then again, some people were still fresh-faced enough to still be awed by the proximity of someone famous. Aaron leered at the woman a little bit. "In the flesh." He placed an extra emphasis on the last word.

The woman shivered and smiled back at him. Her companion blurted, "Can we have your autograph?" She held out a napkin.

"Not that way!" hissed the young man. He unbuttoned his shirt suddenly and flipped it down to reveal his shoulders. Turning his back to Aaron slightly, he asked, "Can you make it 'For Scott'?"

Aaron smiled and pulled out his autograph pen, a large, black, indelible marker. He refused to sign paper, but his autograph had graced skins around the world. He wrote out his autograph on the young man's shoulder blade. *For My Pal, Scott—Aaron Barry.* He turned to the young woman with the napkin. "Where do you want it?"

She turned red and looked nervously at her friends. The man shrugged. The woman gestured to her hip. The young woman with the napkin hesitated, then stuck out her arm. "For Marian, please." Aaron wrote the inscription on her inner arm, signing the *y* in *Barry* with an extra flourish in the hollow of her elbow. The woman looked like she might faint.

The other woman presented herself boldly, opening her blouse partway. "Here," she commanded, indicating the top of the cleavage between her breasts. "Down here."

"Adventurous, aren't we?" Aaron tilted her head up and looked directly into her eyes. "What's your name?"

"Karin. With an *i*."

"Karin with an *i*." He settled his hand for the proper angle. It rested across the woman's breast. She shuddered appealingly. "There's not much room for a proper autograph."

"Just your name is fine." Her words were breathy.

Aaron smiled and signed *Aaron Barry.* On a whim, he added the words *was here.* He capped the marker and looked into her eyes again. "You're a virgin, aren't you?" She didn't say anything, but the flush that came to her face spoke volumes. Aaron kissed her on the forehead and whispered, "You'll have to come see me sometime." She nodded slightly as he sent her and her friends back off into the crowd.

A spotlight came on behind him suddenly, and he turned to find himself blinking in the brightness of a television video camera. A vaguely familiar figure holding a microphone stepped up to stand beside him. "This is Tiffany LaRouche, live on the scene for *Friday Night on the Town*. Tonight, I'm at the fabulously hot club, the Screwdriver, and with me is San Francisco's own Aaron Barry."

Aaron put on his best smile-for-the-media grin. "Kiss-kiss, Tiffany. Nice to see you, too. And you, Kate." He winked at Tiffany's assistant, standing partially hidden behind the cameraman. He was pleased to see Tiffany's smiling mask falter for a moment as she was upstaged.

She recovered quickly, however. "I saw you signing autographs, Aaron. Don't you find it difficult to appear in public? And without bodyguards?"

"I don't use bodyguards at all, Tiffany, and being seen in public has never intimidated me very much. Most people respect my personal space. Unless I invite them to violate."

Tiffany's smile became a bit forced. "So what brings you down to the Screwdriver tonight?"

"A little dancing, a bit of getting to know the old town again." He swept his gaze around the club before letting his eyes settle theatrically on a woman in a short, tight skirt. "Seeing some of the sights."

"Any plans for the weekend?"

"Just hanging out. Maybe a movie. I haven't had time to organize an orgy yet."

Tiffany turned back to face the camera, ignoring Aaron's bait. "Of course, the big news for San Francisco club scene fans in the next week is the opening of the much anticipated new dance club, Pan's, next Friday night. Do you think you'll be there, Aaron?"

"I wouldn't miss it, Tiffany."

"Thanks, Aaron." She smiled into the camera. "For KKBA's *Friday Night on the Town*, I'm Tiffany LaRouche." She gestured for the camera to stay on her. "Care to dance, Aaron?"

"I'd love to." He stepped forward, around the cameraman and took Kate's hand. "How about you, Kate?" The camera wavered between Tiffany and Kate. Both women looked shocked, but Tiffany also looked like she might be ready to chew nails in a moment. The cameraman chose to focus on Kate until Aaron had tugged her into the swaying crowd on the dance floor. He shut off the camera and turned back to face Tiffany with some reluctance.

Aaron Barry was impudent. Kate had to give him that much. He was also, she supposed, a very good dancer. And good-looking. Extremely good-looking, from his carefully trimmed black hair to his handmade shoes. His skin was tanned a gorgeous bronze. Being a Technomancer did not render her aesthetic sense completely inoperative, no matter how much the Technocracy discouraged its mages from enjoying such pleasures. She was almost ready to forgive Aaron for that scene at the airport on the simple appeal of his smile.

"Have you worked for her long?"

"Pardon?" The dance floor was the most crowded part of the club, and naturally the loudest as well. Kate was dancing so close to Aaron that they might as well have been touching, and she still found it difficult to hear him. She considered using magick to make his words more audible, but decided against it. Why risk it on something so trivial?

"Have you worked for Tiffany long?"

"Only about a week and a half. It's an interesting job. I get out a lot more now. I see the clubs."

"Tiffany must be a bitch to work for."

"You didn't make her happy by turning her down on the air."

"What?"

"Never mind." Kate smiled. He smiled in return and flipped back a lock of hair that had fallen across his face. For a second, Kate's heart did cartwheels. She was glad that she had not yet reached Julia's level of detached emotionlessness, although Julia would be the first to reprimand her for letting baser urges interfere with her duties. But Julia wasn't the one dancing with him, was she? Kate wondered briefly what Aaron would look like without his clothes.

A few more people spilled onto the dance floor, and Kate found herself pressing even closer to Aaron. The sudden contact flustered her, especially after her last thoughts, and she lost the beat of the music. Aaron laughed. He stepped behind her and wrapped his arms around her in a casual, friendly way, guiding her motions. He was an excellent dancer. Kate fought back the urge to melt into him. Just dancing with Aaron was sure to create a minor scandal in the cold halls of the New World Order regional headquarters. Truly giving in to the heat of the moment might have serious consequences. Such behavior in public was deemed totally unbecoming to a mage of the New World Order. Some of the Technocracy's views were perhaps a trifle harsh and old-fashioned, but they had to be followed, at least for the sake of appearances.

Aaron bent his head forward, bringing his mouth close to her ear, and asked, "What's your last name?"

"Hmmm? Oh." That hadn't been quite what she had been expecting him to say. She felt briefly ashamed of herself. Dancing with the infamous Aaron Barry did not mean that he was automatically going to ask her something indecent. "Sanders."

"Nice name." He stepped back and let her turn

around. The song ended, fading into something else with a faster beat. Kate looked around for Tiffany. She spotted the light of the camera off in a far corner.

"I should go."

"Back to work? I understand." He shrugged. "I guess somebody has to."

"Thank you for the dance."

"What?"

"I said, thank you for the dance." Kate flushed. That probably wasn't the sort of thing you were supposed to say in a trendy club. She was showing her small-town roots again. "Sorry, I . . ."

"No. It's . . ." Aaron gave her a lopsided grin. "No one has ever thanked me before." The grin grew wicked. "At least not for just a dance."

"Like I said, it takes the job to get me out. Good-bye, Aaron." She turned away.

"Wait." Aaron caught her arm. "Are you going to the opening of Pan's next week?"

"Are you kidding?" She stretched her mouth wide in imitation of the fake, on-air smile she always wanted to wipe off of Tiffany's face. "It's the big news on the San Francisco club scene!"

That made Aaron laugh. "I'll see you there then."

"Just look for Tiffany. I'm sure there will be a big open space around her." She watched him drift off through the crowd. In spite of everything she knew about him, in spite of all the hype that the media ground out and the manner of their meeting at the airport, she suspected that she could like him. The opening of Pan's suddenly didn't seem quite so tedious.

You, she berated herself as she slipped over toward Tiffany and the cameraman, are as bad as a hopeless romantic Sleeper. The opening of Pan's would probably be her first real break in trying to ferret out the identity of the owner and designer. It was not the time to flirt with Aaron Barry. It was work. Real, important work. If she could discover anything, any little clue about the mages behind Pan's, then this annoying cover job would have been worth the trouble.

She had been certain that no entertainment reporter's assistant could dig up information where the Technocracy had failed. As it turned out, she had been wrong. Tiffany had a knack for persuading people to let all sorts of little things slip, and it was child's play for Kate to follow up on those little things with the resources of the New World Order. There had been nothing yet on the owners of Pan's, of course, but she felt sure that she was getting closer. And in the meantime, she had come up with some wonderful new bits of useful information.

Tiffany was not in a good mood. The cameraman saw Kate coming. Tiffany turned to follow his gaze and missed seeing him give her assistant a warning shake of his head before taking off for the doors. She rounded on Kate like an angry cat. "What the hell was that?" she shrieked in her face. There was bourbon on her breath. "You stay with me! You do not run off and dance! Who do you think you are? I am the star here. You are the assistant." She turned away. "Don't think that the station manager isn't going to hear about this."

Kate's lips pressed together until they were a thin line. This was the unfortunate downside of working with Tiffany. The woman had a "star reporter" attitude that had grated on Kate's nerves for far too long. It was unfortunate that she didn't have the time to put Tiffany through one of the New World Order's classes on self-control. Tiffany could have benefited from it immensely. Instead, she pulled the pendant that she wore on a chain around her neck, a ground glass lens in a gold rim, out from under her blouse.

"I don't think he will hear about it, Tiffany," she said quietly, holding it up where it would catch

Tiffany's eye. "I happen to know that you have a rather nasty cocaine habit."

"What? How . . . ?"

"How I know isn't important. What is important is that the station takes a dim view of drug use. Unless you want the station manager to find out about your habit, I suggest that you accept my dancing with Aaron Barry in good spirits." The effect was simple and a traditional spell among New World Order mages—blackmail reinforced with the power of Mind, one of the nine spheres of magickal knowledge. The magick ensured that the subject would agree readily, completely, and happily to any suggestion that she made. The lens was a simple focus, a quick way of doing simple magick when she didn't have a more appropriate and sophisticated Technomancer device prepared. It was almost like hypnotism, though not even that vulgar. Kate decided to push Tiffany a little bit further. "It might also be nice if you understood that I am extremely valuable to you. You couldn't be a reporter without me as your assistant."

"But I couldn't!" Tiffany seemed close to crying as Kate lowered the lens and the magick took full effect. "Oh, Kate, don't you see why I was so angry? You left me! I was absolutely lost!" She took the tissue that Kate offered her with a humble smile. "But your idea of dancing with Aaron was such a wonderful video opportunity! Of course you had to take it!" She dabbed at her eyes, then blew her nose. "You won't tell the manager about my little vice, will you?"

"Of course not, Tiffany." Kate smiled and patted her arm reassuringly. "You just forget all about me even bringing it up."

He was racing down the halls of the Barry mansion, through the darkness, his heart pounding in his chest. He was wearing pyjamas, just like the ones with red stripes he had picked out for himself when his mother had taken him shopping on his eighth birthday. All of his pyjamas after that had had to have red stripes. He had insisted on it until the day that he stopped wearing pyjamas. The thin material flapped around his arms and legs, the buttons of the top half undone so that it fell open, letting the chill night air raise goose bumps on his chest. His feet were bare. He had not stopped to put on slippers when he fled from his bedroom.

Enough moonlight filtered in through the windows along the hall to let him see. The moonlight fell in deep pools, however, leaving even deeper patches of darkness between them. Aaron threw himself through the darkness, from moonlight to moonlight. He wasn't worried about what might be ahead of him because what was behind him was infinitely worse.

Doors lined either side of the hallway, far taller than he was. He could have ducked through any one of them and hoped that he would be safe in the room beyond. He knew what would happen, though—perhaps he had tried it in the past. He would slam the door behind him and jump up onto the bed that was sure to be in the room, huddling at its head, his arms wrapped tightly around the pillow. He would watch the door, but it wouldn't open. Instead, a puddle of darkness would slide underneath the door and stand up, spindly legs unfolding like two long, black sticks. And he would flee again, running out through another door and back into the hall.

The creature that chased him was silent when it ran. Its arms and legs were the same length, as if it had been created by someone who couldn't decide whether it should stand upright or walk on all fours. Its skin was slick and black, its teeth and talons sharp, its eyes yellow, its ears pointed. It had no lips, and that was probably the most inhuman thing about it. There was nothing to hide its teeth, so it seemed to be constantly grinning. Its nose was flat and upturned, nostrils facing out. He had named the creature after its nose. Pig.

He felt teeth nip at him from the darkness at his back and hot, wet breath on his skin. He yelled and tried to scramble away, but those teeth caught in his pyjamas. He went down, the friction of his skin against the carpet burning his chest and palms and cheeks. He felt rather than saw the demon leap over him and back into the darkness. For a moment, he just lay there, breathing hard. Pig was still nearby, sitting in the shadows and grinning. He turned his head slowly and looked.

Pig's eyes and teeth gleamed in the darkness.

Aaron screamed his fright. He felt warm wetness flood down over his legs.

"Goddamn it!" bellowed his father. Peter Barry stumbled out of the gloom on the other side of him. His breath, like Pig's, was hot and wet, but heavy with the smell of scotch. As it had been almost every night since his mother had died three years before. "Son of a bitch!" He hauled Aaron to his feet. Pig was gone, as always. It never appeared except when Aaron was alone. "You little shit! Crying like a baby and pissing your pants! Jesus Christ, you're fifteen years old! Grow up and act your age!" Peter shook his son. "Do you think your mother would be proud of you?"

Aaron tried to tell his father about Pig, just as he always did. The words came out in an incoherent babble, though, and his hands, reaching out to clutch desperately at his father, had no more strength or coordination than the hands of a helpless child. Peter just looked disgusted. He dropped Aaron to the floor and stood over him.

"You're a disgrace. You make me sick. You . . ." Peter raised his hands and his cane was in them, the one that he had used for the last three years. There was blood on its heavy, knobby steel head. Behind him, Aaron could see the servants' stairs and the figure in red-and-white pyjamas that lay motionless at their foot. There was blood around the figure's head as well. Aaron curled himself up into a ball as he listened to his father rant and shout, waiting for the blow to fall. Tears burned his cheeks and sobs wrenched his stomach.

He was covered in sweat and shaking when he woke up. He lay still, staring up at the ceiling for several minutes before even blinking. The nightmares hadn't been so intense in five years. He threw back the covers and went into the bathroom to splash cold water on his face and chest. When he got back into the bed, the woman on the other side rolled over to look at him.

"Are you okay, Aaron?" she asked groggily.

"Fine." He couldn't remember her name, although he remembered the short, tight skirt she had worn. He had left the Screwdriver with her on his arm. "Go back to sleep."

"Can you turn out the light?"

"No." Aaron slid down and pulled the bedclothes up around his shoulders.

"Please?"

"No. I never sleep in the dark."

4

The setting sun dyed the city red and orange. Dusk had been Mike's favorite time of day. The warm, easy color of the light, the fading of the sky into black. The way that the shadows fell and the streetlights came on in the gathering darkness. The magic moment on the very edge of night when day and evening were balanced. He had said once that dusk was like a drug. You got high on it and didn't come down until morning. You really only felt alive at dusk.

Stefan reached for the pint bottle of cheap whisky. Mike had always had a gift for irony. The first night they had spent in the tiny apartment that they had shared, he had turned to Stefan and asked with a perfectly straight face, "Will you be taking the master bedroom or the guest room?" Stefan had laughed all the way down to the mattress they had laid on the floor. Now he took a swig of whisky, looked at the bottle thoughtfully, and then took another.

He leaned up against the side of the open window and looked out toward the northeast, toward the financial district where Mike had . . . He sighed and forced himself to think it. Where Mike had committed suicide at dusk, plunging eighteen stories from an office building to the pavement of Montgomery Street. That had been a month ago. He had tried hard to mourn the loss of his best friend. He had felt knotted up inside. He had suffered a blackout for a day or so after he had heard about it, another memory lapse for the doctor at the clinic to diagnose as stress related. But he hadn't really been able to accept Mike's death. Until now.

Finally receiving Mike's remains from the cops had done it. They had refused to believe Stefan was the closest thing Mike had to next of kin and had insisted on holding the remains for a full thirty days after the medical examiner had finished the autopsy. Stefan snorted. Mike's family back in Tennessee had no idea where their son was—or if they did, they didn't care. Mike had never even told him where in Tennessee he was from. He had his secrets, Mike did, and Stefan had known enough not to try and dig for them. The cops had eventually phoned him up bright and early this morning and told him to come down to the Hall of Justice and get the ashes. The medical examiner had had Mike cremated three weeks ago.

Stefan took another drink from the bottle, then set it down and picked up the urn that the police had given him. Well, not given him exactly. They had charged him twenty bucks for the plain, cheap plastic container, and the medical examiner's office had gouged him for the price of the cremation. He rubbed his thumbs across the smooth surface. He wished he could cry, but he was surprised that he could still even feel loss after all the deaths he had lived through. His parents and brother. His grandparents. His foster parents. Jesus, even every pet he had ever had. Mike was just the latest in a long line of deaths.

He looked down out the window. The roofs of Grace Cathedral lay below. When he had first approached the priests of the cathedral, asking permission to scatter Mike's ashes from the bell tower, they had all but laughed in his face. One of them had taken Stefan aside and carefully explained to him that the cathedral had a policy of not allowing ashes to be scattered on the premises. And certainly not from the bell tower! Yes, he had admitted, it was a very beautiful gesture, but it really couldn't be done.

Getting into the bell tower on his own, however, had been surprisingly easy. Mike had shown him how to pick locks. Stefan had simply found the door, unlocked it, and gone up. No one had stopped him. Security was a beautiful gesture.

He leaned his head back against the stone frame of the window and tried to think of something to say. Mike had told him one night, as they watched the sunset together, that he wanted a twilight funeral ceremony when he died. The real thing, with a eulogy and a priest and the whole nine yards. Stefan opened the urn and looked at the gray ashes inside. A eulogy . . .

He closed his eyes, feeling hollow down to his soul. "Fuck, I loved him."

The Latin words of the funeral service came easily, rolling off of his tongue. Memories of Mike, from the first time he had met him in the little coffee shop on O'Farrell off Polk to the last time he had seen him the morning of the day he had died, played themselves out in his head. As he reached the end of the service, Stefan held the urn out of the window and slowly emptied it. He watched the wind catch the fine ash and blow it across the fiery dusk sky of San Francisco. "*Requiescat in pace*. Amen."

"Amen," someone repeated behind him.

Stefan turned around to find a priest standing at the head of the stairs that led back down into the cathedral. He returned the man's gaze steadily. "Hello, Father." Tucking the urn under one arm, Stefan pulled a pack of cigarettes and a lighter out of a pocket. There was one cigarette left in the pack. He lit it, then tossed the empty packet out the window. The wind caught it and sent it into a whirling, spinning dance on its way down to the street.

The priest watched him without comment. "That can kill you, you know," he observed finally, nodding toward the cigarette.

"We all die. When it's your turn, it doesn't matter how healthy you are."

"Did you get permission to do this?"

"From the bishop himself." Stefan lied easily.

The priest laughed. "So you didn't." He smiled comfortingly and a little sadly. "Even if you had managed to talk to the bishop himself, he wouldn't have given you permission. Bishop Williams would never allow something so irregular to happen."

Stefan realized that the priest was not one of the ones he had been talking to earlier. He smiled back. "I'm sorry, Father. It won't happen again."

"I hope not. No one should have to lay more than one friend to rest." He gestured toward the stairs. "Would you like to talk?"

"No, thanks." Stefan hopped down from the window ledge. The priest's eye fell on the bottle of whisky. Stefan felt slightly embarrassed as he stuffed it into his pocket and started down the stairs. "I have to go."

"You're welcome to come back if you do feel the need to talk with someone. I'm Father Matthews." He hesitated. "You know, your Latin was as perfect as I've ever heard. Better than some of my tutors in college."

Stefan could imagine the confusion the priest must feel. A scruffy, half-tanked hustler dressed in old jeans and a worn leather jacket, dark, thick hair falling almost to his shoulders, and multiple rings gleaming silver in one ear, speaking a language that took intense study to learn. He supposed that he was just so used to it now that he didn't even notice. "Oh. Was that Latin?"

He walked along California Street toward Polk Street slowly. A cable car stopped just ahead of him to make a pickup. He could have caught it if he had run, but there was no sense in hurrying. It was barely fully dark yet. Trade would be slow. Stefan turned south onto Polk, pushing past the occasional family of tourists who had strayed away from the Holiday Inn on Van Ness Avenue. He felt almost as bad now as he had just after Mike's death. He thought about just going home and forgetting about trying to work tonight. The money was the clincher, though, just as it had always been.

A couple of the younger hustlers he knew waved to him as he passed the corner of Polk and Bush. He waved back halfheartedly and caught one of them staring at him as the other whispered in his ear. Half the hustlers on Polk probably knew by now that he had finally received Mike's ashes. He hoped that they would just leave him alone. He had heard enough condolences a month ago to last for a year. He imagined, however, that he would hear more.

He had hardly made it past Geary before he did; a Mexican hustler named Carlos, almost certainly an illegal immigrant although he denied it fiercely, reached out from where he was leaning and stopped him.

"I'm sorry," he said simply in Spanish. "I know how you must feel."

Stefan patted Carlos's arm. "Thanks." He replied in Spanish as well.

"Take this. It'll help." Carlos pulled out a joint and tucked it into a pocket of Stefan's jacket.

"Hey! No way! I gave that up." He started to pull it out, but Carlos caught his hand and pushed it back.

"Keep it, *amigo*. A good binge helps." He wrinkled his nose. "Smells like you're halfway there on the bottle already."

"I . . . thanks, Carlos. I'll be seeing you." He could always sell it, he thought as he walked on down Polk. Some client might buy it, or even another hustler as long as Carlos didn't find out that his gift had been sold.

Stefan's usual hangout for the early evening was a bench on the east side of Polk. The sun shone on it for an hour or so before going down altogether, and the bench retained the heat for a while. The warmth was only good for the very early evening, well before things got busy enough for most hustlers to arrive on the street. Sometimes Stefan liked to come down early, though. It was pleasant to sit and watch people with normal lives go about their business. He took a covert swig from the whisky bottle.

Two hours later, or thereabouts, he was back on the bench, and the level of whisky in the bottle had gone down considerably. Trade was very slow tonight. Mondays were always bad. His mood didn't help. He had already rejected one client he might otherwise have gone with simply because he couldn't be bothered to make it in a car tonight.

Another car pulled up to the curb, a Japanese import. The driver rolled down the window and glanced over at him. Stefan met his gaze and came over. "Nice car," he said, forcing enthusiasm into his voice.

"Thanks. Nice jeans."

"You like them?" Stefan pulled them up a bit to emphasize his crotch. "They're well used."

"Don't say 'well used.' They're experienced." The man grinned at him. "What are you doing tonight?"

Stefan studied him carefully. Blond, good-looking. Seemed healthy. He looked like a doctor—Stefan's "cop-sense" was quiet. "I don't know yet."

"Want to go to a quiet little party in a hotel?"

"Who's going to be there?"

"You and me and . . ." He flashed Stefan a condom.

Stefan raised an eyebrow. Not bad. A client who carried his own protection. "How about Andrew Jackson and six of his brothers?"

The man's smile slipped a little bit. "I think maybe three of Jackson's brothers could make it with him."

Eighty dollars. Far less than he had been able to get when he was a bit younger, less even than he usually made now. Stefan glanced up and down the street. Client traffic was very light tonight . . . and he did not feel like going home to an empty apartment. The man looked good for another forty bucks, though. "I'll bet two more of his brothers would be there if they knew that it was going to be a really, *really* good party." He made deliberate, lingering eye contact with the man. "If you know what I mean."

"I'll bet they would, too." Stefan could practically hear the man's pulse quicken. "In fact, I think they will be there. How about it? Do you feel like the party?"

Stefan opened the door and jumped into the car. "I'm always up for a good time."

Stefan walked into the Princess Café, the shabby little all-night coffee shop on O'Farrell off Polk where he had first met Mike and where he had first heard about his death, about ten o'clock the next evening. The owner and manager weren't particularly selective about their clientele, so the café had become a favorite gathering spot for the various denizens of the San Francisco night. Stefan called out greetings to the hustlers he knew and flirted shamelessly in Korean with the waitress at the counter while she poured him a coffee. Carlos grabbed his arm as he turned away and steered him over to a table.

"I have somebody I want you to meet."

"Another 'I-got-a-language-you-don't-know' bet?" Stefan switched smoothly from Korean to Spanish. He juggled his coffee, the heat scorching his fingertips through the Styrofoam. "How much do you want to lose this time?"

"Let's make it a hundred."

"A hundred and another joint."

"You got it." Carlos sat down with him and gestured for a good-looking, young black man to come over. "Do it," he commanded in English. The black man spoke several sentences in a foreign language, a wicked smile on his face.

Stefan stirred sugar into his coffee. He looked up at the black man and replied in the same language, although his pronunciation was more precise and rapid. The smiled disappeared from the black man's face. Stefan laughed. "Never assume anything in San Francisco, kid."

"Shit."

"Shit piled high and deep." Pulling out a wad of bills, Carlos slid them across the table to Stefan. He set a joint on top. Stefan stuffed the lot into a pocket. The black man frowned.

"Where's my money?"

"I don't get no cash, you don't get no cash," snarled Carlos. "Go get me a coffee."

"You said—"

"Just get me coffee. You got a lot to learn." Carlos glowered at him until he shrugged and headed over to the counter. Carlos turned back to Stefan and said in Spanish, "I hooked up with him last night. Doesn't know shit about hustling."

"Your new apprentice?"

"Yeah." He pulled out a cigarette and lit it. "Someday I'm going to call you out on a language," he said bitterly as he pulled the cheap glass ashtray closer to him. "How the hell do you do that?"

Stefan winked. "I sneak into USF during the day and take classes.What was that?"

"Ashanti. His family are immigrants."

"No shit?" Stefan rolled the language around his mouth, testing the feel of the words. "African?" When Carlos nodded, he asked, "I don't suppose you know what part?"

"The middle someplace, I think. Maybe in the west. How do you do that?"

"Beats the fuck out of me. You ever heard of the universal unconscious? Ancestral memories? I think maybe its something like that—I hear a language and bang!" He slapped the worn tabletop for emphasis. Glasses rattled. "I know it."

"Bullshit. You didn't have ancestors that spoke Ashanti, and Korean, and Navajo, and Spanish."

"Studly bastards, my ancestors. They got around. You got a better explanation?"

Carlos tapped his head. "You're psychic. You pick the languages right out of somebody's mind. That's why you got to hear the language first. You ought to go on talk shows. Big bucks, *amigo*."

"'Psychic hustlers, tomorrow on Oprah'? No way! You get into that business, you need an agent. You have to keep to schedules. I don't want that. I'm a free man. Nobody organizes my life. I don't need anybody."

"Anybody but Mike?"

Stefan froze, coffee cup halfway to his mouth. "Thank you very fucking much, Carlos."

The Mexican's mouth twisted into a grimace. "Hey, I didn't mean it that way. I'm sorry. I really am."

"Fuck off."

"Listen, Stefan—"

"Fuck off!"

"Okay!" Carlos stood up. "You come see me when you're feeling better, right? We're still friends. You know where to find me."

He sauntered off across the coffee shop, intercepting the black man and redirecting him over to another table. A sour smile spread across Stefan's face as he watched them. Mike and he had been both student and teacher to each other. Mike had taught him the hustling business; he had worked his way across the country to San Francisco before they had met four years ago. Stefan had helped Mike cope through the tough times. If there was one thing Stefan knew, it was tough times.

They had been casual friends for a year and a half, drifting independently through hostels and flophouses. For a long time, neither of them had been sure if the other was truly gay. You never admitted being gay to another hustler. There were a lot of antigay feelings on the street, even among the men who sold their bodies. Clients were gay, hustlers were not.

Then Mike had got his hands on some really good marijuana and shared it with Stefan. Sometime during the night, they had admitted to each other that they were gay. Stefan couldn't remember which of them had said it first. He did remember vividly what happened afterwards, though. They had sat on the dew-wet grass of a hillside in Golden Gate Park and just looked at each other. Stefan had felt as if his stomach were tied up in knots, a solid band of nervousness tight around his chest. He had had trouble breathing, and the marijuana had sent him into a coughing fit. Mike had slapped him on the back and asked if he was all right. Stefan had looked up and their eyes had met. Mike had said later that he'd never noticed before how blue Stefan's eyes were. They didn't have to say that they loved each other.

He stared into his coffee. That had been a little more than two and a half years ago. They had managed to get an apartment—only slightly larger than a bread box, but an apartment that was theirs. Together they got some furniture. Mike had hooked up with a good escort service and stopped working the streets. He even had a couple of regular clients. Stefan had tried escorting for services for a while, but it hadn't worked out. Too much of a schedule. He had gone back to the streets, making some money there and running an ad in the models/escorts section of the *Bay Area Reporter*. *Hot Body. Athletic 19-year-old with endurance. Full massage or escort. Call Stefan.* He hadn't even lied too much—nineteen instead of twenty-two, athletic when the most he usually did was run a little and lift weights around the apartment. No clients had complained yet, though.

He pulled out the joint he had won from Carlos and contemplated it. The client he had taken last night had offered him a line of cocaine. Resisting the urge had been very, very hard. He had sworn to himself that he would never get mixed up in hard drugs. In the end, however, the loss he felt over Mike's death had driven him under. He had done the cocaine, then offered Carlos's joint to the client. Later, with the drugs singing in his brain, he had taken the money the client had paid him, gone out, and bought some more marijuana. He had returned to the hotel and shared it with the client, trying to lose himself in the haze of grass and sex. The client must have thought he had died and gone to some indecent, X-rated afterlife. Stefan had slipped out in the middle of the morning before the client had woken up.

Tucking the joint back into his pocket, he left the coffee shop. He would never do cocaine again. Never. He promised himself that. He had no desire to get caught in that trap. Marijuana, on the other hand . . . he could control that habit. He stepped off the street into an alley beside a parking lot and lit the joint. He inhaled deeply, closed his eyes, and held the smoke in his lungs for a moment. In the parking lot, a car started up. A car door opened and closed. Over the noise of the car driving away, he heard the sound of someone in high heels approaching him.

He opened his eyes to face a woman with platinum blond hair, full lips, and slightly too much makeup concealing an aging face. She applied fresh lipstick as she walked, her eyes glaring at him accusatorially. "That better not be what I think it is, Stef."

"Depends what you think it is, Marilyn."

"I think that it's pot." She got close enough to smell the smoke as Stefan exhaled it. "Oh, baby, I thought you quit that stuff."

"Quitting is just the time between fixes, Mother." He leaned forward and gave her a quick kiss. He could still smell the cologne from her last trick clinging to her skin.

She pushed him back. "Don't call me that. I always get cold when the johns say it. Did Carlos get you started again? I'll rip the bugger's balls off if he did."

"No. It wasn't Carlos." He took another hit from the joint.

Marilyn hesitated for a moment, then asked softly, "Mike?"

"I got his ashes back yesterday and finally put him to rest. It hurts, Marilyn."

"Poor baby." Marilyn held out her arms. Stefan stepped closer and let her pull him into a warm, comforting embrace. "You'll get over it. You'll always have the memories."

"Lot of good they'll do me."

"Don't say that." She stroked his hair and squeezed him tight.

He sighed. "I'm not going to be able to keep the apartment without Mike."

"Bullshit. You got money stashed somewhere. I know you do." She tweaked his chin. "You're still young. You look good. You can pull in the bucks for a few more years. Find yourself a sugar daddy to take care of you."

Stefan shook his head. Four years on the street

brought down the amount of money a hustler could bring in. Clients wanted new faces. A hustler on the street too long found his income creeping steadily lower. And a hustler's lifestyle was not conducive to savings accounts and long-term investments. If he still had all the money that had slipped through his fingers . . . "Mike was pretty much supporting us. Between the two of us, we stayed comfortable. He was the one who really paid the rent, though. I just can't make enough on my own."

"You could move to something cheaper."

"Do you know how much trouble we had getting this place? Besides, there are still six months on the lease. I can't afford to lose the deposit. I'm not sure I'm even going to be able to make the rent for next month."

He looked at Marilyn. She looked back at him, her mouth slightly open as if ready to speak but not quite sure what to say. He shrugged off her arms, half guessing at what she was going to suggest next, and took a drag from the joint. "I can't go back to the escort services. I want the free—"

"Don't give me any crap about getting tied down. Remember who you're talking to. Marilyn, mother confessor and career counselor to prostitutes of all flavors." She smiled. Stefan just regarded her with a steady gaze and blew a stream of smoke out the side of his mouth. Marilyn let her lips lapse into a hard, flinty line. "It's good money, Stefan. Better than you make on the street, and enough to get by on. With your looks, it would be steady, too. You might be able to pick up some regular clients."

"What service is going to hire me?"

"That was a fluke."

"Having clients die three times is not a fluke. Service owners tend to notice these things, especially when I get hauled downtown by the cops twice as a prime suspect."

"Those were accidents! It wasn't your fault!"

"Tell that to the services."

"There are new services in town now."

"They'll have heard about it." Stefan stubbed out the butt of his joint carefully and tucked it inside a packet of cigarettes. He sat down on the steel rail barrier that ran around the parking lot. "If not from the other services, then from the hustlers. Do you know that I've had clients reject me on the street because of what they've heard from other hustlers?"

"You could get a straight job."

"On what qualifications?" He slumped, letting his head hang down. "You're right. As usual." He smiled thinly. "Valentine's always been after me to go back to his service. He doesn't care."

"No!" Marilyn snapped abruptly. "If you do one thing, I want you to promise me you'll never go back to Valentine. I'd rather see you starving on the streets."

"I wouldn't."

"Promise me, Stef." Marilyn crouched down beside him, concern written on her face. "Promise me you won't go back to Valentine. No matter what."

Stefan looked at her. Marilyn had been his mentor, even more than Mike had. The old hooker was like a second, or third, mother to him. "I can't, Marilyn. I need to make a living."

"Mike wouldn't have wanted you to go back."

Stefan squeezed his eyes shut. "That's fighting dirty, Marilyn."

"You do what you have to, baby."

You do what you have to, Marilyn, Stefan thought to himself as he climbed the stairs to the second floor of the modern-looking red-brick building. The first floor held a Chinese grocery, a coffee shop that was moderately more upscale than the Princess Café, a restaurant specializing in deserts, and a video store. The upstairs was home to the offices and "boardrooms" of Valentine's Escorts, Inc.

He had promised Marilyn that he would not approach Valentine, and he felt guilty that he had to do it now. But he had no other choice; every other service that he had applied to had turned him down cold. Some had done it in a very nice way, suggesting that they had no need for another escort. Some had done it curtly. A few, mostly the older services, had been thrown into an uproar by his mere appearance on their doorstep. He had been physically ejected from the offices of one escort service. He had no options now but to try Valentine's or face slow deterioration on the streets.

The heavy metal door at the top of the stairs opened easily. Dance music, played relatively softly and floating on air that was warm and scented with a heavy, exotic fragrance, greeted him. Valentine's reception area was small and perhaps slightly heavy with red tones, but it was as lushly appointed as any corporate reception area. There was someone new at the reception desk, a bored young man with very fair skin and blond hair. He wore a light silk shirt that clung ever so slightly to his shoulders. Like all of the staff here, he was also merchandise.

Stefan stepped up to the desk. "I want to see Valentine."

The young man smiled ingratiatingly. "I'm sorry. Valentine isn't a real person—"

"Like hell he isn't. Don't give me the corporate symbol line—I want to talk to Valentine."

"He's not in."

Stefan sat down on the desk and leaned over toward the young man. "Look, precious. I've worked for Valentine before. You know the toys that he keeps in the White Room? If you don't tell Valentine that I'm here to see him, I will drag you down there by your lovely, curly locks and demonstrate the use of each one of them in careful, intimate detail."

The young man blanched and reached for the phone as Stefan stood and paced around the reception area. "Valentine," he said softly, "there's someone here to see you."

"Tell him it's Stefan."

The young man repeated the message. A look of surprise spread across his face, and he hung up the receiver. "He says go on in. Second door on the right."

"I know."

The hall that led back from the reception area was longer than Stefan remembered, and dimmer as well. Maybe it just seemed that way. The scent that drifted back from the reception area couldn't cover up the smell that lingered in the hall, a raw, primal odor that did nothing to inspire confidence in Stefan. As much as he tried to put on a show of bravado, Stefan was scared.

The door to Valentine's office was painted a garish canary yellow. It was a rather unattractive color, but all of the attractive colors had been applied to the doors of the other rooms in the hall. The White Room, the Blue Room, the Green Room, the Red Room, the Black Room. Valentine referred to them as his "boardrooms," but they were actually theme rooms that he was willing to rent out to clients whose tastes were particularly . . . specific. The exotic, unusual, and downright depraved were Valentine's specialty. Stefan raised his hand and knocked on the yellow door. He went in without waiting for an invitation.

Valentine looked up from his desk. He put down his pen and settled his bulk back in his chair. Valentine was a big man. His massive frame was padded with muscle, however, not fat. Stefan had once seen him put an unruly client right through the wall of the Red Room. He regarded Stefan levelly. "I never thought I'd actually see you back here again."

Stefan shrugged. "Neither did I." He sat down in one of the padded chairs across from Valentine's desk. "You're looking good. The offices haven't changed much. How's business?"

"There are a lot of strange people out there."

"Any problems with the cops?"

"I keep my business license up and pay my bribes. I don't get trouble." He leaned forward, his chair squealing in protest. "But enough about me. Things aren't going too well for you, are they? I was sorry to hear about Mike."

"I need money, Valentine." There was no point in trying to hide his situation. Valentine could smell desperation a mile away. Stefan decided to lay his cards plainly on the table. "I'm not making enough on my own, and no other service is willing to take me."

"Ahh . . ." Valentine smiled at him, hands flat on the desk.

There was silence. Stefan ground his teeth in frustration. Valentine wouldn't offer him anything; he wanted him to come crawling back, begging his indulgence. Unfortunately, Stefan didn't have any other choice. "I was wondering if you'd be willing to take me on again."

Valentine's smile grew broader and more satisfied. "I don't know," he said casually, "there's the small matter of your abrupt departure from my employment last time."

"I was the best you had, Valentine. You know it."

"You were lucky that last client was too embarrassed to go to the police."

Stefan shivered. "Do you know what she wanted to do?"

He shook his head. "You knew the rules of the game when you took the job with me." Valentine made a steeple out of his fingers and regarded him carefully. The look in his eyes made Stefan shiver again. "I run a very ordinary service for people with some very extraordinary predilections. You want to work for me, you do whatever the client wants you to do." He smiled again. "I like you, Stefan. You're good-looking. You're generally on time for appointments. You have a talent for acting roles. You're not too squeamish."

"You can make money off the hustler who had three clients die in bed."

"There are people who will pay to sleep with you because of that." Valentine stood up and stepped out from behind his desk. "Same deal as before—sixty percent to you, forty percent to me. This is a specialized business, so I can afford to be generous." He paused, his hand half extended. "But I want to hear those five little words before I hire you again."

Stefan's heart sank. He had hoped that he would never have to do this again. Even on the street, there was a little loss every time he sold himself. Working for Valentine felt like selling his soul. But he needed the money so desperately! He took a deep breath and said numbly, "I'll do anything they want."

"That's my boy!" Valentine pulled him into a rough hug, then suddenly threw him violently to the ground. Stefan found himself looking up with Valentine's foot on his throat. Valentine was smiling hideously. "Just remember, though," he snarled softly, "you foul me up this time, and your ass is mine to play with."

All that Stefan could do was nod weakly and gasp out, "When can I start?"

Valentine took his foot away and walked back around behind his desk, leaving Stefan to stand up on his own. "You're lucky. Do you still speak Russian? I have a couple who want an 'imported' escort. They were fairly specific about the costume." He wrote the information down on a slip of paper. "It's for Friday night, the opening of a new nightclub. A place called Pan's."

Aaron glanced at his watch: 2:27 A.M. He turned up the collar of the black coat that he wore, ready to move. Across the street stood Pan's, its facade hung with a huge banner that proclaimed GRAND OPENING TOMORROW NIGHT! Although the club would be bustling and busy tomorrow, the side street that Pan's stood on was empty tonight. Or almost empty, he thought with a grin as he caught the sound of an approaching vehicle.

A battered pickup truck with the words HAMMER SECURITY SERVICES emblazoned on the side came roaring around a nearby corner and accelerated, heading straight toward Pan's. At the last moment, the driver braked hard. The truck went into a skid. In spite of the driver's efforts, the rear of the truck slammed sideways into a light pole in front of the club door. The pole snapped off under the force of the impact, crashing down to the sidewalk. The light shattered.

The driver of the truck, a small woman in a security guard's uniform, got out and stood swearing at the fallen light pole, the dent in her truck, her no-good husband, and the world in general for several minutes. Finally, she staggered drunkenly over to the club doors, tested them to make sure they were locked, and then continued her stagger around to the back of the building where the construction entrance was located. He could hear her muttering loudly about the trouble she was going to catch even after she was out of sight.

2:34 A.M. Aaron waited exactly two more minutes before racing across the street and up to the doors of Pan's. He skirted the broken light and the strange black box attached to the top of it. He knocked once, then three times in rapid succession on the door. The locks clicked from the inside, and the door swung open. Aaron ducked in and pulled the door shut behind him. "Good work."

"Think they bought it?" The security guard pulled off her cap as she led him further into the club. Her long brown hair had been tucked into a knot at the nape of her neck. "I've been acting like I was piss drunk at least once a week while I made my rounds. Last week I mowed down a bunch of garbage cans."

"Let's hope they did buy it. You're sure that was the only camera out front?"

"Positive. There's another camera in the alley and two out back, but that was the only one on the street. The front door hasn't been opened since we installed it three weeks ago. Why should they watch it?"

Aaron shook her hand. "You're a wonder, Tango."

The woman shrugged. "I try. Hammer Security wants to give me a raise."

"I'll see their raise and double it. I can't afford to lose the best club manager and sabotage artist I've ever seen." He swept her up into a hug and gave her a solid kiss before releasing her. "They might not want to keep you after they find out about the light pole, anyways." He took Tango's flashlight from her and flashed it around the visible portions of the club's interior. "The place looks good."

After almost nine months, Pan's was nearly finished. The final coat of paint had been applied to the walls, and the decorators had finished their work. The cash registers were in place on the bar. Tables and chairs were stacked under a dust cloth in one corner, ready to be set out tomorrow. Kegs of beer and boxes of liquor were piled in another corner. Aaron shone the light up toward the ceiling. Exposed wiring hung down.

"Not a camera in the place yet. Not even any focused lights," Tango commented. "No lenses of any kind at all, as per instructions." She smiled slyly. "The lights were delayed in customs thanks to a friend of mine. The cameras were damaged while they were being unloaded."

"Sometimes I could swear you were a mage."

"We did have to install the monitors for the video wall, but they're still completely disconnected from any outside link."

"Telephones?"

"The wiring is installed, but the phone company's not dropping off the equipment until tomorrow." She shook her head. "Everything is coming tomorrow. It's going to be a zoo around here if we want to open on time."

"It will be worth it if we can deny the New World Order a way to spy inside tonight. Without lenses or a link to outside the building, they can't do a thing. I'm sorry I had to wait so long, but I didn't expect my father to die." Aaron returned the flashlight to her. "I had thought I would be flying in and out of San Francisco rather than staying here."

"I'm . . . sorry about him."

"Don't be. Do you know I actually stayed up one night worrying about whether his death was really just a coincidence or if I had somehow unconsciously caused it? Then in the morning, I realized I didn't really care." He gave a little sigh. "No other problems?"

Tango hesitated. "Apart from Richardson's death? No. The media has been pressing to find out the name of the owner, but I've been telling them that even I don't know for sure." She looked at Aaron sideways. "You're very good at creating corporate mazes."

"Don't ask me who exactly owns Pan's and you won't be lying when you say you don't know." Aaron glanced at his watch again. "I'm expecting my guest soon. She'll probably be a little bit confused."

"What's her name?"

"Kate . . . no, Karin."

"Can't keep your babes straight?" Tango laughed. She pulled her cap back on. "I have to get back out before long and let the cameras see me leaving, or they might get suspicious. Everything is ready for you on the dance floor."

"Good."

Somewhere behind them, the front door of the club opened slowly and closed again. Timid footsteps echoed on the floor. Tango glanced at Aaron. He nodded and faded off into the darkness. Tango slipped back toward the front door, her flashlight off. Stealthily, she crept up on the woman who stood looking around in the coat-check vestibule, a lighter her only source of illumination.

"Can I help you?" she asked the woman mildly.

The woman almost jumped out of her skin. The lighter went out. Tango switched on her flashlight, catching the women in its beam like a deer in headlights. The woman gasped. "I . . . I'm sorry." She swallowed and caught her breath sharply. "My name is Karin. I'm looking for Aaron Barry. He told me to come see him sometime and I just knew that tonight he would . . . He is here, isn't he?"

Tango smiled. "Of course." She walked around behind the woman to re-lock the front doors. "Follow me." She led the woman into the cavernous main area of the club, careful to keep her flashlight trained on the floor. The less the woman saw before the proper time, Aaron had instructed her, the better. In the middle of the floor, she stopped. "Wait here." She turned off the flashlight.

Karin froze in the darkness. "Hello?" she whispered. "Are you there? Is anybody there? A-Aaron?"

Somewhere in another part of the building, a door opened and closed. Startled, Karin whirled around. She turned again at a tiny noise from behind her. And again as something creaked off in the shadows. Alone in the open, echoing space, her panic growing, she seemed like a frightened animal. "Aaron!"

"I'm here."

Light flowered in the dimness as he struck a match and touched it to the wick of a candle. From that candle, he lit another, and another, and another, until Pan's was illuminated with the flickering light of a score of candles. Set in stands of all varieties, the tapers made a circle around the cushions and thick Oriental rugs that had been spread across the dance floor. The mirrors that decorated the club caught the candles' light and turned it into a shimmering web. Half in the shadows, half in the light, Aaron uncovered an ornate incense burner and dumped powdered incense over the coals within. Then, as ribbons of fragrant white smoke began to pour out of the burner, Aaron turned so that Karin could see him fully.

He wore jeans, black boots adorned with silver chains, and a black leather jacket, but no shirt. One of his nipples was pierced. He reached out, gesturing for Karin to come forward. The jacket brushing against his bare skin made a soft sighing sound. Karin walked forward very slowly. For a moment she just looked at him, skin turned coppery by the candlelight, then reached out, almost involuntarily, and traced the muscular lines of his chest, her finger lingering on the pierced nipple. Aaron's sigh of pleasure was almost as soft as the sound of his jacket against his skin.

"Karin," he whispered, "do you know why you're here?"

She nodded, her eyes still fixed on his chest. "You're going to make love to me."

"I'm going to make love to Pan's." Aaron bent his head and kissed her deeply. He pushed her coat off of her shoulders, letting it slide to the floor. From the pocket of his jacket, he produced a recorder. He put it to his lips and began to play, all the while looking into her eyes. The music he made was warm, slow, and sensual, music that called to the sensations of the body. Karin flushed.

Aaron lowered the recorder and reached out with one hand to stroke the side of her face. She shivered at the delightful rapture that the touch woke within her. Aaron smiled. Karin's brashness at the Screwdriver had first attracted his attention. A simple magick had confirmed her virginity—he had been fortunate to find both brashness and virginity so readily. This spell would require both, and the sacrifice of one.

"You are Pan's, Karin. Its walls are your body. Your virginity is its virginity. The ecstasy you feel, Pan's will feel as well."

She nodded silently, eyes barely open. She reached out with her arms and wrapped them around Aaron, submersing herself in his smell of leather and incense. Aaron slid his free hand up her back, and she gasped at the pleasurable sensation. Echoes made it seem as though that gasp came from the club walls themselves. Karin was Pan's. Pan's was Karin. They were one.

"Now," Aaron murmured, "share what you feel with me." He blew into the recorder, producing a single pure note that lingered in the air. The reflected light of the candles trembled around them. Karin and Pan's

opened their lips and drew Aaron's mouth down to
theirs, freely passing him all that they felt. Aaron
touched them. They moaned. He moaned with them.

"Do you believe in magick?" he asked them softly.

"Yes."

He stepped away from them for a moment, drawing
a long piece of fine white silk from his sleeve. Taking
their hand and placing it palm-to-palm with one of
his own, he bound them together. Even the light
brush of the fabric made the breath hiss between
their teeth. Aaron left the ends of the silk hanging.

Where the silk grazed the floor, a soft light began
to grow, spreading up its length until their bound
hands were enveloped in a white glow. "What is it?"
they asked in wonder.

"Tass." Aaron kissed them again. By the time he let
them go, the glow had dispersed out like a mist
through the building that was their larger body. He
smiled. "The energy of reality—Quintessence. Pure
magick bound into something you can hold."

He drew them both down to the carpets.

Aaron stood on the roof of Pan's, barechested and
barefoot as the light of dawn rolled over San
Francisco. Arms spread wide, he reveled in the feel of
the cold, fresh morning air. Too few mages were truly
able to appreciate life, so completely caught up in the
pursuit of Ascension that they did not have time for
its most basic pleasures. The mages of the Cult of
Ecstasy knew the truth, however. The appreciation of
life and its pleasures was the path to Ascension.
Hedonism was transcendent. Ascension could be
found in ecstasy and altered states of consciousness.
Some Cultists used drugs to achieve that ecstasy;
Aaron preferred the delights of physical sensation.
The touch of the breeze, the kiss of the sun, the deep
rapture of sex. Aaron sighed and turned to let the sun

play across his back. He half suspected that the skin cancer panic of the last few years was a Technomancer plot to scare people away from the heady, simple delights of sunbathing.

Karin was gone, sent home in a cab that had been driving past conveniently when he let her out of the club doors. She would remember the night as a pleasant, possibly somewhat embarrassing, dream—he had used magick to blur her memories. The carpets and candles and cushions had already been packed into several large sealed crates that Tango would arrange to have taken away later in the day. He should be going soon as well. The New World Order would eventually send agents to repair the monitoring camera that had been hidden atop the lamppost Tango had knocked down. Depending on the depth of the suspicions they harbored about Pan's, the repairs might occur within a couple of hours. He would hate to be caught inside Pan's without an easy means of escape when the camera went back on-line.

He hoped the New World Order had indeed believed the deception that they had gone through in order to break that camera in the first place. Tango's ruse was complicated, but it had the advantage of being mundane. He could have disabled the cameras easily with magick. An effect of repetition, drawing on the magickal sphere of Time, would have kept the cameras transmitting the same scene back to the Technomancers' monitoring screens over and over again. He could have slipped through the spirit space of the Umbra and into the club using Spirit magick, although he suspected that the New World Order's cameras might be capable of viewing Umbral, as well as physical, events. If he had had greater skill in the sphere of Entropy, he might have been able to render the cameras incapable of recording anything but static. Greater skill in the sphere of Correspondence might have allowed him to teleport himself into the club by stepping through space, avoiding the cameras altogether.

But all of those strategies would have required the use of vulgar magick to rend the fabric of reality, and that carried the risk of Paradox. The use of any magick at all, even the gentler static magick that reality could accept as mere coincidence, might have caught the notice of the New World Order. Who knew what gimmicks they built into their cameras? It was better to risk the complications of an entirely mundane plan. Aaron didn't want knowledge that he was a mage, or that he was involved with Pan's in any way at all, abroad in San Francisco. At least not until the proper time.

And he certainly didn't want the Technocracy to figure out what was happening with Pan's. As soon as Tango had informed him that Richardson, one of the architects, had disappeared and later been found dead, Aaron had known that the Technocracy had taken the bait he had set. He had realized that there was a very good chance that it would stumble across the magick inherent in Pan's sooner or later anyway, so he had deliberately placed false clues as to the club's purpose. The symbols he had planted in the design for Pan's were decoys. They might have spoken of an intent to transform the club into a node, a source of plentiful Quintessence, but the club would never develop into any such thing. Eventually, the Technocracy would grow tired watching the club, assume that the arcane symbolism in the club's design had been accidental, and turn its back on Pan's, leaving Aaron in peace.

The true purpose of Pan's was much less obvious, and last night's encounter with Karin had enabled him to activate the magick behind the building without the Technocracy knowing about it. Pan's fed him power of the kind that only another Cult of Ecstasy mage could understand. Ecstasy Cultists required the transcendent power of some vice to act as a focus for much of their magick. Aaron's vice was sensation, especially the sensation of pleasure. But magick based on a vice was slow. Indulging in a vice took time, and was often . . . awkward. Especially in his case. Pan's provided Aaron with an alternate source for his vice—the pleasurable sensations experienced by its patrons.

The sex he had had with Karin last night had been a complex ceremony based on coincidental magick that had enabled Aaron to rouse the magick in the club. To Karin, the feeling of unity with Pan's and Aaron that she had experienced would have seemed like some kind of drug-induced hallucination, possibly the result of something in the incense. In fact, it had been magick. He had linked Karin with Pan's, then connected with her mind as a symbolic gesture of connecting with the club. The pleasure she had felt represented the pleasurable sensations of every future patron of Pan's, pleasure that the club would feed to Aaron. He would experience those sensations as if they were his own. It was instant vice, a powerful focus for his magick.

Magick of the spheres of Spirit and Correspondence to link Aaron and Pan's. The sphere of Mind to tap into the sensations of Pan's future patrons. The sphere of Prime, the magick of manipulating the power that underlay all magick, to bind Quintessence to the link and make it all permanent. He had learned the theory that had made the ceremony possible during his long years abroad. He smiled. Not all of his time had been spent in the scandals that the media loved and his father had loathed. In fact, much of the scandal had been part of his learning as an apprentice in the Cult of Ecstasy. He had had many different tutors, not the least of whom was his first mentor, a little old Irish woman posing as a music teacher at the British boarding school to which his father had shipped him. She had recognized the ability inherent in him and given him his first lessons in magick. And his first lessons on the recorder.

He went back inside, tugging lightly on his pierced nipple as he climbed down the stairs and shivering at the delightful feedback that it created in him. He felt the sensation once personally, and then again through Pan's, and again, and again. His own sensations inside the club were magnified exponentially. To a limit, of course. There was a ceiling on the amount of sensation that the club would feed him from any source, since otherwise he might easily be overwhelmed when the club was packed. When Pan's was empty during the day he would not necessarily be any more powerful than another mage, but by night . . .

Aaron stepped out onto the floor of the club and gave his nipple ring another tug. Pleasure washed over him in a mind-altering experience, the essence of the reality of the Cult of Ecstasy. By night he would have the full force of that reality behind him.

And he would need it. The reasons why people became mages were varied. Some sought personal power. Most sought after the enlightenment of Ascension in one way or another. Aaron's motivation was far simpler. He wanted revenge, revenge and the destruction of the demon who had tormented him. Pig's first hideous manifestation, an evil, yellow-eyed, inhuman shadow lurking in the shadows of the servants' stairs, had sent Aaron screaming for the relative safety of his bedroom. Later Pig had grown in power, appearing physically, chasing him through the halls of the Barry mansion and actually eating his pets in front of his eyes. No one had ever believed him when he had tried to tell them about Pig—the demon had only been able to manifest at night, inside

the mansion and only when Aaron was alone. Later he
began to manifest during the day as well, and on the
mansion grounds.

Aaron clenched his fists as he picked up his shirt
and jerked it savagely over his head. No wonder his
father and William Pierce had thought he was suffering from some kind of instability. Their decision to
send him away to England had probably been the
only thing to save him in the end. The memory of
Pig's abuses had driven him to find a way to destroy
the demon, though. Pig might still inspire fear in him,
the lingering effects of old terrors, but at least Aaron
was prepared to meet Pig on equal terms now.

The atmosphere of Pan's hit Kate the moment she followed Tiffany through the doors of the club. She
looked around in awe. She had told Aaron the truth
when she said that she hadn't gotten out to clubs
much. Even so, she liked to think that she had seen
something of the ways in which Sleepers amused
themselves. None of those experiences had prepared
her for Pan's. Julia and her other superiors in the New
World Order would have been horrified.

The club was overwhelming. Somehow it managed
to mix elements of a Greek temple, a carnival fun-
house, and a hi-tech brothel in its design. Lights
flashed in a dazzling display across a main dance floor
that was easily as large as a basketball court.
Somewhere at the back of the club, according to
Julia's blueprints, were two or three other rooms with
smaller dance floors. A bank of video monitors occupied one entire wall. Computer graphics, rock videos,
and live shots of the dancers themselves flickered
across it. There were two people in the control booth
above the dance floor, one to program the music and
one to control the video wall.

Stairs and ramps ascended to large viewing and seating platforms raised off the floor to various heights and interconnected by catwalks and more stairs. The space was entirely open, so all of the levels had a view of the main dance floor. Kate felt as though she was in some kind of arena, a latter-day Coliseum. The Roman gladiatorial contests must have had the same feel of spectacle and tense struggle that permeated Pan's.

The walls were adorned with bold, splashy graphic designs. They approached psychedelic proportions, and Kate found it hard to keep her eyes on them. Everything in the club's decoration encouraged the eye to keep moving. More video monitors were scattered throughout the club. There were several large, bright murals depicting people engaged in a variety of stimulating activities. Kate glanced away. The murals came very close to being pornographic. Platforms in the middle of the dance floor and niches in the walls held hired dancers—two dancers moved together in a gleaming steel cage raised up behind the bar. The mirrors that were attached to every surface that was not otherwise decorated made the club seem even more dynamic than it was already, reflecting every movement of lights and people.

And there were people everywhere. It was difficult to move through the crowds without at least brushing another person, and at some points it was necessary to squeeze past people in a way that would have been exceedingly intimate under other circumstances. In a place like Pan's, though, such fleeting physical contact was not only permissible, but, Kate would almost have guessed, deliberately encouraged. It raised the sexual tension in the building. She couldn't shake the feeling that any minute might see the dancing turn into an orgy. Or a riot.

What was even more disturbing was the fact that

the tension called to her. In the pit of her stomach, Kate wanted to join in that sensual, lusty experience.

"Mmmm . . ." Tiffany licked her lips as her eyes followed a young blond man that was just barely half her age. "I think I could like this place." She tore her eyes away and gestured to the cameraman. "Let's do the first spot for the show so I can get a drink."

"Up there," suggested Kate, pointing to a platform. "We can get a good shot looking down." Tiffany frowned at the crowded steps they would have to climb, but sighed and started up after a hard glare from Kate.

The platform was also a good vantage point from which Kate could scan the club for signs of magickal activity. As Tiffany started talking to the camera, Kate pulled out a small set of what might have resembled opera glasses if opera glasses came with blinking lights, tiny internal liquid crystal displays, and a number of New World Order–enhanced features. Kate turned to look out over the club and pressed a button to activate the magick of the device.

The patterns of Life and Matter that made up Pan's and its patrons as parts of the fabric of reality faded out of her sight. All that remained were the magickal elements the Technocracy had first noticed in the building: the arrangements of beams, wiring, concavities, and tile patterns. Kate had digitized the blueprints of the club earlier, then downloaded them into the powerful miniature computer built into the glasses. Using the preprogrammed computer and Technomancer magick, she could selectively block out any extraneous patterns and concentrate on the magickal elements of the architecture. The magick of the glasses drew on the sphere of Prime and allowed her to see any magick that was active in those elements.

A careful scan brought nothing but a faint curse to her lips, however. The magickal elements were no more active than they had been weeks ago! She could identify them more easily, of course, now that she could see them as more than just representations on a blueprint. The tiled patterns on the floor were clear beneath the invisible feet of the crowd. The beams of the ceiling and the fine web of electrical wiring in the walls seemed to glisten ever so slightly. The strange concavities in the walls were disguised as the niches in which dancers performed. But there was no Quintessence moving through them. If Pan's was to become a node, it had not yet been activated.

She had been sure that any ceremony of activation would have already taken place, even though the New World Order's surveillance of the club had been airtight. It seemed unlikely that such a ceremony could be conducted now that the club was open and filled with Sleepers for much of the time. Still, this was the big opening bash. If the mages who had built Pan's were going to be present at any time, this would be the event to draw them out into the public eye. She pressed another button on the glasses. The magickal elements of the architecture vanished. The patterns of the people crowding the club returned, this time illuminated by a dull reddish light. Kate swept her gaze across Pan's, carefully studying its patrons. The reddish light was a scanning function, combining the spheres of Life and Prime to check for extra Quintessence stored in the patterns of the people below. Any mages in the club would show up as blinding glares as the glasses picked up the power inherent in them. This magickal effect was short-lived and unstable, but it would certainly serve long enough for her to pick out the builders of Pan's.

No glares appeared on the dance floor. A strange pattern caught her eye on one of the platforms nearby, however: not brighter than the other patterns around it, but actually shadowy and muted. It was clearly a magickal effect of some kind, though she couldn't identify it. Kate lowered the glasses for a moment. The Sleeper was a handsome young man with black hair, wearing a sun-bleached denim jacket and sitting with a couple in more formal evening wear. She committed his features to memory as someone who might be working with the mages of Pan's and continued inspecting the club.

The light touch on her shoulder startled her, so intent was she on searching out the hidden mages she knew must be present. She almost dropped the glasses. When she looked over her shoulder, though, no one was there. There was another touch on her other shoulder, but this time she was ready for the culprit and simply turned around completely, slipping the glasses into her pocket as she did so. She caught Aaron Barry just as he tried to move over out of her line of sight. He grinned at her impishly.

"I couldn't resist. You looked so occupied." He stepped forward to stand beside her. "What were you looking at?"

"Just the dancers." Kate hesitated. She should be continuing her investigation of the club, not flirting with Aaron. But there was nothing else that she could see from up here anyway. Anything she did now would have to involve linking with the security system to get a better sense of who was in the club. That was complicated, certainly too complicated to perform tonight. The club was not likely to suddenly burst into full activity as a functioning node in the space of the next few hours anyway. She had already done quite enough work for one evening. A little time for herself couldn't hurt. She smiled, surrendering to the mood of Pan's. "So have you been here long?"

"Long enough to follow you up here. It's hard to miss Tiffany. I persuaded her that she could spare your services for a while." He pointed down toward the bar, where Tiffany was buying a drink for a young man. Kate almost giggled. It was the same blond Tiffany had had her eye on earlier.

Aaron grinned at her. His gaze seemed slightly out of focus, as if he were drunk or on drugs. Occasionally he shivered or sighed unexpectedly. "Are you all right?" she asked with a bit of concern.

"I'm fine—it's just the club. Can I get you one of what Tiffany is having?" he asked.

"Sorry," Kate demurred with a straight face, "he's not my type."

Both of them burst into laughter. "A drink," Aaron specified.

"I'd love one."

Besides the major bar on the ground-floor level, smaller bars were scattered throughout the club. Aaron led her to the closest and ordered two of the house special. Kate watched with fascination as the bartender produced a surprisingly small drink that was a startling red in color. She could have sworn that she had seen more liquor flow than could possibly be held in a glass of that size. She waited until Aaron had received his to pick her own up and sip at it cautiously. The reason for her confusion over the amount of alcohol in the drink was instantly apparent: the drink was almost pure liquor. It was pleasantly smooth, though, and she had taken two more fairly large sips before she could stop herself. It was also deliciously warm, something unusual for a cocktail. The fumes tickled her nose, urging her to raise the glass again. She gave Aaron a look of mock severity. "Are you trying to get me drunk?"

The man was suddenly all innocence. "Me? Would I do a thing like that?"

That made her laugh all over again, and he laughed along with her. The warmth of the drink penetrating into Kate's system made her perhaps a little bolder than usual. On a whim, she slammed back the remainder of the glass. Aaron blinked and followed suit. "Would the lady like another?" he asked politely.

Kate shook her head. "The lady is here on business, not pleasure. I'd rather not be completely drunk when I have to rouse Tiffany to do another on-the-spot report." She smiled. "You could buy me something virgin though." She put a finger to his lips before he could open his mouth. "Don't say it."

They returned to the platform where she had been standing before and sat down at a vacant table overlooking the dance floor. Aaron had bought a very nice mixture of fruit juice from the bar's nonalcoholic selection for her and another house special for himself. Kate watched him dip one finger in the drink and then absentmindedly pop it in his mouth. He grinned endearingly when he noticed. "Sorry. I embarrass myself if I'm not careful."

"That's all right." She dipped a finger in her own drink. "If you can't play with your food, what can you play with?"

The smirk that the international media had come to know and love appeared on Aaron's face as soon as the line was out of her mouth. He started to say something, but apparently changed his mind before the words could escape. He glanced away.

Kate caught his chin and turned his face back to look at her. "Aaron! You're blushing!"

"Don't tell Tiffany, okay? I have a reputation to maintain." He gulped at his drink. "Some things are too crude for even Aaron Barry to say to . . ."

He left his sentence unfinished, but Kate filled in the words based on his expression and smiled to herself. *To a nice woman.* Her heart jumped, but she forced it back down and rewarded Aaron with a light peck on the cheek. "That's okay, Aaron. You can be yourself with me."

"Thanks." He turned and looked into her eyes. "You're . . . special, Kate." He raised his glass to his lips again, but paused and set it down without drinking. "Is what you're having good?" She nodded in reply. Aaron smiled again and stepped away toward the bar.

Kate let a slow, slightly guilty smile of pleasure spread across her face as soon as he was gone. Who would have expected it? Aaron Barry had a soft side! She hadn't felt this way since high school when she had had a crush on a quarterback. This was more mature, of course. Aaron was attractive, but she didn't feel any urge to go to bed with him. An urge to hold him and be held by him, maybe, but no urges to have sex. She wanted to take him kite-flying (oh, yes, that was *really* mature). Christmas was in a couple of weeks. She wondered what he was doing. No, that was too personal and too soon. Maybe eggnog on Christmas Eve? Or a dinner of turkey casserole on the day after Christmas? She thought he might like that. New Year's Eve, definitely. There was a little restaurant near Ghirardelli Square. She sighed happily, relishing the brief respite from the rational emotionlessness that the New World Order demanded.

A sudden burst of light down in the DJ's booth caught her attention. Tiffany and the cameraman! Tiffany's voice came on over the sound system—the reporter was clearly tanked. After a second, her image appeared on the club's video wall, a direct feed patched in from the camera.

"This is Tiffany LaRouche, live on the scene for *Friday Night on the Town*. As you can see, I'm still at the opening of Pan's and having a wonderful time!" She pulled the blond man she had been with earlier into the picture. He was flushed with alcohol and excitement. There was lipstick on his face. "This is Chris. What do you think of Pan's, Chris?"

"Incredible!"

Tiffany turned and leaned out of the booth's window. The camera panned across the crowd on the dance floor. "How about all of you? Do you like Pan's?" The club shook with the force of the crowd's response. "All right!" screamed Tiffany. "That's what I like to hear. Pan's and *Friday Night on the Town* are going to bring you a very special treat now. I know that Aaron Barry is out there somewhere tonight. Aaron, this one is going out for you!"

Kate sat up straight, stunned with surprise, as Tiffany held up a videocassette and popped it into a VCR. A horrified thought struck her. The video. Aphrodite's new video. The one that supposedly had Aaron in it. She hadn't seen it herself, and until a few minutes ago, she probably wouldn't have cared if anyone else had seen it. Now . . . She bit her lip nervously. So what if the video did show Aaron? What did it really matter to her? Quite a bit, she realized. She wanted to savor her discovery of Aaron's other side as long as she could. She gathered her will. If the system were to inconveniently eat the tape . . .

"Is this what I think it is?" Aaron's sudden return startled her almost as much as his first appearance that night. The surprise caused her concentration to waver and the magick she had been weaving to fail. The video began, filling the air with a slow rhythmic beat just a little bit too reminiscent of the sounds of lovemaking. A still shot of a totally naked man, his face masked by a simple black bar, flashed up on the monitors. The crowded yelled, and Kate hissed with annoyance.

Aaron glanced at her, then reached over and patted her hand. "Relax. It's nothing, really. I'm used to it."

She was glad that he was, because she was too unbalanced to make another attempt at stopping the performance with magick. As Aphrodite sang about the bittersweet pleasures of sex with a lover who would soon leave her, the video ran clips from home movies that were shockingly explicit. Nothing that the woman (obviously Aphrodite herself) and the supposedly anonymous man did was left to the imagination. The crowd in Pan's seemed to have mixed reactions to the video. A sizable majority hollered in appreciation. A much smaller minority reacted with shock. Kate was quite disgusted to find herself wavering between the two groups.

"Is that really you?" she asked Aaron quietly. He looked at her carefully before nodding slowly. Kate turned back to the monitors. "Oh."

The video brought her back down to earth again. The man sitting at her side was Aaron Barry. *The* Aaron Barry, dilettante, pervert, and sensualist extraordinaire. He had had more lovers than she had fingers, and the majority of them had been unceremoniously and harshly dropped the moment he lost interest in them. Danger signals should have been going off in her head. But she had just seen that he was capable of being deeper than that! Maybe she could reform him. She almost laughed at herself. There was a stupid idea. Women undertook to reform men every day and most failed, ending up in unhappy, sometimes dangerous, circumstances. Of course, most women weren't mages. She looked at Aaron speculatively, then berated herself for the thought that had crossed her mind. She had no qualms about bending people to her will with magick when it was necessary, but she would not do that to a man she wanted to love her!

On the other hand, she did not want to give him up. She had enjoyed the way she had felt only moments before. It would be nice if that feeling could continue. Maybe he was being truthful with her. Maybe he really did think of her as someone special.

She bit her lower lip again as she considered him. She could be into and out of his mind without him even noticing, and she would know for certain. No, that was as bad as manipulating him with magick directly. She made a decision: She would simply move into any relationship with Aaron carefully and slowly, relying on her own instincts just as any woman would. She wouldn't try to reform him. If he wanted to mend his ways for her, he could do it under his own initiative. If not, she could certainly use magick to see that he got what he deserved.

The video ended, and Tiffany's face reappeared on the screen. "Wow! I'll bet that one gets banned coast to coast! They're never going to let us show that one again! Aaron, honey, wherever you are . . ."

Aaron turned to Kate and spoke over top of Tiffany. "I'm sorry. I've embarrassed you." He stood up. "I'll be going now."

"No. It's all right, Aaron. It's not your fault."

"I was the one who dumped Aphrodite. And not nicely, either."

Kate stood as well. "That doesn't give her the right to use those videos like that."

"You know she wrote that song about me."

"I had guessed it." She held out her hand. "How do you feel about turkey casserole?"

His mouth almost dropped open. "You're still interested in me?"

"Let's say I'm willing to give you a chance."

"Kate, I . . ." He put his arms around her and gave her a warm hug. Kate returned the hug happily, a sense of triumph swelling inside her.

Suddenly, Aaron stiffened slightly for a second, then relaxed again. "What is it?" she asked with some concern.

"Nothing." He pulled back a bit and smiled at her. "I was just . . . happy." He hesitated, then kissed her on the forehead. "Thank you, Kate. Would you like to go see a movie next week?"

"That would be nice."

They looked at each other fondly for a moment. Aaron broke the silence with a slight chuckle. "I have to go to the bathroom."

Kate smiled. "I should find Tiffany before she embarrasses the station again." She pulled a pen out of her pocket and wrote her phone number down on a napkin. "Call me," she said, thrusting it into his hand.

Aaron looked at it as if in amazement, then took a business card out of his own pocket. He looked at it for a moment, then borrowed her pen and scrawled something on the back. He handed it to her with a grin before disappearing into the crowd. As she walked down the stairs to the dance floor, Kate looked several times at what he had written. It was a simple heart with *A.B.* + *K.S.* scribbled inside.

But Aaron's thoughts weren't on Kate as he dodged through the crowd. Nor were they on Tiffany (he would have to pay her back for playing that video) or even on Aphrodite. No, they were on a face that he had seen in the crowd over Kate's shoulder. A face he had never seen before, could never have seen. Still, it was a face that he knew or had imagined, a face that commanded his attention by its mere appearance.

He tore recklessly along a catwalk between platforms, searching for that face. He had lost valuable time getting away from Kate. In a crowded place like Pan's, he might never be able to find that face again. Using magick to search for it was not an option—he was too agitated right now to summon up the concentration necessary. But it couldn't be too hard to find the person he sought after. He couldn't have gotten too far.

Then suddenly, he spotted the face. He shoved

through a cluster of people and reached out, grabbing onto a shoulder. There was almost a hint of desperation in his voice as he asked, "Michael?"

He must have said it loudly, because the people at a table nearby, a couple in evening wear and a young man in a faded denim jacket, glanced up. The couple looked away again, but the young man's gaze remained locked on him. Aaron scarcely noticed, however.

The man whose shoulder he gripped was not Michael. The resemblance was there, but the face did not belong to the person he thought it had. Why should it? Michael had died when he was fourteen. Aaron had never been able to see what his face might truly have looked like as an adult. He let go of the man's shoulder, feeling like a complete idiot. "I'm sorry. I thought you were someone else."

The man smiled at him. "You're Aaron Barry, aren't you?"

"Yes," Aaron agreed wearily. He knew from the tone in the man's voice what to expect next. He had his marker out before the man had even finished asking for an autograph. "Where do you want it?"

"How about my arm?" The man rolled up his shirt sleeve and held a bare, almost hairless arm out to Aaron. "This is what I want: *From Aaron Barry . . .*"

In order to sign the man's arm, Aaron had to stand virtually in front of him, almost within his embrace. As he wrote, in fact, he felt the man's other arm creeping across his back. He shrugged it off casually, but firmly. He wasn't into that.

" *. . .to my old friend . . .*"

The arm was back, but Aaron didn't feel it. There was something strange about the man's skin. The marker kept skipping, almost as if he were trying to write on greasy paper. The skin was too smooth, too perfect. It had no pores.

Aaron dropped down out of the creature's embrace, lashing out with a kick as he moved away. The kick impacted, sending the creature sprawling and knocking the last words out of its mouth. Not that they were necessary.

"Pig," he spat.

"Hello, Aaron." The demon rolled to its feet with unnatural flexibility. The people around it shouted in surprise, but they were only reacting to the violence. Pig could mimic human form well enough to pass undetected in most circumstances, even if it had never mastered fine details. The patrons of Pan's had no idea of the true terror that was in their midst. "Surprised?"

"No."

In fact, he was, but the first thing his tutors had taught him about fighting demons was never to give them an edge. Never admit that you were surprised or afraid or tired. When Aaron had left San Francisco fourteen years ago, Pig had been unable to manifest except when he was alone. That it could now do so in a place as crowded as Pan's was frightening. This had been the last place he would have expected Pig to come after him.

The second thing Aaron had learned from his tutors was to press any advantage that you had over a demon. If you could surprise a demon in any way at all, you did it. That was why Aaron had become a mage when the opportunity had presented itself. It all came down to this moment.

Except that he and Pig stood in the middle of a crowd of Sleepers. Aaron hadn't counted on having witnesses to Pig's ending. He didn't dare risk the use of vulgar magick in the presence of so many un-Awakened beings. The backlash of Paradox could kill him. Even coincidental magick presented risks if used incautiously here. If he had had to, though, he would have destroyed Pig in front of the assembled mages of the entire Technocracy.

He wanted to injure Pig, slowing it down and distracting it until he had a chance to work stronger magick. A glass had fallen off one of the tables nearby. If Pig were to step on it, the broken glass would penetrate the shoes that the demon wore, possibly even crippling it. Aaron flung his magick at the glass, bending reality so that the demon would bring its foot down upon it.

But Pig didn't step on the glass. Its foot hovered over it for a second as it took a step forward, then moved ever so slightly to one side. Pig bent and picked the glass up. It gave Aaron a horrible grin, the veneer of humanity slipping away from its features. Someone screamed. "I'm not the only one who learned something in the last fourteen years, am I?" The smile grew wider as Aaron cursed involuntarily. "I watched you and that cute girl in here last night."

Aaron held himself poised on the balls of his feet, refusing to allow the demon to throw him off kilter, even though he cursed himself for not thinking of the possibility that Pig might somehow spy on him. Out of the corner of his eye, he could see the disturbance as Tango and the bouncers began converging on the platform. Ordinary people in the area were beginning to edge away from the confrontation. His own heart was racing with adrenaline as he fought back the fear that Pig aroused in him. He had counted heavily on the element of surprise. Without it, he was reduced to relying on wits and guts.

Pig seemed disappointed at his lack of response, but nodded slowly anyway. "Yes," it hissed, "little Aaron's learned some magick. But did he learn enough?" It dashed the glass to the ground, sending sharp-edged shards scattering across the floor. A couple of people yelped with surprise. Aaron flinched. Far faster than a human could have moved, the demon plucked the largest piece of jagged glass from the ground and skimmed it through the air with tremendous force. Straight at Aaron's head.

Aaron focused his magick on the fragment of glass. To the Sleepers it might have seemed that the glass missed naturally; Aaron knew that the sphere of Entropy had exaggerated the errors in its flight, sending it ever so slightly off course. He heard the shard slice past his ear. There was a sickening, wet, tearing sound as it struck someone behind him. Several people shrieked at once. Aaron resisted the urge to turn around. Instead, he launched himself at Pig. This time the demon was surprised. Aaron locked his hands around the demon's throat and squeezed for all he was worth.

Just as the Sleepers would have seen a fragment of glass naturally, if miraculously, miss its target, so they would see nothing more here than one man trying to strangle another. In essence, that was indeed what he was doing to Pig. Aaron had learned long ago, however, that simple choking wouldn't hurt the demon. It didn't have the human need for air because it wasn't alive. Pig itself actually started to laugh. The Sleepers weren't the only ones who failed to see beyond the obvious.

Pig stopped laughing suddenly and began to struggle, shock on its distorted face. Its efforts were useless. Aaron had already robbed it of its strength.

The demon might not have been alive, but it still depended on its body to exist in this world. The action of choking was only a sham to surprise it as Aaron worked his magick on the matter that made up that body. Pig's manifested form began to unravel under his fingers, becoming unfit for the demon to inhabit. It attempted to flee back into the spirit world of the Umbra. Aaron was able to block its escape there as well, however. His link with Pan's feeding him the powerful sensations of his vice as a focus, Aaron slammed down a spiritual barrier around the demon. Flight to the Umbra impossible and his body destroyed, Pig would die.

"Everybody dies."

The words sounded strangely detached. Aaron wasn't even sure he had heard them. He was prepared to ignore them, counting them as a figment of his imagination until he heard them repeated. And this time, as they were spoken, control of his magick slipped away from him. Pig's body began to rebuild itself.

"No!" he screamed. He renewed his efforts, punching the demon as if they really were just two Sleepers brawling. A patch of Pig's body crumbled after each blow, but reformed before the next blow landed. Strength began to build again in Pig's struggles, though the demon was no longer grinning. It was clear that the demon was fighting to get away. Aaron aimed a final desperate blow at its head, driving the heel of his hand down like a piston. Just before he struck, though, the spiritual barrier that he had constructed fell. Pig vanished. Aaron's hand slammed into the floor, sending waves of pain shooting up his arm. Howling in agony and anger and clutching his arm, Aaron whirled around.

The young man in the bleached denim jacket stood quietly beside the table where he had been sitting. It had been one of his companions at the table, the man in evening wear, who had been struck by the deadly piece of glass meant for Aaron. His throat had been torn open. The woman with him cradled his body, her face a mask of grief. There was blood everywhere. Most of the crowd had stepped back from the spreading pool in shock. Only the young man seemed oblivious to it. His eyes were glazed, and he stared at the dead man.

"Everybody dies," he repeated absently a third time, as if he were speaking only to himself.

This time, it wasn't just magick that was warped. Aaron cried out as reality itself stretched and spun. His connection with Pan's was lost in that stormy sea. He drew desperately on the Quintessence stored within him, pushing back the madness of reality gone wild and trying to find an anchor to hold himself steady. All he could do, though, was allow himself to be buffeted about like a toy boat, riding out the storm. The Sleepers barely seemed to notice what was happening, although Aaron distinctly saw one of them waver and vanish. Only the woman holding the body seemed affected at all: Reaching into the man's ruined throat, she pulled free the shard of glass and drew it swiftly across her own wrist. Tears ran down her cheeks as she watched her blood stream out to mingle with the man's.

When it finally did end, the young man was gone, bloodstained footprints showing where he had simply walked away. The woman was dead. The Sleepers had hardly moved. Aaron was left panting on the floor, as the sensations of Pan's patrons flowed back into his body again in a sweet wave of pleasure. Tango and the bouncers came pouring up the steps of the platform. The entire wild ride had taken less than a minute. All Aaron could do was accept Tango's help in standing and wonder what the hell had just happened.

Saffleur awoke with a start in the darkened bedroom of his home. It took him a moment to recognize the sense of pain and loss that rushed through him, then vanished, only to explode again a moment later. In its aftermath, he realized what had happened. The wheel of the Angel's life cycle had turned! It was impossible, but the connection between the young man and the mage still shook from the event. Saffleur had never experienced anything like that feeling anywhere else. There was no mistaking it.

But this was not the proper time for such a turning! The next event that would trigger a turning should not have occurred for another week yet. Of course . . . He turned on the bedside lamp and sat up. It was possible that the next event had occurred on its own. Or even that . . . No. What Lao-Hsung had suggested was impossible. The stages in the Angel's life cycle were marked by deaths. Specific deaths, the deaths of particular people at particular times and in particular manners. Saffleur ensured that those deaths happened precisely when they were supposed to. It was vitally important that they did!

And yet he tried to remember what Lao-Hsung, one of his past friends, had once said. It was theoretically possible for the Angel's life cycle to be shifted. New stages could conceivably be introduced, new deaths added to the pattern of his life. But the deaths would have to be particularly traumatic, the Angel himself would have to be in a state of instability, and magick would have to be involved in the deaths. Lao-Hsung had attempted several times to make such shifts in order to satisfy his curiosity, casually slaying several of the Angel's bed partners with his magick in order to determine the effects of their deaths. Then Saffleur had caught up to his erstwhile friend. Now Saffleur had three more deaths to schedule into the Angel's life, and Lao-Hsung's bones rested on the bottom of the Sea of Japan. He hadn't told another mage about the Angel since.

Was it possible that a mage had somehow accidentally fulfilled the conditions that Lao-Hsung had identified? Saffleur groaned at the thought of the potentially disastrous consequences of that meeting. The Angel's value depended on the integrity of his life cycle. New events in that cycle were like a wheel slipping. If it slipped too much, the results could be catastrophic.

There was also the question of the strange abilities that the Angel had begun to manifest. The events of his last few cycles had been followed by very brief periods in which reality was distorted around the Angel. Saffleur had been able to end these episodes quickly, but they were still a mystery. With those abilities active, the Angel was a danger, both to those around him and, more importantly, to himself. There was every chance that the Technocracy could discover him or that the mage who had triggered this new event might interfere again. He had to find the Angel quickly and try to counter the mistake that had occurred.

Getting out of bed and pulling on a robe, he walked into his study. The center of the room was clear, and standing in the empty space, Saffleur began to dance. Dancing acted as a focus for mages of his tradition, aiding their workings in certain spheres of magick. The dance he performed in his study tonight allowed him to extend his perceptions across great distances, searching San Francisco for the Angel. He found nothing. He tried again, focusing on the places where the Angel was most often to be found, before beginning a methodical scan of the city. He still found nothing and collapsed into a chair, sweating from the exertions of the dance and cursing. The Angel's blasted powers were interfering with his magick!

Kate was on the far side of the dance floor, heading towards the DJ's booth and Tiffany, when the commotion began. It was sheer coincidence (or perhaps not—she had been thinking about Aaron) that she just happened to be looking up and in the right direction at the right time to see Aaron kick a man in the stomach. The violence was surprising, especially when she had expected Aaron to be in the bathroom. She pulled out her opera glasses again, activating a function that bent light to give her a better view of the fight. She could hear nothing of what was actually happening, since the music was far too loud, but she didn't have to hear anything. What she saw was the last thing she would have expected to see.

Aaron Barry working magick.

That sight shocked her far more than did the realization that the man Aaron fought was not human at all. There was no mistaking what Aaron had done, although the working was so well concealed in coincidence that it would have gone unnoticed by even the most observant Sleeper. Kate triggered the spell in the glasses that scanned for Quintessence just as the man standing behind Aaron died a sudden and brutal death. She scarcely noticed; the glow surrounding Aaron was so intense it was almost blinding. The powerful magick he brought into play as he struggled was astounding. He easily overwhelmed the thing he was fighting. Inhaling sharply, Kate switched the glasses to scan the magickal elements of Pan's. Had the node been activated under her very nose? No, the magickal elements were still inactive. Something was feeding Aaron's power, but whatever it was, it was not Pan's!

She focused the glasses on the fight once more. Aaron had the creature helpless. The movement of someone else—the young man with the dark core of lost Quintessence—drew her eye away from the fight for a moment. She saw him staring at the dead man. He opened his mouth as if to speak.

Suddenly the magick of the glasses went crazy. Kate snatched them away from her eyes instantly, but they left her dizzy and disoriented anyway. She tried to fix her sight on the platform again. It slid and wobbled in her vision, however, and she realized that the problem was not with her eyes but with the platform itself. The reality up there was shifting!

She froze where she stood. That was impossible! It simply could not be happening! Mages manipulated reality, but certainly not in the way that was being demonstrated before her eyes! And the young man was not even a mage! She began pushing her way through the crowd. The platform stabilized before she had gone ten feet. The young man was already down the stairs and crossing the ground floor toward the doors, walking in a daze. The crowd parted before him, obstructing Kate's efforts to reach him, although it seemed doubtful that anyone was really aware of his presence. All eyes were on the carnage above; they did not appear to see what she, as a mage, had seen. Kate tried to follow the young man, but he was moving quickly, reality still occasionally blurring ever so slightly around him. He was out the doors before Kate could break away from the crowd and completely gone by the time she stepped into the street. She raised the opera glasses to search for him, but the only thing they showed her on their tiny display screens was hazy static. They were ruined.

In the same situation, another person might have cursed. Kate merely furrowed her brow and tried to sort out what she had just seen. The young man and the shift in reality were inexplicable. A Sleeper should not have been able to do what he had done. She would report the event to Julia and let her organize an investigation. Aaron, on the other hand, was more of a problem.

He was a mage. And the only reason she had not detected him earlier was because he had been behind her when she scanned the club! She did curse herself for that. There was no doubt in her mind: He was one of the mages behind the construction of Pan's. The evening had paid off. Her duty to the Technocracy was clear. Julia would have to be informed, and Aaron would be taken in by the New

World Order for interrogation. Kate tried to harden her heart against the voice inside that urged her not to betray him. She wanted to love him, but he was the enemy! He was a threat to the New World Order and to the Technocracy, and he had to be eliminated. Except that Kate didn't want that to happen. He didn't know that she was a Technomancer, and he hadn't deliberately concealed his abilities any more than she had concealed hers. Kate crushed the voice of protest resolutely, though. The Technocracy and the dream of Ascension required it.

7

Stefan stayed in bed the next day until after noon, hiding under the covers from the morning sun. Occasionally he was able to force himself into sleep, but most of the time he was awake, his thoughts focused on last night's clients. Two more dead.

He had come home to his apartment after he had left Pan's. Vague recollections of riding the bus through the nighttime streets, the feeble light inside making the dark outside that much denser, paled beside what had happened at the club. The whole trip was like a dream, all hazy and dim. A strange dimness still seemed to hover over his consciousness, as if one of the dense fogs that sometimes moved in off the Bay had attached itself to him personally. He did recognize the feeling; it was the prelude to the blackouts he suffered when people close to him died. When he had first heard about Mike's death, he had been sitting in the Princess Café, watching television. The dimness had overwhelmed him. He had awakened several days later on the beach beside the Pacific Ocean. This time, however, there was no sense that he was going to drop into unconsciousness. The dimness lingered on, far longer than it ever had before.

It was a truly discomforting state. The world seemed distant, as though he were looking at it through smoky glass. Sounds were eerily muted, even those of the traffic outside and a cat in the alley under his window. His sense of touch was obscured as well, as if he were wearing oven mitts. He had difficulty remembering anything clearly. It was a little bit like being really, really drunk, with the room spinning around and a feeling like he had stepped away from the world. Except that the dimness made it feel as if the world were trying to pull away from him. Everything but death and loss seemed uncertain. Death and loss were the only constants in his life.

But everybody died eventually. He vaguely remembered saying something like that last night, though he couldn't be sure. Everything died and everything passed, even memory. Everybody suffered pain, and anguish, and grief. He certainly wasn't the only one, even if he seemed to take more than his share of grief and disappointment. Death was a natural function.

The dimness seemed to retreat the more he thought about that. Death was natural, whether it came today or in ten years. Everybody would die at some point—the clients from Pan's would have slipped into the grave sooner or later, and they had just happened to do it in front of him last night. Even Mike would have died anyway. Even Mike . . . He felt a piercing pang of loss run through him at the memory. The dimness surged in on its heels. He forced himself to relax, willing himself to forget about the clients and not to think about Mike until the dimness had receded again. He pulled the bedsheets away from his face. He was hungry, he realized.

He threw the covers aside and swung his legs over the side of the bed. He sat there for a moment before forcing himself to stand. The air in the apartment was stale; he had been sweating heavily through the night. He walked groggily to the windows and pulled the curtains open. There was a dead pigeon lying on the windowsill. He opened the window, pushing the bird off the sill and into the alley below with a rolled up newspaper. The cat there yowled up, half in feline annoyance, half in feral gratitude. Lunch, even if it was carrion.

There was nothing edible among the scant contents of his own refrigerator. An apple that had been sitting on the shelf was mealy and bruised. The milk was sour. The cheese slices were dried out. The best-before date on half a carton of eggs had passed a week ago; the date on a package of hot dogs two weeks before that. He did not even want to look into the sealed containers of leftovers. For a moment, the dimness grew ever so slightly stronger. He shrugged. Everything passed—even food. Death and an ending was all that there was. The dimness subsided again, like a dull gray headache. He swept everything from the refrigerator into a garbage bag and knotted the bag closed.

He would have to go out to get something. He pulled on some clothes and felt in the pockets of the pants he had worn the night before. The money the clients had paid him was still there. Valentine stipulated payment up front. It had certainly paid off in this case. Stefan took a ten-dollar bill and stuffed it into his pocket. It was part of his cut anyway. He stopped in front of the bathroom mirror to run a comb through his hair. He realized that he had selected an entire outfit of black clothing and smiled to himself. Mourning clothes. Maybe he should wear them full-time.

His neighbor, old Mrs. Donner, was poking uselessly at the elevator buttons as he emerged from his apartment. She was going senile. He could not remember the elevators working once since he and Mike had moved in. He took the stairs down to the lobby and stepped out onto the street. A stray cat was being noisily sick by the mouth of the alley beside the building. A half-eaten pigeon, probably the one he had pushed off his window, lay nearby.

A police officer brushed past him as he walked into the convenience store down the block. A glass bowl of lollipops that usually sat by the cash register inside the store was missing, and a window behind the clerk's head was covered over with a piece of brown cardboard. Something had clearly happened. Stefan walked to the back of the store, his shoes crunching on the occasional piece of broken glass. There was no milk in the refrigerator cases. He took a large jug of orange juice instead, then grabbed a box of Twinkies and some instant coffee on his way back up to the cash. "No milk, Deng?" he asked in Mandarin Chinese.

The clerk shook his head. "Whole shipment went sour."

Stefan grunted as he handed him his cash. "What's the deal with the window?"

"We got held up again last night." The clerk counted out his change. "Some nut with a gun looking for drug money. Bullet grazed the night clerk's head. Jimmy's lucky to be alive."

"We all die sooner or later."

"That's pretty casual. Did you hear about the couple at that nightclub last night? Ugly way to go."

Surely it was only a strange coincidence that Deng should mention the events at Pan's, but Stefan's stomach churned suddenly at the reminder. His vision swam as nausea slammed into his body. The dimness returned with a vengeance, darkening his eyesight and filling his ears with formless noise. He lurched and almost fell, grabbing at the edge of the counter to support himself. He heard Deng shouting something, but it was muffled. Stefan snatched at the thought that had helped him before: Death was natural. Decay was natural. Death came to everyone. In the end there was only death.

He repeated that thought over and over to himself as the dimness buffeted him. All things eventually fell apart. All people eventually died. His parents and older brother, killed in a car crash when he was eight, dying in front of him. He had survived only by a miracle. His grandparents who had raised him until he was thirteen, swept away by illness. His foster parents, dead in a house fire. Mike, committing suicide. Even he was dying, at least spiritually, forced onto the streets, forced to sell himself for money, forced to sell his soul to Valentine. He tried to push himself past the memories of all those deaths, past the sickening heartache of them, even though the act of trying to forget hurt more than the original loss. Death and decay ruled the world. It was natural. He embraced those words, desperately filling his mind with them until he truly believed them.

The dimness was gone abruptly, as if shattered by a pulse that rose up from deep inside him. In its place was a clarity so sharp and vivid that it made Stefan's senses sting. The clarity almost seemed to spread visibly, scouring its way through his surroundings. For a moment, he smiled and took a deep breath, relieved after the clinging confusion of the dimness.

The stink of decomposition made him gag, though. He lifted his head, the clarity of his vision rendering everything around him sharp-edged and bright . . . and rotting. Everywhere he looked, things were falling apart! The orange juice on the counter in front of him turned thin and watery. Loaves of bread were suddenly mouldy. Packages of lunch meat inflated like balloons from the noxious vapors produced as their contents decayed. Deng . . .

He screamed, pushing himself away. Deng was lying on the floor behind the counter, his skin grayish, his hand clutching at his chest, a surprised look on his face. Stefan had seen that look before; one of the clients who had died in bed with him had had it on his face as a sudden heart attack struck him. But Deng was scarcely older than Stefan himself. He should not have had a heart attack.

Stefan risked another peek over the top of the counter. The skin around Deng's eyes and lips darkened and pulled back as he watched. The hustler scrambled to his feet and sprinted out of the store before he saw any more. The door squealed in protest, as though in desperate need of oiling, when he pushed it open. He didn't notice as the rot and decay in the store wavered and vanished with his departure. All was as it had been before he entered, except that Deng was still lying dead on the floor.

Outside, Stefan stopped for a moment to gulp down fresh air, leaning helplessly against a mailbox on the street corner. Only when he heard the sudden, desperate blaring of a car horn and looked up to see a station wagon, its driver's face distorted with horror, careen helplessly through the intersection did he realize that the strange clarity of decay was still pulsing out of him. He clapped his hands over his ears as he fled back toward his apartment, trying to shut out the sound of the station wagon's collision with another vehicle.

What was happening? Had he actually caused all of this? Had he caused the deaths of his clients last night at Pan's? He could remember something like this terrible clarity occurring for a moment last night. Oh, God, he had done it! Did that mean . . . could he have been responsible for Mike's death and the deaths of his family? Oh, God, no!

He could still feel the dimness on the edge of his mind, and he seized it as desperately as he had

pushed it away before. Anything to blot out that clarity!
The dimness was slippery now, however, and refused
to come to him. He almost had to wrestle with it as
he ran. Every sound he heard and every sight he
glimpsed seemed tinged with the appalling and
ghastly. He groped for the dimness, finally managing
to draw a fragment of it over his thoughts like a veil.
The clarity wavered and vanished.

Stefan felt almost calm, sheltered by the dimness,
as he entered the dingy lobby of his apartment building. He stabbed a finger at the buttons of the elevators instinctively before remembering that they hadn't
worked for years. No, that wasn't true. They had been
working only yesterday. His hands felt clammy as he
pushed open the door to the stairwell and began
climbing. Had he caused the elevators to break down
as well? Did this happen every time he had pushed
away the dimness? The rotten food in his refrigerator,
the dead pigeon on his windowsill, the sick cat in the
alley? Had he caused all of that as he roused himself
out of bed this morning? He tried to remember how
long Mrs. Donner next door had been going senile.
Hadn't she been going out to play cards with her
friends a few days before, a merry smile on her face as
she told him how much she was going to take them
for? How could he have imagined her as senile? Was
she, or had he caused it just this morning?

The telephone was ringing in his apartment, the
noise shrill and demanding. He picked it up almost
out of habit as soon as he was in the door. He hoped
it wasn't a client calling. He needed a distraction, anything to take his mind off death, but he was terrified
at the thought of what might happen if the clarity
came over him while he was in bed.

"Hello?"

"This is Valentine. Have you seen today's paper,
Stefan?"

Stefan didn't have to ask what he was talking about. He slumped back against the wall, the telephone cradled limply in his hand. "The clients?"

"Yes!" Valentine chuckled on the other end of the line. "I already have people lining up for you."

"Clients with a death wish?"

"If they're willing to pay. By the way, did you . . ."

"They paid up front."

"I have another appointment for you tonight."

"No," Stefan responded wearily. "No clients tonight."

"Big bucks!"

"Fuck off and die, Valentine." Stefan hung up before the man could say another word. Even the thought of what he might have to do with one of Valentine's customers was enough to make the veil of dimness tremble. He slid down the wall until he was sitting on the floor and put his head between his knees, suddenly overcome with dizziness. This couldn't be happening. He needed to talk to someone desperately.

He picked up the telephone again and dialed Marilyn's number. The phone rang unanswered. He sighed and hung up. The money from last night's clients was on the tabletop, level with his eyes. He contemplated it. The cash would buy enough drugs to get seriously trashed on, enough drugs to bury himself in a haze, if not in the dimness.

The telephone rang as he stuffed the money into his pocket. Hoping against reason that it was Marilyn, he snatched it up. It was Valentine. Stefan unplugged the phone from the wall before he had managed to spit out a complete sentence, and walked out the door.

Aaron let the water from the shower pour down over his head, rinsing the clinging smell of incense from his hair. He had spent much of the weekend after the incident at Pan's engaged in magick. The Barry mansion was now ringed with wards that would limit Pig's access to the house from both the physical and spiritual worlds.

Sunday morning he had attempted to put similar wards in place around Pan's, but they had, of necessity, been weaker. The Technocracy was still watching the club and surely with greater scrutiny after the deaths on Friday night. Now that Pig knew he was a mage, there was less point in trying to hide his magick completely, but it was never wise to flaunt magick in front of the Technocracy. And the link that fed him sensations from Pan's would always be useful. Aaron still wanted to keep his both magickal and mundane connections with Pan's a secret as long as possible.

He had actually been incredibly lucky in the matter of the deaths at the club. The shift of reality that had spoiled his magick and driven the woman to commit suicide had also apparently clouded the memories of the Sleepers present. Eyewitnesses could not remember the events leading up to the deaths. Most recalled a struggle of some kind and assumed it had been between the man whose throat had been slashed and some other man who had run off. None remembered the fight between Pig and Aaron. The police were treating it as some kind of private quarrel, with the woman's death as strictly self-inflicted (as, of course, it was in the strictest technical sense). The deaths had even lent Pan's a kind of strange allure; it had been truly packed on Saturday, more than making up for the early closing on opening night. Tango had hired extra bouncers to discourage any copycat violence.

What truly mystified Aaron, though, was the sheer power that had been demonstrated. A mass memory manipulation was the least of the feats that the young man who appeared to be the source of everything had performed, all virtually simultaneously. The unraveling of Aaron's magick, the shifting of the fabric of reality—even the complete disappearance of a Sleeper! Aaron still had no idea what had become of the vanished Sleeper, although discreet questions had revealed that one of the witnesses had a friend matching the description. The witness claimed that though his friend had wanted to come, a severe illness had prevented her. That kind of reality manipulation was so vulgar it should have produced a Paradox backlash strong enough to level Pan's. It hadn't. Only Marauders, the bizarre, mad mages of the Umbra, could rend reality so casually and escape without harm, but the young man had not looked like a Marauder. At the very least, though, he should have left some trace of the working of magick in his wake. He hadn't.

Whoever the young man was, or whatever he had been, he was not a mage. And try though he might, Aaron could not locate him with his own magick. The Bay Area was big, but when a mage wanted something, he could usually find it. Aaron couldn't find a trace of the young man. It was as if he had vanished out of reality altogether.

Aaron shut off the shower and reached for one of the thick towels hanging on the rack next to it. He shook it out carefully prior to using it. Before he had put the wards up around the house, Pig had slipped in and fouled his bed with various disgusting substances—an old trick it had pulled when Aaron had been younger. It had also fouled every piece of linen in the house, and every towel as well. Just to prove to Aaron that it had escaped him, and, of course, to terrify him. It had worked. Aaron had put up the first of the wards in a blind panic that night, then spent several hours thrashing in the grip of his nightmares as he tried vainly to sleep. The next morning, he had tried to search for the demon with as much luck as always. Which was to say none. Pig was hiding somewhere in the Umbra. At least the young man wasn't plotting against him out of sheer malevolence. He hoped.

That was perhaps the most terrifying thing about Pig. Its sole purpose in whatever kind of life it had seemed to be the tormenting and frightening of Aaron. There was no pattern to its attacks, no reason, no method, no direction except leaving Aaron petrified with fear. It defied rational analysis. Not long after Pig had first appeared, Aaron had tried to stand up to it with a show of bravery. It had reduced him to tears anyway. Even the potentially deadly shard of glass had only been meant to frighten him. Pig had known that Aaron would find a way to deflect or avoid it at the last moment; it was matching its efforts to his new level of ability, and doing so easily. Unable to find the demon, unable to predict its next attack, all he could do was wait for it.

Just thinking about Pig made his heart race as if in an effort to flee. The young man from Pan's gave him something to think about, a problem to solve. As long as he kept his mind busy with something besides Pig, he could carry on a normal routine. The young man and his reality-bending powers was one such diversion. Kate Sanders, with her small-town manners and cool reporter's facade, was another. A game of seduction.

Aaron smiled to himself as he walked into his bedroom and got dressed. He had broken through to Kate last night. He knew he had. The low-key, boy-next-door approach had done it. She was such a sweet girl, but strong, too. She would never fall for him if she saw him as a media star; he had realized that the moment he had first decided to seduce her, a week ago at the Screwdriver. The nice guy forced to play the role of the arrogant star, on the other hand, was an image she could empathize with. He glanced into his underwear drawer and made a mental note to himself to buy plain white briefs, something appropriately ordinary to wear the night she finally and inevitably succumbed totally to his skills.

While he didn't need help seducing Kate, finding the young man was another matter. As much as he disliked admitting it, he was still little more than a disciple, a beginner, in many of the spheres of magick. Most of his research as an apprentice had been devoted to the study of demons and the best way to fight them. His abilities were weak in other, relatively more pedestrian (as mages saw such things) areas. He needed the aid of someone who was more knowledgeable regarding reality-related phenomena, someone who might be able to shed some light on the young man's powers.

Unfortunately, most of his contacts were spread across other parts of the world. Although he knew that there were numerous mages living and practicing in San Francisco, he was unfamiliar with the mages themselves. There was a friend of a friend nearby, however, an old mage of the Euthanatos tradition living at Berkeley. The Euthanatos were strange. They were death mages, pursuing Ascension through endless rounds of death and rebirth. But this mage might be willing to help. And as long as Aaron was going for the drive . . .

He picked up the phone and dug around for the phone number Kate had given him. He caught the faint change of tone as the call was automatically forwarded to another telephone. Kate sounded somewhat frazzled and distracted when she answered, her voice slightly distorted in the way that was distinctive to cellular phones. He could almost hear her surprise when he said hello.

"Aaron? This isn't a good time. I really can't talk now."

"At work?"

"Yes." She paused, and he imagined her glancing over her shoulder toward Tiffany. The reporter would have an impatient look on her face and would probably be tapping her foot.

"Do you think you can get away from the dragon lady?"

Kate gave a choking cough. "Can I call you back, Aaron?"

"No, listen: I have to go over to Berkeley later this afternoon. Do you want to come?"

"I . . ."

"It's a beautiful day. And it's Monday. Nothing important could possibly be happening on a Monday!"

She hesitated, clearly thinking it over. He heard another woman's voice murmur in the background. Kate said something in reply, her hand over the mouthpiece of the phone. "Okay," she said into the phone finally. "But give me a little while to wrap up what I'm working on."

"Okay. I'll pick you up . . ." He glanced at the clock beside his bed. It was already almost noon. "About one. At the television station?"

"Sounds good. I'll see you then."

"Bye." Aaron hung up the phone, a smirk of satisfaction tugging at his face. He went downstairs to see about finding something to eat in the kitchen.

Instead, he found William Pierce sitting uncomfortably in the front hall. His father's friend looked up at him blandly as he descended the stairs. "You've changed the locks," he observed.

"I didn't know what kind of riffraff had keys." William reddened obligingly. "How did you get in?"

"The housekeeper. I've been waiting for approximately an hour."

"What do you want? I thought you had quit."

"I never actually quit. Nor, for some reason I can't see for myself, was I included in the round of firings among your father's former employees." Aaron cursed himself for that oversight—he had crossed William's name off the list of dismissals before passing the list on to the secretary. "I am here because I made a promise to your father."

Aaron stepped down off the steps, confronting William. "Allow me to remind you one more time that my father is dead. I run the show now."

"And poorly." William stood to face him. "I promised your father I would not let you sink his empire too quickly. The cuts you have made to the staff will have exactly that effect, particularly if they have to have all of their affairs in order in such a short period of time."

"I gave them the standard two weeks. Plus a fat severance package on top of their Christmas bonus."

"Your father's . . . I'm sorry, *your* accounts are somewhat beyond two weeks and a fat package." He handed Aaron a copy of the financial section of the *New York Times*. "Word got out about the radical reorganization, and stocks in several of your companies have dropped dramatically. Not irreparable damage, but that's just a start. You let a bunch of people who don't know what they're doing get into those accounts, and you're going to take a huge loss."

Aaron gritted his teeth. The old man was making sense, damn him. He had expected some drop in stocks, but not this much. "I suppose you want me to keep them on for a little while, with you as supervisor."

"To put it bluntly, yes."

"Fine. You've got it. They have an extra two weeks. That should put them into the new year."

"Might I suggest graduated dismissals? Bring in a few new people at a time rather than a great herd all at once?"

"All right!" Aaron snarled. "On one condition: that after this, you leave too, and I never see you again."

"Agreed." William picked up a briefcase and

marched out the door. "And the sentiment, Aaron, is mutual," he threw back bleakly.

Kate turned back to Julia as she switched off the cellular phone. "I'm sorry about that. Thank you for giving me the afternoon off."

Julia shook her head. "There's nothing going on here that I need your help with. It's important that you cultivate this contact. Aaron Barry may prove a useful source of information. It's fortunate that he seems to be attracted to you."

"The feeling is strictly one way, Julia," Kate insisted. "He provides useful insight into club society and from a different angle than Tiffany."

"I want you to keep your eye on Pan's still, of course. Go there frequently with Aaron if you have to. Find out any personal information about him that you can, as well. It may be useful if we decide to make an example of him and his lifestyle in the future."

Kate suppressed a slight chill at the casual way her superior delivered the words. "Yes, Julia. He seems to have no secrets, though. One of his trademarks is his absolute openness with the media."

"Everyone has secrets." She sat back and smiled suddenly. "Even me. He thought I was Tiffany?" She laughed, a musical tinkling sound. "You see? I have a sense of humor." She wiggled her fingers at Kate in an exaggeratedly feminine wave good-bye. "Have a nice time on your . . . date." She laughed again, as though she had just made the world's funniest joke.

The whole effect was actually more disturbing than reassuring, however. Kate forced herself to smile back. "Yes, Julia." She looked back over her shoulder as she left the room. Julia's face had lapsed back into its normal hard, emotionless mask, and she ran her finger thoughtfully over her scar while she leafed through the papers on her desk.

Kate kept her mind resolutely blank as she walked down the cold empty halls of the New World Order regional headquarters. She thought about nothing, a technique that New World Order mages learned early. Idle dreams and thoughts of promotion or disobedience were dealt with swiftly and harshly among the masters of Mind magick. Only when she was about a block and a half away from regional headquarters and heading back toward the television station did Kate allow her thoughts to flow freely. Why had Julia opened up like that? She normally only laughed or even smiled when she was acting during an interrogation or when she was trying to get something out of someone! What could she want from her? Did she know Kate had lied to her about the events at Pan's?

The report Kate had turned in to Julia on Saturday had made no mention of anything even remotely unusual. She had only mentioned Aaron at all because she wanted to cover herself if word of her activities did get back to the New World Order—as Aaron's own, ill-timed phone call had. But Kate still wasn't sure why she had not turned him in as a mage. She knew why she hadn't mentioned the young man and the warping of reality, at least. Any allusion to that would have prompted a full investigation that might have led to the discovery of Aaron.

It wasn't love or attraction! She refused to admit that that was even possible. The New World Order took precedence over her own desires. No, she was withholding her evidence against Aaron until she knew more about what was going on. When she had found out more about Pan's and about the strange young man, then she would go to Julia. She might even be promoted for her work. This was strictly business. What she had felt for Aaron at Pan's had been completely misguided. He was nothing but another informant, albeit one who was about to inform on himself.

So why did she feel so giddy with anticipation as she waited for him to pull up in front of the television station?

"Marilyn!"

The old hooker turned as Stefan called her name. "Stef?" she responded with a smile on her face. The smile faded as she actually saw him. "Oh, Stef. What have you been doing to yourself?"

Stefan mimed taking a hit from a joint. He knew how he must look. He had returned home only two or three times in the last couple of days to take a shower, maybe change his clothes, and get a little bit of sleep. The rest of his time had been spent on the streets, as stoned out of his mind as he could manage. At first he had done some hustling and turned a couple of tricks for money, but clients were afraid to approach him now. At least the clarity that made things die had not returned; he had lived for two whole days under the dubious comfort of the dimness. He smiled unsteadily at Marilyn, squinting in the bright light of the early afternoon.

"You asshole."

"It's not what you think!"

"Then what is it?"

"There were these clients . . . two of them." He had had the story all rehearsed at one point. A simple retelling of the events that had happened Friday night and Saturday, clear and straightforward. Marilyn would understand and know what to do! The story had become tangled with the marijuana smoke, though. Stefan found himself babbling about clients and grocery stores and blood and joints and dimness and rotting things. And death. So much death.

When he had finished, he stood, swaying gently

back and forth, as Marilyn regarded him with a hard stare. "Where did you say you found these clients?" she asked harshly.

"Valentine's," he replied without thinking.

Marilyn slapped him so hard he fell over backward. "You promised me you wouldn't go near him!"

"I had to!"

"Sure. Like you had to go back to marijuana. How much did you smoke before you came up with this bullshit story?"

"It's true!"

"It's fucking bullshit! What kind of an idiot do you take me for?" She turned away from him. "If you're going to screw yourself up like this, you're on your own. Don't come near me again."

"Marilyn!"

She just walked away. Stefan stayed where he was, sitting on the sidewalk, watching her until she turned a corner. The pain of abandonment stabbed through him. Marilyn was gone. Not dead maybe, but she might as well have been. Gone was gone. Another person he loved had been taken away from him.

The dimness began to evaporate in spite of the murk of the drugs. He wrenched it back around himself desperately. He had hoped Marilyn might be able to help him, although he could see now that had been a ridiculous hope. What would a hooker know about the things that had happened to him? What would she have been able to do anyway? What could *anybody* do beyond what he had already done? Except maybe die . . .

He reached into his pockets and pulled out his last cash. Enough to buy a big bottle of booze. If he couldn't keep the deadly clarity away, then maybe he could at least drink himself to death.

8

A smile played across Aaron's face as Kate got into his car. She had taken her time about it, running her hand over its immaculate hood, admiring the perfection of the British racing green paint job. He half expected her to ask him to pop the hood open so she could look at the engine.

"Nice car," she said. She nodded appreciatively as she noticed the stereo system inside.

"Thanks." Aaron pulled away from the curb and merged with the traffic heading toward the Oakland Bay Bridge. "You're a car buff?"

"I never miss an auto show. My living room is piled with brochures from the car companies." Kate leaned back into the leather seats and sighed in contentment. "If I had the money and the space to store them, I'd buy a whole fleet of cars."

"You don't look like the car buff type."

"Let's just say my mother was a little bit disappointed when I preferred playing with my brothers' Hot Wheels over playing with my Barbie."

They passed the drive to Berkeley talking about cars. Aaron found that he had to dig really deeply into his memory to come up with replies to some of Kate's comments. Eventually, he was reduced to responding with simple murmurs of "yes," "uh-huh," and "I see." He made a mental note to himself never to bring up cars in Kate's presence again. She finally changed the subject as they drove into Berkeley and onto the University of California at Berkeley campus. "Who exactly did you have to come here to see?"

"A curator at the Lowie Museum." He pulled into a parking lot and found a space. They got out of the car. "A friend of a friend. Artifacts have started turning up in a Sonoma vineyard I inherited, and I want to get his opinion on what I should do."

"Really?" Kate's ears perked up again. "What kind of artifacts?"

Aaron cursed to himself. There were, of course, no artifacts at all. The lie had been a convenient, though apparently not very successful, invention. "Some Indian things," he said breezily. "Let me guess— you're an amateur archaeologist, too?"

"I haven't had the time to go on any digs, but I like to keep read up on the subject."

"Great." He found a sign-mounted map of the campus and began examining it. Kate tugged him away.

"Don't worry. I know where the museum is. They've changed the name, too. It's the Phoebe Hearst Museum of Anthropology now."

"You've been here before, haven't you?" Aaron asked as they set out across the campus.

"Not since they changed the name." She smiled. "Don't worry. I'll find lots of stuff to look at while you talk to your curator. After you're finished, I can show you around."

Aaron smiled back. The breadth of Kate's knowledge was greater than he had expected. In other seductions, that might be bad or awkward. This time, however, he wanted Kate to feel as if she had things

to teach him. He had originally thought to invite her
along to the museum as nothing more than a pleasant diversion, but he could use Kate's familiarity with
the museum to his advantage. She could take the role
of teacher on their tour, while Aaron took the role of
the student. The vulnerable Aaron he had played for
her benefit at Pan's would gain an added dimension
of pleasant ignorance. He tested the waters, asking
her about some sculpture that stood outside the
museum. She told him about it with a warm smile
and a serious tone. Aaron nodded understandingly
and tried to keep a self-satisfied smirk off his face. He
held her hand as they walked up the steps of the
museum.

At the reception desk, Aaron asked where he could
find the office of a guest curator, Dr. David Brossard.
The receptionist called a security guard to escort him
back into the administrative wing of the museum.
Aaron gave Kate's hand a final squeeze before he left.
"I'll come find you when I'm finished."

Her interest in the museum had another benefit as
well, he realized as he walked after the guard. With
something to keep her busy while she waited, Kate
would be less likely to ask questions. Lies about artifacts in vineyards aside, Aaron would rather not have
her asking more questions about exactly who Dr.
Brossard was and why he had come to the museum to
see him.

Kate watched Aaron follow the security guard through
a door and into the administrative wing of the museum. She was definitely glad now that she had come.
Aaron was obviously up to something secretive. His
fumbling lie, well told but highly unlikely, had confirmed that. She hadn't been kidding when she said
that she knew a little something about archaeology.
At least she knew enough to realize that any artifacts

that appeared in a vineyard should have been turned
up when the ground had first been plowed.
Furthermore, Aaron should have brought some of the
artifacts with him to show the curator. He hadn't even
brought photographs. Whatever he had come to the
museum to talk to this Brossard about, it was not
archaeology.

She smiled at the receptionist. "Can you give me
the telephone number for David Brossard's office,
please?"

"I can ring him for you if you like. Did you want to
join your friend?"

"No. Just the phone number is enough, thank you."

The receptionist shrugged and wrote the number
down for her. Kate thanked her and took the number
across the lobby to a pay telephone. Lifting the
receiver, she punched in three sets of numbers. The
first was an access code that circumvented the need
for her to pay for the use of the phone, a simple magick that the Technocracy had worked into the telephone system early in its development. The second
was David Brossard's phone number. The third,
entered rapidly before the telephone could ring, was a
New World Order spell. The New World Order main-
tained magickal effects on-line, ready to be dialed up
by its mages. The telephone in Brossard's office activated even though the receiver had not been lifted
from the cradle. Kate listened carefully to the sounds
that the telephone relayed to her.

The guard knocked on the door for Aaron, then left
him when a voice from the other side called "Come
in!" Aaron pushed the door open.

The occupant of the office sat behind a desk lit-
tered with pottery shards, measuring implements, and
papers. He was of medium height, with gray hair and
a neatly trimmed beard. His clothing, by contrast, was

shabby, worn in patches, and unraveling at the seams. He looked like any average college professor in his early sixties, but Aaron had learned long ago never to judge a mage by physical appearances.

"Dr. Brossard? I'm Aaron Barry."

The man put down a broken pot. "I've heard of you," he said in a voice tinged with a faint French accent. He made the observation sound like an accusation. "What do you want?"

"A mutual friend told me that you might be able to give me advice if I needed it. Do you remember Adriana Papadimitrios?"

"Ahhh—Adriana." One of Brossard's eyebrows rose and he nodded slightly, but his expression did not otherwise change. He leaned back in his chair as if they really were discussing no more than an old acquaintance. "I haven't seen her in years. How is she? Still living in Venice?"

"She was well the last time I saw her, although she had moved to a small village in Greece."

"And her cats?"

"You must be thinking of someone else," Aaron replied with a polite smile. "Adriana is allergic to cats. Her dogs are fine, though. She told me to ask about your falcons."

"A city is a hell of a place for birds." He ran his gaze over Aaron, then asked suddenly, "Is she still weaving?"

Aaron responded without hesitation. "Aren't we all?"

"What's my real name? What's my Tradition?"

"Saffleur of the Euthanatos."

The older mage regarded him in blank silence. For a moment, Aaron felt a little bit nervous. The exchange of questions that they had just gone through should have convinced the man that he did indeed know Adriana and that she trusted him enough to reveal certain personal details about herself and other mages. In fact, she had been one of his teachers. More importantly, the questions should have convinced him that Aaron was a mage, just as he was. Only a mage would have recognized the true significance of a simple question about weaving. A Sleeper might have assumed that Adriana was nothing more than a weaver of cloth. A mage would know that the question referred to the weaving of reality with magick. Could Saffleur want some sort of further proof?

At last, however, Saffleur nodded and smiled without asking anything more of him. "I'm pleased to meet you, Aaron." He rose and poured himself a cup of coffee from a coffeemaker that was almost buried between boxes of pottery shards. "Are you a Dreamspeaker like Adriana?"

"Cult of Ecstasy."

"Ahh. Help yourself to coffee if you want it. I'm sorry I don't have anything more potent to offer you." Saffleur returned to his chair. He looked at Aaron over the rim of his cup. "But you didn't come to make small talk, did you? What is it—are you looking for information or do you just want someone killed?"

Aaron paused in the act of reaching for the coffeepot. "Just information."

Saffleur shrugged. "You would be surprised how many mages regard the Euthanatos, even one of my standing, as assassins for hire. Too squeamish to do it themselves." He sipped at his coffee. "What do you want to know?"

"I had a strange experience the other night." Aaron shook his head as he poured himself some coffee. "You might not think it's that unusual, but . . ."

"When a snake says the ground is cold, the wise man believes it. Tell me what happened."

Aaron described the incident that had occurred at

Pan's. He told Saffleur about the young man, about how reality had seemed to warp around him, and about how his own magick had been disrupted. He mentioned his inability to locate the young man afterwards. The only things he left out were his relationship with Pan's and the role Pig had played in the attack. In his story, Pig became a drug-using clubgoer that Aaron had tried to disable using magick. He tried to downplay that aspect of the incident as much as possible, in fact. While he was willing to consult Saffleur regarding the young man, he didn't want the other mage to get involved in his struggle with the demon. Pig was his fight.

When Aaron had finished, Saffleur looked at him levelly, as if evaluating him. After a moment, he asked, "Advice doesn't come free. What do I get in return for helping you?"

"Tass." Aaron pulled a small envelope from his coat pocket and extracted a slip of yellowed paper from it. There was Sanskrit writing on the paper, the script drawn out in blood. The paper, like the silk he had used to fuel the enchantment on Pan's, was a storage battery of Quintessence. Saffleur nodded in appreciation, but waved the payment away.

"The offer was more important than the actual payment. It shows your honesty. I think that we can actually help each other." He opened a desk drawer, taking out a folded newspaper clipping that he passed to Aaron. "Read that."

The clipping was from the Sunday edition of the *San Francisco Chronicle*. Two small articles had been circled in bright yellow. The first described the unexpected death of a young convenience-store clerk in one of the more rundown parts of the city early Saturday afternoon. The death was attributed to a sudden, massive cardiac arrest arising out of a previously unidentified heart defect. The second article was about a nasty car accident that had claimed three lives, also early Saturday afternoon and in the same rundown part of town. In fact . . .

"These happened less than a block from each other?"

"Within ten minutes." Saffleur reclaimed the newspaper. "Early on Saturday afternoon, I sensed a tremendous localized fluctuation in the patterns of Entropy in San Francisco. A fluctuation that could be indicative of the reality shifts that you described."

"How . . . ?" Aaron stopped himself in midsentence. He had been about to ask how Saffleur could sense a disturbance in San Francisco when the mage was in Berkeley. Euthanatos, however, were masters of the sphere of Entropy, and Saffleur was a powerful Euthanatos mage. He suspected that if Saffleur claimed to have felt such a fluctuation, then he had indeed felt one. Aaron had some knowledge of Entropy and knew that it was possible. He could perceive the patterns of Entropy himself on a small scale. He rephrased his question. "If it was strong enough for you to sense from out here, how come I didn't sense it when I was actually in the city?"

Saffleur sat back in his chair. "The fluctuation was powerful, but extremely subtle. You would have had to be immersed in the sphere to truly sense it. Think of it as an ocean current, virtually invisible from the surface, but irresistible if you're caught in it." He tapped the newspaper clipping. "For a few seconds, Entropy was out of control. I suspect that the other spheres making up the fabric of reality were distorted as well. I'm old and quite experienced. Most mages would not necessarily have recognized that anything happened. Even I myself have only felt something remotely similar once before. Last Friday night."

"The young man at Pan's."

"Precisely. And like you, I found that my magick

was useless in pinpointing the source of these disturbances. I suspect we may both be looking for the
same person." He pushed the Tass paper back toward
Aaron. "We may well be able to help each other to our
mutual benefit."

Aaron slipped the paper back into the envelope
and returned it to his jacket pocket. "We both satisfy
our curiosity?"

"More. The young man is a danger to himself and
to others, both Awakened and Sleeping. He could suffer a severe Paradox backlash effect. He could damage
the fabric of reality. Worst of all—the Technocracy
could stumble across him and possibly use him to
their advantage."

"That's not good," Aaron agreed. Certainly, he had
toyed with a similar idea himself. If the young man
could shift reality at will, he would be a useful ally.
Saffleur didn't seem entirely amenable to such
manipulation, but if Aaron cooperated with the
Euthanatos, at least he would have the opportunity to
study the young man. "Can you explain what happened?" he asked, changing the subject.

"I . . ." Saffleur hesitated, then said flatly, "No. I
had come up with a couple of possibilities originally.
The disturbances could have been caused by
Marauders. . . ."

"I thought of that. But he didn't look like a
Marauder."

"And the reality shift was too subtle. Marauder
attacks are as subtle as a charging elephant." Aaron
snorted in amusement. The shifts at Pan's had
seemed anything but subtle! But Saffleur shook his
head. "Don't laugh. *Subtle* does not rule out the possibility of *strong*. I don't understand it. I've never seen
that kind of warping of reality on earth."

"But you have seen it before."

"It can happen when areas of stable reality are

created in the Umbra. Mages creating such pocket realms can manipulate most aspects of any of the nine spheres of reality's fabric. On Earth, where reality is already locked into a pattern, it would be extremely difficult to alter that pattern as deeply as he appears to."

"There are spirits that can."

"Pure Forms and Nexus Crawlers? Unlikely. In my experience, they never manifest in anything even remotely resembling human form." The older mage shrugged. "Perhaps the only way we'll know for sure is if we can find the young man."

He held up his hand, forestalling Aaron's question of how they were to accomplish that when they had had no luck before. "We work together, using our magick in concert." He stroked his chin thoughtfully. "The shifts in reality may be making it difficult for magick to fix on him directly, but I think I may know a way to determine his location indirectly. It requires two mages, so I haven't been able to try it before now. How are your skills in the sphere of Time?"

"Competent."

"Good. The effect is simple in theory, but complicated in practice. It also requires a fairly large, open space; it is Euthanatos magick and involves dancing as a focus." He swept his hand around the room. "Obviously my office is unsuitable. Perhaps we can use Pan's."

Aaron blinked in surprise. "What?"

"It's perfect. One of the shifts was centered there. I imagine it has lots of space."

"Except that the New World Order has cameras all around it. Maybe inside it now."

This time Saffleur blinked. "How do you know?"

Aaron shifted in his chair, reluctant to give away one of his secrets, but forced to do so. If he didn't they might lose a shot at finding the young man. "I own it."

"Are they monitoring it because of you?"

"I hope not." He hesitated. Eventually he was going to have to do something about those stupid cameras, but he couldn't even tell Saffleur why the cameras were there without admitting to the secret of his link to Pan's. "They may have recognized the reality shifts on Friday night, too."

Saffleur nodded slowly. "Possibly. Do you think we can disable the cameras for a while in order to get in and use the club?"

"I suppose so." His link to Pan's had already been established, Pig already knew he was a mage—there was no need to go through the elaborate mundane charade he and Tango had used to enter the building unseen before. As long as the Technocracy wasn't able to associate him with Pan's, it would be fine. He forced a tight smile onto his face. "I can put the cameras into a repeating loop with Time magick. It's a little risky, but worth it, I suppose. There's also the problem that the club would normally be open tonight."

"I don't relish the thought of trying to perform magick in front of a crowd of Sleepers."

"I can arrange to have the club closed for the night."

"Excellent. When shall we meet?"

"Ten . . . no, eleven o'clock. At the back doors to the club." Aaron stood up. "Will you need anything special?"

"I'll bring what I need." Saffleur stood as well and shook his hand. "Until tonight, Aaron."

Kate had seated herself demurely on one of the benches in the lobby by the time Aaron emerged from the administrative wing of the museum. Her heart was still racing a little bit. Aaron knew that the New World Order was monitoring Pan's. Did he suspect that they were watching him as well? Did he know that she. . . ? She took a deep breath, calming herself. Why would he have brought her to this meeting if he suspected that she was one of his enemies? His thoughts were clearly on the young man with the strange abilities. She was safe for the moment, but she certainly didn't feel like being around him any more than was necessary.

At least not right now. Eventually she would have to see him again. Her duty to the Technocracy demanded that she watch over him, if not to determine his personal objectives, then to find out more about the young man that he and Saffleur were so anxious to keep hidden. Tonight. She would follow him to his meeting tonight. For now she wanted to be away from him.

She drew another calming breath, then stood up to greet him as he came over to her. "How did it go?"

"Oh, fine. The artifacts the workers turned up in the vineyard were old, broken flowerpots." He smiled. "I'm ready for that tour of the museum you promised me."

Kate shuffled uncomfortably, as if embarrassed at breaking a promise. She was intensely aware that both of them were lying now. She felt so terribly confused. "I'm sorry, Aaron. Tiffany paged me." She held up her beeper. "She needs me back at the station right away. There's some story she wants researched for coverage on tonight's late news. Maybe another time?"

"Are you sure?" He took her hand again. "There must be someone else Tiffany can get to do her research."

"No." Firmly, but with a little hesitation, Kate removed her hand from his grip. "I really need to get back. Can we go now? Please?"

9

The words to a song that she had sung as a child at summer camp came back to Kate as she waited outside Pan's later that night. "Poor little fly on the wall," she sang softly to herself, "no one to love me at all . . ."

She stood in the shadows across the street from the club. Although she didn't know it, Aaron had stood in the same place four nights previously. Where Aaron had watched Pan's, though, Kate's eyes were on the miniature television she held in her hands. Another artifact of New World Order technological magick, it was hooked into the transmissions of the various monitoring devices that had been installed around and, at least since last Friday night, within Pan's. The picture on the screen flipped between the views offered by the cameras on the light poles outside the club, by the security cameras inside the club, and by a few television monitors that were also inside and had been added to the network through Julia's magick. The entire video wall of Pan's main dance floor had been altered to act as a huge window for the New World Order to peer through.

Kate was feeling very much like a fly on the wall.

First at the museum, then again here, she was forced to watch while important events occurred elsewhere. Not that Aaron and Saffleur were likely to allow her inside to view in person whatever spell they were going to weave tonight, but it always seemed to be her role to act as a witness rather than a participant. Working out of New World Order regional headquarters, she usually did no more than paperwork and data analysis. Very seldom had she ever actually interacted with her subjects to the extent that she already had with Aaron.

His passion and drive were so different from the rationality of most Technomancers. Not necessarily totally agreeable to her, but . . . different. And not all bad, heretical though that thought might be in a Technomancer. She wished that just once she could actually share the working of magick with a mage of the Traditions on peaceful, open terms rather than skulking about plotting conflict. It seemed like there were so many things that the New World Order could learn from the Traditions if only they could be more accepting and flexible.

An unexpected movement on the street caught her eye, a cat crossing the sidewalk in front of Pan's. She switched her monitor to show the scene from the point of view of one of the cameras and cursed as she realized why she hadn't spotted the cat before. It didn't appear on the monitor. The street scene was unchanged. Aaron was already jamming the cameras, freezing in time the pictures they transmitted. She shifted to the cameras in Pan's, extending her own senses through them by way of her little monitor in an effort to see if Aaron was truly there.

She was almost caught herself as a wave of magick surged through the cameras in the club. The wave sought out the New World Order devices and spells, locating them by locking on to the magick that powered their transmissions, then encapsulating them in the net of Aaron's own spell. The cameras themselves were not frozen in time, since the internal chronometers on several of them continued to run. Instead, Kate suspected, Aaron had chosen the more delicate effect of fixing the pattern of the light that entered the cameras in time, altering it so that no matter what was actually happening in front of the camera, the picture would always be the same as the moment he worked his magick. Nothing would appear to be wrong to anyone watching the transmissions from afar.

Kate pulled her senses back out of the network as it rapidly became useless. She still had not seen Aaron, but the effects of his magick made it clear that he was present. She waited a few more minutes, then punched a button on the monitoring device that she held. Her own magick reestablished connections that she had made earlier with a single camera and a single microphone inside Pan's. Those connections had been closed down until they were almost inactive, with just barely enough magick flowing to maintain a fine connection. Aaron's spell, searching for more powerful magick, had passed them over. The increased flow of magick now would not draw any attention—if she was lucky. Kate crossed her fingers as the picture the camera transmitted to her monitor slowly grew more distinct. It was possible that Aaron's magick was designed to remain active, seeking out and shutting down any new Technomancer intrusions. She doubted that it was, though she still held her breath until she saw Aaron and Saffleur walk onto the dance floor.

"Adriana taught you how to make demon wards?"

"Some types, yes," Aaron replied, a little bit surprised by the sudden question. He had thought that he had hidden the wards around Pan's well, but

Saffleur apparently had little difficulty in detecting them. The Euthanatos mage had been looking around Pan's with interest from the moment they had entered the club.

Saffleur merely nodded in response to his answer and added, "I'd have recognized her style anywhere. You have a problem with demons?"

"Better safe than sorry," Aaron lied.

He led Saffleur out onto the dance floor. A few security lights provided dim illumination, turning the floor into a murky sea of gloom and the ceiling into a shadow-shrouded sky studded with the irregular projections of the club's light-show system. As new as the club was, the stale smells of cigarette smoke and beer already lingered in it. He turned to face Saffleur. "Do we need music?"

"We make our own." Saffleur removed his coat. Underneath, he was wearing a rumpled tweed jacket, a shirt, and a tie. He also wore a necklace of tiny, polished animal skulls, an incongruous sight against his very civilized jacket. He took two items from the pockets of his coat before laying it neatly to the side of the dance floor. One was a pale wooden rattle, worn smooth with use. The other was a bone, so ancient and strangely shaped that Aaron wasn't sure what manner of creature it had come from. For a moment, he wasn't even sure it was a bone; it was long and very broad, tapering to end in a slightly rounded point. Saffleur smiled when he noticed Aaron staring at it. "A relic of the Mythic Age," he explained. "The breastbone of an ogre. My first master gave it to me as a focus for my magick."

He passed it to Aaron. The bone was surprisingly heavy and dense. "How old is it?"

"About six hundred years." Saffleur smiled fondly. "Only a century older than me."

Aaron whistled in surprise, then laughed. "There

aren't many people old enough to be able to say 'only a century' so casually."

"There are more than you think. Back then, before the Technocracy, there were more. Unfortunately, Paradox makes it extremely difficult to extend your life. Your very presence in the fabric of reality, long after your pattern should have faded away, tends to attract Paradox. It gathers around you until it reaches a critical level and then—poof! Reality restores itself, sometimes in extremely dramatic ways. Accumulated Paradox can kill you or worse."

"You're still here, and you don't seem to have a problem with Paradox."

"There are ways to avoid it. I have been willing to do what was necessary to survive."

The way he delivered his words chilled Aaron. He passed the bone back to the Euthanatos, commenting with false levity, "I've never seen anything like it before."

"I imagine you have actually. All kinds of bones and relics from the Mythic Age are still lying around museums. There are too many for the Technocracy to destroy all of them, so they pass them off as frauds or extinct animals or fossils. You'd be surprised what people will believe when they're lied to by someone with authority."

"Fossils are stone, not bone."

"Some giants and dragons had bones made of stone. Trolls turned to stone in the sunlight. So did their bones. Didn't you learn anything from Adriana besides how to make demon wards?"

"I concentrated on the wards," replied Aaron testily. "Can we get started?" He pulled his recorder from his pocket and shrugged off his jacket.

"Very well." Saffleur walked to the middle of the dance floor and set the ogre bone on the ground, then continued on until he and Aaron were both an equal distance from the bone. "Stay where you are. We remain opposite each other through the spell, dancing around the bone."

"How exactly is this going to work?"

"Time and Entropy in conjunction. You are going to look ahead through time, trying to focus on where and when you will next see our young man."

"But I can't fix on him directly!" Aaron protested. "The only way I would be able to predict when I'll see him again is if I scan my entire life. There are too many possibilities!"

"Which is why my role will be to reduce the number of extraneous and unlikely possibilities you perceive by minimizing Entropy's influence. You should be able to produce a prediction despite not being able to 'fix' on him." He raised his rattle and looked penetratingly at Aaron. "My control minimizes the randomness in your predictions. Do you understand?"

Aaron hesitated before responding. Entropy was a complicated sphere, and he couldn't pretend to understand all of its complexities. Saffleur's explanation of the magick left him feeling like a high school student trying to comprehend a lecture on quantum physics: He knew it would work, but he was not entirely clear on why it did so. But if a mage as old as Saffleur claimed to know what he was doing, then presumably he did. "I understand enough. What about Paradox? Isn't this vulgar magick?"

Saffleur nodded. "It can't be helped. But there are no Sleepers about. Without Sleeper witnesses, chances are good that we can work the magick without attracting Paradox. Follow my lead in the steps and the rhythm, but stay across from me. You can improvise music. You'll know when to begin using magick."

He shook the rattle once. The sound was like wood chips falling against each other, not the softer, maracas-like sound Aaron had expected. It made him wonder what was inside that rattle. Saffleur shook the rattle again, twice this time, then took a slow step to the side. Two shakes and a step back to where he had been. Two shakes and a step to the other side. The rhythm was slow, and Aaron picked it up easily, mirroring Saffleur's steps. After a moment, he put the recorder to his mouth and produced a sliding, slightly flat note that mimicked the slow side steps. Saffleur nodded approvingly, then began to move consistently in one direction, slowly making a clockwise circle around the bone. Aaron circled opposite him.

By the time they had returned to their original positions, Aaron realized that they were dancing more quickly. The shakes of Saffleur's rattle were faster. The notes of his recorder were bursts more than slides, and he had begun to work an increasingly complex tune into the music, weaving it through the rhythm that Saffleur set. That made it easy to follow the steps of the Euthanatos. When he suddenly took a pace in toward the bone, Aaron paced with him. When he began to dance back counterclockwise in a tighter circle, Aaron followed.

Just as Saffleur had said, he needed no signal to know when he was to begin using his magick. It happened almost spontaneously. As they circled, visions of the future began to take form in his sight. The motion of the dance was pleasurable, and he opened himself to Pan's, his link magnifying the simple sensation until it was almost unbearable. He drew on that focus. Time spread out in front of him as though he were standing on top of a mountain. The visions became clearer and more numerous, a bewildering riot of phantom shapes and scenes. He caught glimpses of people he recognized, or thought he might recognize, among a multitude of faces that held no meaning to him at all. These were all of his possible futures, swarming before him. His music was suddenly as full of intricacies as his future was full of possibilities.

They completed the circle and took another step forward. Abruptly, a number of futures vanished from his vision. He knew that they weren't gone completely, only shielded from his sight. He could feel Saffleur's presence, routing the randomness of Entropy away from him. The futures that he saw were still numerous, but now he could at least make out individual events, although they spun away from him faster than he could commit them to memory. He saw the young man from Friday night, however, and quite clearly. He was in his future; they would meet again. But Aaron saw him in many, many ways: dead and alive, joyous and grieving, horribly scarred and gloriously beautiful. Their meeting would have many potential outcomes.

He and Saffleur stepped in and circled back and forth again and again. With each step toward the bone, the future became more clear and his visions more restricted. The music he played imitated them, becoming simpler and simpler until he was repeating two notes over and over as fast as his fingers could move. Time contracted toward the present, shrinking from months to weeks to days. It narrowed as well, until the only figure that he saw was the young man, rushing at him through time until they were about to collide.

The last circle was barely three steps to the side, and suddenly Aaron found himself standing face-to-face with Saffleur, the bone at their feet. The recorder and the rattle both fell silent as Saffleur demanded simply, "Where?"

Aaron's vision of the future crystallized. "Here!" he shouted.

"When?"

"Now!"

Something fell against the front doors of the club with a loud thump.

Kate didn't see the end of the ritual.

She listened with interest to Saffleur and Aaron's conversation about bones and demon wards. She could detect them now that she knew they were there, and she remembered the inhuman creature Aaron had struggled with in Pan's on Friday night. Had he put the wards up in response to its attack? She struggled to understand Saffleur's explanation of the magick that they would work and watched them begin to circle around the bone. Just as the dance picked up its pace, however, she glanced up. A lone figure was stumbling down the street toward Pan's.

It was the young man from Friday night. He looked terrible, the streetlights washing all color from his face until his skin was paper white. He stumbled as he walked. Kate was sure that he would fall over at any moment. Twice he grabbed at lampposts, hugging them for support. A car drove by a second time, slowing down for a moment. Kate watched as the young man turned his hug into a casual lean. The car kept going, and the young man collapsed again, but Kate recognized the purpose behind his sudden change in posture. He had been displaying his body for the driver of the car. The young man was a hustler.

She pursed her lips as she watched him reel on to the next lamppost. This was her chance to find out about him. If she could spirit him away before Aaron and Saffleur had finished their ritual . . . She glanced at the monitor in her hand, then shoved it in her pocket. They were still dancing. If she got the young man away from here right now, Aaron would not see him in his future. The New World Order would have him to itself. She ran out of the shadows and raced across the street.

Stefan forced his legs to push him along to the next lamppost. He had tried to hail a cab several blocks back, but none would stop for him. He had had to walk, lurching through a world that was muddy with the alcohol he had consumed. He had drunk an entire quart of some kind of liquor over the last few hours. It hadn't helped. After he had seen Marilyn, nothing seemed to help. The more he drank, the thinner the veil of dimness around him grew. Drinking did keep back the terrible clarity on the other side of that veil, though. His only shield against the clarity had become the haze of drunkenness. When that finally evaporated, he knew that the clarity would still be there, waiting for him. He didn't want that to happen.

He had finished the liquor and come here, his legs growing heavier with every step. The world was already spinning around him. He hoped he would make it in time. All he wanted to do now was sit on the steps of the club where the nightmare had begun and wait for the alcohol in his blood to kill him.

Somehow, he realized, he had managed to walk past the lamppost he had been heading toward. It was already several paces behind him. The next one was right in front of Pan's. He blinked as one lamppost briefly became two in his sight, then squinted until there was only one again. He didn't take his eyes off the lamppost this time, not wanting to miss it and end up down the block, searching vainly for the club. Only a few more steps . . .

A hand came down on his shoulder. Stefan swung around, perhaps too quickly. He fell to the ground. A woman, the one who had touched him, helped him stand again. He shook off her hands and swore at her.

"What?" she asked, startled.

He laughed. Whatever language he had just produced, it had not been English. He continued to curse her as he staggered on toward the club, vomiting out all of the languages that he spoke and maybe some that he didn't.

"My God!" he heard her whisper between clenched teeth. The words were a combination of frustration and awe. She caught at his arm again just as he was setting foot on the steps of Pan's. "Come with me!" she said urgently.

"Piss off, lady. I'm busy."

"Come with me!" This time, the words were an order. He glanced back and saw that she was holding something in her hand, a magnifying glass or something on a chain around her neck.

Something sliced painfully into his mind, commanding him to do as she said. He might have done so, except that the command also cut through the haze that staved off the clarity. The magnifying glass in the woman's hand came into focus so suddenly it made Stefan want to throw up. The glass shattered with a thin snap. The woman gave a little shriek. The intrusion into his mind vanished.

"Who are you?" she gasped.

Dark blotches began to swim in front of Stefan's eyes as the alcoholic stupor settled back over his brain like a wet wool blanket. He tried to keep his eyes on the woman while he took another step upward. She had done something to him. He didn't know what, but he didn't want it to happen again.

"Who are you?" she asked again.

She took a step toward him, her arms open wide, ready to seize him. He whirled, desperate to get away from her. The doors of Pan's were abruptly in front of him, though, and he slammed into them hard. He went down like a bag of dirty laundry.

He couldn't see anything, he wasn't sure which way was up, but he felt someone holding him. "Mike?"

"Is that your name?"

"It's me, Mike." He wasn't sure what language he was speaking, but he knew Mike would understand. "It's Stefan. Wait for me—I'm coming." A door opened somewhere, and he fell through it.

"Kate?"

Aaron had the doors of Pan's open and was looking down on her as she cradled the young man in her arms. Aaron was clearly surprised to see her. She returned his gaze but couldn't think of anything to say that would explain her presence. She was extremely conscious of the monitor that weighed down the pocket of her coat and of the shattered lens hanging around her neck. Aaron still held his recorder in his hand. Kate let the first intelligible thing she could think of roll off her tongue.

"His name is Stefan. We have to get him to a hospital."

"How do you know his name?"

"I asked him. He told me."

Saffleur, still pulling on his coat, pushed past Aaron and knelt beside her, one hand over Stefan's heart. Kate felt the faint pulse of simple Life magick as he examined the hustler. "Alcohol poisoning," he pronounced.

"Can you do anything about it?" asked Aaron. "Can you heal him?"

"I'm Euthanatos. I study death, not healing."

"The best I can do is cure a hangover."

"A hospital it is then."

Kate allowed herself to relax slightly. If they were caught up enough in Stefan's unconsciousness to discuss magickal healing in front of her, then they had all but forgotten she was there. That gave her a chance to get away before Aaron or Saffleur could ask any more awkward questions. She might have been able to take on Aaron alone, but Saffleur was old and knowledgeable. He was much more powerful than her. Kate did not want to try defending herself against both mages. She pushed Stefan into Saffleur's arms and jumped to her feet. "My car is just around the corner. We can take it." She ran off down the street as fast as she could.

They watched her go; then Saffleur glanced up at Aaron. "You know her?"

"Kate? She's a friend."

"Well, what the hell was she doing out here with him?"

Aaron pulled the door closed and locked it behind him. That question left a sour feeling in his stomach. "I don't know."

"Find out." Saffleur shifted the young man—Stefan, Kate had said his name was—in his arms until he had a better grip on him. "I can get him to a hospital faster than her car."

"San Francisco General is closest. Take him there. I'll meet you after I've had a talk with Kate."

Saffleur nodded and stood up slowly, Stefan a dead weight in his old arms. He managed a few rough dance steps to focus his magick, and vanished, taking the young man with him. Aaron ran after Kate. She was perhaps only half a block ahead of him. Her shoes had not been made for running. Saffleur's Euthanatos dancing and his own sensation-based magick had tired him as well, however, and Kate dashed around the corner of the street before he could catch up to her. When he did reach the corner, there was no sign of her. Several cars were making their way along the street, though, and he waited for one of them to turn the corner, knowing it would be Kate on her way back to pick up Stefan.

None of the cars turned. Aaron frowned. She hadn't come back. He risked the use of a little bit of vulgar magick, trying to sense whether she was still in the area. He found nothing. She was gone completely.

Aaron hesitated, torn between tracking Kate down in order to question her and going to the hospital to see what was happening with Stefan. He opted for the hospital and Stefan. Kate could wait until tomorrow. He trudged back to Pan's to retrieve his coat and his car.

Aaron Barry had no idea what he was dealing with. That was clear to Saffleur as he gritted his teeth against the pain of the Paradox generated by his vulgar use of magick and threw himself and the Angel across space to his study in Berkeley. If he were to take the Angel to a hospital in this condition, there was no telling what havoc he might cause. He would have to go the hospital very soon, of course. The young man was suffering from acute alcohol poisoning and could die without medical attention.

But first, he was going to have to find a way to stabilize the Angel's powers. Saffleur laid him out in the center of the room. Aaron had believed his story about sensing fluctuations of Entropy. The Ecstasy Cultist really must have spent all of his time with Adriana learning about demon wards, or he would have realized that such an explanation was rather unlikely. In fact, the last three days had been hellish for Saffleur. The ties that bound him and the Angel together had stretched and strained. The wheel of the Angel's life cycle had been grinding back and forth, and the powers that had at first been a minor nuisance were growing more and more serious. They had to be stabilized, at least temporarily!

Saffleur sat back on his heels. Normally, he would simply have completed the ritual that surrounded the turning of the life cycle. The final component of the turning ritual wiped the turning from the Angel's memory, and it had served in the past to quiet his abilities. There was no time for the full ritual now, however. He was lucky to have located the Angel in time to do anything. Indeed, he was lucky even to find the Angel at all after the activation of his abilities had shielded him from direct magick. Aaron's visit had been fortuitous, since it had provided him with the second mage he needed to perform the ritual of Entropy and Time. And because Aaron had already had a brush with the Angel, Saffleur wasn't forced to reveal the young man's existence to another mage.

The delay had still been too great, though. He would have to skip the beneficial part of the turning ritual and proceed directly to the amnesia magick. He hoped it would work. Without the full turning ritual, the magick would not be as strong. The Angel might be able to break past the shield across his memory. The next scheduled turning would happen in three days' time, however. If the Angel could be kept quiet, without anything that might jar his mind, the turning ritual then would be enough to stabilize him properly. Saffleur's eyes narrowed in thought. Aaron. He might be able to trick Aaron into watching over the Angel for the next three days. That would provide the Angel with a guardian, and it would release him to arrange the events of the turning. Yes, that could work out quite well, although he would have to be careful to refer to the Angel by his given name around Aaron. It would feel odd to call him by any other name. He had long ago decided to name the spirit rather than the body it occupied.

He stood and went to his desk. A plain box of age-blackened wood sat atop it. He drew a deep, calming breath before he opened it, just as he always did. The Great Lady was nestled in the box, shrouded in dark velvet. The power of the talisman never ceased to awe him, even though it had been his constant companion for several centuries. He took the statuette out of the box gingerly, although the years had proved it to be virtually indestructible, and returned to kneel beside the Angel. He set the talisman on the Angel's chest.

In spite of the fact that the only light in the room was shining over Saffleur's own shoulder, the Great Lady cast a shadow as if the light were coming from directly behind it. That long shadow fell across the Angel's face, and he groaned. His eyes fluttered open to stare at the beetle head staring back at him. He screamed, a brief terrified yell that was cut short as Saffleur clapped his hand over his mouth.

"Great Lady," Saffleur murmured, "let him sleep. Let his memories, like dreams, slip under the black waters."

A soft humming and whispering filled the air. The Angel relaxed. As the humming and whispering grew quiet, his eyes drifted shut. Saffleur waited a moment longer, then removed the Great Lady and returned it to its box.

The emergency room of the hospital was crowded. In fact, crowded was putting it mildly: The emergency room was a zoo. Babies and small children were screaming and crying uncontrollably. Adults were trying to talk over the din. Somewhere behind thin walls and white curtains, a man was shouting incoherently. A doctor yelled for help in restraining him. There was a sudden shriek, and that produced a shocked silence in the waiting area for a moment. Then the children started crying again, the adults started talking, and the volume rose even higher.

Aaron stopped the first medical-looking person he spotted, a doctor in a lab coat and slightly stained surgeon's greens. "I'm looking for someone——"

"Ask at admissions."

He glanced at the long line that had formed in front of the admissions desk. The drive from Pan's to San Francisco General had taken long enough. He didn't want to wait any longer. He smiled charmingly at the doctor, putting a little magick behind the charm. "The name is probably Brossard. A young man with black hair brought in by an old man with a beard."

The doctor's eyes glazed slightly, lost in that smile. "In back. Already treated and just waiting for reexamination before we let the young guy go."

"Thank you. It's not a problem if I go see them?"

"Not at all."

"Good." He tapped the doctor lightly on the cheek. "Have a good night." He walked away, leaving the doctor slightly bemused and wondering what had just happened.

Stefan was lying on a gurney out in the hallway, still unconscious and looking as if he had been stretched on a rack. Saffleur sat patiently on a chair beside him, largely oblivious to the chaos around him. Or perhaps he was only oblivious to the physical chaos. Aaron saw his eyes shift to glance into a nearby cubicle as the patient there arched her back in a final, long convulsion before relaxing with a quiet sigh of release.

"You're enjoying this, aren't you?" he asked in disgust.

The Euthanatos shrugged. "Death and suffering are natural parts of life. It's important that mages study them as we study any other part of our reality. And hospitals are as much places of death as they are places of life."

Aaron couldn't help feeling cold suddenly. Saffleur's tradition and his own were the antitheses of each other in many ways. One celebrated life; the other, death. He changed the topic. "Did you have any trouble getting him in?"

"There were some delays, though not many. I could have pressed for a bed, but we won't be here that long anyway."

"He looks like hell." Aaron pressed his hand to Stefan's face. The young man's skin was clammy with slowly evaporating sweat. He stirred restlessly at Aaron's touch.

"They pumped his stomach. Not a pleasant procedure. It seems he has been drinking and using illegal drugs quite heavily recently, while hardly eating at all. What came out of his stomach was almost entirely alcohol."

"Stupid shit. What was he trying to do? Kill himself?"

"Apparently."

Aaron found another chair and pulled it up beside Saffleur. "I don't suppose you've been able to find anything out about how he was warping reality?"

"No," Saffleur responded with a shake of his head. "Perhaps when he's awake. As far as I can tell, he is a perfectly normal human being. Not a Marauder, not some kind of spirit. He's not even a mage or Awakened at all as far as I can tell, just a Sleeper."

"Did he have any identification on him?"

"Just keys and some loose change."

"I think I could use the keys to track down the matching locks with magick and figure out where he lives. That could be a clue."

Saffleur smiled. "Who's being morbid now? You talk like he's not going to wake up. The doctor says that he should be completely all right in a few days, provided we keep him away from any more booze and make sure that he remains in a quiet, very restful environment. Nothing is to disturb him." He paused. "I was thinking he could stay at my house while he recovered and we examined him."

"I was going to suggest my place." Aaron tried to keep the tone of demand that crept into his voice low. He wanted the opportunity to study Stefan without the older mage around, and he certainly wouldn't have it if they were going to be together constantly. "I imagine that I have more room."

"What if there is another reality shift?"

"I think I'll be able to handle it this time. I know what to expect."

"I would have to . . ." Saffleur stopped and raised his eyebrow. "Actually, I suppose one of us would have to drive somewhere, no matter where we let him stay. Very well. He stays at your place." He gave Aaron a little smile. "Since you insist."

10

The receptionist answered the phone with a bright, cheery tone. "KKBA Television in San Francisco—may I help you?"

"Yes." Aaron, cordless telephone in hand, sat down on the large sofa that graced the living room of the Barry mansion. "Can you connect me to Kate Sanders?"

"One moment, please." Bland background music hummed in his ear as she put him on hold. Aaron grimaced at the sound. The receptionist was back on the line quickly, however. "I'm sorry, but she's not in today. Can I take a message?"

"No, I left one earlier. Look, I really need to talk to her. Can you tell me if she's expected in at all?"

"I'm afraid she called in sick today." The receptionist's voice was so nauseatingly perky that he suspected she herself had never suffered anything more debilitating than a minor cold.

He growled in frustration. "Thank you." Aaron hung up, punching at the release button on the phone hard enough to make his fingertip tingle. He waited a moment, then dialed again. The phone rang five times at the other end before it connected, and he heard the words he had been hearing all morning.

"Hello, this is Kate. I can't come to the phone right now, but please leave—"

He cut the answering machine off with another stab at the phone's release button. Where was she? He had been trying to get hold of Kate since eight-thirty and it was now almost noon. She wasn't at home, she wasn't at work. He had tried to find her once using magick, but without any luck. Perhaps she had left the city. He would try again later, this time searching across the entire Bay Area. What had she been doing outside Pan's last night? He wanted answers!

With a grunt of dissatisfaction, he put the phone down and picked up a large mug of extremely black coffee. He had finally gotten home from the hospital with Stefan at five o'clock last night. Hospitals and emergency wards had never exactly been his favorite places under the best of conditions, and sitting in one for four and a half hours with a Euthanatos certainly did not improve the experience. Saffleur was a nice enough person, but Aaron never wanted to interact with him socially again. He had put Stefan to bed in a guest room, then spent twenty minutes under a hot shower trying to scrub away the hospital smell and Saffleur's observations on death before collapsing into bed himself. Three hours of sleep was far too little to make him happy, but he had survived on less during some Cult of Ecstasy celebrations.

The doorbell chimed, and Aaron forced himself to his feet to get it. He almost wished he hadn't told the housekeeper to take the day off. She could be answering the door while he napped. The doorbell rang again as he reached for the locks. "Hold on," he muttered, "I'm here."

The woman on the doorstep was dressed in an

unflattering cream-colored uniform and carried a small black bag. "Mr. Barry?" she asked politely in accented English, extending her hand. He murmured an acknowledgement as she introduced herself as the private day nurse he had hired. His second call of the morning, after failing to reach Kate, had been to an agency that specialized in providing reliable, discreet temporary staff. He had promised the agency a bonus if they could get him someone before noon. They had been as good as their word. The nurse seemed competent, professional, and, most importantly, just large and tough enough to double as something of a security guard. He explained her basic duties as he led her upstairs. She would be required to watch over a young man and attend to his needs during the next couple of days until he had recuperated from a case of alcohol poisoning. While he was expected to be fairly quiet and inactive, if he did happen to get up, she was to see that he did not leave the suite of rooms where he was. Aaron offered no explanation for this confinement, and she didn't ask for one. He unlocked the bedroom and opened the door quietly.

Stefan lay sprawled naked on top of the bed, the sheets and blankets kicked off and pooled down around his feet. He was still sweating slightly in his sleep. The nurse went directly to the bed and pulled the bedclothes up over her charge in a brisk manner, but not before Aaron had caught the slightly disapproving look on her face. "No," he snapped, guessing what she was thinking. The notorious Aaron Barry with an attractive young man buck naked in one of his beds. "We are not lovers."

"Yes, Mr. Barry. Are there any pyjamas around?"

Aaron pointed at a chest of drawers. "The kitchen is downstairs at the back of the house. You can help yourself to anything there. Come and get me only if there's a problem." He handed her the key and headed back downstairs, massaging his temples and trying to remember where he had left his coffee.

The doorbell rang again just as he reached the foot of the stairs. He stopped, staring at the door. He wasn't expecting anyone else. Saffleur would not be coming by until this evening sometime. Aaron had insisted that Stefan be given a chance to recover before they talked to him. He peered through the peephole, then blinked in surprise and opened the door slowly.

It was Kate. "Good morning, Aaron."

"Morning."

"May I come in? I have some things I have to say."

He stood aside and let her pass. Aaron was abruptly and acutely conscious, in a way that he had not been with the nurse, that he was wearing nothing more than old jeans, a T-shirt, and yesterday's whiskers. His feet were bare. By contrast, Kate was carefully, almost primly, dressed in a shirt and jacket. He led her into the living room, then, almost as an afterthought, shut the big, old sliding wooden doors that sealed off the room from the rest of the mansion. "I've been trying to call you."

"I know." Kate sat perched on the edge of an armchair, her purse in her lap, her knees together, and the fingers of her hands tightly interlocked. "I know you own Pan's," she said bluntly.

"What?" He sat down in a chair across from her, separated by the length of a coffee table and by the stunned shock that he felt. That was his best-kept secret! Only he, Saffleur, and Tango knew that fact. At least, they should have been the only ones.

"I know you own Pan's. Don't deny it." She glanced up to catch his eye. "I've suspected since opening night. Seeing you there last night just clinched it. I have a talent for figuring things out."

"I don't own Pan's!" Aaron gritted his teeth. "I

needed to meet someone in private and a friend is the manager. What were *you* doing there last night?"

"I followed you," Kate admitted frankly. "I got someone else to do Tiffany's research. I wanted to confirm my hunch."

Aaron stared at her for a moment, then asked, "Does Tiffany know about me and Pan's?" The last thing he needed was to have his connection with the club splashed all over the city on one of Tiffany's gossip-column news reports. The New World Order would certainly notice that.

"No." Kate met his gaze without blinking.

Aaron let his breath out slowly. The secret was safe, then. Or at least relatively safe. Kate herself still knew, but that wouldn't be a problem. Suddenly, he was very glad that his seduction of the reporter had been going so smoothly. He was certain that he could convince her to keep his secret.

He rose to his feet and walked around the coffee table to kneel beside her chair. "Kate," he said in a carefully pleading and vulnerable voice, "please, please don't tell Tiffany?"

"Why shouldn't I?"

"Because." He took her hand, rubbing it between his, then kissing her fingers tenderly. "I don't want anybody to know. Please, Kate?"

She was weakening. She looked confused, as if she were trying to decide how to react. He played on her confusion, drawing her to her feet before she could make a decision and holding both of her hands lightly.

Kate tensed, then replied slowly, "Aaron, I don't know what to say."

"You don't have to say anything." He looked into her eyes, then slowly brought his lips closer to hers. Moving in for the final seduction. "Kate, you're—"

Abruptly, the nurse was shouting from upstairs. Kate, startled, pulled away from Aaron. He cursed under his breath and turned to throw open the heavy wooden doors. "What is it?" he bellowed.

"Your . . . guest is having a seizure!"

"Damn! I'll be right up!"

Kate grabbed his arm. "Who is that? What guest do you have?"

He hesitated before telling her. She didn't need to know about this, at least not all of the details. "Stefan," he confessed reluctantly.

"What? He's here?" She charged upstairs before he could stop her.

The revelation of Stefan's presence was like a godsend to Kate. She had come to the mansion expecting to get information out of Aaron by playing the part of a woman trapped between her job and her love for a man. Aaron's own performance and pleading appeal had been more powerful than she had expected, however. When he had taken her hand and asked her not to tell his secret, she had not merely been acting confused! His charm had brought all of her conflicting emotions about him to the surface, where they had fought with her rationality.

He was using her, Kate reminded herself. He was using her to hide the secret of his ownership of Pan's. That was all! He didn't care for her, whatever she might think. She was the one allowing him to believe that she had fallen for him. She was the one in control.

If only she could believe that herself.

It was simple to find Stefan's room: She just followed the shouts and screams. Aaron was at her heels all the way up, almost bowling her over as she froze in the bedroom doorway. The sight was startling. Stefan was thrashing about on the bed, yelling incoherently, the red-striped pyjamas that he wore half stripped off. The nurse, a big, brawny woman, was crouched over his chest, trying to pin his arms and legs down while at the same time struggling to keep his pyjamas on him. Stefan was throwing her about as though she were a small boat on a storm-tossed ocean.

Aaron pushed past her to seize one of Stefan's arms and give the nurse some respite. "Epilepsy?" he demanded of her.

"Epileptics don't usually scream in the middle of a seizure." The nurse gestured imperiously for Kate to take Stefan's other arm. She did, straining to hold him still. Stefan wasn't heavily muscled, but his seizure seemed to make him stronger. "Is he epileptic?"

"I don't know."

The nurse cursed in some language that sounded vaguely Scandinavian to Kate. She couldn't tell what the nurse had said, but whatever it was, it did something to Stefan. The young man suddenly began to buck so violently that the nurse was thrown to the floor. Kate's own grip on his arm was shaken off, and Aaron was pulled off of his feet. Stefan began to shout at the nurse, his ravings taking on the forms of individual words in whatever language she had spoken. The nurse appeared astonished, though Kate couldn't tell whether it was from her fall or out of surprise at Stefan's words.

"What is he saying?" she demanded as she grabbed for his arm again.

"Nothing." The nurse climbed grimly to her feet and clapped her arm around Stefan's thrashing legs. "Yelling for his mother, that's all." She grunted as Stefan kicked her a glancing blow in the shoulder. "All we can do is wait for the seizure to pass."

"It will go away soon enough."

Kate knew what Aaron was going to do as soon as she saw him reach toward Stefan's head. She would have done it herself had Aaron not been present. Mind magick could calm Stefan easily, disguised as nothing more than a soothing touch to the forehead. She sensed Aaron's split-second spellcasting and, probably unconsciously, allowed her grip to grow slightly slack, certain that the worst was over. That was a mistake. Stefan gave one last convulsion as Aaron touched him, lifting the nurse clear off the floor and flailing out with his arm to deal Kate a hard punch to the jaw. Kate pulled back belatedly. Stefan was already relaxing, though, his eyes closing.

He had not, however, stopped babbling. If anything, in fact, Aaron's magick appeared to have opened a door, releasing a storm of words that poured out of Stefan's mouth. He was no longer yelling, but his constant, shifting whisper was now almost more disturbing. She let go of his arm, letting it fall limply to the mattress. It was almost like listening to a crowd of people trying to talk at once, each person speaking nonsense phrases of their own invention. Or not nonsense phrases, perhaps. Suddenly she heard him murmur, clearly and distinctly, "Grandfather, please don't go." In Japanese.

The plaintive words were lost so quickly she wasn't sure she had actually heard them. She listened again, but could make out nothing else that she recognized. Stefan's voice began to grow as quiet as his body. Then Aaron frowned. "Italian?" he muttered half to himself. Kate looked up at him, startled, just as Stefan spat out something in German. Both of them stared down in surprise, then glanced at each other.

"Was that German?" There was bafflement on Aaron's face.

Kate had to force herself not to ask what exactly he had done to Stefan's mind. After all, she wasn't supposed to have noticed his magick. Instead, she merely nodded. "I heard Japanese earlier. And you heard Italian." She turned to the nurse. "What was he speaking to you?"

"Norwegian." The nurse checked Stefan's pulse as his final words drifted into silence and his lips stopped moving. She looked up at Aaron. "It might be a good idea for a doctor to have a look at him."

Aaron shook his head, frowning. "No."

"Mr. Barry—"

"No." He put his hand over hers and smiled confidently at her. "He'll be fine without a doctor."

Kate sensed Aaron's magick flow again as he charmed the nurse into accepting his wishes. She turned to Stefan, hoping that Aaron would not try the same trick on her. "Strange that a hustler should speak so many languages," she commented aloud, trying to shift the direction of the conversation.

"How do you know he's a hustler? I thought you said you didn't know anything about him."

There was suspicion in Aaron's voice, and Kate winced before she looked at him over her shoulder. "I know what I saw on the street outside Pan's. He's a hustler as sure as you're rich." She frowned as other details of last night came back to her. "He did the same thing then, too—said a bunch of stuff to me that I didn't understand. I thought he was just drunk."

Aaron looked at her steadily, then turned to glance at the nurse. "We'll be downstairs."

He took Kate's hand and led her from the room. Once they were partway down the stairs, he stopped and turned to her. "What exactly did Stefan say to you last night?"

"I don't know. I think he was swearing at me. At least, that's what it sounded like." Kate looked into his face. "What did he say in Italian just now?"

"What did he say in Japanese?"

"You tell me first," she replied defiantly. Her heart was beating wildly. He could use magick on her anytime, but Kate didn't dare use any to try and find out what she wanted. She tried to think like Tiffany might in interviewing some recalcitrant celebrity, confusing him with a flurry of questions. "Just what is Stefan to you anyway? Why have you got him here?" She stepped away from him, the distance giving her more confidence. "What do *you* know about him? Are you . . . ?"

"No! Jesus Christ, the nurse asked the same thing!"

"He is a prostitute."

Aaron sighed and reached out to her. Kate recognized the look of wounded pride that she had seen on men's faces before. "Believe me, I'm not interested in him that way."

At least he was back to trying to charm her with promises of love. She allowed him to take her hand again. She even went so far as to give him a little hug before whispering in his ear, "So why are you interested in him?" When she felt him stiffen, she laughed lightly, realizing even as she did so that she reminded herself of Julia, flirting in the middle of an interrogation. "There must be something about him."

"Stefan was asking how someone could betray him."

"What?" Kate looked at Aaron in confusion.

"When he was speaking Italian. That's what he said."

"Don't change the subject. I want to know why you've got such a concern for someone you don't know."

Aaron pushed her gently away without saying a word and walked on down the stairs. Kate hesitated for a moment before catching up to him. "Wait. Aaron . . ."

He turned to look at her, then said slowly, "I have to go to see where he lives. To look around. If you've got such a talent for figuring things out, why don't you come with me?"

"I'm no detective, Aaron." He was trying to lure her more deeply into his seduction, attempting to pique her interest. She wanted more information, though.

"Is this something you should take to the police?" she asked, baiting him

"They wouldn't be able to help. I need to go myself." He looked down at his feet. "I'll need to put on shoes."

"I'm not going anywhere with you until you tell me exactly what is going on with Stefan, why you're going to search his home, and," she added as she sat down obstinately on the stairs, "why you want me to be there."

He was sitting beside her in a flash, and she swore to herself as she realized that he had been waiting for her to demand just such an explanation. He wanted to look suitably hesitant to speak, yet still sincere. "I know I can trust you, Kate." He looked deeply into her eyes. She forced herself to look into his, softly and sweetly, in return. "And I want you to be able to trust me. I think you would figure it out on your own anyway, so I'm going to tell you now. Maybe you can help me that way. Kate . . ."

Kate pressed her finger to his lips before he could say anything else. "No. Not another word, Aaron. You don't have to try to explain yourself to me."

Because if you tell me one more lie, she thought, I will be physically ill.

Aaron had hung a key, suspended by a fine gold chain, from the rearview mirror of his car. It was, he said, the key to Stefan's home, and he claimed that he wanted to be sure he didn't lose it. Kate thought she might have been able to believe that, except that she had felt Aaron work a magick that she didn't recognize on the key as he looped the chain over the mirror.

He chatted incessantly as they drove, talking about the weather, his memories of San Francisco as a small boy, her job—anything but his interest in Stefan and where they were going. His apparently mindless babble, combined with the constant swaying of the key as Aaron turned the wheel of the car, made her feel as though she were seasick.

She realized that they were driving in circles after they passed the same corner store three times. They had been driving in circles the entire way. The key wasn't swaying as the car turned. The car was turning because the key was swaying. Aaron was using the key as a pendulum, his magick causing it to point toward its matching lock on Stefan's door. He didn't know where Stefan lived, but he was triangulating as they drove, drawing slowly closer to Stefan's home.

They finally parked in front of a squat, old apartment building they had already passed twice. "This is it!" Aaron said with an enthusiasm that sounded forced to Kate's ears. He took the key down from the mirror, but Kate noticed that he didn't untie it from the chain. He would need it to find Stefan's apartment. She looked dubiously at the building. The cement was cracking close to the ground, and the paint was peeling around the door. An alley that she would be unwilling to enter even on the brightest of days ran to one side. The little lobby, when Aaron had fished out another key and let them in, smelled of old urine. The elevators stank of stale cooking odors.

They rode from floor to floor as Aaron watched his pendulum and lied about how it was the elevator's fault that they kept stopping. They finally got off on the fifth floor. Kate followed Aaron down the hall. His eyes were on the swaying key. He almost ran into her as he spun suddenly and walked back to stand facing a door he had just passed.

"His apartment?" Kate asked, putting a tinge of excitement into her voice.

Aaron nodded and wiped his hands nervously on his jacket. He looked at her with a smile. "I'm excited."

"I can imagine." *You're scared,* she thought to herself.

Scared that someone who can do what Stefan can might have left something behind to surprise unwelcome visitors. And, frankly, that seemed like a sensible concern to her. She stepped to the side, away from the door, just to be safe. Key in hand, Aaron reached for the doorknob.

The door swung open at his touch. It wasn't locked. Aaron stared into the apartment and gestured for Kate to look as well.

Sometime after Stefan had left, the apartment had been ransacked. Clothes and a few books had been strewn about. The apartment's meager furnishings had been overturned. Dishes from the kitchen had been thrown against one gray-painted wall. The smell of rotten food was strong in the air. They walked in carefully. A cheap television had been set in the center of the room and smashed with a set of weights. Kate drew Aaron's attention to the wall above the telephone. Knives and forks had been driven into it, roughly tacking up a number of photographs. Stefan and another young man with long blond hair. The blond man's face had been deliberately cut from the picture with the knife driven through it. A younger Stefan with a smiling middle-aged couple. Stefan as a child, holding the hand of an elderly woman, a puppy at his feet. A black-and-white photo, burnt along one edge, of a young couple emerging from a wedding. Pinned neatly in the middle of the photos was a note. Aaron took it down.

"Stefan," he read aloud, "I haven't seen you lately, so I thought I'd drop by. Please excuse the mess. Remember our agreement. Call me when you get in." He looked up. "It's signed *V*."

Kate plucked a black address book out of a pile of clothes and flipped to the back. "Only one entry under *V*, and it's been scratched out. Valentine's Escorts."

"Valentine's?" Aaron made a sickened face. "He's been working for them?"

"You know about this place?"

"By reputation only."

"Really?"

Aaron scowled at her. "Yes, really. Believe it or not. Some . . . friends told me about Valentine's a few years ago. They'd heard about it while they were visiting San Francisco. Some of the rumors about it are truly foul."

"I'm sorry." Kate patted his cheek and tried not to wonder what kind of sexual practices a Cult of Ecstasy mage might frown upon. She turned to gesture around the small apartment. "What should we be looking for?"

"I don't know. Anything." Aaron began to push around clothes and set some of the furniture back on its legs. He looked under the bed, the only piece of furniture still standing, and shuddered. "Check the bathroom for medicine."

The tiny bathroom was so dirty that Kate almost had second thoughts about walking in. She did, however, and flipped open the medicine cabinet. It was mostly empty except for a few bottles of over-the-counter medicines, some toothpaste, a disposable razor, and two toothbrushes. She could feel Aaron out in the apartment, probing discreetly with magick, hunting for anything that might tell him something about Stefan and his abilities. She heard him curse; apparently he had found nothing. She didn't listen too closely, however. She was focused on the two toothbrushes as she realized their significance.

"I wonder where his lover is," she commented, emerging from the bathroom.

Aaron turned to stare at her. He was standing by the apartment's sole window, facing out over that unsavory-looking alley. "What?"

"He had a lover. One bed, two toothbrushes. Two styles of handwriting in the address book, so they were very close. I'd bet they lived together." She prodded a pile of clothes delicately with her foot. "Only men's clothes."

"A gay lover?" Aaron shook his head. "There aren't enough clothes for two people."

Kate crossed the room to stand behind him. "I doubt Stefan could have afforded a wardrobe like yours. They may have shared clothes." She picked up a shirt and regarded it carefully. "He was talking about someone named Mike last night, right before he passed out. Maybe that was his lover."

"Mike? He had a lover named Mike?" Aaron turned around, an unreadable expression on his face. "And why do you say 'was'?"

"It sounded like this Mike was dead." Kate found her gaze meeting Aaron's and tore it away. There was something in his eyes, an old devastation, that was truly discomforting. "Stefan was calling for him to wait, that he was coming. Maybe he thought he was dying, too. Maybe . . . maybe he was trying to commit suicide last night. Over Mike's death."

"Maybe he was."

He started to turn away, but Kate caught his shoulder, suddenly genuinely concerned. "Is something wrong, Aaron?"

Aaron laughed bitterly. "No. Nothing."

"There is."

"No!" he spat vehemently. "There isn't . . ." He froze. His face tightened, and he reached out for her abruptly, pulling her into an embrace without warning. "Kiss me."

"What?" she started to gasp. Then, suddenly, something stepped out of the air in the center of the apartment.

She didn't get a good look at it because Aaron spun her around and clasped her to his chest. "Trust me, Kate." He sounded genuinely terrified and desperate. "Just kiss me."

His voice was so urgent that she did it without even really thinking. Aaron kissed her as deeply as if they were intimate lovers, safe in a bower. But surely he could feel what she did! The thing that had appeared was unnatural. Distinctly unnatural. Its very unseen presence was enough to make her stomach twist in panic. She pulled away and started to turn, to see what it was, but Aaron grabbed her jaw and held her head still with one strong hand.

"Don't look at it," he whispered. "Please." He drew her in closer to him, pressing his body against hers, rubbing his hands along her back. It felt very strange, this combination of sex and danger. It reminded her of how much she had wanted Aaron at first, before she had discovered that he was her enemy. Her body began to react to Aaron's caresses. His body was reacting as well. She kissed him back and returned his caresses roughly and sensuously, even as her mind screamed at her to push him away and defend herself against the dark presence that was growing closer.

Something was stirring within Aaron. She could feel it as he sighed at her touch. There was a purpose to his passion. A drive behind his ill-timed lust. He was kindling his magick from their sensual contact, she realized, and suddenly she felt very close to him. For the Technocracy, magick was a cold tool. For Aaron, it was warm, alive, and pleasurable. She looked into his eyes.

All that she could see there was hard-edged lust, angry, vengeful power, and the reflection of the thing behind her. She didn't see herself. A chill blossomed in the pit of her stomach. Her heart dropped sickeningly in fright. Aaron didn't see her as anything more than another body to thrust against. She was wrong. Magick was cold for Aaron, too. The creature that had appeared in the apartment was the true center of his attention.

Just as suddenly as he had embraced her, Aaron shoved her away, his eyes bright and his breathing hard. Kate managed to catch a glimpse of a spindly, smiling black creature, but then her senses were overwhelmed as Aaron lashed out at it with powerful magick. The fury of his attack was staggering. He made no attempt to render his magick palatable to reality—it was vulgar magick, pure and raw, intended to shred the pattern of the monster. The creature just laughed and vanished.

The magick died, and Aaron screamed in anger and pain as Paradox overcame him, punishing him physically for his action. He fell to his knees, his breath still hissing between his teeth, to grab at a scrap of cloth the thing had dropped. White with red stripes. Kate moved every so slightly. Aaron's head whipped around to bring a burning gaze to rest on her. If the desolation in his eyes a few minutes before had been discomforting and the hardness a moment ago frightening, the obsession that raged there now was truly terrifying.

"Forget this happened!" he snarled, pointing at her. The power that flowed from him was staggering. Kate could not have resisted it if she had tried. Where she had previously worried about concealing her identity from Aaron, now she fought to protect her memory. She pulled herself back into her mind, like a turtle into its shell, leaving only a false, hollow memory behind to be scoured away by the rush of Aaron's magick. Even so, she found the attack growing faint in her mind. When she looked at Aaron again, it was as if the creature's appearance had happened years ago.

What she had seen in his eyes, though, was still very clear. She was nothing to him when compared with it. Aaron hated that creature with all of his mind and passion. Beside it, she truly was nothing to him.

He helped her quickly to her feet. There was haste

in his manner, but it was not directed at her. "You passed out," he said simply.

"Can I rest a minute?"

"No." He stuffed the note from Valentine's Escorts in his pocket, then pulled the pictures off the wall. The red-striped cloth that he clenched in one hand caught her eye as if she had never seen it before. "We have to get back to the mansion. Right now."

Aaron braked so hard in front of the door of the Barry mansion that his car went into a short skid. He was out of it before it had even really stopped moving, however, and fumbling with the locks on the door. He had run two red lights and almost sideswiped a van in his reckless haste to get here; none of his magick was the sort that could have got him back any faster. Behind him, Kate, still in a daze, climbed out of the car. He had barely spared her a thought during the drive back. He had been fortunate that she had been there when Pig appeared. With Pan's closed during the day, the main source of the vice that fueled his most powerful magick was cut off, but he had been able to derive enough pleasurable sensation from his brief contact with Kate to at least make an attempt at destroying the demon. She would recover.

But Pig's appearance at Stefan's apartment had really been only a taunt. The demon had wanted to leave him the scrap of pyjama cloth as a sign that it had just come from the mansion. Aaron got the door open and left his keys hanging in the lock as he burst inside. He checked the demon wards instinctively as he ran—they were all still intact. He cursed. Did they have no power over Pig at all?

Something was burning in the kitchen. He could smell it. He charged toward the back of the house. Smoke was pouring out of a pot on the stove, an empty soup can beside it. Aaron had no eyes for the pot, however. The servants' stairway ended in the kitchen, just behind a little, narrow door. There was a body blocking the door open, blood in a little pool around its head.

For a moment, he was paralyzed. He had seen something like this before, sixteen years ago. He screamed and threw himself across the kitchen, not even daring to think who the body might be.

It was the nurse. She was alive and groaning weakly as he touched her. Kate came running up behind him just as he stood and looked up into the darkness of the stairwell. "What happened?" she gasped.

"Fell down the stairs, I suppose." His expression twisted bitterly. "They're very dark and very steep and there's a turn in the middle. I should have told her not to use them." He gestured for Kate to look after her as he started up the stairs himself.

Once, the stairs had been his favorite place to play. He had sat on them for hours as a child, reading books by the light at the top or the bottom and then moving into the shadows of the landing to imagine that he was the hero of the stories. He had still loved the stairs when he was a little older, slipping confidently down them in the middle of the night to raid the kitchen. But the last time he had used them had been sixteen years ago. When he was thirteen. He had crept down them with Michael. . . . He crushed that thought. He wasn't going to think about that, he told himself. He wasn't!

But he paused, only five or six steps up. On the edge of the shadows. Pig had first appeared in those shadows, a pair of yellow eyes staring at him.

He could hear Stefan distantly, screaming.

He could still see Pig's eyes in his memories.

Aaron whirled around and jumped down the stairs, back into the kitchen. Kate started to ask him what he was doing, but he was already past her and racing through the house back to the main stairs. His teeth were clenched, partly in fear, partly in anger at his own weakness. He couldn't bring himself to use the servants' stairs! He dashed up the main staircase, two steps at a time.

Muffled shrieks and screams came from inside Stefan's bedroom, and he wrenched at the doorknob, thrusting his weight at the door. He bounced off ineffectively. The door was locked. Aaron swore. The key was probably with the nurse. He bent down to peer through the keyhole, though, and saw that the key was still in it. The door was locked from inside. He swore again and pointed at a light fixture hanging from the ceiling above.

A bolt of blue electricity arced down from the light and blew the bulb, the fixture, and the heavy door to splinters. Aaron shook as the agonizing, painful numbness of Paradox overtook him for the second time that day, punishing him for his use of magick. He would someday pay for the Paradox he was accumulating, but for now he pushed past it. It would always be there, waiting for him.

The first things he saw inside the bedroom were the shredded remains of the pyjamas the nurse had put on Stefan. They lay on the floor, just beyond the doorway. Aaron ground his teeth, then raised his eyes to the rest of the room. All of the furniture and knick-knacks in the room were completely undisturbed. Even the nurse's bag and coat sat neatly by the bed. The walls of the room, however, were marked and scored with claw marks until there was barely a palm-sized patch of clean wall left. In places, the scratches and gouges resembled writing in some weird language. In others, they looked like nothing so much as disturbing works of art, eerie landscapes and crude portraits. Aaron recognized himself in many of the savage sketches.

He felt as though he were being hypnotized by the marks on the walls as he crossed the room to the bed. It seemed like he was walking in slow motion, every movement of his arms and legs taking place in the infinity that it took for his eye to trace the intricacies of the claw marks. He blinked, breaking the spell of Pig's drawings, and kept his eyes on the ground.

At first he had missed seeing the figure that lay on the bed, mistaking it for a bundle of sheets. It didn't move, and only the helpless, terrorized cries that it made drew his attention back to it. The bedclothes had been bound about the figure like a shroud, so tightly that Aaron couldn't find the end of the sheets, or even an edge. In desperation, he pulled out a pocketknife and rolled the figure over. It screamed and began to struggle.

"Don't move!" Aaron yelled frantically, grappling the figure and pinning it between his legs, body, and the bed. "Don't move!" He guessed at where the cloth might be the thinnest and slid the knife in. The figure shivered, but held still as he carefully worked the blade up its side, revealing bare skin that flinched involuntarily away from the cold metal. When there was enough of a tear, he began grabbing the sheets and ripping them away.

Stefan clutched at Aaron as his arms were freed, throwing them around him and holding on as if he were drowning. The cloth that Aaron pulled away from his face, only a single layer thick so Stefan would be able to breathe until he was found, was soaking with tears. "Holy fuck!" the hustler sobbed. "Holy fuck!"

Aaron threw the knife aside and held him. "It's all right," he said soothingly. "It's gone."

"It was so fucking scary!"

"I know."

"No!" Stefan looked up into his eyes. His hair was plastered back around his head, and he looked paler than the sheets that had been his bonds. "No, you can't! It was black, and thin, and it had teeth, and eyes . . ."

"And a nose like a pig?" Aaron held him close. "Believe me, Stefan, I know."

"Aaron?" Kate's voice echoed down the hall, and he looked up in time to see her peer into the bedroom, flush, and step through on the doorframe, studiously ignoring him and Stefan. "The nurse is okay. She just hit her head and bled like crazy."

"Good."

He knew what this must look like. Aaron Barry embracing a sobbing, naked man so tenderly. He was barely conscious of it, though. Someone else had finally seen Pig. Not just in some human shape as at Pan's, but in its real, inhuman form.

Kate's eyes traveled around the room, looking anywhere but at the bed. "What happened in here? Who did this?"

"A demon." He felt too tired to make up another lie. He didn't even attempt to explain the wreckage of the door.

She finally looked squarely at him. "A demon?"

"The same thing that . . . never mind. You wouldn't remember."

Her silence was suddenly cold. "Don't be silly," she said at last. "There are no such things as demons."

Aaron nodded and shifted Stefan in his arms. "That's what everybody told me once, too."

11

The attack had come as a total shock to Stefan. He had woken suddenly to find himself in a room he didn't recognize, with a terrifying black monster standing over him. Its hands had moved like darting birds, stripping the pyjamas that he wore off of him and then wrapping him up tightly in the bed sheets. He had hardly been able to scream, almost too frightened to believe that this was really happening. He had heard its claws raking the walls around him, over and over. Then it had gone, and he had filled the silence with desperate cries for help, trying to get the nurse's attention. After an eternity, he had heard someone at the door and then what sounded like thunder. And Aaron had freed him, clasping him tightly as he sobbed out his horror, telling him that he would be safe now, that the demon was gone.

Aaron believed him when he had been sure that no one else would. A monster? It was too ridiculous to be real, too improbable—but too horrible to be just his imagination. But Aaron said that it was real, that it was a demon, that it had attacked him, too, and that its name was Pig. He held Stefan in strong arms and promised that he would fight Pig if it came back. Someone else, a woman, came into the room, but Stefan was only conscious of Aaron and his arms. He couldn't even remember Aaron telling him his name or if he ever actually told Aaron his own. The woman left eventually. Aaron stayed with him through the rest of the day and all night, whispering comfortingly to him or else just holding him.

At some point he left for a few minutes to make a phone call. Stefan could hear him telling someone that they wouldn't be able to come over, that tonight was bad, that he, Stefan, was still asleep. After that, Aaron took him to another room, one without the scars of the demon's visit, and put him in a new, warm bed. Somehow, Stefan managed to sleep, in spite of his terror and in spite of the light that Aaron kept on through the night.

In the morning, Aaron left the nurse with a bandage on her head to watch over him, although he still looked in frequently. Stefan slept a lot, dressed in the pyjamas that the nurse made him wear. Occasionally he dreamed about the demon and woke up in a cold sweat, but the terror was slowly receding by the light of day. In the evening, Aaron came back again, this time with a bowl of soup that he fed to him when his own hands proved unsteady. Stefan found himself actually looking at Aaron's face for the first time. Although he seemed drained from a lack of sleep, he was good-looking. Very good-looking, and strangely familiar.

"You're Aaron Barry."

"Yes." He ran the spoon around Stefan's mouth to catch a drip of soup as if he were feeding a baby. "Pay attention. This is harder than it looks."

"Was that really a demon last night? A real, honest-to-God demon?"

"Yes."

"It's not going to come back, is it?"

"No."

"Good. What am I doing here?"

Aaron paused, then fed him another spoonful of soup. "You passed out on the steps of a club I own. I took you to the hospital, and now I feel responsible for you."

Pan's. He dimly remembered being very drunk and very stoned and going to Pan's. To die. He couldn't remember why, though. Another blackout, goddamn it. The last thing he remembered clearly was . . . Friday. Pan's again, opening night. His clients. The man dead. The woman committing suicide in grief. And then nothing. Except for Pig. He strained to recall anything at all before the demon's attack and the fuzzy memory of Pan's, but all that came back to him was darkness, a disorienting hum, and a vague feeling of nauseating dizziness. And Marilyn. Marilyn had found out that he was working for Valentine, and she had walked away from him. "Fuck. What day is this?"

"Wednesday. Wednesday night. I took you to the hospital Monday night."

"Fuck. Fuck, fuck, fuck, fuck." Stefan leaned his head back against the pillows of the bed and stared up at the ceiling wearily. "Was I with you on the weekend?"

Aaron's mouth tightened. "I'm not into gay sex."

"I didn't ask if you were! I wanted to know if you knew what I was doing Saturday and Sunday." He looked Aaron in the eye. Aaron met his gaze calmly, so calmly it almost seemed unnatural. There was something Aaron was holding back, something he couldn't tell him even though he might want to. Stefan suddenly found himself trying to keep his stomach level. Maybe it was because he still felt a little light-headed, but Aaron reminded him so much of Mike! A veneer of strength and confidence, with a core of secrets. Holding and protecting, yet at the same time quietly wanting to be held and protected himself. His stomach twisted again but he forced a hard edge into his voice, just as if Aaron were no more than another client on the street. "You must want something from me. Taking a stranger to the hospital, bringing him into your house—"

"I didn't say this was my house."

"I didn't tell you I was a hustler, but you figured it out, didn't you?" The warmth of the soup was making him drowsy, and he yawned in spite of himself. "I bet it has something to do with whatever I did over the weekend. Am I right? What was I doing?"

Aaron frowned and stood up. "Actually, I wanted to ask you the same question."

"Well, you're fuck out of luck then 'cause I don't know anything either." He turned away.

"I'd like to ask anyway. Later. I have a friend who wants to talk to you, too." Aaron hesitated, then added, "How many languages do you speak, Stefan?"

So it was about that. He must have been spouting off. There had been other people who wanted to exhibit him as a freak-genius. He had always rejected them and their moneymaking schemes. He had rejected all of them and he could reject Aaron Barry, too. Stefan rolled over to look at him again. "Twenty-six," he said harshly, picking a number out of the air.

Aaron just nodded slightly, clearly impressed although he didn't say anything else. Not even a "Where did you learn them?" or a "Why does a street hustler speak so many languages?", the responses that most people had. Aaron merely walked out of the room and closed the door behind him. He wasn't interested in the languages his guest spoke so unnaturally, Stefan realized. There was something else. Something Stefan couldn't remember.

What *had* he done?

————

He fell asleep still racking his brains for an answer. Once, he woke up enough to hear the bedroom door closing and the murmur of voices in the hall outside. He recognized Aaron's voice easily. The other voice, with its faint French accent, seemed ever so slightly familiar to him as well. He couldn't place it, but for some reason it made him shiver.

"Have you felt any further Entropy fluctuations? Are you sure that it's him causing the reality shifts?"

"I am positive, but no, I have felt no more fluctuations. You saw the way that the pattern of his being was muted? There is some magick at work. He has had contact with mages before, somehow. I will need to talk with him and examine him more closely. As soon as he is able."

"Why the hurry?" Aaron sounded strangely defensive.

"In case another uncontrolled reality shift should occur—or do you want the Technocracy here looking for him?"

"I want Stefan to be safe and recovered. And I have other things on my mind."

"I will want to see him alone."

"No!"

There was a moment of silence, and then the voice with the accent said quietly. "I see. Why did he have the relapse? I told you that he was to have absolute quiet and rest."

"He has epilepsy," Aaron lied.

Stefan slipped back into the deepness of sleep without hearing any more. This time he dreamed. He was in Pan's again, sitting where he had sat Friday night, but this time with a young blond woman and an old man. Both seemed familiar. The woman was the one who had been in the room after Pig's attack. He couldn't place the man. Aaron was nearby, too, wrestling with another man. No. He was wrestling with Pig. A man. Pig in the shape of a man. Just Pig. Aaron was crying and sobbing in terror, but he refused to let Pig go. The demon turned away from Aaron for a moment to grin at him. Stefan rose to his feet. He stood in a pool of blood deep enough to spill over the tops of his shoes when he walked.

He began to back away from Pig, from Aaron, and from the man and woman sitting at the table. The man nodded and smiled at him. His tongue was a shard of glass, and Stefan knew that if he were to talk, he would have a French accent. The woman peered at him through a pair of opera glasses held in a hand adorned with dripping rubies. Something bumped into the back of his legs.

A body floating on the shallow blood. It rolled over as he watched. Deng, the clerk from the convenience store near his apartment. Other bodies began to surface, rising out of the blood like misshapen bubbles. Mrs. Donner. The immigrant couple from Pan's. Mike. His family and stepfamily, appearing one by one. He turned around and around. The blood stretched away from him, a flat red plain distorted only by bodies enough to fill a multitude of graveyards. He no longer recognized the corpses that were emerging in the distance, although in a strange way he knew who they were, as if they were half-forgotten friends from his childhood. The air was clear here, though the sky was overcast, and he could see to the very edge of the plain. Behind him, a scarlet sun was setting, its bulk settling slowly below the horizon across a wide river (or maybe an ocean) of dark water.

Strangely enough, he felt calm, or at least numb. Aaron and Pig still struggled, splashing in the blood and setting the bodies around them bobbing. He was frightened of Pig, but what was the worst it could do to him? He had already lost all of the people whose bodies filled the landscape. All of them. For a moment, he felt fragmented, as if he were viewing the plain and the bodies from a dozen—no, a hundred— different perspectives, all overlapping. In that instant, he knew all of the dead intimately and felt a sober grief at the loss of them. Then he was drawn back to the spot where he stood watching Aaron, just as a heavy cane appeared in Pig's hands. It brought the cane down with a deep bellow of incoherent rage.

Stefan felt the blow as though he had been hit instead of Aaron. Aaron fell. Stefan yelled out, shouting at Pig, and charged toward the demon. The grief and fear of loss that sliced through him suddenly was hot and fresh, and it made the entire plain tremble. He didn't want to lose Aaron, too! Pig looked up at him, suddenly frightened itself.

Something dove at him, swooping out of the sky with a loud hum, as he reached for the demon. He tried to dodge, but it swooped under him, rolling him up and onto its back. Stefan could do nothing but hang on as he found himself clinging to the carapace of a huge flying beetle. Aaron was left behind. He could see him slowly toppling over into the plain of blood. Pig was nowhere around. The old man with the glass tongue stood over Aaron, laughing. Stefan screamed and pounded uselessly on the beetle's armored head as its thrumming wings carried him up into the mistiness of the clouds.

He woke up just as the beetle carrying him in his dream broke through the top of the clouds. Aaron sat in a chair beside the bed, eyes closed and his handsome, haggard face twitching as he himself dreamed a nightmare. Stefan stared at him, his own dream still vivid in his mind. He reached out to touch him, to assure himself that Aaron was really there and not gone like all the others in his dream. He hesitated before putting his hand on Aaron's leg, but Aaron didn't vanish and no giant beetles swooped down to tear him away. Aaron shivered slightly at his touch. Stefan sighed in relief and withdrew his hand slowly.

"What were you doing?"

Stefan froze as Aaron's eyes opened. "Nothing. I . . . had a nightmare."

"With Pig in it?" When he nodded, Aaron grunted softly. "Join the club."

"Aaron, where did Pig come from?"

"Don't ask me that."

"Sorry." He settled back into bed as Aaron twisted around in the chair. "My dream was really strange. *Really* strange."

"They all are. You'll get used to it."

"Aaron? Would you hold me?"

He turned his head to look at him. "I told you I'm not into men. I'm not gay."

"I just want you to hold me. You did it last night." Stefan shifted over. "Please?" he pleaded.

After a minute, Aaron moved to the bed wordlessly.

"Thank you," Stefan said as Aaron's arms slid around him from behind. Then he asked quietly, "Why do you think Pig attacked me?"

Aaron replied slowly. "To hurt me."

He sounded so lonely and tired that Stefan twisted in his arms to hug him back. Aaron stiffened momentarily, then relaxed. "Thank you," he whispered.

The man with the tongue of glass came to visit the next afternoon.

Aaron had sent the nurse home after she pronounced Stefan well enough to cope on his own. He had found Stefan a robe and then helped him downstairs to a sunroom. Unfortunately, fog and rain blotted out the sun, but the open, comfortable room was a delight after the better part of three days spent in bed. Stefan reveled in the simple pleasures of a peanut-butter-and-banana sandwich as Aaron talked about the places he had visited abroad. He had been checking his watch frequently, so Stefan was not particularly surprised when the doorbell finally rang. The housekeeper came back to announce that Dr. Brossard had arrived. Aaron nodded for her to show him back. "This is the friend I mentioned to you. You can call him Saffleur. Just do me one favor: Don't talk about Pig. That's between you and me."

"I doubt he'd believe it anyway."

"You would be surprised. If he asks, tell him you're an epileptic."

"Why?" Stefan took another huge bite of his sandwich.

"Just do it." He stood up as someone rapped on the doorframe. Stefan turned around in his chair. When he saw Saffleur, he began choking on the sandwich. Aaron pounded on his back and handed him a glass of milk. "What's wrong?"

Stefan pointed at Saffleur, his voice rough. "I know you!"

Saffleur's eyebrows rose, and he sat down. "I took you to the hospital after you collapsed."

"No." He huddled back in his chair, wrapping his robe around himself tightly. "You were in a dream I had last night." He huddled back in his chair.

"Really? Let's start there then." Saffleur pulled out a pad of paper.

"Are you a psychologist?"

Aaron shifted his own chair around so that he sat closer to both of them. "He's an archaeologist."

"I'm here to try and figure out what happened to you over the last weekend. Tell me about your dream."

Stefan looked from one of them to the other. Both gazed at him with a hungry expectancy that made him nervous, as if he were about to tell them the meaning of life. He thought he could trust Aaron, but there was something about Saffleur that disturbed him, a strange feeling he couldn't shake. For one thing, he couldn't remember even being at the hospital, so he doubted if that was where he remembered the old man from. For another . . . he shook his head. The thought was gone. All that was left was a vague humming sound (like the wings of the beetle in his dream) in his skull and a fading sense of *déjà vu*. Still, he could have sworn that he had met Saffleur before. He stole another glance at Aaron, who smiled encouragingly. Stefan exhaled sharply and began describing his dream. Leaving out Pig, of course.

When he had finished, Saffleur questioned him about exactly what he could remember of the events of the previous weekend. When that produced no results beyond establishing that Stefan's memory ended with the deaths at Pan's and started again when he came out of an epileptic seizure (Stefan saw Aaron give him a slight nod of approval for the lie), he asked if Stefan had ever experienced previous periods of amnesia.

"Once or twice."

"Under what conditions?"

He balked. "I'd rather not say."

"We need to know if we are going to be able help you."

Stefan sighed. "When somebody close to me died," he confessed.

"So those people at Pan's were what?" Saffleur twitched his pen back and forth as he spoke. "Aunt and uncle? Cousins? Friends?"

"Clients," he snorted in response. "They hired me through an escort service for the night."

"But they were not close to you?"

Stefan flushed with anger. Saffleur's voice was probing and cold. He had heard that tone before, from mission workers and other do-gooders, people who saw him only as an immoral, uneducated street rat. "No, you bastard frog," he spat in perfect French, using his gift with languages as a weapon, "they were not close to me. I don't like working as a hustler, but it's the only way I've got of earning a living. You got a problem with that, I don't need your help!"

Saffleur stared at him in some surprise, then replied evenly in French. "I'm sorry."

"You should be."

Aaron cleared his throat, dragging the conversation back to English. "Stefan, we're not passing judgment on you. We just want you to answer some questions."

"I have!" Stefan took a deep breath, calming himself. He looked up at Aaron, ignoring Saffleur. "Look, I really don't remember anything. Why don't you tell me something about why you're interested in me?"

The two older men glanced at each other, communicating silently with gestures. Aaron quirked an eyebrow. Saffleur shook his head. Aaron scowled. "I think we should tell him," he said aloud. "He can't help at all if he doesn't know what we want."

"It's dangerous."

"It's always dangerous. We have to."

Saffleur muttered something in French, but finally agreed reluctantly. Aaron turned to Stefan. "Do you know what a mage is?"

The hustler had to shake his head. Aaron nodded slightly. "A mage is sort of like a wizard. Saffleur and I are both mages."

Three days ago, Stefan wouldn't have believed that. He would have looked at Aaron and tried to guess how long he had been out of the asylum. A demon attack made a lot of things believable, though. If there were demons, maybe there were wizards or mages. Maybe there were vampires and werewolves and ghosts, too, but right now he tried to focus on what Aaron was telling him. Stuff about reality, and something called entropy, and car accidents, and convenience stores. He felt weighed down when Aaron had finished.

"I live near that convenience store. I go there to buy milk." He stared out into the fog beyond the window. "Last night, I dreamed that Deng—he's a clerk there—was dead. Jesus Christ." He blinked, clearing his eyes as the window frame blurred and the fog seemed to spread into the room. "Did I kill him?"

"Maybe," Aaron admitted. He produced a large brown envelope and pulled out several pictures. "Who are these people?"

"These are mine!" Stefan gasped.

"I found your apartment while you were unconscious and went there. We needed clues. I'm sorry, but what about the people?"

"They're my family. They're dead." His fingers lingered over the torn photographs, tracing the rips. He picked up the picture of Mike tenderly. "Did you do this to them?"

"No. Someone had ransacked your apartment before I got there." Aaron paused as he thought, then asked cautiously. "How did your family die?"

Saffleur reached out so suddenly that his touch made Stefan jump. "Don't answer that," he commanded. "Don't even think about it!" Stefan nodded mutely in shocked surprise. The old mage turned to Aaron and whispered. "That's not a good thing to bring up, Aaron."

"Why not?"

"I felt the beginning of another fluctuation in Entropy as you asked it. Definitely from him." He furrowed his brow as he looked over Stefan, absorbed in the pictures. "Deep thoughts of death seem to trigger the reality shifts."

"At least we know that, then." Aaron dropped the envelope on the table beside the remains of Stefan's sandwich and stood up. "Stefan, has anything really strange ever happened to you? Anything you couldn't explain? Besides in the last few days, I mean."

"Aside from everyone I love dying and my life being a constant hell?" Stefan blinked again, as his vision threatened to go hazy once more. Saffleur shushed him to silence and glared at Aaron.

"I don't believe we should pursue this line of questioning," he told Aaron in a cold, warning tone. "It could prove dangerous."

Aaron nodded, but smiled. "I think I've figured out what's happening anyway." He put his hand on Stefan's shoulder. "We know he's had contact with a mage before, right? What if he's had a curse put on him?"

Stefan's jaw dropped as he sputtered out "A *what?*"

Saffleur managed to constrain his reaction to polite surprise and an amused chuckle. "Curses went out with the Mythic Age."

"Well, the Order of Hermes still clings to the past," Aaron pointed out. "What if a Hermetic mage was angry enough at somebody to put a curse on Stefan as revenge?" He gazed off into space speculatively. "Something that might activate every so often to kill somebody he cared for?"

Saffleur sat back in his chair, his face impassive in thought, tapping his fingertips together. "It has problems," he replied blandly after a moment. "Most of all, it would be extremely vulgar magick, and we've seen no sign of Paradox anywhere in this. And it doesn't explain the shifts in reality. There would be simpler ways to kill somebody."

"A degenerating spell? Something gone wrong? How long have people been dying around you, Stefan?"

"Forever." He tried to smooth out one of the photographs. "No, I'm sorry. Since I was eight." He touched another photo fondly. "My parents and brother died when I was eight. Fourteen years ago."

"Fourteen years isn't a long time for magick," Saffleur pointed out.

Aaron shrugged. "Long-term exposure?" He frowned as an idea struck him. "What if a curse like that were placed on someone with the potential to be a mage? If they were going through an incredibly traumatic Awakening to their powers of magick . . ."

This time, Saffleur couldn't stop himself from guffawing. "You're beginning to talk nonsense! Some things aren't possible, even with magick. How could an Awakening be stretched over years? Besides which, why would a mage do such a thing?" He shook his head, then looked at his watch and stood. "I have to go now, but perhaps we can continue later." He offered his hand to Stefan. "I am sorry if I insulted you earlier."

Stefan looked at the proffered hand for a moment, then finally took it. He didn't smile, but he did force himself to say grudgingly, "That's okay."

Saffleur shook hands with Aaron. "I don't think I'd bother anymore with that curse theory," he advised.

"You're probably right. I'll show you to the door. You'll be okay, Stefan?" The hustler nodded, and Aaron ushered Saffleur out into the hall. Just beyond the door, he paused. "I forgot to ask you about the languages Stefan speaks."

"I don't know. But that's another thing your theory doesn't explain." Saffleur glanced back into the sunroom, meeting Stefan's gaze for a fraction of a second before following Aaron to the door.

Stefan drew a sharp breath before the force of that gaze. It made him feel dizzy for a moment. Suddenly, he was more certain than ever that he had met the old mage before, although he was no more sure of where that meeting had taken place than he had been before.

He found his hand resting on the table and on the envelope from which Aaron had taken his photographs.

Those photographs were the only things he had left to remember his family by; the fire that killed his foster parents had burned almost all of his possessions. Having them nearly destroyed now was devastating. As much as he was angry at Aaron for going into his apartment, he was glad that he had brought the pictures to him. He looked into the envelope to see if there were any more.

All there was inside the envelope was a note. Stefan shook it out and read it. He didn't need to see the *V* at the bottom to know that it was from Valentine, punishing him for running off with the money from last Friday. Or just for running off. Valentine had been the one who destroyed his pictures and trashed his apartment. He clenched his jaw so tightly his teeth hurt, and he began methodically to tear the note into very small, very ragged pieces.

12

Stefan went to bed not long after they ate dinner, claiming a lingering weariness and disturbed feelings after Saffleur's visit. Aaron could hardly blame him. When he had returned to the sunroom, he had caught him in the process of attempting to hide the shredded remains of Valentine's note. It was hard to tell which had upset the hustler more: the interview by Saffleur or the discovery that his apartment had been ransacked by this Valentine. Aaron decided that it must be the ransacking after Stefan told him about Valentine and the way the man ran his escort service. He felt rather glad that he had never used Valentine's and even briefly considered finding the other Cult of Ecstasy mages in San Francisco and suggesting that they discontinue any use of the service.

Over dinner, Stefan had also pressed him to discuss magick and how it was performed. Aaron had given him a level look. "You want me to use magick to take out Valentine, don't you."

Stefan had flushed at his directness. "Yeah. Or teach me."

"No." Aaron had taken a sip of wine. "First, I don't

kill people. Ask Saffleur. He does. Second, by the time
you'd learned magick, you would have forgotten about
Valentine. Magick isn't for revenge."

He had told him a little bit about magick after all,
though, describing the war between the Traditions
and the Technocracy and the way that mages sought
to control reality in pursuit of Ascension. His words
about revenge came back to him after Stefan had
retired, however. After all, revenge had driven him to
learn magick as a way to destroy Pig. He tried to come
up with some reason why magickal revenge against
Pig was justifiable, while magickal revenge against
Valentine was not.

At least Pig wasn't human, so he hadn't lied when
he said that he didn't kill people. For a long time,
Aaron sat blankly in front of the television, a cup of
tea virtually ignored in one hand, thinking about
nothing. The sound of the cook leaving finally broke
him out of his trance, and he turned off the television
with a sigh. He considered phoning Kate, a task he
had been putting off for the last two days. She had left
a couple of messages on his answering machine, saying that she wanted to see him and asking about
Stefan. But he didn't feel like facing her. He just
wasn't up to the effort of seduction right now. Hell, it
wasn't even really seduction anymore. He just wanted
her to keep her mouth shut about Pan's.

And frankly, he didn't want to have another person
around while he was trying to deal with Pig. Saffleur
was bad enough. The demon's reappearance and
attack on Stefan had thrown him off balance. More
than ever now, he wanted to deal with it once and for
all, before he had to try and explain it to anyone. He
had never actually told any of his mentors about Pig,
although he was sure that some suspected or knew
that he was demon haunted. He even found it difficult
to talk about Pig with Stefan, and the hustler had

seen Pig with his own eyes and experienced the terror of its attacks.

A reluctance to talk about the demon had been . . . conditioned into him. The two years of constant torment that Pig had visited on him were worse, far worse, than anything Valentine might have forced Stefan to do. They had left deep scars. His habit of sleeping with the lights on. The driving need to be around other people at night. The nightmares. Oh, the nightmares. He drained his teacup and took it into the kitchen. He deliberately avoided looking at the base of the servants' stairs until he had set it down.

Last night he had dreamed that he was wrestling with Pig, just as he had been back at Pan's. The ground had been covered in blood, again just as it had been at Pan's, and just as it had been when the nurse had fallen down the stairs (although he was sure Pig had had something to do with that), and just as it had been . . . He spun around and leaned against the kitchen counter, gasping for breath. He didn't want to remember that! He didn't! He wouldn't!

He pushed himself blindly out of the kitchen and began the task that he had performed at least once a night for the last several nights: strengthening the network of demon wards he had spun around the mansion. It was a long and tedious process, but it made him feel better, and it calmed his thoughts. Sometimes he had performed it twice a night. Only on the night after Pig's attack on Stefan had he failed to perform it at all, and then he had stayed awake the entire night himself, alert in case Pig should try to attack again. By now the wards must be so strong that Aaron hoped the demon would have trouble coming within a mile of the mansion, but he couldn't help reinforcing them. The stronger they were, the safer he, and Stefan, would be.

The wards here took the form of arrangements of flowers and greens, distinctly different from the subtle spiritual wards around Pan's. He had learned to make these from a witch mage of the Verbena Tradition in Australia, adapting the practice to better suit the Cult of Ecstasy style. The Verbena wards were created with wildflowers, grasses, and sprigs of herbs, watered with concoctions brewed up in the Verbena's cauldrons. His version used cut flowers and wine. The flowers were still vulnerable to decay, however, and if the housekeeper had wondered about the shipments the florist delivered every day, she didn't ask about them. Aaron paced through the house with armloads of damp roses and freesias and carnations and chrysanthemums and ivy trimmings, a bottle of good white wine balanced precariously amidst the greenery. Drawing on his link with Pan's for focus, he carefully renewed the magick around each ward, the act of working the magick slowly restoring his own balance.

He had almost finished his rounds when he paused in front of a door on the second floor. His father's bedroom. He hesitated, the last few flowers dripping water onto his already wet clothing and onto the carpet around him. This was the only room in the entire mansion that had no ward. He had stopped here every night and thought about creating one, and every night he had decided that it didn't really need a ward. Surely the other wards around the house were enough to cover for this one weak spot. His father's bedroom was also the only room in the house he had not entered in the weeks since his return. The door had remained firmly closed.

Tonight, though, a room without a ward seemed more like a fatal flaw than a mere weak link, no matter how strong the wards around it were. He had to set a ward in his father's bedroom. His fear of Pig, as much as he tried to deny that fear, demanded it. Aaron took a deep breath, hesitated once, and then pushed the door open.

The air was musty in the room, still carrying the faint odors of disease and death, even though it had been aired out for days after Peter Barry's demise. Aaron snapped on the lights and looked around. He had not been allowed in here as a child, just as he had not been allowed in his father's study. He stepped inside, torn between a desire to put a ward in place and get out as quickly as possible and a curiosity about what his father had accumulated in his private haven. He tried to accommodate both, looking around as he set the nearly empty wine bottle on top of a bureau and stuck a few flowers into it. The big four-poster bed his father had died in was neatly made. There was an old clock on the night table beside it, unplugged and stopped at the time his body was discovered. Quarter after eight in the morning. His slippers peeked out from under the bedspread. There were a few trinkets on top of the bureau: a pocket watch, cuff links, a little bowl of pocket change. There was a photograph on the wall nearby, his mother and father on their wedding day. A smaller photograph was tucked inside the frame. He peered at it, then completed the ward and wiped his hands carefully before taking it.

His mother holding him after he had been born. Barbara Barry had been a strong, healthy woman. She looked like the very image of motherhood in the snapshot, as she smiled and held a sleeping Aaron up for the camera. Aaron found himself suppressing tears. He had never seen this photo before, or at least not that he could remember. His mother might have shown it to him once, but she had died when he was twelve. A fluke case of something nasty and contagious that she had picked up on a trip abroad with his father, the same disease that had weakened his father's leg and forced him to use a cane. Aaron hadn't even been able to hug his mother before she died in the hospital. Peter Barry had blamed himself for her death.

That had been the beginning of the end of his love for his father. Peter Barry had fallen into a mood of perpetual grimness and taken to drinking heavily, limping around the mansion with the aid of his cane. Aaron almost didn't have to look for that cane. He knew it would be in the room somewhere, its heavy steel head gleaming brightly. Gleaming brightly and cruelly and malevolently, red with blood . . .

He fled from the room, the little snapshot clutched in his hand. Downstairs, he jammed the plug of a pair of earphones into his stereo and dropped random CDs into a five-disc carousel. He was just settling the earphones on his head when the phone rang. He snatched it up, almost hoping that it was Kate or any other woman he knew. He wanted sex tonight. Desperately. "Hello?"

"This is William Pierce, Aaron."

He swore into the receiver and almost hung up. William shouted at him to listen. "There are some changes that I want to make to your accounts, Aaron! It might be risky, but it could stabilize the losses you've been taking! The changes will take effect in a few days. I need your permission."

"Do it, William! Just fucking do it! I don't care!" He threw the telephone completely across the room and turned the volume on the earphones up as high as he could stand. Then Aaron threw himself into his link with Pan's, drowning himself in the pleasurable sensations of all of the club's patrons until he forgot about his father and his cane and Pig and the servants' stairs and even that Aaron Barry was a person at all.

"William? Are you going to come to bed soon?"

"In a little while, Jean." He hung up the phone. "I have some work to finish."

His wife stepped up behind him and put her hands on his shoulders. "You've been working so hard these last few days. Can't you take a break?"

"Aaron Barry has me riled up. I want to be rid of the little bastard as soon as I can." He sighed and began shuffling papers around on his desk. "I have to keep my promise to Peter, even if I detest his son."

"I think you're letting this affect you too much. I'm worried about you, William." She kissed him on the forehead.

William patted her hand comfortingly. "Go to sleep, Jean. I'll be up when I can." He turned back to his desk as his wife went up to their bedroom. She didn't understand. She didn't understand how much he hated Aaron Barry, how much he longed to put him in his place. The solution for his revenge had come to him last weekend. A uniquely fitting solution. His visit to the Barry mansion on Monday has set things in motion, and he had only needed Aaron's permission tonight to bring it all together. Tomorrow . . . He stopped suddenly, surprised and a little shocked at the violence of his thoughts. Maybe Jean was right. Maybe he was letting this whole affair with Aaron get to him. People at the office had glanced at him strangely several times recently. Sometimes, he would look down and discover that he had gone through a pile of paperwork without really noticing. And surely this plot was mad. He could fudge the books with the best of them, but the scale of this sort of forgery was incredible. He was sure to be caught himself! But he did dislike Aaron so intensely, and the boy was destroying everything that he had built for Peter over the years. Aaron was a walking affront to the very society and morality that he held dear!

By God, he did hate him enough to do this!

He went to work, grinning sharply and cruelly, his mouth stretched across his face until his lips were

thin red lines. He wrote quickly, initiating the rearrangement of accounts he had mentioned to Aaron,
but leaving the rearrangement half completed and
deliberately stopping his work as he reached certain
accounts. He had modified those accounts himself
earlier in the week, backdating some of them and
forging Aaron's signature with almost unnatural accu-
racy. His hands had never felt as loose and limber as
they had recently, as if his arthritis were clearing up,
and he had often surprised himself by writing out
whole pages with what seemed like inhuman speed.
Anything to destroy Aaron.

Pig looked out of William's eyes and grinned
through his face and prodded him to begin writing a
short letter to the police telling them what he had
found in Aaron Barry's accounts.

Stefan crept quietly down the stairs. He was wearing
his own clothes again and his own leather jacket. That
made him feel more like a normal person, and less like
some kind of patient. He had made a point of casually
asking Aaron where his things were before going up to
bed. He actually had slept for a while, too. Maybe for
four hours. Enough that he felt like he had gotten his
energy back again before the alarm clock had woken
him up. He felt awkward, slipping out on Aaron like
this, but he had to do it. He had to go see Valentine.
He wasn't sure what he would do once he got there.
Take revenge on Valentine for ransacking his apartment, presumably. He wasn't exactly sure yet how that
could be accomplished, but he had known that he had
to do it ever since he had read Valentine's note.

There had been no sign of Aaron as he had gotten
dressed and slipped out of his room. He was actually
a little disappointed that he had not been sitting by
his bedside. Disappointed but glad that he didn't
have to try to explain what he was doing. He stepped

down off the stairs and began to cross the hall to the front door, then froze.

Aaron was lying on the sofa in a room just off the front hall, earphones on his head. Stefan could hear the music, a muffled whisper, from where he was standing. There was no way Aaron could hear him, yet somehow he had turned his head just as Stefan had passed in front of the doorway. Stefan hardly dared to breathe. Aaron didn't move anymore, however. After a moment, Stefan realized that he was asleep. Deeply asleep, in spite of the music blaring deafeningly into his ears. The turn of his head had been nothing more than a movement in his slumber. Stefan sighed with relief. He ran the rest of the way to the front door and threw it open.

Saffleur was standing on the doorstep. Stefan couldn't quite suppress a little yelp of surprise. The night was as foggy as the day had been, and Saffleur loomed like a living shadow out of that fog. The old mage held a finger to his lips, silencing him. "Where are you going?" he asked softly.

"Just out for a walk." Saffleur gave him a look so sharp that it made him wince. "Okay," he confessed, "I have to go see the person who broke into my apartment."

"Ah. Revenge."

"Yeah." Inspiration suddenly struck him. He didn't like Saffleur, and being around him made him feel uncomfortable. But he had done a lot of things that made him feel uncomfortable because he needed to do them to survive. "Aaron said you kill people."

"I kill people when it is the proper time for them to die. That is the way of my Tradition. Why? Does your revenge require that someone die?"

Stefan hesitated, then shrugged. It felt very strange to be standing in the doorway of a mansion in Nob Hill, discussing death with this man as he might discuss cookies with a Girl Scout. "I don't know. I don't really know if I want anybody dead. Aaron . . ."

"Aaron doesn't really understand vengeance, I think." Saffleur took his arm, drawing him away from the door. "As I said, I kill people when it is the proper time for them to die. There is a proper time for everything, especially death. You want to go to Valentine's Escorts, don't you?"

"Yes! How did you know that?" He pulled away a bit and Saffleur laughed softly.

"I'm a mage. I've been waiting for you. Why do you think Aaron is asleep right now?" He touched something in his breast pocket, something about a handspan high. "I put him to sleep to help you get out of the house."

Stefan swallowed and took a step back toward the mansion, suddenly nervous. "You can do that to another mage?"

"If I surprise him and if my magick is strong enough." He reached out and seized his wrist with a hard grip. "Stefan, tonight is the proper time for you to go to Valentine's. I am here to make sure you get there."

"I think I've changed my mind!"

"You can't. In fact, you haven't." He tugged Stefan irresistibly along toward a black car that was parked in the mansion driveway. "I know you. You want to go where you can have your revenge." He opened the door of the car. "Am I right?"

The car's interior was dark. The smell of leather seats drifted out of it. Stefan stared into it like it was a bottomless pit. "Yes. Yes, you are, fuck it."

"Good. Get in." He went around to the other side of the car and got in the driver's-side door.

I could run now, thought Stefan. I could run back to the house and wake up Aaron. He can deal with Saffleur. I don't have to go to Valentine's.

But he did, of course. He climbed into the car, slammed the door behind him, and stared straight ahead. Saffleur nodded. The lights from the car's dashboard turned his face into an eerie green mask of shadows and planes as he turned the key in the ignition. "You made the right choice." His voice was harsh. "I have been trying to see you alone, to talk to you about this, but Aaron wouldn't let me. He doesn't understand. You don't know how critical it is that you be at Valentine's at exactly the right time tonight, Stefan. It is a part of the pattern of your life."

"How do you know that?" Stefan looked at the old mage. "Where do I remember you from?"

Saffleur didn't say anything. He just put the car into gear and pulled out of the driveway.

Rationality and order were the highest principles of the New World Order. Kate had struggled to remain rational for the past two days. Two days since Stefan's strange seizure. Two days since the appearance of the demon in the hustler's apartment and her . . . encounter with Aaron. Two days since the demon's attack on Stefan himself. And two days in which Aaron hadn't called her. She knew nothing about what was happening in the Barry mansion. She couldn't even spy inside as she had spied on Saffleur's office. Aaron had somehow blocked his telephone and even his cable television lines against tampering by the Technocracy. Her curiosity was driving her crazy!

She had all of the evidence she needed. She should have turned Aaron in instead of waiting. His crimes against the Technocracy were clear. He was a mage of the Traditions. He was the driving force behind Pan's. He was concealing Stefan and whatever dangerous powers the young man had. He had traffic with demons (even if he did seem to be the enemy of the demon that had appeared, it was a serious offense). If she was being rational, she should have called down all of the forces of the New World Order on Aaron Barry. So why wasn't she being rational?

It wasn't love on her part. It wasn't lust either. Kate knew that he certainly didn't love her. He was more interested in his enmity with this demon, that was clear. He was even more interested in Stefan! She was a game and that was all. His manipulation hurt, but strangely not as much as she had thought it might.

She just could not bring herself to turn him in. She couldn't even bring herself to truly hate him for the bastard that he was. Why? Why? It was the rational, orderly thing to do! But no, she was on her way back to the Barry mansion. Intending to confront Aaron alone. She leaned on the horn, urging a more slowly moving driver out of her way. The only orderly aspect to the whole mad caper was that she had waited precisely forty-eight hours after she had left the mansion before returning. And that had more obsession about it than precision.

This kind of confusion felt alien to her. She hadn't grown up with anything like it. Her childhood had been orderly. A small town with shady streets. A regular curfew imposed by her parents. Her model cars lined up neatly on shelves in her room. Even her entry into the Technocracy and the world of magick had been orderly. Her parents would have told her that she was being ridiculous now. Julia would say that she was letting her emotions get in the way of her thoughts.

Yet on another level, she felt as calm and rational as she ever had in her life. She had plotted her arrival at the mansion in exquisite detail. She would again play the role of the love-besotted woman, worried about Stefan. How cruel Aaron was not to let her know how he was doing! How upset she was! Kate wasn't sure exactly how Aaron was going to react to that. She supposed it still depended on whether he saw her as useful or not. In any case, it would be enough to get her inside and close to him. She spun the wheel, turning onto the street that led to the mansion. This time, she wasn't going to dissemble in front of Aaron. She would reveal herself as a Technomancer—and the magick she had prepared would overwhelm Aaron easily. She would find out his secrets.

Presumably, Stefan was still in the mansion as well, and he would have to be dealt with. She almost felt a little bit sorry for Stefan. He had been a victim of Aaron's demonic enemy. He was in a strange place. He had apparently lost someone special to him recently. The powers he was manifesting must be extremely stressful. She wondered if Aaron had made any progress in figuring out the hustler's abilities. If he had, of course, he could be made to tell her. In any case, Stefan would be better off under the protective guidance of the New World Order.

Or would he? Julia would stop at nothing to discover the nature of Stefan's powers. She would kill him if she had to. At least Aaron wouldn't kill him.

Kate cursed herself and hammered her hand against the steering wheel. Was she going to start feeling the same way about Stefan now as she did about Aaron? They were the subjects of an investigation, damn it, not friends! She was letting emotion get in the way of her duty again!

Just as she was about to pull into the driveway of the Barry mansion, another car came barreling out of it. Kate braked hard, her tires squealing on the pavement. Her headlights caught the white faces of the other car's occupants. Saffleur, driving, and Stefan, sitting in the passenger seat. The car sped off down the street without even stopping.

Where were they going in such a hurry? And why wasn't Aaron with them? Kate bit her lip as she tried to decide what to do. She had not really expected Saffleur to be present at the mansion. She wasn't capable of taking on both Aaron and him. That the older mage was definitely not there now was a bonus. She would be able to tackle Aaron one-on-one. But Saffleur had Stefan with him, and she had wanted Stefan as well. Aaron or Stefan? Aaron would know where Saffleur had been taking Stefan. That made the decision easy. She wheeled into the driveway.

The front door of the mansion was standing wide open, light streaming out into the foggy night. She stared at it as she got out of her car. That didn't seem right. A trap? It didn't feel like one. Aaron should still have had no idea that she was a Technomancer. Crouching behind her car for protection, Kate opened a briefcase and pulled out several items. One was a flat black automatic pistol that she put into a shoulder holster under her jacket. Another was a cellular telephone, a convenient, portable link to the New World Order's on-line magick. She set the phone on the ground at her feet. The last item was a pair of electronically enhanced binoculars. Raising the binoculars to her eyes, she began adjusting their focus. They were a more advanced model of the opera glasses she had used at Pan's. Like the glasses, they were capable of making active magick and the flow of Quintessence visible, although the binoculars did not have to be preprogrammed with target patterns.

A glowing meshwork sprang up around the house as she focused the binoculars. She recognized it as the result of extremely strong demon wards placed inside the mansion. While they wouldn't affect her or her magick, she was suddenly worried about what Aaron was trying to protect himself from. Surely the demon that had appeared in Stefan's apartment hadn't been that powerful! She frowned and continued to manipulate the dials on the binoculars. There was no other magick at work around the house that she could see from here. The doorway, even open as it was, was not magickally trapped. She flicked a switch and scanned the doorway for the electrical activity that would mark more mundane traps like infrared beams and security alarms. There was an alarm system, but it was inactive. Kate checked again carefully. There must be something!

There wasn't. Not a thing. The door was simply open, and that was perhaps more worrisome than a trap. Kate picked up her telephone and dialed Aaron's number. His answering machine picked up the call after a couple of rings. She hung up without leaving a message. Tucking the phone back in her pocket and pulling out her pistol, she sprinted in a crouch toward the door.

Aaron was lying sprawled on a sofa in a room off the main hall with his eyes closed. A pair of earphones blasted music into his head. He was oblivious to her presence.

Kate hesitated. With those earphones on, he wouldn't have heard anything. Not the telephone. Not the departure of Stefan and Saffleur. The question of the why the front door was open was still a mystery, although it would all be answered soon enough. She walked boldly across the room to stand over Aaron. Flicking off the safety switch on her gun, she placed the cold metal barrel against Aaron's temple.

He didn't flinch. His eyelids didn't even so much as flicker. Kate gave him a sharp slap to the side of his face, something she wished now that she had done the first day she met him. He still didn't react. Surprised, Kate checked his breathing. He was alive, just asleep. Very deeply asleep. She took the gun away from his head and stood back, once again biting her lip as she thought.

It was unnatural. That was clear. She pulled the earphones off his head. This time, Aaron did move, his head lolling to the side. It was still no more than someone might move while they were dreaming, though. Kate frowned. What was going on? She raised the binoculars to her eyes, manipulating them with one hand while keeping her pistol trained on Aaron with the other.

The magnification of the binoculars was a hindrance at this close range, but the enchanted electronics showed her what she wanted to see. Aaron was virtually surrounded by highly active magick! Luminous waves of energy lapped at his body as if he were submerged in a pool of glowing water. A stream of the energy ran from him into the distance, flowing away through the Umbra. More properly, actually, the stream flowed to Aaron. Kate snarled. She was willing to bet money that that energy was coming from Pan's. Whatever it was, though, it was not the Quintessence that she would have expected from an active node. It didn't explain Aaron's strange sleep, but the reason for that was equally obvious.

A black beetle as big as her hand crouched on Aaron's forehead.

Kate sucked in her breath and took the binoculars away from her eyes for a moment. The beetle was not visible in the physical world. It was entirely magickal, either the manifestation of a spell or a spirit of some kind. It was what was keeping Aaron asleep. Gritting her teeth, she reached out to touch Aaron's forehead. She felt nothing more than his skin, warm and slightly damp from sweating. The binoculars showed her hand passing through the beetle, though, and a murmur of whisperings tugged at her ears. She pulled her hand away. The whispers disappeared. The beetle raised its head, antennae feeling the air as if it sensed something amiss. A spirit, then, intelligent enough to react to her presence. It began to crawl down over Aaron's face.

Coolly, Kate set her gun down and took the cellular phone out of her pocket. Watching the movements of her hand through the binoculars, she reached out until the phone was just touching the beetle. The whispers returned as soon as she came in contact with it. The spirit turned, putting its front legs on her hand, climbing onto her. With a hiss of fright, she punched a number into the phone with her thumb, dialing up a spell.

The tone of the phone clarified and narrowed sharply. The spirit shivered as the pure sound bombarded it. It tried to scuttle away, but Kate moved with it. After a second, the beetle shattered, exploding in a silent cloud of dark, shadowy fragments. Aaron gasped and opened his eyes and sat upright with a start. Kate dropped the binoculars to snatch up the gun. "Don't even think about moving," she commanded.

13

He had felt the subtle workings of magick brush him as he lay cradled in the arms of pleasure. He had tried to fight back, countering the magick with his own, but the attack was too strong and too unexpected. It was like trying to dam a river with a single plank. Aaron had slipped under the surface of that river and into darkness. A woman's soothing whispers replaced the roar of music from his earphones. He knew he was asleep, but he didn't dream and there was no way of telling how much time had passed. He was helpless. When the whispers were suddenly overwhelmed by a shrill, piercing blast of sound and he had woken up, he had expected to see Saffleur standing by him.

Instead he saw Kate. Kate with a gun, and with a look on her face that was so cold and hard that he froze instantly. "You? What are you doing here?"

"Saving you." She stepped to one side and sat down on a chair, keeping the gun trained squarely on Aaron's chest. "Although I'm not entirely sure why I bothered. It would have been easier to deal with you while you were asleep."

"But you . . . *you* woke me up? How . . .?" He started

199

to rise, but Kate brought up her arm to point a cellular phone at him. If anyone else had made that gesture, the effect would have been laughable. Kate made it seem very, very threatening. And suddenly he realized what that meant. "You're a Technomancer?" he asked with a sinking feeling.

Kate didn't respond. She just glared at him harshly. Aaron cursed himself. The thought that she might be a mage at all had never occurred to him. That she might be a Technomancer had been totally inconceivable. No wonder she had been outside Pan's that night! And he had performed magick around her. He had even led her to Saffleur and to Stefan. After all of his plotting and careful planning, he had brought the Technocracy on top of himself, and now it was sitting in his living room with a gun pointed at him.

Kate looked like she knew how to use the gun, too. He wasn't sure exactly what the telephone could do, but the way Kate held it made it clear that she considered it a weapon. She was grim. Very grim, and as dour as any Technomancer he had ever encountered. He wondered where Stefan was—presumably asleep upstairs. If he could escape from Kate, he would have to try to get the hustler away from her as well. . . .

What was he thinking? It was every man for himself! Stefan was on his own! If he could rescue him, Aaron would try, but he wasn't about to get himself killed doing it. He looked Kate straight in the eye suddenly and asked boldly, "How long have you known?"

"Long enough. I—"

"What did you do to put me to sleep like that? What have you done with Stefan?"

With a very slight puffing sound, a bullet hole appeared in the upholstery of the couch beside his right arm as if . . . by magick. Aaron swore involuntarily. "Technocracy science, Aaron," Kate said quietly as she released the trigger on the pistol. "Totally silent and extremely accurate. Just answer my questions, or do you want to find out what my telephone can do?" She set her finger lightly on the keypad of the cellular phone. "For the record, though, you were already asleep when I got here. Some kind of beetle spirit. I used my phone to destroy it. Believe me when I say that the phone can do the same thing to flesh and blood that it can do to spirits."

Aaron stared at her in stony silence, hoping desperately that his heart's pounding didn't show. His arm stung from the close passage of the bullet. He felt as though sweat was running from his palms like a river. "You didn't attack me before?"

"Didn't I just say that? Maybe it was this demon that you're so afraid of." She gestured ever so slightly with the gun, an unnecessary reminder of its presence. "But I have a few questions I want to ask you. About that demon. About Pan's. About Stefan."

"I'm not going to tell you anything."

She shrugged. "I didn't really expect that you would immediately. I'm patient, though." She set down the phone to slip a tiny device out of her pocket. "A portable mind probe developed by the New World Order. I won't hesitate to use it if I have to. Not as powerful as some of our models, but very efficient. You can't hide anything from me."

"So don't even try?"

"Exactly. Where did Saffleur and Stefan go tonight?"

Some of the surprise he felt must have escaped to be displayed on his face, because Kate's eyebrows rose. "I find it difficult to believe that you didn't know anything about this."

"I . . ." Stefan should still be here. Saffleur wasn't supposed to come by again tonight. He had wanted to, but Aaron had firmly told him that Stefan was still weak and needed rest. Saffleur had capitulated reluctantly. He would wait to return until tomorrow. Had he come again? Suspicion struck Aaron, and he sat back on the sofa. "You're trying to trick me," he hissed at Kate. "Divide and conquer?"

"I know what I saw. I passed Saffleur and Stefan as I arrived. But why would I want to try and trick you? I already have you in my hands." She leaned forward hungrily, just as he had pulled back. "You'll have to come up with a more convincing lie than that, Aaron."

But he was genuinely confused! All of his clever words seemed to have abandoned him. If Kate didn't believe the truth, what was she going to believe? "I loved you?" he said weakly, probing desperately for a weakness in her rational, unemotional armor.

She replied with a derisive snort. "No, you didn't. First you wanted me in your bed, then you were trying to get me not to tell Tiffany about you and Pan's. You were acting the whole time." She smiled and added venomously, "But you weren't the only one."

He saw the opening he was looking for. "Sour grapes, Kate?" he shot back. He was rewarded by seeing her flush briefly as he broke through her icy Technomancer shell. He pressed her further. "This is what it's all really about, isn't it? You don't care about Pan's or Stefan. You're just really pissed because I was stringing you along!"

Kate turned livid. "If I was pissed at you, I wouldn't be here, and the New World Order would already have you in custody! Is love nothing more to you than something to be exploited? Do you have any sense of loyalty to people other than yourself? Do you ever do anything without some ulterior, selfish motive?"

As she spoke, Aaron reached out and seized the power of his connection with Pan's. He didn't listen to Kate's words. They weren't important, only the angry, distracting tirade that she was delivering. At the height of her rage, when her attention was the weakest, he drew hard on the sensations of Pan's and worked magick on himself.

Time suddenly jumped and surged, actually accelerating around him for a few moments. But a few moments was enough. He was out of the room before Kate had even had time to fire two silent shots into the upholstery of the sofa and scream after him.

The Paradox of the act was mercifully small and the pain that accompanied it little more than a dull ache. He charged upstairs, then streaked down the hallway to Stefan's room. "Stefan!" he yelled as he burst in. "We have to get out of . . . here?"

The room was empty. The bed was made. Aaron ripped open a closet. Stefan's clothes were gone. Had Kate been telling the truth? Had Stefan really left the mansion with Saffleur?

Who had attacked him and sent him into a magickal sleep?

Aaron's eye fell on a folded note atop the pillow on Stefan's bed. He snatched it up and read it over. *Aaron*, it said, *I'm sorry to leave you like this. I've gone to see Valentine. I have to do it. I don't know if I'll be back, but I'll try. Thank you—Stefan.* At the bottom of the page he had added, as if it were an afterthought, P.S. *Thank Saffleur for trying to help, too.*

"Shit," he muttered.

"Shit, indeed." Kate stepped into the room, gun steady in her hand.

"Stefan's gone." He tossed the hustler's note to her resignedly. It fluttered to the ground at her feet.

"I told you that." She picked the note up, careful to keep the gun on him. Aaron collapsed onto the bed, his forehead creased in thought, as she scanned it. Kate frowned. "So you really didn't know where he went."

"I told you that," he mimicked, then sighed. "But did you read the last line?"

"A thank-you. It doesn't sound like something you'd ever say."

"Leave me out of this for a minute, okay? You said he left with Saffleur?" Aaron pointed at the note. "Why would he ask me to thank Saffleur if he was going to Valentine's with him?"

"Maybe he ran into him as he was leaving."

"Coincidence? When mages are involved? I would have expected a little more skepticism from a Technomancer." Aaron stood and began to pace back and forth. Kate moved the gun in time with his pacing, keeping him covered. "Do you think it was just coincidence that I was attacked just in time for Stefan to leave? I wouldn't have let him go if I'd been able to stop him!"

"Why?"

He froze. Why would he have stopped Stefan? There was no reason not to let him go with Saffleur. No reason except that Aaron wanted to know everything that Saffleur might discover about the young man's powers. He had heard enough of Kate's accusations of his selfishness downstairs that the realization disturbed him a little bit. He had actually begun to enjoy having Stefan around, but was his only real interest in the young man his power to warp reality? Stefan had originally just been a diversion from Pig, something to occupy his mind. What was he now? A . . . friend? Gritting his teeth, he pulled himself away from that thought. He couldn't afford to become emotionally attached to anyone. "The point is that Saffleur attacked me so that he could whisk Stefan away!" he snapped. "What would you make of that?"

"I would wonder whether Saffleur was a friend or an enemy."

Aaron laughed bitterly. "I thought *you* were a friend."

"Why do you think Saffleur took him?"

"How much do you know about Stefan?"

Kate hesitated, then admitted, "Everything except what you two may have found out in the last couple of days. I saw what happened in Pan's. I know what Saffleur has said about Entropy fluctuations and reality shifts. I know that you're trying to keep him away from the Technocracy."

"Well, then you know everything we know. All we were able to figure out is that what sets everything off is the death of somebody Stefan knows and that he blanks out after it happens. I tossed out a few explanations and Saffleur shot them down."

He paced in silence for a minute until Kate said suddenly, "But Saffleur knows something that you don't." She looked up at him as he stopped. "Why else would he take Stefan and not tell you?"

"He wants his power for himself!"

"Possibly." Kate shook her head slowly. "But if he didn't think that he could unlock Stefan's abilities somehow, why would he go to the bother of taking him away? He could have left Stefan with you until you and he could have figured them out together—then he could have killed you."

"Why didn't he kill me now?"

"Do you think you would have woken up if I hadn't come along? Even if someone had taken you to a hospital, no doctor would have been able to wake you. Eventually, you would have died. All very coincidentally." Aaron gave a little shudder, and she nodded. "He could have killed you when you had figured out Stefan's powers. Instead he tried to do it now. E*rgo*, he knows something about Stefan that you don't. Maybe one of the explanations you suggested was a little too close for comfort."

"Goddamn it!" Aaron slammed his fist into the top of a bureau. He bit his knuckles and stared at Kate. "I suppose you're going to turn me in to the New World Order now."

"No."

"No?"

"No." Kate opened her jacket and slid her gun into a shoulder holster. "I'm sorry, Aaron, but compared to Stefan, whatever you're doing with Pan's is nothing."

He frowned. "You think I'm just going to let you take him?"

"How strong was Saffleur's attack on you?"

Aaron remembered the feeling of a dark river washing over him and the whispers that drew him down into sleep. A spirit, Kate had said. Only Dreamspeakers normally had traffic with spirits, and Saffleur was no Dreamspeaker. He could have learned, however, and who knew what kinds of spirits a Euthanatos might deal with? "You want us to work together?"

"It would give us a better chance against Saffleur."

"Who gets Stefan once we've rescued him?"

She gave him a bleak stare. "Maybe we should wait and see if we *can* rescue him. Where do you think they've gone? They could be anywhere."

"The New World Order is supposed to have eyes everywhere. Why don't you use a few of them?"

Kate nodded in slow agreement. "It will take . . . time. I can't be seen cooperating with a mage of the Traditions."

"You think it will do me any good if other mages find out that I'm working with a Technomancer?" He sighed. "See what you can set up. I'll get some stuff together, and we'll try some hit-or-miss searching while we wait for your results. Did Stefan and Saffleur look friendly when you saw them?"

"Yes."

"Then presumably they were on good terms and Saffleur was taking Stefan where he wanted to go." Aaron indicated Stefan's note. "Valentine's."

The ride in Saffleur's car was silent. Stefan didn't have anything to say, Saffleur didn't appear to have anything to say, and no sounds entered the car from the outside world. It was like watching television with the volume turned off. The silence lent an eerie, surreal quality to the dark world on the other side of the glass. The fog had turned into a light, cold drizzle. They rolled smoothly past busy shopping districts and past Grace Cathedral, all without a sound. An ambulance pushed quietly past them, its lights flashing madly. They turned down Polk Street. Stefan spotted Carlos being pushed into a police cruiser. His mouth was open, and he was clearly yelling loudly in protest, but Stefan couldn't hear a thing.

He was beginning to wonder if Saffleur hadn't cast some kind of spell on him when the car stopped and the mage gestured for him to get out. Noise returned as soon as he opened the door. Stefan consumed it gratefully: the rumble of traffic, the wail of distant sirens. Saffleur was already striding off down the sidewalk. He had produced a voluminous black trench coat from the backseat of the car, and it gave a stiff, unnatural look to his movements. He reminded Stefan chillingly of some kind of modern-day Grim Reaper. The hustler hurried to catch up with him, the collar of his leather jacket turned up against the rain.

"You parked far enough away from Valentine's," he muttered.

"I know."

"If you'd parked closer, we wouldn't have to move so fast."

"If I had parked closer, my car might have been associated with Valentine's and what's going to happen there tonight."

Stefan stumbled in the darkness. "What's going to happen tonight?"

"What must happen." Saffleur stopped suddenly.

They were standing in front of the Chinese grocery below Valentine's. The door upstairs was just around the corner. "Go ahead."

"Where will you be?"

"I'll be there when you need me."

Stefan swallowed and stepped around the corner. He paused, looking at the door with its inscription VALENTINE'S ESCORTS, INC. painted on a glass window. Through the glass and beyond the painted words, he could see the bottom of the stairs. He heard the heavy steel door at the head of the steps open and close, the change in air pressure making the lower door shudder slightly. Someone began making their way down, high heels tapping on the stairs.

"I don't know, Saffleur," he said hesitantly. "I don't know what I'm going to say to Valentine. I want revenge, but I don't know how to do it. Maybe this isn't the right time. Saffleur?" He glanced around. There was no sign of the mage. Legs and a short, leather skirt came into his view on the stairs. Nervous, he began to turn away. He could let this person pass before going in.

Some force scooped him up and shoved him toward the door. Saffleur's voice echoed out of the shadows, vicious with urgency. "Get in there *now*!" The door flew open before him. He fell to a sprawl on the cold floor. His head and torso cracked painfully against the steps, right at the feet of the descending woman. She shrieked.

"Stef?"

He twisted his head to look up. "Marilyn?"

"Oh, my God!" The hooker backed up a couple of steps. "Stef! What are you doing here?"

"Marilyn? You wouldn't believe what I've been through!" Stefan grabbed at the banister and hauled himself to his feet on the stairs. "Look, I came here to split up with Valentine. I'm not going to work for him anymore! I've got a friend with me. He's going to help me take care of . . ." His voice faltered suddenly as he looked at Marilyn. Her face was pale and her legs were shaking, trembling on her stiletto heels. She just stared at him.

"What are *you* doing here?" he asked in a whisper.

"Oh, God, Stef!" She whirled and began to climb desperately back up the stairs. Her heels and skirt slowed her down though. Stefan was easily able to close the space between them and grab her arm. These stairs led only to one place. Valentine's.

"You're working for him too, aren't you?" he screamed angrily. "Fucking hell! You're working for Valentine after you made me promise not to!"

"Please, Stef!" Marilyn's carefully applied mascara began to run as tears spilled out of her eyes. "Listen! I had to do it! An old whore runs out of options!"

"How long, damn it? How long have you been working for him?"

"A couple of years, on and off. Stef, I'm sorry! I need the money!"

"Where have I heard that before?"

She grabbed on to the sleeve of his jacket. "You know how it is, Stef! It's good money when you need it, and then you can't get away! It's even worse when you're old. It poisons your soul. I know you've felt it. The streets are tough, but this is like crawling into a sewer." She looked into his eyes. "I wanted to keep you away from it—"

"Shit." He pushed her away. There were deep, corded red marks on her wrists. The marks of rope tied too tightly. Deliberately too tightly. "A great example you are then."

"Stef—"

"Fuck off!" he shouted in her face. "Didn't you tell me a couple of days ago that you never wanted to see me again? Well, don't worry. You won't have to!" He turned his back on her and started down the stairs.

"Stef!"

The steel door at the head of the stairs crashed open. Valentine filled the doorway. "Stefan!" he roared.

Stefan whirled around and gave him the finger with both hands. "Fuck you, Valentine! Fuck you!" He glared at Marilyn, collapsed against the wall, tears and mascara streaking her face. "Fuck you, Marilyn!" He turned again, running down the rest of the stairs and out into the night. The drizzle outside hid his own tears of hurt and betrayal.

Saffleur seized him as he came out the door and pulled him into the shadows. Stefan lashed out at him. He didn't want to be with the old mage. He wanted Mike, or Aaron. Someone warm to hold him. Saffleur was cold.

His blow didn't connect with Saffleur, only with a fold of his overcoat, the cloth swallowing his arm. "Let me go, damn it!" he cursed.

"No. Not yet." Saffleur was stronger than he looked, or else he was using magick. Stefan struggled, but he couldn't break free. "How do you feel?"

"How do you think I feel?" spat Stefan. "I feel like shit! It's like having your mother sell you down the river!" His tears were falling faster than the rain, and his words were almost a sob.

"And Valentine?"

"I want to kill the son of a bitch!"

"Good."

"Good? What kind of . . . ?" He clenched his teeth. "Is this the big thing that was supposed to happen tonight? That I was supposed to get mad enough to kill Valentine?"

"Yes and no." Saffleur swept one side of his trench coat around Stefan. "It's not over yet."

In a roar of engines, the street was suddenly swarming with police cars, their flashing lights cutting through the night. A couple swung around to form a barricade near Valentine's door. Police officers came charging around the corner, their guns out. Two carried a battering ram. They poured up the stairs to Valentine's. There were several loud bangs as the cops swung the battering ram against the steel door, then a crash as the door gave way.

"Christ," whispered Stefan. It was a raid.

"Hush." Saffleur pulled out a small figure of a woman with the head of a beetle. Stefan felt a cold sensation run through his gut as he saw it. It triggered a memory somewhere inside him, a vague feeling of terror and distrust. He tried to pull away from Saffleur, but the mage held him tightly. "Don't move," he ordered firmly. He held the figure up. "Great Lady," he murmured, "make them blind."

A cop paused directly in front of them as though she had heard Saffleur's words or sensed his movement. For a moment, she looked straight at them; then her gaze drifted off and she continued on her way. Saffleur released Stefan. "If you move," he warned him, "they will see you."

Shouts began to filter down from above as the police raided Valentine's. "There's a back way out," Stefan said quietly. "Valentine will get away."

"No. They already have Valentine. Don't worry about him."

There was a sudden gunshot from somewhere inside. In its aftermath, everything was silent for a moment. Stefan glanced at Saffleur, but the old mage's face was impassive. His gaze was trained on the door and the stairs. The police on the street brought up their guns, training them on the door as well. From inside, there came the sound of one voice shouting loudly.

"If I see anybody move a muscle, I swear I will kill her! And tell that to your boys downstairs, too!"

It was so quiet on the street that the noise of the falling rain pattering off the roofs and hoods of the police cars was clearly audible. Once again, Stefan heard the tapping of high heels descending the stairs, this time accompanied by the heavier footfalls of a man. The same shouting voice as before called out. "I have a hostage."

One of the police officers stood up from behind a cruiser and waved at the other cops to lower their guns. "Come out and we'll talk," she yelled in reply.

"Anybody tries anything funny, and this whore will have an extra hole in her head!"

"Our guns are down. Come out."

Stefan's heart stopped as the man and his hostage slowly emerged from the building. The hostage was Marilyn, her arms twisted behind her back and handcuffed, the man's gun held to her ear. The man, wearing the pants from a business suit but no shirt and with a dog collar around his neck, pulled her around so that his back was to the wall and she stood in front of him. "I've got a family," he screamed. His eyes were crazy. "They wouldn't understand. You've got to let me go! I haven't done anything!"

They were only a few feet from Stefan and Saffleur. *I could stop him if I move quickly,* Stefan thought to himself. He tensed his body, preparing to leap at the man.

Saffleur put a heavy hand on his shoulder. "No."

"I can save Marilyn!"

"You can't."

The mage's face was hard. Stefan's breath hissed between his teeth as he finally realized what Saffleur was doing. He shrugged his hand off his shoulder. "You're going to let her die! *That's* what's supposed to happen here tonight! Not Valentine—Marilyn!"

"It is her time to die. It is necessary." Saffleur slipped a hand into one of his pockets and pulled out a strange, knobby, pointed bone. "There isn't anything you can do. There never has been. If you move, the police will see you and you will die as well. Just watch."

"Like hell I will!"

Stefan jumped for the man with the gun. Even as he did so, he saw a look of angry shock come over Saffleur's face. The mage flicked his bone at a police cruiser, and suddenly sirens tore through the silence. The man started. His finger tightened on the trigger of the gun just as Stefan dragged at his arm. There was a deafening crack and a spray of warm blood.

The man staggered and fell. Stefan fell as well, landing painfully on his arm. He didn't notice the pain, though. Marilyn lay by his feet. The bullet had torn its way across one side of her chest before sinking into the other. She was still alive, though, gasping for breath through the blood that bubbled out of her mouth. Stefan scrambled over to cradle her. "Marilyn!"

Her eyes were rapidly losing focus, but he knew that she saw him. She moved one arm awkwardly, and her lips tried to move. The tears came back, and he squeezed his eyes shut as he blurted out, "I'm sorry! I'm sorry, Marilyn! Oh, God, I'm sorry for everything." He opened his eyes again. She was already dead. He screamed.

Someone, one of the cops, gently pried him away from Marilyn's body and helped him to his feet. He barely noticed. Another one dead. Another of his friends, another person he had loved and cared for— possibly the last—had died. Just like Mike. Just like everybody. He felt cold. The world seemed distant. Everything seemed dim. There was nothing but . . . death.

And suddenly the deadly clarity exploded out of him again, wiping aside his amnesia as though it were a thin curtain. He remembered everything abruptly. The aftermath of the client's death at Pan's. Deng's death. The binge of drugs and alcohol trying to erase the clarity. Returning to Pan's. Saffleur, using that beetle-head figure he called the "Great Lady" to lock his memories away. Saffleur. Saffleur had killed Marilyn with his magick.

The man from Valentine's began to shout again as Stefan looked up. He was surrounded by police officers, but somehow he managed to raise his gun again. Bang! Bang! Bang! Two of the officers around the man went down as the clarity touched them. The third shot found the cop holding Stefan's arm. He fell, blood blossoming around his shoulder. Not a fatal wound normally, but Stefan could smell the stench of gangrene setting in almost immediately. People were screaming somewhere.

Saffleur was abruptly at Stefan's side, his face a mask of rage. "Stop—"

Stefan aimed a punch straight at the mage's head. "You!" he screamed. Saffleur whipped up the arm of his trench coat in shock. Once again, Stefan's hand sank into the cloth as though there was nothing behind it. This time, though, a burst of clarity accompanied his blow. The magickal cloth rotted away, and Stefan grabbed Saffleur's arm. "Are you doing this to me?"

"You little fool! You'll destroy everything!" His free arm came up holding the Great Lady. Stefan tried to block it, but Saffleur pulled his arm away at the last moment, then darted in to press the statuette against the side of his head.

He wasn't sure what Saffleur whispered, but suddenly all of his senses seemed to fracture. The world became disjointed and broken. He couldn't think straight. The clarity seemed to evaporate, though he couldn't be sure. He couldn't be sure of anything. It felt as though he were trying to see the world through a badly cracked window. Only occasionally did anything make sense.

Saffleur was leading him somewhere and cursing him madly.

His feet were wet. He was standing in a puddle.

He heard his named shouted. It was Aaron, running toward him. There was someone with him. The woman from outside Pan's, the woman with the opera glasses from his dream.

He smelled dirty water as Saffleur released him to scoop up water from the puddle and sprinkle it over the two of them. "Great Lady," he heard the old mage cry, "take us away!"

And then all of the smells and sights and sounds and sensations that he was familiar with vanished.

Aaron drove to Valentine's more quickly than he had driven from Stefan's apartment to the Barry mansion two days before, pushing Kate's car to the limit of safety on the wet San Francisco streets. Kate herself complained only briefly when two hubcaps came loose and fell off to roll in the gutter behind them. Kate's love of cars had proven fortunate. She had installed a magickally modified radio, altered by the Technocracy to pick up police-band transmissions, in her own car. They had heard about the imminent raid on Valentine's only a few minutes after leaving the mansion. Aaron had glanced at Kate. "I don't suppose you know enough Correspondence magick to be able to teleport us there?"

She had shaken her head. "No. You?"

"Uh-uh." And he had settled back in the driver's seat and floored the gas pedal. Kate had dialed up a number on her cellular phone, tapping into a traffic control system somehow, and punched in a long sequence of code numbers. All of the traffic lights along their route turned green. "Bless you," Aaron had whispered between tight lips.

Kate had just nodded and pulled a flashing police

light out of the glove compartment, setting it on the dashboard before Aaron's startled eyes. Cars had pulled over to let them pass. They drove past two police cruisers at top speed without the officers inside giving them more than a second glance. It was coincidental magick of the simplest kind, indistinguishable from pure chance and luck.

About a block from Valentine's, Kate pointed at a parked car as they sped past it. "That's Saffleur's!"

"Good," Aaron replied, slowing down and pulling over. "We can't get any further anyway."

Police cars filled the street in front of them. Gunshots echoed in a building ahead just as they got out. Kate jumped up on the hood of the car and looked ahead using her binoculars, flicking a switch to activate some kind of magick that would let her see through the nighttime darkness.

"They're there," she confirmed. "Saffleur is using magick to keep them hidden." She bit her lip. "He's holding some kind of talisman, Aaron. An extremely powerful talisman."

They had to push the final few yards through a small crowd of people. Just as they reached the edge of the crowd, though, there was another gunshot. A moment later, Aaron felt reality begin to slide as it had at Pan's. This time he was ready for it. "Hold on!" he yelled, grabbing Kate's hand.

He drew on his connection to Pan's as the changing reality broke over him, clinging to the sensations of pleasure as he might cling to a lifeline. He let the pleasure fill him and lift him up in the mind-altering reality that the Cult of Ecstasy sought. Aaron focused on that ecstatic reality, driving himself to ignore the shifting reality around him. He concentrated on bringing himself into perfect alignment with his Tradition's paradigm of reality.

It worked. The shifts in reality washed around him

as though he were a rock. He could function in a limited way, and he drew Kate after him, walking slowly toward Valentine's. Briefly, he tried to push his reality outward in order to encompass her in its security. He could feel Paradox waiting for him the moment he tried to extend the effect beyond his own body, though. He stopped his attempt and simply pulled her along, stumbling and blind. How was Stefan able to do all this without creating any Paradox at all?

The fabric of reality solidified and rewove itself as abruptly as it had begun to unravel, leaving Kate gasping in relief. Aaron released his connection to Pan's and looked around. He spotted Saffleur and Stefan almost immediately, the mage leading the hustler and swearing at him abusively. Aaron ran toward them, shouting Stefan's name. Saffleur looked up, surprise on his face. He reached down to scoop up water from the puddle that he and Stefan were standing in and splashed it over the two of them. He yelled something.

Aaron stopped, flinging his arms out desperately.

Stefan and Saffleur vanished.

Aaron crumpled with a hissing sigh. Kate caught him and lowered him gently to the ground. "Are you all right?"

"Just Paradox. I'll be okay in a moment."

She looked at the puddle. "They teleported."

"Not exactly. They stepped sideways into the Umbra. Vulgar magick." He smiled grimly. "At least that will have hurt Saffleur, too."

"So they could be anywhere. They got away!"

"No." Aaron eased himself onto his knees and then to his feet. "Look at this."

He pointed to the air above the puddle. Amid the spitting drizzle of the rain, a number of dark droplets hung suspended in the air. "I caught some of the water Saffleur used with a spell of Time and Spirit.

The passage that they used to reach the Umbra is still open." He stepped directly into the puddle. "We can follow them. Come on."

Kate hesitated. "I've never actually been in the Umbra before. The Technocracy forbids it."

"Do you want to help Stefan or not?" Aaron demanded in annoyance. "You're already breaking the rules of the Technocracy by working with me, remember?" He nodded toward Valentine's. "And the police are beginning to notice us."

She turned to look. Aaron reached out to grab her arm and pull her into the puddle. Before she could protest, he released the spell that held the gateway to the Umbra open. They vanished just as Saffleur and Stefan had.

14

At first, Kate wanted to slap Aaron for dragging her into the Umbra so underhandedly. Her anger swiftly turned to wonder, however. She had seen the Umbra before, of course, viewing it through devices like her binoculars or a variety of other Technomancer instruments. The Technocracy was afraid of the Umbra; its static paradigm of reality couldn't affect the spirit world, so the Technocracy had no control over it. When Technomancer instruments scanned the Umbra, they inevitably rendered it in dull, two-dimensional images. Even though she was as frightened as any good Technomancer should be at entering this forbidden place, Kate couldn't help feeling a sense of awe as well. The Technomancer scans were like faded pictures compared to the real experience of the Umbra.

The streetscape outside Valentine's simply faded away, replaced by an unearthly counterpart. Buildings became huge obelisks, cubes, and other geometric shapes, overgrown with reddish vines. The light of the Umbrascape came from large crystals that hung high in the air, pulsing in time with each other. Above them was a network of heavy, old steel cables, the pattern web that gave structure to reality. Spider spirits crawled among the web, spinning out fine silvery threads that were slowly replacing the heavier cables. It was a beautiful sight.

A tendril of energy flowed past her like white silk, arcing up through the Umbral sky from somewhere in the city and then down to somewhere just behind her. She touched it experimentally as she turned to see its grounding point and was almost overcome with a sudden rush of passion and pleasure. Aaron gasped at the same time she did. The energy terminated in him, and Kate realized that this was the same stream of energy that she had seen when she had scanned him with the binoculars earlier. "What is it?" she asked without thinking.

Aaron shook his head. He wasn't saying anything.

Now they began to move, or at least they seemed to move. Kate's hair flew back as if caught in a strong wind, but she could feel no wind on her face. Something lifted her and Aaron up, carrying them along faster and faster until everything was a blur, and they passed through the pattern web in the blink of an eye. It was like flying through outer space, if outer space was color and sound instead of void and vacuum. They were fading across different levels of the Umbra as they moved as well, so that they were flying not so much up as through. It made no sense—at least no physical or logical sense. She shivered with panic and excitement.

Within moments, San Francisco had been left far behind, and suddenly the world was growing solid around them once more. Or perhaps it would have been better to call it *a* world rather than *the* world. It was like nothing she had ever seen before. Even Aaron stared around him in astonishment.

They stood atop a raised platform built of ancient rough-hewn stones and timbers, surrounded by an open space or plaza of hard-packed earth. The soil was dry and a deep, rusty red-brown. There didn't seem to be any plants around. It was dusk and a huge reddish sun was poised on what they could see of the horizon. Much of it was hidden, however, by the profusion of buildings that cluttered the world. Kate spotted a fine wooden Japanese summerhouse. Next to it was an English country home. Next to that was a stone-walled farmer's cottage. A Bedouin tent was staked out on the red ground.

And unless she was truly hallucinating, a French chateau loomed in the distance. Beside it was the Kremlin.

Movement at the edge of the plaza caught her eye, and she pulled Aaron down to the platform. Saffleur was just leading Stefan away behind a mud-walled compound that looked African.

"This is insane!" she muttered, half to herself. "Where are we?"

"A pocket realm in the Umbra," Aaron whispered in reply, "I think."

"What about these buildings?"

"Who knows?" A series of rough steps led down from the platform. Aaron walked down them cautiously. "Anything can happen in the Umbra. This whole realm could be under Saffleur's control."

She joined him. "Let's hope not. They went that way."

Their first step took them all the way to the edge of the plaza. Kate glanced back at the platform, then at Aaron. He shrugged. "A mage can define the rules of reality in his pocket realm however he wants. Distances are shorter here."

"That *is* insane."

"This isn't Earth. The Technocracy has never imposed itself on this place. There's no Paradox. You can't assume that science and logic are going to apply here." He looked at her sideways and added pointedly, "You're in the minority, Kate."

She returned his glance with a steady stare. "So what are the rules, then?"

"Is fixing reality all that Technomancers ever think about? Why do you need rules?"

"Because without rules, everything is unpredictable. Nothing is safe." Kate drew herself up proudly. "The Technocracy defends Earth against the madness and danger of unpredictability."

"At the price of self-will and freedom? That's not defense, it's oppression. I'd rather face madness and danger."

"Like that demon you're so afraid of?"

Aaron's face hardened, and he spat on the ground. Away from the plaza, it was like a fine powder, and the impact of his spittle raised a little puff of dust. "Pig is none of your business."

"So it has a name."

"Shouldn't we be looking for Stefan?" Aaron asked testily.

"I didn't start the argument. Shall we go?" Kate turned away from him, content that she had the last word for now.

A trail through the dust showed where Stefan and Saffleur had gone. In fact, the trail was so well worn that it seemed likely Saffleur had been here many times before. Kate frowned to herself as they walked. If each of their steps carried them approximately ten yards, shouldn't the trail have been a series of widely spaced, worn patches? She stepped off the path to walk though the dust for several paces, then looked back.

Her footprints were an unbroken line, as if she had been walking normally. She scowled at the impossibility of it. The Umbra was wondrous, but it was also frustrating. She looked up to find Aaron grinning at her.

Kate might well have lost her temper and hit him, but suddenly he started and pulled her aside. She glanced over her shoulder and caught sight of several big black things moving ahead of them. Beetles. Beetles as big as small cars, their carapaces clicking as they moved. She stared at them in shock as she and Aaron pressed themselves into the doorway of an Art Deco–style office building. They scuttled along the path that the mages had been following, and for a terrified moment, Kate wonder if they might be tracking them.

The beetles turned aside well before reaching the plaza, though, disappearing between the Bedouin tent and the English country home. Kate realized that she had been holding her breath and exhaled nervously. "The spirit that Saffleur used to put you to sleep was a beetle," she said without looking at Aaron. "Do you think that they're his servants?"

"If they are, then we're surrounded by them." Aaron picked something off the wall beside him and held it up for her to see. Another beetle, but at least normally sized. "They're all spirits."

"What do we do?"

"Ignore them, I guess, and avoid the big ones." He stepped back out onto the path. After a moment's hesitation, Kate followed him.

The path ran straight toward the setting sun. There were no hills to obstruct their view, and they could see Saffleur and Stefan some distance ahead of them. If Saffleur had turned around, they would have been discovered. Fortunately, he didn't turn around. Kate realized that there was no reason why he should. To the best of his knowledge, they had been left behind on Earth. She suggested to Aaron that they should leave the path anyway, but he just pointed to one of the buildings off the path. Giant beetles stood quietly beside it, watching them. She nodded in understanding.

As long as they were on the path, they would see anything that came toward them.

They continued to pass buildings in styles from all over the world. There seemed to be no order to their placement and no reason for their presence. Beyond the Kremlin was a tavern that looked like something out of the seventeenth century and a grim factory from the Industrial Revolution. A Spanish *hacienda*. A plantation mansion from the American South. A shantytown hut. So absorbed was Kate in examining the buildings that she almost failed to notice that the path had ended. She stood on the edge of another packed-earth plaza. Aaron was crouched at the base of a building nearby, gesturing fiercely for her to join him. She did so instantly, as quietly as possible. Saffleur and Stefan had stopped not far ahead.

Aaron tapped the side of the building as she squatted down beside him. "Recognize it?" he asked in a whisper.

Kate looked up, then leaned forward to stare around the corner at the front of the building. "Pan's?" she gasped, settling back again. Aaron nodded. "How?"

"I don't know, but it's almost identical. Almost, but not quite." He looked concerned. "I want to know why."

The plaza at this end of the path was much larger than the other. There was a wide . . . pool, she supposed, in the center of it. At least, *pool* seemed to be the best word to describe the dark waters lapping at Stefan and Saffleur's feet. It was big, at least fifty feet in diameter. And it was deep. She knew that without even having to look into it. The water was as deep as a well, or deeper.

A platform of stone and wood, much like the platform in the other plaza, rose out of the pool. Atop the platform stood a statue fully ten feet tall. A woman

with the head of a beetle. The setting sun shone down
from behind the statue, casting a long shadow across
the water and halfway across the plaza. "That's the
same as the talisman Saffleur was holding!" Kate
whispered urgently to Aaron.

Aaron shook his head and pointed. "He's still holding it."

Beside the water, Saffleur released Stefan and
touched him on the forehead with the small figure in
his hand. The hustler staggered suddenly, looked up
at the statue, and screamed. Saffleur slapped him
sharply, hard enough that the stunned young man fell
to the ground. Kate winced and began to rise. Aaron
grabbed her arm.

"Where are you going?"

"To rescue Stefan!"

"Wait." He pulled her back down. "Maybe we can
learn something."

She gave him an incredulous look. "Don't you care
about Stefan at all?"

He growled at her and turned back to the scene at
the edge of the pool. Reluctantly, she did the same.
Saffleur was shouting at Stefan now, berating him for
interfering in the death of a woman at Valentine's. It
had been time for her to die! There had been nothing
he could have done! Stefan was only lucky that his
actions had not disrupted his life cycle altogether!
Kate risked a glance at Aaron, whispering, "Life cycle?"
Aaron shrugged.

Stefan just looked up at Saffleur accusatorially.
"You killed her. You killed her before I could tell her I
was sorry."

"That was the way it was supposed to happen!
That's the way it has always happened!"

"I could have saved her."

Saffleur slapped him again. "I didn't create you to
save people!"

Aaron's breath hissed between his teeth so loudly that Kate felt sure Saffleur would hear it. She herself frowned. The literal creation of people through mag-ickal cloning was fairly common among certain branches of the Technocracy. The thought of a mage creating someone was not totally alien to her. She had scanned Stefan, though, back at Pan's. He was no clone. And Saffleur was a Euthanatos. A death mage. It seemed strange that he should be creating life at all. "Now?" she asked Aaron.

"Wait."

Stefan, struck speechless, did nothing more than gape at Saffleur. The mage nodded sourly. "Why shouldn't I tell you? You know entirely too much already anyway, thanks to Aaron Barry's interference." He scowled. "When this cycle is over, I am going to have to deal with him."

"No!" spat Stefan.

"What are you going to do? Warn him?" Saffleur hauled the hustler to his feet. "You won't remember this any more than you remember any of our other trips here. When we're finished, I will destroy your memory of this place. Hold out your hands."

"No!"

"Do it!" Saffleur's voice was like a whip. Stefan cried out in sudden pain. His hands opened reluctant-ly, and Saffleur placed the talisman into them, folding his own hands over top. "Great Lady," he commanded, "bind us together!" He smiled expectantly as Stefan tried to pull away.

The smile faded abruptly, though. His grip on Stefan's hands and the talisman grew tighter. "Great Lady, bind us together!" he repeated desperately before cursing loudly. He glared at Stefan. "What are you doing?"

"What does it look like, you asshole!" Stefan screamed. "I'm trying to get away from you!"

"Don't you feel loss? Don't you feel pain? Your mentor betrayed you and died while you watched helplessly!"

"I feel angry! I could have saved Marilyn!"

"No!" Saffleur's voice cracked and shook suddenly, and Kate realized that the mage was as terrified as Stefan. Perhaps more so. He was clinging to Stefan and the talisman with all of his strength. "You can't! You must feel pain! You must, or the wheel won't turn!" Saffleur gasped for breath. "What about your lover? Mike? He's dead! They're all dead!"

Stefan froze. Relief washed across Saffleur's face. Stefan looked at him and said quietly. "They are all dead."

"Yes! Yes!" He stood up straighter. "Save your hate. Only for a little while, a few days. Hate is for the final turn of the wheel, the last death of the cycle."

Kate didn't remember rising, but she found herself on her feet, Aaron's hand on her shoulder holding her back just a little bit longer but with one finger indicating Saffleur. She should take him when the time came. Her teeth were clenched, cold, Technomancer rationality forgotten in her anger at what Saffleur was doing. All her attention was on Stefan and Saffleur as Stefan looked at the mage and asked, "The last death? There have been others?"

"All of them." Saffleur looked Stefan straight in the face. "Marilyn, dead because she worked for your tormentor, Valentine. Mike, dead by suicide. Rita and Chuck, by fire. Jean-Claude and Hélène, by influenza. Richard and Marie-Claire and Luc, in—"

"Enough!"

"Such pain, Stefan. You feel their loss, don't you?" His voice was as sharp and cutting as a razor. He smiled again as Stefan's face sagged and his struggles became weaker. "Such pain in your life. It was all necessary. I know what you feel. Haven't I felt it myself?

Such pain." He inhaled deeply. "Great Lady . . ." he began.

Aaron gave her the signal to move. She dropped to one knee, pulling out her gun with a smooth motion and aiming squarely at Saffleur. Aaron ran toward Stefan, surging through the strange space of the pocket realm. Saffleur looked up in the midst of his words, blurting out, ". . . bind us . . ."

The shift in reality surprised all of them, so suddenly did it come. It was not as powerful as it had been on Earth, more like a ripple moving through the landscape, emanating out from Stefan. It was still strong enough to affect them, however. Saffleur gasped and barely managed to hang on to the talisman. Aaron, caught in midstride, fell on his face as the rules of space changed around him. Kate's gun fell apart in her hands even as she squeezed the trigger. Somehow a bullet managed to fire, but it went wild, impacting in the dust by Saffleur's foot.

Kate cursed and pulled her cellular phone out of her pocket. She could dial up a sonic attack, or some other spell! Nothing happened, though, and she almost wept. The phone depended on a network to access its magick, and there was no network in the Umbra, so far from the reach of the Technocracy. She screamed in frustration, and, without thinking, flung vulgar magick at Saffleur as a mage of the Traditions might have. Her mind struck out at his like a psychic knife.

He turned her attack aside easily, but not before she had touched his mind briefly. Great age. Fear. Pain. Most strongly, the desire to live, backed up by a ruthlessness that made her shy away from further contact. Kate forced her eyes open, just in time to see Saffleur glare at her with icy hostility and spit out, "Great Lady, bind us together!"

The smile that suffused his face was short-lived. Aaron's fist swooped down and slammed into his jaw.

Saffleur went down, stunned, pulling the talisman of the Great Lady out Stefan's hands. A startled cry escaped his lips, but before he could do anything else, Aaron hoisted the old mage in his arms and flipped him into the pool of dark water. He sank without even a splash.

"Go!" he yelled at Kate. "Go, go, go!" Stefan was still in shock from the grief that Saffleur had inspired in him. Aaron threw him across his shoulders and climbed awkwardly to his feet, lumbering down the path.

"Where?" Kate screamed. "How do we get back without the talisman?"

"Shit!" Aaron paused for a moment, then indicated the replica of Pan's. "In there! Back door!"

They sprinted behind the building just as Saffleur rose up out of the pool with a roar. Kate didn't want to try to imagine what he might look like in his rage, but she could certainly hear him as he bellowed, "Great Lady, send me your servants!" She prayed that the door was unlocked.

It was. They darted into the replica of Pan's. Behind them, a deafening hum of wings and clicking of carapaces filled the air as the beetles of the realm responded to the magick of the talisman. Kate slammed the door and threw the lock. As if it was really going to help. "What now?" she demanded.

"There are two ways we can leave," explained Aaron, sliding Stefan from his shoulders. The hustler groaned, but managed to stay on his feet with Aaron's support. "I can move us sideways into the Umbra easily and we can travel back to Earth under our own power. That could take days, though." He hesitated, looking at Kate as if he were evaluating her. "Or," he said at last, "I think I can open a portal that will take us straight back to Pan's."

Something thudded against the door. Something big. "So do it already!"

"You have to promise not to tell anyone about how I do it."

Kate glared at him. "You sound like a child!"

"It's important! Promise, or I'll leave you here!"

"You wouldn't!"

"I would!" But he was the one holding Stefan. He had what they had come for. And he knew that she couldn't travel the Umbra herself.

"You bastard!" Kate spat. "Fine! I promise!"

With a grim smile of triumph, he led her quickly through the replica of the club. It was empty, although chairs and tables and glasses and drinks were all in place, as if it had just been vacated. Except for their footfalls and a repeated heavy thudding at the door, it was also dead quiet. Behind the bar, he ushered her through a door and into a spacious office. "The manager's office," he explained. "We'll cause less of a disturbance if we appear in private."

"What exactly are you going to do?"

"You know that white silk you saw in the Umbra? It's a connection to Pan's." Briefly, he described the nature of that connection to her. "I think I can use the power of the sensations to pull us back to the real Pan's. The similarity of this place will help to make the transfer."

Kate looked at him in amazement. "We thought Pan's was going to become a node!"

"You were supposed to." There was a trace of pride in Aaron's voice. That was replaced by a note of urgency as the back door of the club finally fell in with an echoing crash. "Here! Hold Stefan!" He passed the hustler to her, then pulled a small envelope from his jacket pocket. Out of it, he extracted a slip of yellowed paper with brownish writing on it. He chuckled almost ironically. "I offered this to Saffleur once as payment for helping me."

Stefan groaned weakly in Kate's arms. "How are you doing?" she asked him quietly.

"It hurts . . ."

"It's going to be okay." She hugged him. "We're going back to Earth."

Stefan's eyes snapped open. "No! Everything's still clear! I'll kill people!"

"What?"

"I'll kill people! Things will die!" He began to struggle. "I'm not hurting anything here! Leave me!"

"No. You're coming with us!"

"Everything will die! It's all clear!"

She gasped as another ripple in reality washed over her like a breaking bubble. Aaron hissed in frustration as it disrupted his spell. "I wish he would stop doing that!"

"He was trying to tell me something!" Kate's hand dipped into her pocket for her miniature mind probe. The tiny machine would help her sort out what Stefan wanted to say. The mind probe, however, came out in two pieces. "Goddamn it!" She glared at Aaron. "I promised you I wouldn't tell anyone about your link with Pan's. Don't you tell anyone you saw me do this." Without waiting for a reply, Kate used vulgar magick again, reaching desperately into Stefan's mind.

She pulled away in shock almost instantly. "What is it?" Aaron asked quickly.

"I can't tell you now." She rubbed at her head. The brief contact had given her a headache and made her want to sob in shared grief with Stefan. "But we have to calm him down. He can see the shifts in reality—it's like his vision becomes extremely sharp and clear. His pain is being reflected onto the fabric of reality. I don't know how." She looked up at Aaron. "Something's muting it here, but if we take him back to Earth, the shifts are going to be deadly."

"Can you use magick?"

"His pain is too strong. Jesus, it's so deep!"

"Drugs," Stefan whispered. "Give me drugs. I can blot it out. Anything to make it dim."

Aaron sucked in his breath. "Can you make a link between my mind and Stefan's?" he demanded.

"You won't like it."

"My connection with the sensations from Pan's will drown out his pain like drugs." He gritted his teeth. "Trust me and do it."

She didn't even hesitate. From the other side of the office door came the clicking of one of the giant beetles. The door bowed as the huge insect crashed into it headfirst. The beetle backed up for another charge. Placing one hand on Aaron's head and the other on Stefan's, Kate forged the link with raw, vulgar magick. Both men cried out in unison, Stefan in sudden pleasure, Aaron in agony. Tears dripped from the mage's eyes as he looked at her. "Oh, God!"

"I know. Just do the spell."

He dropped the slip of paper and seized hold of her and Stefan. The paper dissolved into writhing purple light as it hit the ground. Tendrils of the light crackled out to hit all three of them. The energy felt cold, but Kate saw a warmer white light spring up around Aaron. For an instant, she thought she saw the stream of white silk that tied him to Pan's. Then the purple energy was all around her, shaking her as though she were caught in an earthquake.

With a sound like a wrecking ball, the giant beetle smashed through the door and came rushing straight at them. She screamed in spite of herself. The Umbra seemed to explode around them for a fraction of an instant, wiping away the beetle, the fractured door, and the office in a haze of deep, shadowy purple.

Kate fell to her knees, bruising them against the solid, earthly floor of the real Pan's. She had never been more grateful to feel pain.

15

The pleasures that Pan's fed to him through Aaron were almost enough to blot out Stefan's sorrow entirely. Almost, but not quite. Stefan still felt grief, a hot ache in his chest for all of the past deaths that Saffleur had reminded him of so sharply, plus the closer deaths of Marilyn and Mike. Everything twisted suddenly in his sight. For a moment, it felt as though another wave of clarity, another shift in reality, would rush out of him to devastate Pan's, but the sensations of pleasure blocked it. His vision wavered on the edge of clarity and then fell back to normal. He could feel the dimness, the unthinking state that had blocked the shifts before, still on the edge of his consciousness. The pleasures of Pan's, though, were better than the dimness, better than alcohol or marijuana. He still felt in touch with the world and his anger.

Saffleur had used magick to make sure that Marilyn died. And if he had been able to do that . . . Mike's suicide had been unexpected. The fire that had killed his stepparents had been suspicious. The deaths of his grandparents had been strange. All possibly natural, but none entirely probable. Just the way Aaron had explained the workings of magick to him. And Saffleur had known the names of his dead family. Grief and anger and pain began to build inside him again, threatening to crush his heart. He sobbed once and tried to lose himself in Pan's pleasurable sensations. They took away the worst of his pain.

Stefan became aware that he was lying on the floor, carpet fibers rough against his face. Aaron was on the floor next to him, exhausted by his magick and the link that Kate had forged between them. The link was two-way, feeding each of them what the other felt. Stefan turned to look at the mage. "He killed them all."

Aaron reached out and took his hand. "I know." He winced, and tears ran from his eyes. "How can you stand this?"

"I had to. You get used to it." He held out his other arm. He needed contact, to know that there was somebody there for him. "Hold me."

Aaron looked at him for a moment, then glanced at Kate, on her knees and drawing slow, deep breaths in an effort to calm herself down. "I have to use the phone." He let go of Stefan's hand and staggered to his feet. "You're okay?"

He turned away without really waiting for an answer. Stefan watched numbly as he dialed a number and asked the club's switchboard to page the manager with the message that Aaron was waiting in her office. He sat up himself, an emptiness beginning to mix in with all of the other emotions running through his system.

There was a light touch on his shoulder. "Are you feeling all right?" Kate asked.

"I'm good enough," he replied as she helped him up onto a sofa. "What was that place? How long were you there?"

"Aaron says it was a pocket realm in the spirit world, like a separate little reality. And we were there long enough to hear everything." Kate flushed. "I'm sorry we didn't stop Saffleur sooner. Aaron wanted to—"

"No." Stefan cut her off. "It's okay. I'll get over it, and I know more about Saffleur now. I know why I felt like I knew him when we met at Aaron's." He sighed and rubbed his face. "I've been having blackouts whenever somebody died since I was eight. Has he been taking me to that place every time and wiping out my memory afterwards?"

"It looks that way."

"But why whole days at a time?"

"Who knows?" She sat down beside him and put her arm around him as Aaron had refused to. "Who knows why he's done any of this?"

Her tongue tripped over itself as she said it, though. Stefan looked at her. "You're lying. You know something."

Kate looked away from him just as Aaron hung up the telephone. Silence fell over the room. Aaron turned a chair around to sit down facing the couch. "Do you know something, Kate?" His voice was cold.

She glared at him and said stiffly, "Nothing I have to tell you."

"Really?" Aaron glanced at Stefan. "Remember what I told you about the Technocracy, Stefan? Kate's a Technomancer."

He must have pulled away from Kate a bit at Aaron's news, because suddenly she stiffened and took her arm away. He looked over at her. The flush on her cheeks had returned and deepened in anger. Aaron nodded. "She wants to turn you in so that the New World Order can take your mind apart."

"I do not! Stefan, Aaron has been giving you a one-sided picture of us." She wasn't looking at him as she spoke. Instead, all of her attention was on Aaron.

He smiled at her and sat back. "Then why don't you tell us what you know?"

"You're not—"

"Stop it!" Stefan screamed. "Just fucking stop it!" His head hurt, and he felt confused. He pushed himself to his feet and walked over to lean against the office desk, his back to them. "You two are the damn almighty mages. I'm the one who is being screwed over here." He turned around again to look at Kate. "Why did you lie and say you didn't know anything?"

She looked down at her lap. "I didn't think it was the sort of thing you'd want to hear right now."

"What? It might upset me?" He gave both Kate and Aaron a twisted smile. "Upset me more than finding out that my entire life has been scheduled and my family and friends murdered with magick? Upset me more than finding out that I can barely think about them without fucking up reality and killing more people?" He felt reality reacting to his pain even as he said that and drew on Pan's to block the pain out. "Tell me."

"You . . ." Kate began. She hesitated, gesturing vaguely with her hand. "This is going to sound a little weird, but when you try to use magick to touch somebody's mind, you get a certain sense about them. Everybody's mind has a unique texture. Sort of like psychic DNA. I felt your mind tonight, Stefan. Mostly I sensed your pain and grief, but I felt the texture under all that as well." She shifted uncomfortably. "I felt Saffleur's mind tonight, too. His mind has the same texture as yours."

"*What?*" Stefan slid down to sit on the floor with his back against the desk.

Aaron's eyes narrowed in thought. "They're the same person?"

"They have the same mind." Kate shook her head. "I can't explain it. It doesn't seem possible."

Stefan looked up. "I've heard things about twins. . . ."

"But you're not twins. Saffleur is centuries old. You're not. I've never scanned his Life pattern, but I'm positive it wouldn't be the same as yours." Kate bit her lower lip as she concentrated. "But somehow your minds are the same."

"What if . . . ?" An idea was taking form in Stefan's mind. He didn't like it, and it scared him, but it was a possibility. "What if I'm centuries old, too? Saffleur kept talking about my *life cycle*." He swallowed again. "Doesn't that mean I've been alive before?"

"Reincarnation?"

Aaron nodded thoughtfully. "Reincarnation is part of the Euthanatos paradigm of reality. Everything dies so it can be reborn." He looked up again. "It makes sense another way, too. What if all those languages you speak are holdovers from previous lives? Those buildings in the pocket realm correspond to some of the languages we heard you speak." He began checking them off on his fingers. "Japanese. French. Italian. Maybe Norwegian or German."

"English," Kate pointed out. "If nothing else, Pan's is there right now."

Stefan's heart suddenly seemed to be pounding in his chest. "I had a dream about a plain of blood that was covered in bodies. I knew all of them, but I didn't know how." He drew a faltering breath. "How long has Saffleur been controlling my life?"

Aaron shrugged. Kate shook her head. "We should be asking *why*. I don't think there's any doubt that he is."

"Why then?" Stefan blinked. Tears rolled down his cheeks. "Why is he doing this to me? Why this hell, over and over and over?"

"Why the buildings in the pocket realm?" Aaron asked.

"Why are you able to warp reality, and how? What does Saffleur get from any of this?" Kate sighed. "I'd be willing to bet that that talisman he calls the Great Lady has something to do with it."

"What he said about it binding us together?"

"Yes." She stood and walked toward Stefan, reaching for him. "Will you let me probe your mind again with vulgar magick? I might be able to locate this bond and—"

Aaron held up his own arm, blocking her before she could reach him. "We're on Earth again, remember?" he reminded her. "This isn't the pocket realm or the Umbra. You try doing vulgar magick here and Paradox is going to get you."

Kate cursed in frustration. "He's right, Stefan," she apologized, "I can't do anything for you until I get a new mind probe."

"Maybe we could sneak back to the pocket realm!" suggested Stefan desperately. "Could you do it there? Could Aaron?"

"I can't do it, Stefan," Aaron said sadly, "My knowledge of Mind magick isn't strong enough. Even if I could, it would be too dangerous to go back. We can't even stay here for much longer. Saffleur has problems finding you when your powers are active, but it should be fairly easy for Saffleur to figure out how we got out of the pocket realm and follow us here." He exchanged glances with Kate. "I'm not absolutely sure that even the two of us together would be able to stop him."

"So what do we do?" Stefan demanded.

"I could call in the New World Order," Kate suggested. "We could wait for him and fight."

Aaron made a sour face. "You would take Stefan in afterward and destroy Pan's around me."

"He would be safer with us. We could help him figure out his reality-warping powers." Kate scowled and crossed her arms. "What do you suggest?"

"We hide." Aaron stood and then helped the hustler to his feet. "Like I said, Saffleur has problems finding Stefan when reality is shifting around him. The reality shifts interfere with active magick. Saffleur got really worried when he wasn't able to conduct his little ritual with the Great Lady. And he said that the last death in the cycle would happen in a few days. If we hide out for the next several days, it should be too late for Saffleur."

"But we don't know what will happen if this last death doesn't take place! We don't even know who is going to die the last death!"

Stefan turned away from the arguing mages. A terrible certainty had sprung up in him. "I am," he said quietly.

Kate and Aaron stopped bickering and looked at him as one. He stared back at them. "It makes sense, doesn't it? If it's the last death of the cycle, and the cycle is based on reincarnation, then I must be the last one to die."

"But Saffleur said that the last death involved hate," Aaron pointed out.

"Can you think of anyone else?" asked Stefan.

Aaron shook his head, abashed. Kate grimaced. Stefan nodded. "I'm it."

The door to the office swung open, admitting a short woman with long brown hair and a wave of sound. The sudden noise was a shock after the quiet tension of the room. Stefan had virtually forgotten that they were in the middle of an active nightclub. The office was very well soundproofed. The woman shut the door and stared at Aaron. "Where have you been?" she demanded.

"In the Umbra, Tango, escaping from the threat of a dire and rather unpleasant death," Aaron replied curtly. He introduced Stefan and Kate to the woman. Tango frowned when he identified Kate as a Technomancer of the New World Order.

"You're in this kind of trouble *and* you're messing around with the Technocracy?" she asked, shaking her head.

"What kind of trouble?"

Tango looked at him in wonder. "Where have you been for the past four days?"

"Mostly at home."

"If you were, you were invisible." Tango pulled several newspapers out of a desk drawer and tossed them down in Aaron's lap.

"*Gaaaa!*" said Aaron, gaping.

Shock and surprise suddenly flooded down the link from him to Stefan, shock strong enough to make the hustler feel faint as his heart began to rush. It displaced the sensations of Pan's. Stefan seized onto those sensations tightly before they could disappear altogether and looked over Aaron's shoulder. A headline on the front page of the top paper read, Aaron Barry Linked to Smuggling Ring.

"That's the paper for Saturday!" Kate gasped.

"And Friday, Sunday, and Monday," Tango affirmed, "with more details every day and coverage on television. This is Tuesday. Aaron, you're wanted for everything from embezzlement to drug running to money laundering to insider trading. The cops and feds are cooperating to track you down. Which leads me to ask again"—she leaned across her desk to shout at him—"*where the hell have you been?*"

"In the Umbra," Aaron said weakly.

"Maybe the pocket realm had strange laws governing time as well as space," suggested Kate. She glanced at Stefan. "That could explain why you black out for several days. Saffleur was only erasing your memory of the trip to the realm, but while you were there, days passed on Earth."

Aaron nodded. "It's possible." He flipped through the paper. "This can't be happening," he commented distantly. "They've frozen everything!"

"Everything they could find, plus they've had the mansion staked out. They haven't been able to link you to Pan's yet, though."

"Could Saffleur have done it?" Stefan asked. The surprise that Aaron had felt and that he had shared was slowly ebbing.

"He was in the Umbra with us." Kate was biting her lip nervously again. "If time does pass more slowly in the pocket realm, we might have several hours before he can get back."

"There must be some mistake." Aaron shook his head in disbelief. "This must be something my father was into."

"No mistake. The changes in your accounts were made after your father's death and by you, according to the evidence. And guess who squealed to the cops?" She pulled the last paper from the bottom of the pile and flipped it open. A small picture accompanied one article.

"William!" Aaron spat. He hurled the paper in his hands across the office. Pages scattered everywhere. His sudden anger made Stefan's head hurt. "Goddamn him! He said he was going to make changes to my accounts—he must have done this, then leaked it! It's a setup!"

Kate retrieved part of the paper and read the story over. She looked up at Aaron. "He couldn't have been that thorough. It won't stick."

"No," he agreed, "it won't, but it will be a hell of a mess to clean up."

"You didn't seem to mind your name in the media before."

"That was different! Who would have suspected bad-boy Aaron Barry of being a mage? High profile and reckless, yes, but nothing to suggest I had any kind of serious side." He kicked a loose page of the newspaper. "It was a cover. This . . . this makes me look like a criminal genius. Do you think the Technocracy is going to let this one rest without an investigation?"

"Not really," Kate said frankly, "no."

"Shit," added Stefan.

"You can say that again." Tango handed Aaron several slips of paper from her desk. "William has been calling and leaving messages for you."

This time, Aaron was stunned into complete silence. Finally, he whispered, "How did he find out about me and Pan's?"

Tango shrugged. "I don't know. He's staying at the mansion, helping the feds go through things there. He wants to see you." She hesitated. "I think I have his last message still on my machine."

"Play it."

Tango hit a couple of buttons on the answering machine atop her desk, and William Pierce's voice filled the room. His message was simple. He wanted to see Aaron out at the Barry mansion. There was something strange about his voice, though. It seemed distorted somehow, with a peculiar echo in it.

Aaron growled loudly and crumpled the messages in his hand. "Pig!" he hissed. "That's how William knew about me and Pan's! Pig has possessed him!"

Stefan hadn't realized how much Aaron feared and hated the demon until a wave of emotion slammed down the link between them. His own fear was feeding into that wave, making it almost unbearable. He gasped and staggered. There was old pain in Aaron's feelings about Pig. Immense pain.

Kate didn't see him sway. "Your demon?" she asked Aaron quietly.

"My demon." He turned to Tango. "William's waiting at the mansion?" She nodded. Aaron glanced at Kate and Stefan. "I have to go."

"What about Saffleur?" Kate's voice was flinty, and she was slowly turning an angry red.

"Hide. I'll find you. Can I borrow your car, Tango?"

The short woman nodded and pulled a set of keys from her pocket, throwing them to Aaron. Kate caught them in midair. "You're running out on us at a time like this?" she said harshly. "I thought you had more of a sense of priority than that!"

Aaron turned on her, snatching the keys away. "I do

have a sense of priority! Unfortunately, Pig happens to have higher priority than you do!"

"It's just money!"

"It's not just money!" He glared at her as if he might blast her away with his gaze. "You wouldn't understand. Pig is just waiting for me. I know where he is. I have to go!"

"It sounds like a trap."

"Of course it's a trap!" He smiled, almost insanely, "But this time it's going to be Pig that gets caught. I'm going to make sure of it!"

He stepped toward the door. "Aaron!" Kate screamed in rage, reaching for him. Stefan caught her arm just as Tango slid smoothly between the two mages. Suddenly, there was a large knife in her hand, the blade gleaming like silver.

Stefan only had to glance at the way Tango stood to tell that she knew how to use that knife. He only needed to see her face once to tell that she wouldn't hesitate to use it, either. He tugged slowly on Kate's arm. "He's right, Kate," he said, "he does have to go. I've seen Pig." He looked up and met Aaron's gaze. "Pig is a little bit like his own Saffleur. He'll be back when he can."

Aaron met his gaze steadily for a moment, then nodded once. Stefan felt his gratitude. "Tango," Aaron instructed the woman, "help Kate and Stefan. Stay with them. Just don't let Kate follow me." Tango nodded in acknowledgement. Aaron stepped out of the office door in another blast of noise.

Kate shrugged off Stefan's arm with a curse and glared at Tango threateningly. "I could have taken you down in the blink of an eye!"

"Then why didn't you?" Tango grinned. She straightened up but didn't put her knife away. "Give the boss a break. I don't know much about this demon, but I do know that it's given him a lot of grief. He hates it almost as much as he hated his father."

Kate looked after Aaron. She knew just how much he had hated his father, and she had seen how he had reacted to Pig when it materialized in Stefan's apartment. She let herself relax slowly. "What do you know?" she asked Tango softly. She slipped her arm away from Stefan and urged the hustler to sit down in a chair. "I was with him when it attacked once. I just caught a glimpse of something black. Has it bothered him for long? Where did it come from?"

Tango seemed to hesitate, unsure of what she should be telling a Technomancer. "Yes and no," she said finally. "Long enough. I don't know where it came from. He won't talk about it. It couldn't leave San Francisco, so he got away from it when his father sent him to England, but I think it was tormenting him for a couple of years before that. Now he's back and Pig wants to play."

"Aaron has had nightmares about it for years, even when he was away from San Francisco," Stefan added.

"How did you find that out?" Tango asked. She crouched down beside the hustler's chair.

"He told me. I saw Pig, too. It attacked me at Aaron's mansion."

Tango whistled. "What was it like?"

"Black. Skinny. Ugly. Really mean. It only attacked me once and I had nightmares for two nights." He shook his head. "I can't imagine what Aaron must have gone through. He told me some of it, and that was bad enough."

Tango frowned and looked into Stefan's eyes. "Are you gay?" she asked bluntly.

"Yeah."

"Does Aaron know?"

Stefan nodded. "He must—he's told me he's not

interested in gay sex a couple of times. But he held me through the night after I had my nightmares."

Kate allowed herself a brief, cynical chuckle. "Don't let him fool you, Stefan. He doesn't care."

"Sometimes he can." Tango looked up at Kate with a cool stare. "Sometimes he can. I take it you had a thing for him?"

"Once, maybe." Kate felt herself flush. "Nothing now, though. We have a strictly professional relationship."

Tango shrugged. "It's nothing to be embarrassed about. Lots of women have had the hots for Aaron. Plenty of men, too."

"Technomancers don't get 'the hots.' Besides which," she commented casually, "Aaron is callous, cruel, and self-absorbed."

"Give him a chance. He'll grow on you. Once you get to know him he'll open up."

"Will he?" Kate scooped up her binoculars and cellular phone from the floor where she had dropped them after returning from the Umbra. She sighed. "I thought he was opening up once. I thought I was seeing the real Aaron Barry. Sweet, bashful—like the boy next door." She smiled a bit. "The real Aaron is nothing like that, is he? Sometimes I think that maybe I could like him, and then he turns around and does something that makes me want to slap him."

"I think you could be friends with Aaron."

"He's the absolute antithesis of a Technomancer. He's spontaneous, open, emotional, irrational. It's intriguing to be around him. And when we forget that we're supposed to be at each other's throats, we actually work well together."

"Stranger things have happened than a New World Order Technomancer and an Ecstasy Cultist as friends." Tango went to her desk and opened a locked drawer, pulling out a handgun. "Not many, but a few. Can you use a gun?" Kate nodded. Tango tucked her knife into a sheath up her sleeve and took a second gun from the drawer. She handed it to Kate with a smile. "Stefan?"

"Yes."

The short woman glanced at him. He returned her gaze levelly, but she shook her head. "Bullshit."

"I have!"

"Maybe, but not enough that I want to trust you with one around me." She took a big folding knife out of the drawer instead, then relocked it. "Fighting a mage is no work for someone without experience, but I don't want you to be completely unarmed. I assume you've at least carried one of these before?" He gave her a withering look as he took the knife. She shrugged. "Have you ever killed someone?"

That made him hesitate. "No," he admitted after a moment.

"Good. Don't get in the habit." She turned back to Kate. "Anything you need for your magick?"

"No, but do you have a calculator?" Tango pulled one from another drawer and passed it to her. Kate punched some numbers into it. "What time is it now?"

"Just after midnight."

Kate finished her calculations and nodded with satisfaction. "Judging from the time that seemed to pass in the pocket realm versus the time that actually passed here, a pocket realm minute is equal to ninety-six Earth minutes." She frowned. "Aaron thought it would only take Saffleur a minute or two to figure out where we had gone. That would give us anywhere from an hour and a half to three hours before he can get back. Plus time to locate Stefan—apparently he has trouble doing that."

"Less the time we've spent since we got back," Stefan pointed out. "That doesn't give Aaron a lot of time to deal with Pig."

"Hopefully he won't need that much time." Tango looked at Kate. "What are we going to do?"

"We . . ." Kate was suddenly conscious of Stefan's eyes on her. Her first instinct was to stand and fight, calling in New World Order support. But that would mean turning in Aaron and Stefan. Besides which, she didn't have Aaron to help her fight anymore. There was always Aaron's suggestion, of course. They could hide. She wasn't completely confident in Saffleur's inability to trace Stefan, though, and if Saffleur did find them, they would be backed into a hole with no choice but to fight anyway. Without Aaron or New World Order support. But it would take Saffleur time to find them, and Aaron might be able to rejoin them in that interval. "We hide," she said reluctantly. "Not here, obviously, since this will be where Saffleur comes first. Not the Barry mansion or Stefan's apartment, since he'll probably look there as well."

"Somewhere defensible and easy for Aaron to locate," Tango added. "Your place?"

"He doesn't know my address, and my apartment is protected against magickal eavesdropping. He wouldn't be able to find it."

"So neither would Saffleur!"

"He's a lot more powerful than Aaron, though. He might be able to penetrate the magick. This would be a lot easier if Aaron hadn't left and knew where we were going." She racked her brains for a good hiding place. "How about—"

At that moment, her cellular phone rang. She answered without thinking. "Hello?"

"Hello, Kate," replied the voice on the other end of the connection. "This is Julia."

Kate's heart stopped. Grabbing a pen from the desk, she scrawled "New World Order!" on the nearest convenient piece of paper. "What can I do for you, Julia?" she said calmly as she wrote. She shoved the crude note at Tango. The other woman understood instantly, grabbing Stefan and pulling him into a corner, well away from Kate. Kate herself walked into the opposite corner of the office, as far away as she could get from Tango and Stefan.

"I've been trying to get you for several days, Kate," Julia said pleasantly. Kate's knees quaked suddenly, both from Julia's words and from her tone. It was her soft interrogation voice. "I have the results of a search that you requested last Thursday night on my desk. They're very interesting. I'd like you to come in and discuss—"

Kate hung up. "Get down!" she screamed.

There was a faint click as the connection was reestablished, even though her finger was still on the phone's release switch. "Kate?" said Julia with a little laugh. "I don't know if you're aware of the retrieval system we install in the cellular phones we supply to our field agents. It's really quite amazing. The latest in digital conversion and transmission technology."

The phone in Kate's hand emitted a sudden series of tones, followed by a steady drone that seemed to go right through her head. Kate tried to resist the magick, but it was no good. She shrieked as her body was converted into energy and drawn into the telephone.

Stefan watched the process in horror. Kate seemed to blur and streak as the phone sucked her in. The last bit of her to vanish was the hand that actually held the phone. When that was gone, the phone fell to the floor. The cutting drone lasted a moment longer, then cut out with a beep and a click, to be replaced by a normal-sounding dial tone. He started to take a step forward, but Tango motioned him back and stepped out toward the phone herself. She stopped at the desk, unlocked the drawer, and took out a silencer, screwing it onto her handgun without taking her eye off the cellular phone.

Then she took aim at the phone and blew it apart with two well-placed shots.

"Holy fuck!" breathed Stefan finally. "What happened?"

"I think her superiors in the New World Order called her back to regional headquarters." Tango shook her head. "Shit. What timing."

"Well, this is just fucking great." Stefan sat down heavily on the sofa. "Both of our mages are gone and the bad guy is coming to take me away. What the fuck do we do now?"

Tango looked at him steadily. "We hide you, just like we planned."

"Where? How is Aaron or Kate going to know where to look for us? If they ever come back."

"Aaron will come. You can count on it." Tango looked at the remains of the phone sadly. "I don't know about Kate."

"So where do we hide me?"

"The only place we can. Right here."

Stefan looked at her incredulously, then got up. "Fuck that. I'm running."

"Don't be stupid."

"Hey!" He whirled to face her. "This isn't your life! You heard what's happening. Saffleur is going to be coming straight here! This is the first place he's going to look for me. He might have trouble finding me with magick, but there's nothing wrong with his eyes!"

"Do you want to be alone when he finds you?" Tango poked at the knife in his pocket. "With that to protect you? You stay here, and Kate and Aaron may be able to find you again. And I'll be with you. You run off, you're dead meat for sure."

"What if Aaron and Kate don't come back in time?"

"Then we make our last stand here in Pan's. You and me against Saffleur." She smiled crookedly at him. "Should be a hell of a fight."

16

The Barry mansion was mostly dark as Aaron drove past. There were a few lights on: the living room, one of the bedrooms, and his father's study. Aaron felt his stomach twist. The bedroom that was lit was the one where Pig had attacked Stefan. The marks of the demon's talons still covered the walls. The cops and feds must have had a ball when they found that!

Although Tango had said that the mansion was under surveillance, there was no sign of the authorities in the area. Only one car was in the driveway, an old but well-maintained sedan that belonged to William Pierce, and no other vehicles parked nearby. Aaron didn't doubt, however, that the mansion was being watched. He stopped Tango's car about two blocks away, pulling into an ordinary parking spot at the side of the street. He hadn't really expected that he would be able to simply walk up to the door of the mansion.

Aaron leaned his head against the steering wheel wearily. His first big problem was going to be getting into the mansion. The authorities would undoubtedly have the house watched on all sides in the physical world, and he was willing to bet that the mansion's own alarm system was fully activated. There was no getting in that way. Pig would probably be watching the Umbra, waiting for him to try and enter via the spirit world. There would be means of getting in either way, but neither route would be easy. Once again, Pig was forcing him into a guessing game. Which was the safer means of entry, the physical world or the Umbra? The demon was good at forcing difficult decisions out of him, and good at choosing Aaron's weakest moments in which to strike. And Aaron was weak now.

Of course, there was no way Pig could have known what Aaron had just gone through. Its trap had been timed to catch him several days ago. Aaron managed a smile. The waiting must have driven the demon mad and the authorities to desperate boredom. But the physical world and the law or the Umbra and the demon? Which did he want to face first? He made his decision.

He took hold of his connection to Pan's, drinking the pleasure of the club's patrons in greedily, priming his magick for whatever might happen. The sensations were weaker than normal, and he could sense Stefan drawing on them as well. The hustler was frightened. For a moment, Aaron wondered vaguely if he shouldn't go back to the club. Pig had waited four days for him at the mansion. Surely it would wait a day longer while Aaron stood with Kate and Stefan against Saffleur. Was he being obsessive?

But what if Pig chose to follow him? It might attack at some critical time in his battle with Saffleur. And what if Saffleur killed him? It could easily happen. He would die without taking his revenge against the demon. Pig would be left on Earth and, as it had demonstrated, its power was strong enough now that it could influence other humans. Aaron didn't want to allow that power to get any stronger. His grip tightened on the steering wheel. No! He had to destroy the demon now, even if it killed him in the process.

Aaron stepped sideways into the Umbra without getting out of the car. In the spirit world, the machine did not exist, and he simply found himself sitting by the side of the Umbral street, sucking in his breath against the pain of the Paradox that stepping sideways had caused. He suspected, however, that this was only going to be the beginning of the Paradox that he would accumulate tonight.

The landscape of the Umbra in Nob Hill was much like that of the seedy district around Valentine's, with geometric building-shapes reaching up toward a dim, silver-web-choked sky. There was a greater sense of history here, however, and several of the anonymous geometric shapes actually looked like their real-world counterparts. These were homes that had been lived in long enough to acquire a sort of spiritual presence in the Umbra. Aaron walked down the street, back toward the Barry mansion. While he was safe here from the eyes of the authorities, and the New World Order would not have had time yet to install Umbral cameras, Pig would certainly be watching for him. Obstacles were as opaque here as they were in the real world, though. He hid behind the corner of the dark, glassy obelisk that was the Changs' house and peered at the mansion.

The Barry mansion was one of the buildings that had a presence in the spirit world. It was as real here as it was on Earth or as real as the buildings in the pocket realm had been. The demon wards he had set surrounded it with a glowing, golden meshwork. The glow was fading slightly as the flower arrangements of the wards died, but it was still strong. It should have been more than enough to keep Pig away from the house. Yet if Pig was inside, then somehow the wards had failed to keep it out. Aaron gritted his teeth. It had been a vain hope that he could bar the demon from the mansion. Although he didn't want to think about it, Pig had first been summoned there. The mansion had been its domain for sixteen years. Nothing he did was going to be able to keep it out completely. The wards might inconvenience its passage, but they would be no barrier no matter how powerful Aaron attempted to make them.

He risked another glance around the corner. Pig would surely have rigged some sort of trap or alarm that would be tripped if he attempted to enter through one of the mansion's doors. If he broke a window to get in, Pig would hear the breaking glass. A master of the sphere of Matter magick might have been able to simply walk through the walls of the mansion, avoiding traps and broken glass. Unfortunately, he wasn't a master of Matter. He might, however, be able to accomplish something similar.

Aaron slipped around to the back of the mansion, toward the sunroom where he and Stefan had sat and talked with Saffleur. The trust he had placed in the Euthanatos made him feel almost sick, but he tried to put that behind him for now. The sunroom had nice, big French windows. There was also a telephone in the room, and he wanted to put his hands on a telephone as quickly as possible. And, if he remembered correctly, there was a large clear space without furniture just on the other side of the windows. He took a deep breath, cast his magick, and charged out of the concealing shadows toward the sunroom.

The spell was Time magick, and much like the effect he had used to get away from Kate, it accelerated his movement through the flow of time for a brief moment. This magick, however, was much more potent, worked in the Umbra away from the threat of Paradox. He streaked across the lawn of the Umbral mansion in a fraction of a second. To anyone watching, he would have been little more than a momentary blur, if they had noticed him at all. As he reached the windows of the sunroom, he leaped, arms protecting his face in case what he intended did not work. He stepped sideways out of the Umbra and back to Earth in midleap.

Accelerated in time, he passed through the windows in the moment that his body was between the two worlds. If his timing had been the slightest bit off, he might have broken the glass in either the Umbra, alerting Pig, or the physical world, alerting William and the authorities. Instead, he vanished from one world before hitting the windows and reappeared in the other on the other side. The passage had left him cold and shaking, but it had been successful. He landed back in the sunroom with no more than a soft thump that was not likely to carry through the well-constructed walls of the Barry mansion.

Still, he was quick to locate the telephone in the dimness of the room. Not bothering with coincidental magick, he used vulgar magick to freeze the mansion's entire telephone circuit in time, just as he had the New World Order cameras at Pan's. William wouldn't be able to call out to alert the authorities. Aaron grinned in spite of the shiver of Paradox that passed through him, and in spite of the sudden wilting of the floral demon ward in the sunroom, a minor manifestation of the Paradox that was building within and around him. Now he just had to find William and the demon that had possessed him before either one could realize that anything was wrong. He slipped off into the dark silence of the mansion.

Kate came slowly back to consciousness. Her mind was a haze of pain and speeding lights. Nausea wrenched at her stomach. Her body still felt the sensation of her rapid travel through the telephone system, and it took her a moment to figure out that she was sitting still again and upright in a comfortable chair. She moaned slightly and opened her eyes, squinting at first against a blinding glare of white light.

She was sitting in the parlor chair in Julia's interrogation area. The lights in the room had been left on. Kate could clearly see the big mind probe looming above her. Julia herself sat on the sofa, reading through a pile of papers, her fingers tracing her scar as she read. She looked up at Kate's moan. "Good evening, Miss Sanders," she said merrily in her interrogation voice. "How are you tonight?"

Kate gasped and started to rise. A searing pain burned through her head. She sat down again promptly, glancing back over her shoulder to see a man in black taking his hand off a small box at his belt. She knew what it was, of course: a pain stimulator. She had seen such devices used many times. She had used them once or twice when it was necessary to quiet an unruly prisoner of the New World Order. She had never expected to be the victim of one.

She had never expected to be a prisoner herself.

Her heart began to race in fright. She was in terrible, grave danger. Julia had mentioned the results of the search that she had requested. It could only be the search using the New World Order's resources that she had requested in her attempt to find Stefan and Saffleur. Julia must have found the results while they were in the pocket realm. She would want to know everything. They would know that she had strayed from the Technocracy, that she had been working with Aaron. . . .

The slightest of frowns crossed Julia's face. "A mage of the Traditions, Miss Sanders?"

They were probing her mind, she realized. Kate twisted around to glance at the two-way mirror that concealed the monitoring room. Her panic increased.

She could blot out her thoughts easily, thinking of nothing as the Technocracy itself had taught her. They would know that she was concealing something, though, and they would turn up the power on the probe until they broke through her barriers. Even the middle settings on the mind probe could make the pain stimulator look like a joy buzzer. There was no point in resisting. She turned back to Julia, resignedly. "What do you want to know?"

"Tea?"

Kate looked at the delicate cup that Julia offered her, then met her gaze. "You can spare me the games, Julia."

"Very well." Julia set the cup back down again, but her voice did not lose its soft accent and pleasant tone. She indicated the papers she had been reading. "What are these?"

Kate told her. The results of a search, requested by her four days previously, for the whereabouts of an old man and a young man matching certain descriptions, the search to be conducted using all available New World Order surveillance data. Julia nodded. "Do you know the results of that search?"

"No."

"The search located the individuals at the site of a police raid on an escort service." Julia glanced down at one of the papers. "One of the individuals, the young man, was on file in the police computer for a number of prostitution-related offenses. The other appears in none of the New World Order's databases. A witness on the scene claims to have seen both individuals vanish into thin air." She looked up. "The same witness claims to have seen a man and woman vanish at the same location only moments later. Because they were not part of the search request, no attempt was made at identification. However, your car was later found abandoned at the scene." Julia sat back on the sofa and looked at Kate expectantly. "The search results found their way onto my desk when you could not be located to receive them. Where have you been for the past four days, Kate?"

"In the Umbra. In a pocket realm."

Julia's eyebrows rose sharply. "You weren't authorized for Umbral access."

"I went with a mage of the Cult of Ecstasy in pursuit of another mage of the Euthanatos," she reported truthfully.

"Was this in connection with your assigned monitoring of Pan's?"

"Yes."

Kate glanced up. There was a clock fixed to the lab wall behind Julia. Over half an hour had passed since she had been snatched from Pan's. She bit her lip nervously, then forced her face to relax, returning to the inscrutable emotionlessness of the New World Order. If she was going to tell Julia everything, then at least she still had a chance to help Stefan. She hoped that Aaron, Stefan, and Tango could forgive her for what she was about to do, but she might yet be able to enlist the New World Order's aid in defeating Saffleur. Julia wouldn't dare pass up the opportunity to capture Stefan. At least the hustler would be saved, though she felt sorry for Aaron and Tango. She picked up the tea that Julia had offered her, sipped a bit of it, and began to tell her the whole story.

The living room was empty, although it was abundantly clear that people had been using it recently. The furniture had been pushed back against the walls, and a number of long tables set up. Papers were laid out on the tables in neat piles. Filing boxes were lined up on one table as well. Aaron peeked inside one. It was full of more papers and account books. He recognized some from his father's study. Some papers had his signature on them, others had his father's. It seemed that the authorities weren't taking the chance of overlooking anything in their search.

He clenched his jaw so tightly that his teeth hurt. Pig had outdone itself this time. As he had told Kate, he could extract himself from the legal trap the demon and William (it seemed impossible to separate the blame, since the demon couldn't have done all of this without William's knowledge) had laid for him. The real danger came from the possibility of an investigation by the Technocracy. He felt hopeless when he contemplated it. He was certain that Pig would have planted clues to give away Aaron's identity as a mage to those who knew what they were looking for. He would live in fear of investigation, and Pig would enjoy every moment of his torment.

So why was the demon waiting for him? A trap to get him arrested? It had never before waited around for him to come to it. Aaron climbed silently up the main stairs. Pig must have realized that he would attempt to destroy it. Perhaps it wanted to make him angry enough that he would kill William Pierce in an effort to get at the demon possessing him. He would be guilty of murder then, with the perfectly mundane motive of revenge against the man who had framed him. He was almost angry enough to do it, too. Almost. He knew that Pig was the true culprit and William nothing more than a dupe.

The tricks that he had picked up over fourteen years of studying with mages around the world should still surprise Pig. He hoped. The demon's growing power disturbed him. He had never thought Pig could be capable of possessing someone. Of course, he had never thought the demon could be capable of appearing in public until it had done so. What else could Pig do?

The upstairs hallway was dark except for the light that spilled out from under the door of his father's

study and from the open doorway of the room where
Pig had attacked Stefan. And, he realized, except for
the moonlight that spilled into the hallway. Just as it
had in his nightmares and just as it had on those
nights so many years ago when Pig had first tormented him. He felt his heart begin to pound in his chest,
though he tried to remain calm. It was nothing more
than a chance occurrence that the moon was shining
tonight. He slid his hand along the wall, feeling for a
light switch.

He found one and almost flipped it on out of
unconscious fright before he caught himself. The light
would give him away. He didn't need it. He took a
deep breath and forced himself to walk calmly down
the corridor to the doorway of the room with the claw-
marked walls. All of the doors in the hall were open,
although the rooms beyond were dark. They looked
like gaping mouths, lipless and wide. The moonlight
that filtered in revealed that all of the rooms had been
neatly ransacked for evidence. The bedroom where
Stefan had been attacked had also been searched.
Boxes had been pulled out of the closet. One had
overturned, spilling old photographs of Aaron across
the floor at the foot of a camera on a tripod. The
authorities had been taking pictures of the marks and
drawings that Pig had left on the wall.

He turned off the lights in the room and stepped
back into the hall, facing the door at its far end. His
father's study. Pig and William had to be in there. It
was going to be over. All of the terror, all of the torment. He was going to end it here. He walked down the
hall, one silent step at a time, past empty doorways
and past the broken grandfather clock until he stood
directly in front of the heavy door to his father's study.
Putting his hand on the knob, he opened it quietly.

William was sitting calmly at Peter Barry's desk.
There was an old revolver in his hands, and he had it

aimed directly at the door. "I've been waiting for you to come, Aaron," he said blandly. "I've been waiting every night for four nights. I knew you would come in the dark."

"Put the gun down, William."

"No." He smiled. "You're a desperate criminal, Aaron. Who knows what you might do." He gestured with his free hand to one side of the door. "I believe you know Miss Tiffany LaRouche of KKBA Television?"

Aaron hardly dared to turn his head to see if the possessed man was telling the truth, but he did. Tiffany sat back in one corner, out of the line of fire. She held a video camera steady on her shoulder.

"What are you doing here?"

"Getting a scoop," she said very seriously. "Mr. Pierce invited me to wait with him. Aaron Barry's big secret captured on tape."

Pig's final joke. This was why it had wanted him to come here. Aaron drew in his breath sharply. Tiffany might think that she was about to catch some kind of exclusive confession on tape, but she was more likely to record him in the act of working magick. The magick he had intended to work against Pig's possession of William, a sort of exorcism, simply could not be performed as coincidental magick. There was no way that it could be rationally explained as chance or a natural event, as his struggles with the demon at Pan's could be, and Tiffany would see it all. One more piece of evidence against him should the Technocracy ever get hold of that tape. Tiffany herself was one more witness to his magick. All more for him to worry about.

He could try to deal with Tiffany and her camera, but that would leave him open to William's gun. If he used magick against William first, Tiffany would record it.

The atmosphere in the room suddenly seemed oppressive and unnaturally still. The shadows had a hard edge to them. Hard and bitter. Once he had told himself that he would destroy Pig in front of the entire Technocracy if he had to. Now he would have to live up to those words. "Damn you to hell, Pig!" he spat, spreading his arms wide and letting all of the sensual power of his connection with Pan's flow through him.

William cried out and convulsed as the Spirit magick swept him up, lifting him bodily out of his chair. His finger squeezed the trigger of his revolver uncontrollably. Three bullets impacted in the wall and doorframe around Aaron. A fourth slammed into his right arm, tearing into the muscle. The arm fell to his side. There was probably pain from the wound, but Aaron barely felt it. Paradox had him in the fierceness of its own numb, aching pain. Aaron just let sweet pleasure push all the pain away. In the coarse language of the Brazilian shantytown priest-mage who had taught him this spell, he shouted at Pig to come out of William!

A fiery red light, like dying coals, flashed around William's body, turning the shadows that clung to him into a ruddy glow. The old man groaned and gasped. He writhed.

But nothing more happened. The magick died, and William sank back down into the chair. Aaron stared at him, shocked. "Nothing," he said slowly in disbelief. He stepped forward and tried to reach out to touch William's face. His arm screamed in protest, and he looked at the wound for the first time. Blood was soaking into the cloth of his shirt. He gritted his teeth. The pleasures of Pan's held the pain back. "Nothing! He wasn't possessed!" He looked up at Tiffany.

The reporter was grinning at him as she popped the videotape out of her camera. Grinning widely. Grinning cruelly. Grinning liplessly.

Aaron lifted his arm again with an incoherent yell of rage, pointing at Tiffany, raising his magick. Tiffany lifted the camera and threw it at him with Pig's strength. He dodged, trying to hold his concentration on the exorcism spell, but the camera struck his injured arm, hard enough to knock him to the ground. This time, the sudden pain was so intense that it overwhelmed all pleasure. He gasped in shock. Tiffany laughed and walked calmly out the door of the study.

Julia looked at Kate for several minutes after she had finished reciting her story. Kate tried to endure her gaze stoically, but found that she couldn't. Julia's stare was penetrating. Kate found herself beginning to sweat under it as she might have sweated under a hot light. She wondered if the mind probe was still on, then realized how ridiculous that thought was. If she had been monitoring the probe, she would have left it on until the subject had left the room.

Finally, Julia glanced away from her. "Is she lying?" she asked in her normal, flat tone of voice, looking toward the two-way mirror. The answer that came back to her over her earphone must have been negative, because she asked stiffly, "Did she lie at any time during the interview?" She nodded at the answer and added, "Did the images from the mind probe correspond with her story?"

Listening to the one-sided conversation was eerily disconcerting. Kate shifted in her chair and glanced again at the clock behind Julia. Too much time had passed in her storytelling! If she was going to get help to Stefan, it would have to be done very soon.

Julia rose suddenly, pointing at the man in black with the pain stimulator. "You may go." He nodded and left the room. Julia walked silently to one wall of the interrogation room and picked up a small device from a shelf. Kate recognized it as a pattern inhibitor, a piece of equipment commonly used to block certain memory patterns from the conscious recollection of prisoners. Memories of their visit to New World Order regional headquarters, for example. She stiffened as Julia approached her with it, fearing the worst. Julia was going to block out her memories of Aaron and Stefan!

But her superior merely paused for a moment beside her chair. "Remain seated," she said simply. She crossed the room and entered the monitoring office, closing the door behind her. Several minutes passed before a young Technomancer that she had occasionally seen around the lab walked out of the office and left the interrogation room. He nodded at her in greeting as he passed. She looked after him in wonder. Several minutes was just enough time to use the pattern inhibitor on a subject. Julia emerged from the monitoring office a moment later and took her seat on the sofa again.

"The mind probe is off, Kate. The files of the interview have been erased from the system." She looked directly into Kate's eyes. "You are an extremely lucky woman. Your behavior would normally merit severe disciplinary action. I remind you at this point that the New World Order does not tolerate repeated mistakes."

"Yes, Julia," Kate said dutifully. Her mind, however, was racing. What was Julia doing? "Why am I not being disciplined now?" she ventured.

"Because you are, as I said, extremely lucky." Then Julia glanced up at the clock. "We'll have to hurry if we want to get back to Pan's." She stood and began selecting a variety of devices from the shelves and benches lining the walls of the interrogation room. "Take what you need."

Kate's jaw dropped. Literally. "You're going to help rescue Stefan?" She rose from her chair and took a few devices for herself. One was another cellular phone. She hesitated before taking it, but the magick she could work with it was worth the risk of the New World Order retrieval circuits inside.

"I'm going to help rescue Stefan in order that he may be brought back to New World Order headquarters for study. Aaron Barry, if he survives, will also be returned to regional headquarters." There wasn't a trace of frivolity in her voice. She meant what she was saying. "Pan's will be destroyed after we are finished."

It was no more than she had expected, yet the violence of Julia's intentions struck Kate with surprising impact. She swallowed her emotions just as she had swallowed her pride when Julia had first assigned her to monitor Pan's. Stefan would survive, and that was the really important thing. "Yes, Julia," repeated Kate. "What about Saffleur?"

Julia picked up a handgun and shoved it into a holster beneath her jacket. "He's mine," she said viciously. She turned to Kate. "I told you once that everybody has secrets." She tapped the scar that marred her face with a finger. "This is one of mine. When I was a girl in Georgia, before the war with the North and before I became a mage, an old man did this to me after I almost rode him down in the street. He used a willow switch, nothing more, but it festered and scarred like a cut with a dirty knife. Later I figured out that it had to have been magick." She flushed at the memories. "People that my father talked to said he was from Louisiana, but I know that he didn't sound like he was from Louisiana. My father managed to find out his name. Saffleur." She smiled. "They say that where mages are concerned, there can never be such a thing as true coincidence."

Kate just looked at her in surprise. Julia nodded. "I think it must be the same man. People said that they'd seen him sometimes with a boy from the town. A male whore whose family had all died in nasty ways."

"Stefan in a previous life."

"I don't remember the boy's name. It wasn't important to me. I just remember the old man." Her finger traced her scar. "I can't even take this away with magick."

So it was revenge. Plain and simple and possibly the last thing Kate would have expected from the rational old Technomancer. She kept her thoughts to herself, however. "Saffleur is powerful," she said instead. "I'll order a squad of men in black to accompany us."

"No!" Julia's rejection of the idea was so strong that Kate wondered if she had just made a grave mistake. "You and I are the only ones who are to know about this. I don't want anyone else to find out." She smiled at her, a smile heavy with threatening implications. "I know I can trust you. After all, I know about your indiscretions with Aaron."

Her words left Kate with a cold feeling gnawing at the pit of her stomach. "Yes, Julia." She hesitated and then added, "I think we will need Aaron's help, though."

"That's fine. He won't be telling anyone anything once we get him back here anyway. Let's go." There was a frightening gleam of vengeance in Julia's eye, eerily reminiscent of the way Aaron looked when he talked about Pig. The obsession was as frightening in Julia as it was in him.

He wished that he had greater skill in Life magick. He could have healed himself. But he had never taken more than a cursory interest in the magick of Life. After all, Pig wasn't alive. What use was Life magick to him when there had been so much more to be learned, knowledge that he could put to better use against Pig?

Aaron forced himself to rise to his knees and then to his feet. The pain in his arm had ebbed back to a dull, throbbing ache, partially masked again by the sensations from Pan's. Pig had left William to possess Tiffany. Peter Barry's old friend moaned from the desk behind Aaron, weak from the magick the young mage had cast, but he paid no attention to him. The demon-ridden

Tiffany was already disappearing into the darkness down the hallway. "Pig!" Aaron shouted sharply.

Tiffany turned to look at him. Aaron caught the gleam of moonlight on her face. He flung out more magick, slowing time to a crawl around her. Paradox rippled painfully about him, but he trapped her. She moved as if in slow motion, reacting in sluggish surprise as he walked calmly down the hall. The demonic smile was still on her face, her lips moving too slowly to erase it. Pig stared out at him from her eyes. It had managed to resist Aaron's magick, but Tiffany hadn't. Her body had become a prison for it now. Aaron grinned harshly at it as he raised his arm again, preparing the exorcism spell. He dropped the Time magick and shouted the first words of the exorcism.

Pig did what the creator of the magick had probably never expected any demon to do. It came out of Tiffany's body on its own, using the pull of Aaron's magick to explode out like an immaterial bomb. Tiffany was knocked backward into a wall with the force of the demon's leaving. Aaron staggered, stunned, watching as the shadows beside the reporter swirled and coalesced, forming into Pig's body. The demon squatted and plucked the videotape out of Tiffany's hand. It smiled at him, yellow eyes bright. "You're no fun anymore."

"I never was any fun."

"Oh, but you were. The way you ran, the way you shrieked."

Aaron felt the old fears begin to return as the demon toyed with his memories. He slammed a shield down around his mind with a hiss and drew lightning out of the light fixtures in the hallway, just as he had to destroy the locked door of Stefan's room. Shattered glass rained down and thunder rolled in the hall. "I'm not going to run anymore!" The lightning lashed out at Pig.

The demon leaped out of the way with unnatural speed. The lightning tore a hole in the wall near Tiffany's head. Her body jerked and she opened her eyes, but Aaron didn't notice. He struck out again and again, arcs of electricity and smoke filling the air as Pig continued to dodge and Paradox wracked Aaron's body. Pig was laughing.

"I was wrong!" it shouted over the crash of the lightning and Tiffany's terrified screams. "You are still fun! You're as frightened now as you ever were!"

Aaron let go of the lightning. He was breathing hard. Pig was lost in the shadows and smoke. "I am not frightened of you!" he yelled at the unseen demon.

There was silence for a moment, then Pig whispered, "You are." Its breath was hot on the back of his neck.

In spite of himself, Aaron cried out in sudden panic and jumped away from the demon. Pig grinned and sprang at him like an animal. Aaron fell backward through an open doorway. The demon disappeared into the shadows of the room beyond.

The stench of ozone and burned wood from the lightning in the hall covered up the smell that lingered in the room, but Aaron still knew exactly where he was. His father's bedroom. He rolled over instantly, putting his back to the wall and climbing cautiously to his feet. His hand found a light switch, and this time he turned it on.

Peter Barry was lying on the bed, his emaciated face turned toward his son. "So you finally came back," he wheezed.

Aaron froze. His father's arm came up, and he gestured him closer. Aaron stepped hesitantly to the bedside. "I wanted to talk to you. I wanted to tell you I was sorry." His voice caught in his throat, and he felt for something hidden in the bedsheets. Aaron touched his other arm gently. Peter looked up at him. "I'm so sorry. . . . Sorry I didn't kill you when I had the chance!"

Peter's other arm came up holding his cane, the one with the heavy steel head, and he drove it straight at Aaron's face. Aaron dodged easily, at the same time sending his magick ripping into the pattern of the arm that he touched. The arm crumbled into dust. Peter shrieked in startled agony, his features contorting into Pig's terrifying face. The demon swung the cane again, and this time it connected, smashing into the side of Aaron's chest. Aaron heard a crack and felt a sharp pain before the sensation of his link with Pan's could cover up this new hurt.

Pig leaped out of the bed, teeth clenched. It held the cane pointed at Aaron, holding him at bay. "You're going to pay for that!"

"I think I've already paid." Aaron threw up a wall between the demon and the Umbra as he had at Pan's. Pig sensed it and snarled. Tiffany's videotape was lying on the bed. Aaron snatched it up, using magick to shred it like Pig's arm. Paradox swept over him yet again. Itself immune to the human consequences of working magick, the demon seized his moment of distraction. It lunged at him as he fought the pain of Paradox, sweeping out with the cane. Aaron stepped back. Pig broke for the door, running out into the hallway. Aaron followed.

Just as he did so, there was a gunshot from the study. He glanced back down the hall. William Pierce was lying facedown on the desk. There was a spray of blood on the fabric of the chair behind him. Aaron swore, pausing for a moment in hesitation. He saw Pig disappear around a corner in the other direction and knew where the injured demon was going to ground. The treacherous servants' stairs at the back of the house, the place where it had first appeared. He

would be able to find it easily. First, though, Aaron
went to the study.

William was dead. He had put the revolver to his
ear and used one of the last two bullets to kill himself. He had written something on one of the scraps of
paper that the authorities had left in the study. His
blood was running out over the note now, smearing
the man's final message. All that Aaron could read
was the single word *hate*. He felt numb as he walked
back out into the hall and knelt beside Tiffany.

"Can you hear me?" he asked. She nodded mutely,
her eyes wide with shock. Aaron tilted her head, forcing her to look at him. "You saw nothing tonight," he
told her, opening her mind with magick. "You passed
out. You don't know what happened except that
William finally snapped." Aaron licked his lips.
Suddenly his mouth seemed dry. He felt sorry for
William. "He told you that he framed me. It was all a
setup."

"Framed," she repeated weakly, "a setup."

"Good." On impulse, he kissed her, then stood and
strode down the hall after Pig.

Peter Barry's cane lay in a pool of moonlight at the
top of the servants' stairs. Aaron looked at it for a
minute before reaching down and picking it up. He
had never held it in his hands before. The weight of it
was less than he had expected, but then he had only
felt that weight with the force of one of his father's
blows behind it.

There was a sudden, loud, wet crack from below
and then a thud, as of something falling. Aaron
looked up, startled at the sounds. The thud was followed by a scream and a shout of anger and a confused series of blows and cries. The sounds echoed up
the stairs from the kitchen below. An illusion, a recre-
ated memory. Aaron knew what he would hear next.
The sound of a cane clattering to the floor. "Stop it,

Pig," he commanded bitterly. He looked down into the darkness. "William is dead," he said. "He shot himself."

"I thought he might do that once I left him." The demon's voice drifted out of the shadows. "He had some regrets at the end."

"Did you force him to do this to me?"

"I don't force people," Pig hissed. "William hated you already. Tiffany wanted her big story—and she hated you, too. There are a lot of people who don't like you, Aaron."

"I don't get along with most people. They don't really understand me." He stared into the gloom. "They don't understand about you."

"That's right. They couldn't believe that a demon could really exist. Your father couldn't. And then you were afraid to tell the people who could believe. They might not have understood, either, and where would you have been then?" It paused. "Do you think Michael would have believed in me?"

"Leave Michael out of this!"

"Oh, I'm sorry. Have I upset you?" The demon laughed faintly. "By the way, you might be interested in this." A thin black arm appeared out of the darkness. There was a pale string tangled in its narrow fingers. "Listen. Peter Barry's last words."

It shook the string out, and Aaron heard his father's voice whisper, "My God. You are real."

He had known in the end. He had seen Pig for himself before he died. Aaron felt stunned.

His father's last words were intended as a distraction. Aaron just barely caught the blur of movement as Pig leaped up the stairs and at him, single arm reaching out. He didn't have time to react before its talons were at his throat. But Pig's body was fading as it moved. It wasn't leaping at Aaron. It was leaping into him.

Aaron screamed as the demon's voice suddenly echoed gleefully in his brain. "Did you know that you don't like yourself very much either, Aaron?"

"Get out!"

"No." Pig seized control of his legs, propelling him closer to the top of the steep stairs. "It's so easy to fall down these stairs, Aaron. That's what happened to Michael, isn't it? You remember—you must."

"No! Damn you, get out!"

"You can't make me."

Aaron forced his arms up, fighting the demon for possession of his own mind. Suddenly, Pig let go, and the exorcism spell took effect. The pleasures of Pan's, the ache of Paradox, and the tearing pain of the spell all surged through Aaron at once. He screamed and fell to his knees, teetering on the edge of the stairs. Pig just laughed. "You can't get rid of me, Aaron! I'll get stronger and stronger, and there's not a thing you can do about it. Don't fight it!"

He could feel the demon's presence in his mind, the magick of the exorcism flowing harmlessly around it, and suddenly an idea struck Aaron. "All right," he spat.

He turned the exorcism inside out. Instead of trying to force Pig from his mind, he held it there. The demon's laughter abruptly became a yelp of surprise as the magick solidified around it, slowly squeezing it into a tiny pocket of Aaron's mind. A prison that locked it harmlessly away. It began to fight to get out.

And Aaron reversed his magick again, pushing the demon along in the direction that it wanted to go. The pain of Paradox was becoming excruciating, but Pig flew out of Aaron's body, just as he had flown from Tiffany's. Before it could reform its own body, though, Aaron had stabbed the steel head of his father's cane into the middle of it. Through the haze of Paradox, he worked a final act of magick. Pig screamed as its immaterial form was drawn into the cane and trapped.

Aaron stood still, gasping for breath after his struggle. He felt numb. The bullet wound in his arm, the deep pain in his side from Pig's blow, even the crushing weight of Paradox seemed remote. He felt strange. Light-headed. There was a crash from downstairs as the authorities finally realized that something was happening in the house and responded to it. Aaron calmly stepped sideways into the Umbra to avoid them. Strangely, no further Paradox touched him as he did so.

He walked back to his car through the Umbra in a daze, his hands rubbing the smooth cold surface of his father's cane and his enemy's trap. It was over. But he felt as though his grip on reality was weakening.

The drive back to Pan's passed in a fog. Aaron suddenly found himself walking through the doors of the club. He hoped, distantly, that he wasn't too late to help Stefan. The hustler understood what he had had to do. He would appreciate his triumph.

A coat from his car covered the blood on his arm, but he must have looked like hell, because people shied away from him in the crowded club. The bouncer at the door almost refused him entry, but Aaron overwhelmed his mind with magick (and again there was no Paradox) and walked on. He stopped a bartender and asked for Tango. It seemed as though she had her hand on his arm before the words were even out of his mouth. Stefan had his other arm, and they quickly eased him to the floor. A crowd was gathering around him to watch. Kate hovered over him and another woman, older and with a horrible scar on her face.

"Aaron," Tango asked, "what's wrong? What happened?"

He held his good arm up. Somebody took it. Stefan. "I beat Pig," he said weakly. "I won."

Suddenly he felt dizzy. Tango was saying something to him, but she might as well have been miles away. Stefan's hand twisted in his grasp. "Help," Aaron managed to gasp before reality spun away from him, and he found himself in darkness.

17

Stefan looked up at Kate desperately. She shook her head, answering his unasked question. "I don't know what's wrong with him."

She and Julia had arrived only about ten minutes before. Kate had been relieved to find that Tango and Stefan were still waiting for them at Pan's. Tango had regarded Julia with instant suspicion. She had looked upon Kate almost as a traitor until the Technomancer had been able to take her aside and explain what had happened.

Julia touched a device to Aaron's temple and nodded as it produced a readout of brain activity. "He's in Quiet."

Kate winced. Stefan saw her reaction and tightened his grip on Aaron's hand. "What's that?"

Tango gestured for some bouncers to keep the crowd around them back, then said quietly. "Something that happens to mages when they build up too much Paradox. They lose their hold on reality and retreat into their mind. Like a dream." She shook her head. "It can last for hours or days."

"Or weeks or months," Kate added. "There's no telling when they'll find their way back to reality." She cursed suddenly, frustrated with the Ecstasy Cultist. Julia gave her a displeased look. Technomancers didn't allow themselves to become irrational enough to curse. Kate ignored her, however. "I was counting on him to help us against Saffleur."

"We don't need his help," Julia said confidently.

"It would be easier if we had it!" she snapped back.

Stefan turned his gaze from one of them to the other. "Is there anything we can do for him?"

"No." Julia put her device away and stood. "He's stuck in his own mind. There's nothing we can do but wait for him to come out on his own."

Tango looked up at her. "He's going to be a sitting duck when Saffleur comes."

"Unavoidable."

"Convenient for you."

"Yes." She turned to the crowd of patrons that had gathered to see what the commotion was about. "Move along," she said imperiously. "There's nothing to see here. It's all under control. He just fainted. He'll be all right." The crowd began to disperse.

Kate hissed in frustration with Julia. Couldn't she see past her obsession for revenge and the rivalry of the Technocracy and the Traditions? If they could come up with a way to bring Aaron out of his Quiet, they would have a better chance of defeating Saffleur! She put her hand on Aaron's arm, then suddenly pulled it away as something warm and sticky soaked through the cloth. "He's bleeding!"

Tango pulled out her knife and carefully cut away the sleeve of his jacket. She inspected the wound in his arm but didn't attempt to remove his shirt sleeve. The cloth had become embedded in the clotting blood. "He's been shot. Not too serious."

Stefan swallowed suddenly. "He's not going to die, is he?" He rubbed Aaron's hand between his palms as if that would wake him up. "Fuck! Not him, too!"

"He's not going to die from this, if that's what you mean." Tango knotted the cutoff sleeve of Aaron's jacket around his arm like a bandage. "Saffleur might well do him in, though."

"Shit!" Stefan looked beseechingly at Kate. "Isn't there anything we can do?"

Kate glanced hotly at Julia, bit her lip, and said cautiously, "Mages have been helped through Quiet before. Another mage can sometimes slip inside their mind and guide them out."

"So do it!"

Julia scowled harshly at her. Kate turned her back on her superior. "We can't spare a mage right now. Both Julia and I have to stay conscious for Saffleur's arrival."

"Send me," suggested Tango.

"His mind will be sealed. I could put you inside him, but you wouldn't be able to get through to him." Kate touched Aaron's head gently. "You would need magick to break through the barrier of Quiet." She looked at Stefan. "But if the person going in already had a link with Aaron's mind, they wouldn't have to worry about a barrier."

Stefan nodded. "I can still feel Pan's and I can feel him. He's frightened, Kate. The link is still active." He took a deep breath. "I'll do it."

"It will be dangerous. You could be stuck in his Quiet as well."

"Am I waiting for anything better to come from Saffleur?" He grinned madly. "And won't it piss him off royally if I do get stuck?"

"That would all be vulgar magick, Kate," pointed out Julia with a frown.

"I've done it before."

"In the Umbra, not on Earth. You will be threatening the stability of reality just as any mage of the Traditions might!" She pressed her lips together in a hard line. "He is not that important. I won't permit you to do it."

Kate reached out and abruptly touched Stefan on the forehead. The hustler dropped to the ground instantly, falling across Aaron. Kate looked at Julia defiantly, even as Paradox stabbed into her. "Too late," she hissed through the pain.

Julia turned red with rage and reached into her coat. "You—"

"No." Tango caught the Technomancer's arm and looked her squarely in the eye. "We have to work together. What does your New World Order rationality tell you about that?"

Kate climbed slowly to her feet, watching the standoff. Julia could have burned out the small woman's mind in an instant. Tango looked like she could have killed Julia with her bare hands and working on physical reflexes alone. They stared at each other like fighting tigers. When they finally broke apart, it seemed to be by some kind of mutual consent. Julia glanced at Kate. "I will deal with your disobedience later. You," she said tightly to Tango, "are going to regret that we ever met."

"I already do." She pointed to Aaron and Stefan and signaled for the help of a bouncer. "Let's get these two somewhere less conspicuous."

Before they could do more than lift Stefan off the floor, though, Kate motioned them to stop. She swept her gaze around the club, looking for something she couldn't quite locate. "Saffleur is here."

"Aaron?" called Stefan hesitantly. "Aaron?"

He had recognized the upstairs hallway of the Barry mansion as soon as he opened his eyes. But the scale was all wrong. Everything was larger than it should have been. The doorways and windows were taller and broader, the ceiling was higher. The hallway itself seemed longer. It was eerily silent, too. Moonlight shone through the windows, creating bright pools on the floor.

"Aaron?" he called again.

"Stefan?" Aaron stepped out of the shadows beside him. The mage was wearing red-and-white-striped pyjamas. So, Stefan realized, was he. Aaron was sweating and pale. "What are you doing here?"

"Kate sent me. You passed out in Pan's. Julia says you slipped into Quiet."

Aaron looked over his shoulder as if something might be behind them. "Who's Julia?"

"Kate's boss in the New World Order."

"She brought her to Pan's?" he asked in disbelief.

"She's going to help us fight Saffleur, but I have to get you out of here." He frowned slightly as Aaron looked back over his shoulder again. "Is something wrong?"

"I'm living my nightmare, Stefan." He nodded into the darkness and whispered, "Pig is out there somewhere."

"It isn't real, Aaron. This is all in your mind."

"I know what Quiet is!" he spat harshly. He motioned Stefan to follow him and slipped stealthily along the dark hallway. "I know what I have to do to get out, too. I have to destroy Pig."

"But you said that you already beat him."

"I have to do it again."

"Why?"

"I just have to!"

"Aaron . . ." He reached out, putting his hand on Aaron's shoulder in concern.

The mage yelled and turned on him. "Don't touch me! Don't you ever touch me!"

"But I just—"

"I told you I'm not into gay sex! I'm not interested in men! Jesus Christ, will you just leave me alone!" He whirled away from Stefan.

Two yellow eyes opened in the shadows in front of him, and a cruel smile of sharp teeth blossomed. Aaron screamed and grabbed for Stefan. Suddenly the hustler found himself being shoved in front of Pig as Aaron ran into the darkness. Stefan froze as the demon's eyes settled on him. It stepped out of the shadows, moonlight running like water over its skin, and stalked around him like a hungry cat. Then it dropped to all fours and took off after Aaron.

Stefan felt sick. Aaron had been willing to sacrifice him to get away from Pig. Not in an attempt to capture the demon—he might have agreed to that—but in a desperate, panicked attempt simply to flee from it. This wasn't the real Pig, just a replica in Aaron's dream, but the mage's action might as well have been real. His rejection stung as well, of course. It had been as harsh a rejection as he had ever felt. But his betrayal . . . that hurt more than words could describe. As much as Marilyn's death or Mike's suicide.

Hot tears of pain welled up in his eyes, and he felt the clarity of a reality shift wash out of him. This time he didn't feel like fighting it. He pushed aside the protection of the pleasant sensations of Pan's and let the clarity flow. On the walls around him, the wallpaper began to peel and the wood to twist and warp. Even the silver moonlight turned muddy. Death and loss were his reality. They were all he had ever known. Saffleur had ensured that with his manipulations of his life . . . or lives.

Somewhere down the hall a door slammed. Stefan looked up through his tears. He was going to die, just as all things died, but he would be damned before he allowed Saffleur to control his life any further. He needed Aaron. He had to get him out of here. And even if Aaron had rejected and betrayed him, he still felt a warmth in his heart for the mage. Kate might have been cynical about Aaron, but Stefan wasn't going to let his developing friendship with him die so easily. He wasn't going to lose Aaron as he had lost everybody else.

Grimly, he set off in the direction Aaron and Pig had gone. Reality curdled as he walked. He didn't bother trying to control the reality shifts. If this was all a dream in Aaron's mind, what harm could they do?

"Saffleur?" Julia had her hand on her gun. "Where? How do you know?"

"Someone was using magick." Kate looked around the club again. She had felt something stir in the air. A shiver, a trembling. "It wasn't me. It wasn't you. It certainly wasn't Aaron. That means it was probably Saffleur." She gestured to a nearby table, just vacated by some of the club's patrons. "Sit them at that table and hide their faces. We want to create as little stir as possible. Saffleur is here."

Tango glanced at the bouncer and nodded. They had Aaron and Stefan at the table in an instant, their heads down as if passed out. Tango commandeered two half-empty glasses of beer from a passing waitress and arranged them on the table.

Julia followed Kate's gaze. "Correspondence magick?"

"Probably. I've seen him use it before."

"What now?" asked Tango.

"We hope that we find Saffleur before he finds Aaron and Stefan. Pan's is a fairly big place. Where is the control room for your security system? We can use the system to locate him."

"I'll show you."

"Stay here." Julia stopped the small woman, earning an angry glare from her. She returned the glare coolly. "Someone has to stay with Stefan and Aaron. Saffleur has no idea who you are, you can't help us with what we have to do, and," she added, "I suspect that you could take care of yourself reasonably well. You're the logical choice."

Tango growled at her, but could not dispute her reasoning. "Show them to security," she ordered the bouncer. "Tell whoever is there that I said to let them have free run of the place." She grabbed Kate's hand. "Good luck." Pointedly ignoring Julia, she sat down at the table, her eyes alert.

The bouncer led them to a little room somewhere past Tango's office. The first thing Julia did was order the bouncer and the security guards to get out. She shut the door behind them and locked it, then settled herself behind a console of monitors. She sneered. "This is primitive."

"They're not Technomancers."

"Aaron could have done better."

"He didn't want to arouse anyone's suspicions." Kate sat down, watching the monitors intently. "This would be much easier if I were to use vulgar magick."

"That's an extremely bad habit to get into, Kate. There is a reason we don't teach vulgar magick to young Technomancers." Julia pulled the scanner she had used on Aaron out of her purse and began tinkering with it. "The retrieval effect that drew you through the phone was vulgar. Even though the retrieval circuitry in the phone was acceptable by New World Order standards, the technology is too advanced for reality to accept. But a Technomancer using vulgar magick is more damaging to reality than a mage of the Traditions using vulgar magick. After all, we are the ones who created this reality. We must work our magick coincidentally whenever possible in order to preserve and maintain it." She snapped the cover of the scanner closed with a satisfied nod. "Besides which, there is nothing that vulgar magick can accomplish that coincidental magick, given time and patience, cannot."

She set the scanner on top of the master controls for Pan's security system and pressed a button. Instantly, the security monitors began to flicker, switching rapidly between the views offered by different cameras. Each view was held for only a few moments, just long enough for the powerful miniature computer inside the scanner to analyze the picture. One of the monitors froze after a moment, one figure in the picture highlighted. "Is that him?" asked Julia sharply.

"No." Kate shook her head. "Far too young. Saffleur is probably the only old person in Pan's. Basically similar facial structure, though." Julia made some adjustments to the scanner, reprogramming the parameters of its pattern-recognition instructions, and started the search again. "Your initial search was remarkably accurate."

"I programmed his description from memory. He doesn't seem to have changed substantially from the day I encountered him. And if he is as old as you say, he must have built up incredible amounts of Paradox in extending his life."

"I touched his mind once," Kate confessed. "He's obsessed with maintaining his life. Maybe he spends a lot of time in the altered reality of the pocket realm we entered."

"Mages who spend too much time away from Earth in the Umbra tend to become insane. From your description of his behavior, he seems very sane to me. Obsessed perhaps, but sane."

"What about what he has done to Stefan?"

"He appears to have felt that it was necessary." She turned back to the monitors. "There is a difference between necessity and insanity." The monitor froze again. "There," Julia breathed.

There was no doubt that it was Saffleur this time. Kate manipulated the controls of the security system.

The picture jumped suddenly as the camera caught up to him again. "Camera thirty-nine." Kate consulted a diagram of the club's security system on the wall above the monitors. "He's at the back of the club, moving toward the front."

"Good. That will give us a chance to intercept him." Julia stood. "We'll deal with him quickly, before he can react."

Kate frowned at the monitor suddenly. There was someone walking with Saffleur, but just behind him, drifting along in the wake of the Euthanatos like a zombie. A big man. "He has someone with him."

"Hit Saffleur first. We can figure out who the other person is afterwards." She checked her gun as she walked briskly out the door, then slid it back into its concealed holster. Kate followed, cellular phone in hand. The phone was far less conspicuous than the gun, but no less deadly. She just wished that she had had time to remove the Technocracy's retrieval circuits from the device.

It was difficult to move quickly through the crowd, but at least they had the consolation that Saffleur would have to face the same problem. The many patrons of Pan's also provided them with cover, although their conservative clothing stood out painfully in comparison with the attire of those around them. Something was subtly wrong, however. The crowd seemed more irritable than Kate remembered it being before. The air seemed heavier, smokier. The music had a rough edge. She glanced up toward the front of the club and the dance floor. Static was shooting irregularly across the big video wall. A fight broke out. A waitress dropped a tray of drinks. A woman stood up suddenly and slapped the man she was sitting with before walking away angrily. The man looked after her and began to cry. It was as if everything was falling apart, decaying in small and subtle ways.

Kate stopped Julia. "Stefan is altering reality again!"

"Are you sure? Could Saffleur be using Entropy magick?"

"Why would he?" Kate shook her head. "It's Stefan. The shifts aren't nearly as strong as they usually are, but they're covering the whole club."

Julia gritted her teeth. "If we know it, then Saffleur must know it as well. This close, he may be able to find their center and track down Stefan. We'll have to hurry."

There was light shining out from under one of the doors in the dark hallway. Stefan opened it.

He walked into Pan's and the middle of an orgy.

The club was filled with people. They were having sex, drinking, taking drugs, eating, and indulging in other vices that Stefan wasn't sure had names. The air was hazy with incense and filled with powerful, throbbing music. The connection that he had, through Aaron, to the real Pan's suddenly swelled to a torrential rush of pleasure that almost drove him to his knees. The clarity of his pain vanished into that pleasure. He wanted to throw himself into the orgy that was before him, indulging himself in all of his desires.

He resisted the urge, however, and waded into the sea of flesh only in an attempt to cross it. Hands reached out to pull at him insistently, but he pushed them away. It wasn't hard to spot Aaron. He was on the dance floor, reclining on a high couch built out of video monitors and covered in billows of white silk. A number of women were lavishing their attentions upon his body.

Stefan stepped up to him boldly. "What is this?"

Aaron sighed with blissful satisfaction. "Ecstasy, Stefan, ecstasy. The real source of magick. Relax. Enjoy yourself. Join in."

Two of the women left Aaron to approach him. He glanced at them. "I'm not interested."

They changed smoothly into men in midstride. Stefan still turned them away. "No. Aaron, what are you doing? What about Pig? Why did you throw me in front of it?"

At the mention of the demon's name, the entire room froze for a moment before resuming its orgy with a suddenly desperate intensity. Aaron sat up, pushing the women away from him. They came back, though, and he didn't shove them away again. He just looked at Stefan as if they weren't even there. "I had to," he said simply. "I had to get away from it." He gestured around the room. "Pig can't touch me here. There are too many people for it to appear. And I gather power to use against it." He hissed in sudden sharp pleasure as one of the women did something to him. "I'm safe here, Stefan! I'm safe!"

"You have to go back, Aaron. Don't you care about me at all?"

"Stefan . . ." Aaron reached out as if to touch his face, but his fingers didn't quite make contact. He held them just inches above Stefan's cheek. Stefan leaned toward him. Aaron pulled his hand back. "I can't."

"You can't go back or you can't care about me?"

"I just can't!" His hands moved convulsively, drawing one of the women up to kiss him. "I can't," he repeated in a mumble, his lips pressed against hers.

Cold pain filled Stefan's belly. "You're afraid. You're afraid of Pig and you're afraid of me." The pain rolled through his body. "Why? You have the power to stop Pig! You've already beaten him, but you're still afraid!" He pulled the woman away from Aaron. "And why the hell are you afraid of me at all? I love you, Aaron!"

"No!" He reached for another woman, but Stefan

thrust all of them away from him. "Give them back to me, Stefan! I need them! They keep Pig away!"

He jumped off the bed of monitors, leaping into the orgy. Women's hands stripped off his pyjama top with their caresses, leaving him barechested. They tugged at the ring piercing his nipple. People offered him rich food, red wine, and drugs. Sensation. Vice.

Stefan spat on the ground. "You're hiding, Aaron. You're hiding behind your ecstasy!"

"I need it! You wouldn't understand the pain, Stefan!"

"Wouldn't I?" he asked angrily. He dragged the pain of loss and death out of his stomach and heart and let it fill his whole body. "Wouldn't I?" He struck out deliberately with the clarity, focusing it.

The wine in Aaron's mouth turned to vinegar. The food in his hands turned to foul mush. The drugs disintegrated into stale powders and age-yellowed crystals. The woman around him and all of the people at the orgy shriveled suddenly, wasting away. "You say that you're trying to fight Pig," Stefan shouted, "but you're still afraid of it! You're still afraid of me! You're hiding yourself in pleasure and trying to say that it's a weapon!"

"It is!" Aaron met his gaze.

The sensations that the mage threw at him were so sharp that they stabbed into him, threatening to overload his mind. His legs shook with sudden, rapturous delight. Sweet delirium tried to engulf his pain. Stefan held on to the pain, though, and drove it back at Aaron. He sent it flooding into the flaws in the mage's pleasure that were Aaron's own pain and twisted it sharply. Aaron screamed as his shield of ecstasy shattered. He staggered to his feet and fled from the room, splashing through the puddle of darkness that was sliding under the door and forming into the dream-Pig. Stefan followed him recklessly, back out into the dark hallway of the Barry mansion. Pig followed as well, but he had no eyes for the demon.

Saffleur had definitely sensed the reality shifts emanating out of Stefan. When Kate and Julia finally spotted him in person, he was weaving through the crowds of Pan's, heading more or less in the direction of the unconscious hustler. "He still can't locate him directly," Kate observed.

"He'll be able to see him if he keeps going, though." Julia drew her gun but kept it hidden under her jacket.

"You're going to have a hard time shooting him without hitting someone else. You could kill someone."

"I want Saffleur dead," Julia said pointedly. "I'll do what I have to. How about you? Do you want him to get hold of Stefan again?" Without waiting for a reply, she indicated a staircase that led up to one of the platforms suspended above the main dance floor of the club. They would hide behind it and emerge after Saffleur had passed, surprising him from behind. "Besides, the bullets are magickal." She smiled grimly. "They'll pass through anything but their target."

They slipped in behind the stairs. Saffleur walked by not ten feet from them. The big man still followed him. Whenever the mage stopped, he stopped as well. He was large enough that Saffleur disappeared completely when he was behind him. Julia touched Kate's arm, and they stepped out in Saffleur's wake. Julia brought out her gun, and Kate began to dial a spell on her cellular phone.

Suddenly, reality in the club changed again. Where everything had been hard-edged and dark, with the hint of death and violence in the air, now the mood was . . . sexual. Kate could feel it tugging at her and even Julia seemed discomforted. The Sleepers were drawn into the reality shift instantly, groping and kissing. The movements of the dancers suddenly lost all relationship with the beat of the music.

"Is this Stefan, too?" Julia demanded.

Kate shook her head. "I think it's Aaron."

"He can do this as well?"

"No." She frowned. "It might be the link between them. Aaron is connected to the pleasures of Pan's, and his magick is based on pleasurable sensations. Stefan is connected to Aaron. If Aaron's pleasures overwhelm Stefan's pain . . ." She put one hand to her head and screwed up her eyes. "I don't know! It doesn't make any sense!

"Now you see why Technocratic reality makes things so much easier?" Julia looked ahead. "Saffleur must have stopped."

The large man was standing stock still, immobile amid the sudden orgy that Pan's had become, hiding Saffleur with his bulk. Julia motioned for Kate to go around to one side of him. She would take the other. They moved.

Saffleur was gone.

"Damn it!" swore Julia, "Where is—"

She got no further before a hand reached out of the crowd and grabbed for her gun arm. A second hand appeared to clutch her throat, and Saffleur reappeared from the masses of people around them. Julia's face began to turn purple even before Kate could take the two steps that separated her from the Euthanatos. His leg kicked back. She dodged, then brought her cellular phone up to his ear and pressed a button. The scream of the phone was piercing. He released Julia in shock and pain. Kate grabbed her arm, dragging her away. Saffleur whirled after them. He pulled a bone from his coat pocket—Kate recognized the ancient ogre bone—and thrust it at them. Kate felt a deep ache in her own bones as his magick seized her.

Then reality changed again, spinning madly between wild pleasure and bitter, painful loss and decay like an out-of-control pendulum. The shifts broke Saffleur's magick and sent him reeling as though he had been kicked in the stomach. Kate pulled Julia off into the crowd. Reality settled down again after a moment, going back to the darkness of Stefan's projections. It was stronger, though, and Kate could feel the loss and pain behind the reality shifts.

Julia gasped for breath and croaked, "Where are we going?"

"Back to Aaron and Stefan! We'll make a stand around them!"

"We'll lead him to them!"

"He would find them on his own anyway!"

Tango looked up at them as they pushed through the crowd. "What has been going on?" she demanded. Her silver knife was in her hand.

"You resisted the reality changes?"

"I have my secrets." She saw Saffleur elbowing his way through Pan's patrons behind them. "Oh, shit." Kate pulled her back to stand with her and Julia.

The mage's face twisted in anger as he saw them clustered protectively in front of Stefan and Aaron. He pointed at the hustler. "I want him."

Julia stepped forward. Her gun was in her hand and trained on him. "Do you remember me, Saffleur?" she challenged him coldly.

"No," he snapped. "Should I?"

Julia hissed in outrage and fired. Saffleur's ogre bone flicked out. Kate wasn't sure exactly what happened to the bullets, but Saffleur was unharmed. With a howl of anger, Julia dropped the gun and charged the Euthanatos, any vestige of Technomancer rationality forgotten in her thirst for revenge.

"No, Julia!" Kate yelled.

Saffleur whipped the talisman of the woman with

the beetle head from his pocket and shoved it at her. "Great Lady," he shouted as he stepped to the side, "swallow her mind!"

Julia's momentum carried her past him and into the chest of the big man who was with him. She bounced off and fell to the ground. She was still breathing, but her eyes stared blankly as though she were already dead. The mage looked up at Kate, lips drawn back from his teeth.

"Who was she?" he asked.

"Her name was Julia," replied Kate numbly, staring at her superior's mindless body. "She wanted vengeance. You scarred her when she was young."

"I have scarred a lot of people." He stepped closer to them. "You're Kate, I believe? You seem sensible enough for a Technomancer. I want the Angel. You can go."

Kate looked up from Julia's body. The Angel? Presumably, he was referring to Stefan. Rationally, she should let the Euthanatos have him. She didn't want to end up like Julia. Stefan's pain should have been nothing to her. If she gave him up now, she could track Saffleur down at some time in the future and deal with him then. This was what the training of the Technocracy told her to do. Rationally.

But she had seen the Technocracy challenged in so many ways recently, and her faith in it had been challenged as well. Rationality wouldn't save her if Saffleur decided to go back on his word and kill her anyway. It didn't seem unlikely that he would do just that. And she did care about Stefan. She cared about his pain, and she didn't want to see him die. Against all rational thought, she looked at Saffleur, put on the cold mask of the New World Order, and stalled desperately for time.

"Who do you mean by 'the Angel'?"

Saffleur pointed the Great Lady at her. She forced her face to remain neutral. "Stefan, you fool! Stefan!"

"Then why didn't you call him Stefan?"

"I might as well have called him Juan or Alexander or Marc or Johnathon or Shih or any of the other names he's had. His name in this cycle is as unimportant as it was in any of the others!"

"Is he really some kind of angel?"

"No! He's only human. 'Angel' is just a name. A convenient name."

"He's no good to you right now anyway," Kate said calmly. "He's in Quiet."

She thought Saffleur was going to foam at the mouth, so agitated did he become. "That's impossible!" he screamed.

Kate took advantage of his distraction to punch a few numbers into her cellular phone with her thumb. She could feel Tango tensing beside her and shot the woman a warning glance. "It's not his Quiet," she explained. "He insisted on trying to help Aaron."

"Then wake him up! I need him now!"

"I can't." She punched a few more numbers into her phone, building up a spell. "There's no way to reach him."

"Then I'll kill Aaron."

"You'll kill Stefan, too."

"What's your hurry?" asked Tango, getting into the game.

Saffleur scowled. "It is time for the final event in the cycle of his life. The final turning. The final death."

Kate gaped in surprise. Her thumb hovered over the next-to-last digit in her spell, forgotten in the aftermath of the mage's announcement. "But you said in the pocket realm that the final death wouldn't come for a few more days!"

"I'm used to speaking in Earth time, even in the Great Lady's realm. I'm sure you noticed the differences in the flow of time between Earth and that realm? Those days have passed." His scowl turned into a sudden grin as he realized that his news had caught her off guard. "Tonight Pan's will see the final turning of Stefan's life and the end of another cycle in the Angel's existence."

The shifts in reality ended abruptly. The world returned to normal inside Pan's. Both Kate and Saffleur turned simultaneously to glance at Stefan.

Stefan tackled Aaron roughly, bringing him crashing to the floor. Something—Pig—sailed over them in the darkness, but Stefan ignored it. Straddling Aaron's chest and pinning his arms to the floor, he gasped for breath. His pain was still raging in him, but he wasn't angry with Aaron any longer. The mage was afraid, so desperately and deeply afraid that the fear was ruling his life. Had ruled his life, Stefan realized, for years. He looked into Aaron's eyes. He could feel his fear like a hot knife through his guts.

Aaron was crying. "Nobody believed me!" he sobbed. "Nobody else could see it!"

He didn't have to ask what Aaron meant. The dream-Pig's eyes gleamed at him out of the shadows, just as yellow and frightening as the real demon's eyes. He stared back at them. This was the desperate fear that had caused Aaron to throw him in front of the creature. This was the fear that had caused him to run out on the hustler and Kate at Pan's. Fear— Aaron's pain.

He turned back to Aaron. "Nobody else could see it?"

"Nobody! There was nobody that I could tell who would believe me."

"What about your father? Couldn't you tell him?"

Aaron screamed suddenly and cringed away. Stefan could feel a presence nearby. Not Pig. He looked up.

A big man loomed in the shadows, frozen like a statue. Another element of Aaron's nightmare brought into the Quiet, Stefan guessed. He held a cane upraised in his hand, a cane with a heavy steel head. Stefan recognized the cane. Aaron had brought it back with him from the Barry mansion. The man's pose was unmistakable. He was preparing to strike. Aaron began to scream for the man, begging him to listen and babbling to him about Pig. Finally, he collapsed into shuddering sobs.

"Your father beat you?" Stefan whispered in shock. "Why? Because of Pig?"

Aaron just stared at him, his chest heaving as tears fell from his eyes. Stefan was reminded again of how much the mage reminded him of Mike, deep secrets aching inside a shell of strength. Impulsively, he bent down and kissed him tenderly.

"Goddamn it!" Suddenly, Aaron's father was moving, lashing out with the cane. Stefan rolled off Aaron with a gasp of surprise. The cane whistled through the space where his head had been. Peter Barry grabbed Stefan with his free hand, hauling him to his feet. "Son of a bitch! You little shit!" He shook Aaron roughly. "What the hell are you doing?"

"It was the demon again! It was Pig!"

Peter's face twisted in disgust . . . and, strangely, fear. "There are no such things as demons. You're going crazy on me, aren't you? You're going to tell!"

"No, Father!" Aaron shrieked. "There is a demon! There is! I'm not going to tell! I'm not going to tell!"

Stefan watched, stunned and puzzled. The dream-Pig winked at him and disappeared toward a pool of white light blossoming in the shadows. Peter threw Aaron to the ground.

"You are going crazy! But you aren't going to tell, are you? You aren't going to tell!"

"No!"

"No what?" He raised his cane.

Aaron shrank back. "No, I'm not going to tell! There isn't a demon! I'm never going to do it again! I promise!" He screamed as the cane came swinging down.

"Stop it!" Stefan wrenched the cane away from the dream-figure of Aaron's father before he could hit his son again. He couldn't just watch this, no matter how much it mystified him. The man turned on him. Stefan struck out with the cane, but he dodged, slipping in with surprising speed to punch him hard on the jaw. A second punch landed in the pit of his stomach, doubling him over. "Aaron!" he gasped. A double-handed blow to his back sent him to his knees.

The mage stared at him. He was caught up in confusion, Stefan realized. Afraid of Pig and afraid of his father, beaten into mysterious silence. What had he done? What couldn't he talk about? No wonder he hated his father. No wonder he was afraid of Pig. For two years, he had faced an unbeatable terror, and not only had he been alone in facing it, he had been battered every time he mentioned it. But why?

"Aaron?" he gasped again, pleading with his friend for help. Peter Barry pulled the cane from his grasp and lifted it over his head.

"No!" Aaron finally moved, coming to his feet with a yell. "Not again, damn you! Not again!" He struck out with his magick. Stefan wasn't sure what he did, but suddenly Peter was gone. Aaron was helping him to his feet and hugging him desperately. Stefan hugged him back. The mage was trembling.

They held each other silently for a moment, until Stefan asked, "What couldn't you tell?"

"I can't say."

He was still afraid. Stefan put a hand under his chin and lifted his head to kiss him again. At first, Aaron was stiff, but gradually he relaxed. Stefan pulled back, though not too far. "You're going to have to face your fear before we can get out of here."

"I know. But it's hard, Stefan." Aaron swallowed. "It

was two years like that! Pig on one side, Father on the other."

"Your father is dead, Aaron. And you said yourself that you've beaten Pig." Stefan stroked his hand soothingly over Aaron's back. "What caused it all?"

Aaron pointed numbly at the pool of white light where Pig had disappeared. Stefan looked.

It was the base of the steep, dark servants' stairs in the Barry mansion kitchen. There was a body lying there, that of a red-haired boy dressed in a pair of Aaron's red-and-white-striped pyjamas. Blood spilled out across the linoleum of the kitchen floor. "Who is he?" Stefan asked quietly.

"Michael. A . . . friend."

"You know that I had a friend named Mike, too?"

"That's what Kate told me."

"What happened to him, Aaron?"

"Don't ask. I don't want to remember."

But Aaron's denials were useless when everything around him was formed from his memories and dreams. The scene of the kitchen and the stairs shifted. There was no body. Instead, Stefan watched as Michael and a dark-haired boy that could only be Aaron stood on the bottom step of the servants' stairs. They kissed.

"He was staying over." Aaron stared at his younger self and his childhood friend. "He did that a lot. We were only thirteen. We were experimenting."

Suddenly, there was a large shadow looming out of the darkness of the stairs. Peter Barry's heavy cane came down on Michael's head. He fell, and all young Aaron did was stare at him in shocked silence for a moment. Then he screamed. Peter shouted in anger and slapped him viciously. Aaron cried out. Peter hit him again. And again. And again. The two slowly faded from sight, Peter still beating Aaron, until all that was left was Michael, lying on the cold, bloodstained kitchen floor.

"Jesus," whispered Stefan weakly.

"My mother had died the year before. My father had been drinking a lot." Aaron pulled away from Stefan to kneel beside Michael's broken body. "He made me promise never to tell what happened and never to kiss another man again. He called the cops and told them that Michael had fallen down the stairs in the middle of the night. He bribed them to make the story stick."

"And then Pig came and started frightening you. Your father was scared you were breaking down and would tell the police what really happened."

"More than that." He rose, taking Stefan's hand and leading him to the base of the stairs. Pig's eyes peered at them from the darkness above.

"When someone becomes a mage," Aaron said softly, "we call it their Awakening. Sometimes an Awakening is linked to traumatic events, and sometimes the mage works magick unconsciously." He wiped tears away from his eyes. "I Awoke the night my father murdered Michael. I summoned Pig into this world out of my fear." He started to shake uncontrollably.

Stefan pulled Aaron into a hug, holding him and rocking him gently. "I did it to myself, Stefan!" Aaron whispered. "I summoned Pig out of fear, and it just kept terrifying me. I was too scared even to work magick again until a mage found me in England." He buried his face in Stefan's hair and sobbed. "I should have told someone what my father did. I should have tried to stop him. But I couldn't! There was nothing I could do! No one would have believed me about Pig or about my father!"

"Shhhh." Stefan held him close. "It's over now. You can let it out."

"No." Aaron pushed him back. "There's no time. We have to get out of here and rescue you." He looked up the dark stairs to where the dream-Pig lurked. "I have to face my fears." He took Stefan's hand. The hustler could still feel his fear, but he could also feel confusion. Fear and pain had controlled Aaron for sixteen years. He would have a long struggle before he could control them. Aaron started up the stairs, drawing Stefan after him.

Stefan's eyes fluttered open. He was sitting at a table, his head pillowed on his arms. He could smell beer somewhere very close by. He could feel Aaron as well. He lifted his head.

Aaron sat across the table from him, his own head down but moving slightly as though he were waking from a long sleep. Kate stood nearby, and Tango.

Saffleur stood beyond them. He hadn't expected to see the Euthanatos here already. He hadn't expected to see the big man who stood by his side at all. "Valentine?" Stefan said in surprise.

Saffleur smiled at him. "Come here," he ordered.

Something seized control of Stefan's body abruptly, moving it like a puppet. He tried to scream for help from Aaron or from Kate or from Tango or from anybody, but his mouth wouldn't respond. Kate just stood aside mutely and let him walk past her to Saffleur's side. Aaron's head jerked up in reaction to his fear. He tried to climb to his feet, but Tango put a hand on his shoulder, restraining him. The mage looked like he was ready to incinerate Saffleur on the spot.

His body stopped just beside Saffleur. The mage took hold of his hand. "Good."

Kate looked at Saffleur. "You said you'd let us go." Aaron howled incoherently, and Tango had to use both hands to keep him in his chair.

Saffleur shook his head. "I'm sorry. I can't do that." He lifted the talisman in his hand as Stefan watched helplessly in horror. "Great Lady, swallow all of their minds!"

18

Kate's fingers were moving even as Saffleur spoke. She punched the last two digits of her spell into the cellular phone, holding down on the final digit and praying that the spell would work.

The squeal that erupted from the phone was enormous. Everybody in the vicinity clapped their hands over their ears and turned to stare at her. She wished she could do more than cover only one of her own ears, but she needed a hand to hold the phone. She squeezed her eyes shut as if that would make the sound more bearable. If the spell didn't succeed, she wouldn't see anything anyway.

The effects of the Great Lady seemed to manifest as attacks by spirit-beetles. The spell that she had dialed up was very similar to the one she had used to destroy the beetle that had kept Aaron asleep, but this spell was intended to destroy a number of beetles over a larger area. She was targeting the spell randomly too, unable to see the spirit-beetles this time. But the spell would work—as long as the spirit-beetles that swallowed minds were similar to those that put people to sleep.

She kept the magick up until she felt someone rapping her shoulder, trying to get her attention. She opened her eyes. It was Aaron. Saffleur and Stefan were gone. The squeal vanished as she released the spell, although the ringing in her ears didn't go away. "That," she said with a gasp, "is not like any talisman I have ever seen before!"

"Me neither. What the hell has been going on?" Aaron stared down at Julia lying on the floor. The Sleepers in the club, now released from Stefan's reality shifts, had only just noticed her and were crowding around. He hesitated for an instant, then added, "First I thought you had turned us in to the New World Order, then I thought you were handing us over to Saffleur."

"I did what I had to. At least we're still alive. We have one more chance to save Stefan."

Kate started to dash off into the crowd, heading back to the security room. Julia's scanner should still be there. She could run another search for Saffleur! But Aaron caught her arm. "What do you mean 'one more chance'?"

She shrugged him off. "Saffleur is here for the final death in Stefan's life cycle. Stefan is going to die tonight!" Quickly, she explained what had happened while he had been in Quiet.

He stared at her in shock, then muttered, "Shit. Saffleur could already have taken them anywhere!"

"No. He said it was going to happen here." Tango joined them. "In Pan's."

"Shit," muttered Aaron again.

Kate frowned at him. "I should be able to find them again, but it will take a few minutes."

"Wait!" Aaron closed his eyes. "I can use—"

Tango's hand struck out like a snake and slapped him. "You just came out of Quiet! If you try to use vulgar magick right now, you're going to go right back

under, and we don't have time to get you out again!"
She pushed him and Kate in the direction of the security room. "Do it her way! I'll take care of Julia!"

Kate grabbed his hand, dragging him off into the crowd. He pulled away long enough to snatch up a cane with a heavy steel head. There was an odd quality to the polished steel, a dark shadow that slid continuously and unsettlingly across the surface, as if of its own accord. She started to ask him what it was, then thought better of it.

She almost lost him in the crowd. His wounded arm and side slowed him down, and Kate had to go back for him several times. "Is it bad?" she demanded as they stepped into the calm of the security-system control room. The security guards grumbled as she gestured at them to get out, but her glare got them moving quickly.

"I can control it." His eyes were glassy and his gaze was slightly distant. "My link with Pan's blocks it for now. I had forgotten about the wounds while I was in Quiet. I didn't have them there."

Julia's scanner was still in place, and Kate started a new search for Saffleur, then pulled out a device of her own and ran it over Aaron's side. "Two of your ribs are broken." She checked his arm. "There's a bullet lodged against your humerus."

"Kate." Aaron seized her hand, brushing her analysis device aside. "Something happened while I was in Quiet. I didn't realize the significance of it until just now. Kate, Stefan deliberately caused and manipulated reality shifts! He fought me with them!"

"We felt the shifts here." Then suddenly she understood what he was talking about. "Only mages can deliberately manipulate reality! But Stefan's not a mage! I scanned him myself!"

"So did I!" He squeezed her hand. "Didn't you say that he and Saffleur had the same mind though?

Wasn't Saffleur saying something about a link between them? What if they do have the same mind somehow? Couldn't Stefan have the potential to be a mage like Saffleur? Mages can do incredible things when they're Awakening."

"Oh, my God." Kate pulled her hand away and sat down in one of the chairs by the security monitors, stunned by the implications. "He's undergoing an Awakening right now?"

"No." Aaron sat down as well and took a deep breath. "I think he's been in the process of Awakening for centuries."

"So the reality shifts . . ."

"May be his magick working uncontrollably as he finally starts to Wake completely. And our involvement has hastened the Awakening."

"But the shifts are so strong! And he doesn't suffer from Paradox!"

"I summoned Pig during my Awakening and look what happened." Aaron blinked away tears, and Kate realized that he had just shared a deep secret with her. He continued without stopping though. "I Awoke overnight. Imagine what might happen to a mage who has been Awakening for such an incredibly long time." He shook his head. "I suggested the idea that he might be an Awakening mage to Saffleur, and he laughed at it! I wonder if he knows?"

"He must." Kate tapped her fingers on the surface of a monitor, her fingernails making a hollow sound on the glass. "But even Awakening mages usually suffer Paradox from their magick, don't they? I wonder . . ." She looked at Aaron. "Saffleur has been manipulating Stefan for centuries, killing his family, and maybe controlling his entire life. Julia thought she knew Stefan before the Civil War, and she said he was a hustler then. How many lifetimes has he lived that way? As many as the languages he speaks or as there are buildings in that pocket realm? And in all of those lives, all Stefan has known is loss and death."

Aaron started to say something, but Kate waved him to silence as she thought. She stood and began pacing across the small room, building the evidence in her mind, piece by piece. Aaron turned to watch her. "The shifts happen when he's really feeling touched by that loss, and the nature of the shifts is always toward loss, death, failure, and trouble. That's the reality he's Awakening into. It's part of him. It isn't necessarily any different from his everyday reality. If he's projecting that desperate reality with magick, it might even feel more real to him. More clear, maybe—just the way Stefan sees the reality shifts!" The speed of her pacing began to increase. "He's doing all of it naturally and unconsciously! There's no Paradox because it's the way he conceives of reality!"

Aaron reached out and stopped her. "He lives in death and loss the way I want to live in pleasure or you want to live in scientific order. He's almost perfectly at one with his vision of reality. Kate, you make it sound like he's on a path to Ascension."

"Maybe he is, although it must be an extremely unpleasant path. Why would Saffleur be doing this at all? And even to a Sleeper, let alone to a mage? Why are their minds the same?" She sat down, resting her forehead in her hands and tangling her fingers in her hair. She sighed in frustration, then stopped suddenly, staring at the console. "Aaron, how long has this monitor been frozen on this picture?"

He swiveled his chair around to look as she pointed at Saffleur, Stefan, and the big man the hustler had called Valentine. The frozen picture showed them standing in the middle of the main dance floor, just beneath the big video wall. There was a clear space around them, a near impossibility on the crowded dance floor. "I don't know."

Kate fiddled with the controls, and the security camera's current picture appeared on the screen. Stefan and Saffleur appeared to be talking. Kate inhaled slowly. "Well," she said, "we've found them. What are we going to do now?"

Aaron stared at the monitor. "I'd say kill Saffleur, but I want some answers."

"So do I. But how? He may be too powerful for us to capture." Her eye fell on her cellular phone, sitting beside her hand. She bit her lip and narrowed her eyes as she thought.

Aaron reached over and pulled her lip out from between her teeth. "Stop that!" he said irritably.

"Sorry. It's a habit. I have an idea, but it's going to take a little time. You'll have to try to stall Saffleur and keep him from killing Stefan."

"I can do it."

"And we're going to have to get the Sleepers out of Pan's."

Aaron caught his breath. "Why?"

"Fewer witnesses, and I don't want any of them to get hurt." She glanced at him. "Is there a problem with that?"

"Without people inside Pan's, I won't receive any sensations from the club." Aaron met her gaze. "I won't have a focus for my magick."

"Damn." Kate's stomach dropped. It had been a perfect plan, but they couldn't go through with it if Aaron wasn't going to be able to use his magick. "Let me think. . . ."

"No," Aaron said suddenly. "We'll do it this way."

"You'll be helpless."

"Not entirely." He smiled grimly. "I can't hide behind pleasure forever. And anyway, like Tango said, if I use vulgar magick right now, I could fall back into Quiet."

Kate nodded. "All right. We just have to get rid of

the Sleepers." She started to bite her lip, then thought better of it. "I can use Mind magick, but it's going to have to be vulgar."

Aaron held up his hand. "Let me. I know a way to do it with coincidental magick, and it might delay Saffleur even more. Just tell me when you want it to happen." He swallowed, clearly nervous. "I'll be ready."

Saffleur had traced out a circle around them using the long pointed bone he had used at Valentine's. The people on the dance floor of Pan's had begun avoiding that circle, the random patterns of their dancing carrying them away from it. Stefan knew that the mage must be using magick, and suddenly he felt even more frightened than before. He hoped that Kate, Aaron, and Tango had survived the Saffleur's attack with the Great Lady.

Kate had done something just before the Euthanatos had turned to push his way through the crowd. Stefan's body had followed him of its own accord. Valentine had followed as well; Stefan had caught glimpses of him from the corner of his eye. He hadn't been able to turn his head and look directly at the big man. He hadn't even been able to look back and see if his friends were all right.

He tried again to force his body to obey him, but he could no more feel and control it than he could feel and control the clothes he wore. He glared hatefully at Saffleur, although he wasn't sure that the expression would even show on his face. Something must have got through to Saffleur, because the Euthanatos glanced at him. "You have something to say? Speak, Angel."

Stefan's face and mouth were his again. "You fucking bastard!" he spat. He tried to summon up a reality shift as he had in Aaron's Quiet, but he was too angry.

Saffleur slapped him. None of the people dancing around them appeared to notice. It was as if the three men did not even exist to them. "You were never this much trouble in any previous life!" he said savagely. "Never!"

"Wait until I'm free and then you'll see trouble! You can't keep me like this forever!"

The old mage laughed at the expression that Stefan's troubles brought to his face. "I won't have to keep you like this for even another hour." He stepped up to Stefan and began going through his pockets, coming up with the knife that Tango had given to the hustler. "Excellent."

"What are you going to do?" asked Stefan with a sinking feeling.

"I'm not going to do anything, Angel." Saffleur opened the knife and put it in Stefan's hand. "You're going to kill him." He pointed at Valentine, still standing quietly with a blank look on his face. Stefan was willing to bet that he was as terrified inside as he was himself.

"Why?"

"It's the final event of your life cycle, the murder by stabbing of your tormentor. The last turning of the wheel before it all begins anew."

Stefan blinked in disbelief. "You mean I'm not going to die? My death isn't the last event of the life cycle?"

"Oh, no," said Saffleur with a cool shake of his head, "this murder is the last event, but you do die. You stab yourself to death as well, in remorse. I just don't consider your death—or your birth—as events. They're merely transitional states." He smiled again. "Now, you must feel hate for Valentine when you kill him."

"I hate you. How about that?"

Saffleur gestured Valentine over to stand a few

steps away from Stefan, just out of his reach. The big man obeyed meekly, walking helplessly toward his death. "I wish that this event could have come about more naturally, but Aaron and Kate's interference has forced me to become directly involved. I can make the event happen, and I have done so in previous cycles when necessary, but there are still some conditions that must be met. The stabbing, for instance. And the murder must take place in rage."

"I'm not angry at Valentine," Stefan said stubbornly. He tried to release the knife from his grip and let it fall, but his fingers wouldn't move.

"If this had all come about as it should have, you would be." Saffleur stepped around behind Stefan, placing his hands on his shoulders, to whisper in his ear. "Think of all the things that Valentine forced you to do, things that made you feel ill. Things that made you feel inhuman. He led Marilyn into betraying you." He whispered into his other ear. "Don't you hate being forced to sell your body? Valentine represents all of that, all of your life on the streets, all of the times that you . . ."

The mage began to recite a litany of all the perverse things that the hustler's clients had wanted him to do and that Stefan had agreed to so that he could eat or pay the rent. All of the things that he had done to himself with drugs and alcohol. Stefan clenched his teeth and squeezed his eyes shut. Saffleur's whispers were seductive. Every sordid detail of his life came back to him, every moment that he had felt shame or disgust at himself. And Valentine became the symbol for all of those moments. More than just the man that he was, Valentine was his tormentor, responsible for every failure and loss in his life. . . .

"No!" Stefan choked. "You did this to me before. In the pocket realm. You made me upset over Marilyn's death. It's not going to work this time!"

"What I did to you in the Great Lady's realm was nothing. I can do more, and there is no way you can resist it. Don't you see that there has always been someone like Valentine? It is part of your life cycle— you must kill him for what he has done." Stefan felt the cool hardness of the Great Lady as Saffleur pressed it against his head. "Great Lady, let him remember."

It was like drowning, being plunged beneath the surface of waters that were at once dark and bright, filled with memories that rushed in on him. All of his previous lives, with so many memories that he could barely sort them out. So many memories of events that were so much alike. They blurred and ran together as he drowned in his past, sinking back through time.

He was Stefan, and this was San Francisco, and his tormentor was Valentine.

He was Alexander, and this was Moscow at the height of the cold war, and his tormentor was Captain Petrov.

He was Miguel, living in the shantytown on the outskirts of São Paulo, Brazil. His tormentor was Pedro.

He was Johnathon, living in the slums created by the Industrial Revolution in England. His tormentor was Master Grunge, a factory overseer.

He was Ryuji, living in a village in southern Japan. His tormentor was Yoshiro.

He was James, living in a prosperous town in the American South. His tormentor was Arthur Smithson, a local plantation owner.

The memories overwhelmed him with names and places and languages. Many of the places he didn't recognize. Often they were small, and he had known them only with respect to the geography nearby, never conceiving of them as a real part of a larger country. Occasionally, he knew where he had been, or could guess: an Arabian city, a French chateau, a colonial American settlement. He had had a score of names in a dozen languages. He had lived everywhere, he realized as he went back. Every life had left a language waiting in his head, and every life had left the shadow of a building in the Great Lady's realm. The shadow of the building where he had died after killing his tormentor.

And in every place, his life had been the same. The same pattern of deaths, the same losses. There had always been one person, one Valentine, who had made his life hell, and he had always hated him. His earliest memory was of a city in France called Poitiers, and it was the year of our Lord 1543, and King Francis I had been on the throne for twenty-eight years, and his tormentor's name was Bald Louis, and the name his parents had given him was Jean-Marc. But his parents were dead. All of the people he loved were dead. He made a living by prostituting himself, with Bald Louis as his pimp. He didn't feel like Jean-Marc. He had renamed himself after a plant that an old herbalist in the city had told him about. A bitter, poisonous plant. Saffleur.

"Yes," hissed the mage into his ear.

"Kate said we had the same mind."

"We're almost the same person. I lived through everything that you lived through, Angel. I know your pain! I've shared it! Once you kill your Bald Louis, we will be the same again!"

"I don't remember dying in Poitiers." Stefan felt numb.

"We didn't. I Awoke as a mage when I tried to kill myself after murdering Bald Louis. I was on the brink of death, but that old herbalist pulled me back. He was a mage, too, and he became my first master." Saffleur wrapped his hand around Stefan's, his arm resting beside the hustler's. He raised the knife, then turned Stefan's arm free. "Now kill him! Kill your tormentor!"

Stefan looked at Valentine.

"Think of Bald Louis and how much we hated him! Remember him and strike!"

By God and king, how he *hated* Bald Louis! The power of that hatred rolled over him. He *wanted* to kill Valentine, for everything that he and his predecessors had ever done to him! His fingers tightened convulsively on the knife.

Suddenly a clanging bell cut the air, and his own mind struggled through the wash of memories. The bell was a fire alarm, he realized. Saffleur was looking around in surprise. Stefan's arm, raised up above Valentine, wavered, then began to descend. Saffleur stopped his arm, ordering, "Wait!"

His body, still obedient to the mage's spell, froze. Saffleur spun around, peering through the crowd that was now beginning to panic and press toward the emergency exits of Pan's. His magick kept them out of the circle he had drawn, even in their terrified evacuation. Saffleur jabbed his finger out, pointing toward a figure that was moving toward them against the rush of people. "If you think this is going to help you, Aaron," he screamed above the mingled noise of the alarm and the crowd, "you're wrong! The lack of Sleepers is going to make it as easy for me to work magick as it is you! You can't stop me so simply!"

"I have to try!" But suddenly the young mage staggered, his face contorting, although he continued toward them.

Aaron was hurting, Stefan realized. He was in pain from the wounds inflicted on him by Pig at the Barry mansion. As the people fled out of Pan's, all of the pleasure that the club fed to him was disappearing. Stefan could feel its withdrawal through the link that bound them together. He could feel Aaron's sudden shock at the sensation of the pain, too. Without the pleasure, Aaron would face the full pain of his wounds. He hadn't thought of that. He wouldn't have the strength to face Saffleur. He felt Aaron rub at his nipple ring, trying to raise any sensation of pleasure in himself, but the attempt failed. The pain was too great! Where was Kate? Unless Aaron had help, he was surely going to die. Like Mike. And all he could do was watch helplessly!

Or perhaps . . .

Stefan released the hatred that he felt for Valentine and Bald Louis and all of his hundreds of tormentors. It was difficult, but he forced himself to do it. He strained instead to remember the loves of his lives, all of the Mikes and all of the Aarons. He reached deliberately for the pain of their loss.

There were so many Mikes. One for every life, and every one of them taking his own life in suicide. He had loved all of them, and it hurt him almost too much to bear to recall them. Nicholas. Antonio. Hugh. Kotaro. Matthew. Jun. Christophe, Saffleur's own love so long ago. The loss was so overpowering that he almost didn't notice that there were no other Aarons. The mage was unique. Stefan had never before fallen in love after his first love had died.

Just as he had in Aaron's Quiet, Stefan summoned up his pain and the clarity that came with it. But he didn't release the clarity this time. He held on to it, wrapping himself in the clarity, using it to fight the magick that gripped his body, forcing the reality shifts to obey his will and weaken Saffleur's spell. And a new hatred grew in him—for Saffleur.

"Why are you doing this to him?" demanded Aaron as the last Sleepers fled from Pan's. He could see Tango by the doors, telling the bouncers to leave the mages alone. She swung the doors closed behind her. He and Saffleur and Kate and Stefan and Valentine were the last people still in the building. Using the fire alarm to evacuate the building had been the simplest of coincidental magick. And Tango had disconnected the alarm from the emergency response network, so no firefighters would come to interrupt them. A new wave of pain from his wounds shook him as he took another step. He hoped that Tango might at least have the sense to have an ambulance waiting for him when this was over, though. "Why?" he called again. "What purpose could it serve?"

"It serves my purpose!"

Saffleur had the Great Lady in one hand and his ogre bone in the other. Aaron hoped that Kate would be ready to spring her surprise on the Euthanatos soon. Before Saffleur could use either the talisman or his magick against him. "What is your purpose, then?"

"To live, Aaron!" Saffleur laughed. "To live! You're young! When you get older, then you'll realize how important and precious life is! I told you once that I was willing to do anything that was necessary to extend my life." He gestured behind him with the Great Lady, pointing toward Stefan, frozen with a knife in his hand. "This is how far I'm willing to go."

"Forcing someone into a hellish, endless cycle of reincarnation?" Aaron took another painful step closer. "There must be easier ways to extend your life."

"All of them involving vulgar magick and the risk of Paradox. The longer a mage lives that way, the more his extended presence becomes a flaw in the fabric of reality. But," he said triumphantly, "what if the mage is able to die occasionally, removing himself from reality in the natural cycle of birth and death?"

Aaron paused in the act of taking another step. "The similarity of your mind and Stefan's?" he gasped. "He's dying for you? That's impossible!"

"No!" Saffleur rapped his chest with the Great Lady. "I'm dying for myself! His mind is a reflection of my own. His life is a reflection of my own, the events of a single cycle the same as the events of my own life until a point when I could easily have died myself. A mind—some might say a spirit—so similar, a life so nearly identical . . ." He spread his arms. "We are one person in the eyes of reality!"

"My God." Aaron swallowed, praying more desperately than ever that Kate would be ready soon. "How could you do such a thing?"

Saffleur held out the Great Lady. "With this."

"A talisman?"

"More than a talisman!" He rubbed his fingers across the statuette. "The Great Lady is old. Incredibly old. I sought it out when I decided that I was going to live for a very, very long time. One of my master's oldest books referred to a tale that told of this talisman and its power, hidden away from the world." Saffleur glared at him. "The Great Lady commands the spheres of Spirit and Mind. Using it, I created the Angel from myself, to cross into the realm of death and to return again. With it, I can perform the ritual that binds the Angel and me more tightly together with each turn of his life cycle. It was the Great Lady's power that bound the Angel to the wheel of reincarnation!"

"You used it to create the pocket realm in the Umbra?"

"Oh, no. The Great Lady's realm existed long before I found the Great Lady. *That* is the extent of the power bound up in this little figure!"

"What if I were to destroy the Great Lady?" Aaron asked suddenly, trying to throw the Euthanatos off balance.

He didn't. Saffleur simply shook his head definitively. "You couldn't."

"What if I were to destroy you?"

"You could try, but you wouldn't succeed. And if you did, the Great Lady would protect me." He smiled ghoulishly. "When my spirit leaves this world, the Great Lady's power will ensure that I am reincarnated with all of my memories intact. I will live again."

"What," asked Aaron slowly, trying to project a dangerous and threatening air, "if I were to kill Stefan?"

Saffleur's grin grew even wider, and Aaron suddenly felt very, very frightened. "If you kill the Angel or if you interrupt his life cycle at all, you will break the larger cycle of death and rebirth that staves off the Paradox of my extended life. All of that Paradox will strike down on me. That much Paradox is sure to cause an extremely damaging backlash of energy." His smile vanished. "I, of course, will be reincarnated, but I believe that a Paradox backlash of that magnitude would certainly result in the devastation of a very significant portion of the city."

"Holy fuck," Aaron breathed softly, all thoughts of Kate's plan suddenly driven from his head.

Saffleur nodded. "Indeed. You see, you have no choice but to allow the Angel to die as a normal part of his life cycle. And you have nothing at all to gain by killing me. I, on the other hand, have no compulsions at all against killing you." He raised the Great Lady and the ogre bone.

The knife that Stefan had been holding fell to the floor with a sudden clatter. Saffleur swung around to look at the hustler, just as Aaron yelled out, "Stefan, be careful!"

His warning came too late, or perhaps it was ignored. Stefan leaped into Saffleur, grabbing his arms and pushing them back. The old mage was no match for the younger man's strength. The pointed ogre bone, held by Saffleur's own hand and propelled by Stefan's, was swept around and thrust through his chest.

———

Kate looked down on the dance floor from the disc jockey's booth, her hand poised to activate the Technomancer device that she had cobbled together and attached to the control panel for the video wall. She had heard every word of Aaron's exchange with Saffleur. Stefan's sudden freedom and attack had surprised her no less than it did him. She grabbed for the disc jockey's microphone. "What now?" she asked quickly over Pan's sound system.

"Do it anyway!" screamed Aaron desperately, his voice almost swallowed by the cavernous space of the club. "Do it!"

"But it's set to capture a body, not a dying spirit! It will take a minute to adjust it!"

"Do it! He's not dead yet! I'll slow him down!"

Kate nodded and dropped the microphone. She flicked a switch on what had once been Julia's scanner and dialed a short number to activate certain circuits in what had once been a New World Order cellular phone. Then she took the controls of one of Pan's remote video cameras and carefully focused on Saffleur's dying body.

Stefan lowered Saffleur to the ground as Aaron crossed the dance floor, moving as quickly as his wounded body would allow. "I'm sorry," he said, looking up at the mage, "I didn't really think. I just wanted to stop him once and for all."

"You weren't listening to us, were you? He'll be back unless we can stop him." Aaron stopped, gasping for breath. Even the short jog across the dance floor had left him winded. He lowered himself to kneel beside Saffleur. The old mage glared at him, then smiled, trying to say something. Only blood bubbled out of his mouth, though. His eyes rolled back in their sockets. "Shit."

"Can you save him then?" Stefan asked desperately.

He had wanted this all to be over so badly. He had just wanted to save Aaron. He had just done what seemed necessary. He felt sickened as he realized that he had also completed the final event of his life cycle after all. Saffleur, not Valentine, had been his true tormentor, the one behind his misery and loss and pain. And he had stabbed him to death in hate. "Can you use magick?"

"No. I'm too weak. That kind of effort could kill me."

"The Great Lady?"

"I don't even want to touch it." He rubbed his hand gently over the polished steel head of his father's cane. "Pig," he whispered, "come out."

The shadowy reflection that had stained the steel suddenly slid off of it, dripping to the floor like a liquid shadow. Stefan let out a little whimper of fright, although for once he felt none from Aaron. The shadow swirled up and turned into Pig.

"You fool!" the demon said with a grin.

Aaron just met its eyes with a glare, staring it down. Pig actually looked nervous. "I summoned you Pig. You *will* obey me."

There was power in Aaron's voice, power that Stefan hadn't heard before. It wasn't magickal power, but rather a newfound confidence. Aaron had conquered Pig. Now he expected its obedience. Pig must have recognized that confidence, too. The demon struggled against Aaron's will, fighting it.

"You can't command me." Pig loomed over Aaron, its talons reaching out to play in his hair.

"Kneel, Pig!" the mage snapped. With a look of surprise, the demon fell to its knees. Aaron stared into its eyes. "I summoned you, I beat you, and now you are mine to command. I'm not afraid of you anymore!" He pointed at Saffleur. "You caught my father's last breath. Can you catch his spirit and hold it?"

"Yes," it hissed angrily, "if . . ."

Stefan didn't hear its words, because suddenly Saffleur groaned loudly. A final gush of blood spilled out of his mouth. He died.

The rush of memory Stefan had felt before was nothing compared to what he felt now. He still remembered everything that had happened through his life cycles, all of the death and all of the losses. But now, abruptly, a second set of memories settled onto his mind. Memories of his life cycles seen from the perspective of another person. Memories of years between his life cycles. Knowledge of magick. Deep knowledge, vast knowledge, knowledge gathered over more than five hundred years. The knowledge of his other self. Saffleur and Saffleur's mind. One mind divided, his new memories informed him, seeking to be reunited in one body. Saffleur had never expected his shadow to outlive him.

As if from a distance, Stefan was conscious of what was happening around him. Valentine blinked, came out of his daze, took one look at what was happening, and fled. Aaron shouted, "Catch it, Pig!" Pig's hand darted out and caught at something, a slippery, ghostly, eel-like shape that was wriggling from Saffleur's mouth. The demon had to use both hands to grapple with it, holding it firmly in this world as it sought to escape. Stefan could feel the struggle in his own mind. Saffleur's mind and spirit were trying to go in two directions, into him and on to the afterlife, while Pig was trying to hold them in a single place. The eel-thing was pulling itself apart in Pig's hands, slipping between the demon's fingers. If it escaped, Saffleur would return.

Stefan pushed the old mage's memories from his mind, blocking their attempt to lodge in him. A few scraps clung, bits of magick and shreds of thoughts, but most left easily. The eel-thing began to struggle to go in one direction only. Pig was able to grasp it easily.

"Adjustments made! Get back!" ordered Kate over the sound system. Aaron grabbed him and they scrambled away.

A spotlight came on up by the ceiling, illuminating the demon and the spirit that it held. Both looked up. Both screamed, the eel-thing suddenly shifting to resemble Saffleur. The demon and the spirit were drawn up and away, their essences distorted as they were sucked into a video camera. It was exactly like watching Kate disappear into her cellular phone.

But one of Saffleur's spectral hands reached out and grabbed at the Great Lady, still in the grip of the mage's body. Somehow the immaterial spirit was able to grasp the talisman, and it provided the spirit with an anchor against the pull of the camera. Pig clung to Saffleur's spirit. "Make it let go!" Kate yelled.

Stefan reacted without thinking. He lunged forward before Aaron could stop him, and put his hands over the ogre bone protruding from Saffleur's chest. Bearing down with his own weight, he drove it deeper into the body. At the same time, he funneled a reality shift through the bone.

Perhaps it was remnants of Saffleur's mind in his own. Perhaps it was the deliberate desperation with which he pulled at reality. Perhaps, perhaps . . . perhaps didn't matter, because abruptly, awareness bloomed in Stefan. But it wasn't memories of the past this time. He was aware of the fabric of reality around him right now, the way that it was woven, and the ways in which he could manipulate it. Some scrap of Saffleur's memories told him what was happening.

He was Awakening. He was a mage.

The reality shift that he forced through the bone became magick, consciously worked and directed.

Stefan gasped as a numbing pain that could only be Paradox racked his body for the first time. But he grimly drove the power of his will against the solidity of reality until it broke, and Saffleur's corpse collapsed into dry dust as though it had been rotting for centuries. Freed of its grasp, the Great Lady came loose. Saffleur's spirit and Pig, along with the talisman, vanished into the video camera.

19

There were perhaps half a dozen or more voices shouting his name as he emerged from San Francisco's Hall of Justice, but one voice stood out from the others, brazen and bold. Aaron sighed as he pulled his sunglasses out and put them on one-handed. "Tiffany?"

"How did the hearing go, Aaron?"

"You were a witness, Tiffany." Aaron smiled at the reporter. It had been just slightly less than two weeks since her experiences at the Barry mansion. She seemed to have recovered fully. His magick had worked successfully; she remembered nothing except William's confession and suicide. "What do you think?"

"Viewers want to hear it from the horse's mouth, Aaron."

"All right." He gathered his thoughts for moment, then said, "I'd give a four point five for technical merit and a six for artistic performance. The prosecution tripped all over themselves trying to explain how they could have been fooled by an obvious framing, but they did give me a very nice apology when they dropped the charges. Oh, and one of the prosecuting attorneys had a very cute tush."

Some of the reporters who specialized in covering the courts were a little bit taken aback by his flip answer, but Tiffany just laughed. "What happened to your arm?"

"Banged it up while I was skiing in Canada. Incidentally, that's where I was while the authorities were looking for me. Not holed up in a Nevada brothel, as some reports are stating." Aaron patted his injured arm, which was suspended in a sling. "Doctors say it'll be fine in a few more weeks." He smiled at her again. "Can you imagine how I'd do something like this in a brothel?"

"Actually, I can."

"Good—do you want to come over and help me practice so I can get it right next time?" Everybody laughed this time.

One of the other reporters caught his attention. "What about the marks that authorities found on the walls of one of your bedrooms? Inside sources say that the marks and other evidence in confiscated papers link you to occult practices."

The small crowd of reporters suddenly grew still. Even Tiffany was silent, although her nostrils twitched as though she was smelling the beginning of a new Aaron Barry scandal. As well she was. The possibility of an investigation by the Technocracy was still heavy in Aaron's mind. He had no idea how much evidence of his mage status Pig had slipped into the documents gathered by the authorities. So he had leaked his own counterrumors. There were no inside sources, only phony memos on forged letterhead mailed anonymously to a random newspaper. And shortly, it would be revealed that Aaron Barry was flirting heavily with sex spells, love potions, and ritual orgies so outrageous that the media would have a field day and so blatantly nonmagickal that no Technomancer would possibly believe that Aaron truly was a mage.

For now, however, he said simply, "I'm doing a little experimental interior decorating."

"And the occult practices?"

"Well, let's just be thankful the authorities didn't raid the mansion during a full moon!" He smiled mysteriously as the reporters began to scratch their heads trying to figure that out, then proceeded down the steps to the waiting Rolls-Royce.

"Wait, Aaron." Tiffany followed him for a couple of steps. "What are you doing for New Year's Eve tonight?"

The question was too innocent. She was hunting for information. Just as he had hoped she might. He wasn't going to satisfy her curiosity just yet, though. "Not what, Tiffany, who. But to answer the spirit of the question, I have tickets for the New Year's party at Pan's."

Tiffany raised an eyebrow, clearly frustrated but unwilling to admit defeat. "Who's your date?"

Aaron grinned as he climbed into the Rolls. "You'll just have to come and see."

"Miss Sanders?"

Kate looked up briefly from her computer and the report that she was finishing. "Yes."

The lab technician at the door of her office held out a small, narrow plaque. "Your new nameplate just got dropped off."

"Excellent."

"And the maintenance staff wants to know what you want done with Julia's sofa and chair from the lab."

"Have them disposed of."

"The new cabinets for the walls of the lab look good. They hide all the equipment."

"They're functional, not aesthetic. I disliked having the New World Order's equipment in plain sight for anyone entering the lab for mundane reasons." She glanced up at the technician again. "Is there anything else, Stephen?" she asked coldly.

"No, Miss Sanders."

"Then you can go."

She turned back to her computer and waited several moments after the technician had gone before allowing herself the briefest of secret smiles. Julia had never recovered from Saffleur's attack; her mindless body had been taken away to a nameless Technomancer clinic for "examination." After some consideration, the New World Order had given her Julia's old position, office, and lab (although with something less than Julia's authority, but that would come in time), largely on the strength of her report concerning the events at Pan's. She was quite proud of it herself, having turned the entire affair into a vendetta formulated by Julia to take revenge (so irrational!) against an old enemy. The inclusion of magickal elements in Pan's design, she said, had been accidental, and they would shortly be removed under a falsified building-code violation. There was no magickal activity at Pan's. All cameras and monitoring devices were to be removed from the club as a waste of New World Order resources. Case closed.

It had actually been remarkably easy to slip back into something approximating a Technomancer mentality again. She hadn't been sure at first that she could pull it off successfully, but she had. It felt odd, sometimes. She had had a few arguments with Aaron about going back to the Technocracy. He had tried to persuade her to defect wholeheartedly to the Traditions. But for all its present flaws, Kate still believed in the basic principles of order and science that were the Technocracy's foundation. And she suspected that she could do more to change it from within. It would be a very slow process, however.

She saved the file and turned the computer off. On her way out of the New World Order regional headquarters, she stopped to look in on the lab. Stephen was still there, supervising the removal of the sofa and chair. He nodded at her and she nodded back.

She almost wished him "Happy New Year" but caught her tongue. The New World Order didn't approve of New Year's Eve. It would have been happier if the revelry of the night could be officially banned. It would not have been at all pleased if it had known that she would be spending the evening at Pan's in the company of two mages of the Traditions.

Stefan signaled the cabbie to pull over to the curb and yelled out the window, "Hey! Carlos!"

The Mexican hustler looked up in surprise. A wide smile spread across his face, and he came over to the cab. "I haven't seen you around for a couple of weeks. What's happening?"

"Big changes. Get in."

"Is this a job?"

"Just get in, asshole." Stefan opened the door for him, then slid over. "Around the block a few times," he told the cabbie.

Carlos whistled as he looked him over. "Wow! You're looking good!"

Stefan was wearing all black, a style that had come to suit his tastes in the last ten days. All of the clothes that he wore were new, too, from new shoes to a black silk shirt and a new black leather jacket. Courtesy of Aaron, who claimed that even in black, Stefan was the most unconventional Euthanatos he had ever met. "Like I said, big changes."

"You heard about Marilyn?"

Stefan nodded sadly. "I was there, man. It was bad."

He really was sad, too. It felt incredibly good to be able to mourn without triggering a shift in reality. Aaron and Kate were helping him work around the scars that had been left by Saffleur's control over the centuries. Soon he would have to seek out other Euthanatos to learn about the Tradition that he had Awakened into. If Aaron was right, he would be a powerful mage someday.

For now, the scraps of Saffleur's own memories, as well as Kate's and Aaron's instructions, helped, and he had learned to channel his pain into magick. Now that he was conscious of working magick, in fact, he wasn't even sure that he could cause a reality shift anymore without attracting Paradox. But he was glad to give up that kind of power for a little control. Unfortunately, he hadn't learned control in quite enough time. "I feel sorry I didn't get to see her funeral."

"Whores and hustlers as far as the eye could see. She touched a lot of people."

"And got paid for it!" They both broke up laughing. Stefan wiped at his eyes. "I heard that they tried to bury her in a suit."

"They didn't know squat about her. But some of the girls got busy while we held the preacher down. Marilyn went out with a woman's face. Like she would have wanted." He started as Stefan slid a piece of paper into his hands. "What the hell is this?"

"A green card. I've got friends that can pull some strings when they have to."

Carlos looked like he might cry. "Why?"

"I felt like I owed you. For that marijuana."

"Shit, man." He pulled Stefan into a hug. "Thanks."

"You're welcome. Do you want to get dropped off where you were or do you want to get out here so you can wipe your face before you have to look at any of the guys?"

"You better drop me off here." Stefan signaled to

the driver, and they pulled over again. Carlos got out of the car. "Are we going to be seeing you around here anymore?"

"Maybe." Stefan grabbed Carlos's hand. "Good luck, man."

"Good luck, *amigo*. And Happy New Year's!"

Stefan watched him go, then settled back in his seat. "To Pan's," he told the cabbie. Kate and Aaron would be waiting for him.

HarperPrism

SMALL GODS by Terry Pratchett. International bestseller Terry Pratchett brings magic to life in his latest romp through Discworld, a land where the unexpected always happens—usually to the nicest people, like Brutha, former melon farmer, now The Chosen One. His only question: Why?

0-06-109217-7 — $4.99

MAGIC: THE GATHERING™—ARENA by William R. Forstchen. Based on the wildly bestselling trading-card game, the first novel in the *MAGIC: THE GATHERING™* novel series features wizards and warriors clashing in deadly battles. The book also includes an offer for two free, unique MAGIC cards.

0-06-105424-0 — $4.99

SEAROAD:Chronicles of Klatsand by Ursula K. Le Guin. Here is the culmination of Le Guin's lifelong fascination with small island cultures. In a sense, the Klatsand of these stories is a modern day successor to her bestselling *ALWAYS COMING HOME*. A world apart from our own, but part of it as well.

0-06-105400-3 — $4.99

CALIBAN'S HOUR by Tad Williams. The bestselling author of *TO GREEN ANGEL TOWER* brings to life a rich and incandescent fantasy tale of passion, betrayal, and death. The beast Caliban has been searching for decades for Miranda, the woman he loved—the woman who was taken from him by her father Prospero. Now that Caliban has found her, he has an hour to tell his tale of unrequited love and dark vengeance. And when the hour is over, Miranda must die.... Tad Williams has reached a new level of magic and emotion with this breathtaking tapestry in which yearning and passion are entwined.

Hardcover, 0-06-105204-3 — $14.99

and Tomorrow

WRATH OF GOD by Robert Gleason.
An apocalyptic novel of a future America about to
fall under the rule of a murderous savage. Only a
small group of survivors are left to fight — but they are
joined by powerful forces from history when they learn how
to open a hole in time. Three legendary heroes answer the
call to the ultimate battle: George S. Patton, Amelia Earhart,
and Stonewall Jackson. Add to that lineup a killer dinosaur
and you have the most sweeping battle since *THE STAND*.
Trade paperback, 0-06-105311-2 — $14.99

THE X-FILES™ by Charles L. Grant. America's
hottest new TV series launches as a book series with
FBI agents Mulder and Scully investigating the cases
no one else will touch — the cases in the file marked X.
There is one thing they know: The truth is out there.
0-06-105414-3 — $4.99

THE WORLD OF DARKNESS™: VAMPIRE—
DARK PRINCE by Keith Herber. The ground-
breaking White Wolf role-playing game Vampire: The
Masquerade is now featured in a chilling dark fantasy novel of
a man trying to control the Beast within.
0-06-105422-4 — $4.99

THE UNAUTHORIZED TREKKERS' GUIDE
TO *THE NEXT GENERATION* AND *DEEP SPACE
NINE* by James Van Hise. This two-in-one
guidebook contains all the information on the shows, the characters, the creators, the stories behind the episodes, and
the voyages that landed on the cutting room floor.
0-06-105417-8 — $5.99

HarperPrism
An Imprint of HarperPaperbacks